SING, GODDESS!

SING, GODDESS!
A YA Anthology of Greek Myth Retellings

SING, GODDESS!

A YA Anthology of Greek Myth Retellings

EDITED BY JANE WATSON

Snowy Wings
PUBLISHING

TURNER, OR

CONTENTS

INTRODUCTION

"SING, GODDESS, THE wrath of Achilles, and his devastation."

After we read Homer's *The Iliad* in my Greek Mythology class in college, those words echoed in my head not only when I would walk into that classroom, but for years to come. I always found something stirring and profound about those words—especially when I would sing them in my head, as our professor taught us to, since epic Greek poems were performed aloud in the original language to an audience in the form of a song so long ago.

Just as those words have stuck with me, mythology and stories from ancient Greece have withstood the test of time—when you hear names like Zeus, Aphrodite, Arachne, and Icarus, you know who they are. Even if their myths differ depending on the source, you still immediately recognize their names. Greek myths have something for everyone— happiness, sorrow, victorious triumphs, danger and mystery. Putting together an anthology of Young Adult stories based on these classic myths is something I have been brainstorming for several years, so it is my and the other authors of Snowy Wings Publishing's pleasure to present *Sing, Goddess!* and bring you eleven stories that echo these tales… with a new twist.

THE MYTH OF ARES AND APHRODITE

LIKE MARS AND VENUS

JANE WATSON

I THINK THAT'S all we have for today," Ms. Demetrius said, glancing at the clock. "Class dismissed!"

Alexandria 'Lexi' Cypress grinned, closing her textbook and reaching for her pale pink messenger bag. Though she actually didn't mind Ms. Demetrius's class—AP Bio was one of her favorite subjects—her next period was Lunch, and she was *starving*. Probably because she skipped breakfast, her morning walk with her beloved German Shepherd-Labrador mix, Cupid, having taken longer than usual. He just had to keep pausing to inspect every large shrub or fir tree on their path.

You'd think after living here for six months, Cupid would be used to their new neighborhood in Mountainview, Oregon. But, no. He still sniffed the landscape with extra care and cast wary looks at the neighbors and other animals. It was almost as if he was worried that he wouldn't be able to lead Lexi back home should they get lost in the sprawling neighborhood peppered with evergreen trees that towered over them, tangles of ivy climbing up their trunks. Poor Cupid. Moving to a small town in the Pacific Northwest surrounded by firs, oaks, maples, and lush greenery, versus the cliffs and sandy beaches of their home in California, took some getting used to—for both of them. When her father got a job transfer partway through her junior year of high school, Lexi was upset, especially when she learned that they would not only be moving out of state, but to a colder, considerably wetter, small town in Oregon. With long blonde hair that fell in soft ringlets down her back, bright blue eyes, and sun-kissed skin, Lexi was every bit the stereotypical beach girl. She even loved to surf and swim. Couldn't her parents have at least moved to the Oregon Coast? The one bright side was that they had moved to the Western side of the state and were therefore not *too* far from the beach—just over an hour—but it still wasn't quite the same.

Lexi rose to her feet, smiling at Ms. Demetrius as she made her way to the door and into the crowded hallway. "Food, food, food," she sang under her breath as she pulled her phone from the depths of her bag and turned it on, hurrying through the throng of students toward her locker. Blowing a lock of hair out of her eyes as she spun the combination, she had just opened the door and begun switching out her books when she felt her phone buzz. Sliding her thumb across the screen, her eyes quickly scanned the text.

Don't forget, extra practice tonight. Got to get the Spider-Man stunt down in time to wow the crowd and show those Trojan cheerleaders who's boss.

xo Erika

Lexi smiled. Erika Pomo was *very* enthusiastic about the big Homecoming game coming up, and even though she wasn't the team captain, she had taken it upon herself to be extra helpful—getting everyone on the team matching hair ribbons (the nice kind that were already attached to a hair tie and glued in place, so no worries about the bow coming undone) and sending videos with fresh routines and cheers. She even sent texts reminding the squad members about practice—even though Hallie, the actual captain, already helped the coach post the schedule and made sure to send any necessary reminders. Still, Erika meant well, and the more help, the better, right? Taking a breath, she quickly typed, *Of course, I'll be there! :-D*

"Hey, Lexi."

Lexi turned to find Helen Swan standing there. "Oh, hey, Helen," she began. "How's it— "

Hazel eyes shining, Helen eagerly interrupted, "I voted for you!"

Lexi blinked. "What?"

"I voted for you," Helen repeated. "For Homecoming."

Lexi tilted her head and gazed at Helen in surprise. "You did? I mean, thank you, that's so sweet of you, but…" She paused, pulling a thick binder stuffed with papers out of her locker before continuing, feeling confused, "I'm not on the ballot."

Helen tucked a strand of thick, dark brown hair behind her ear. "I know that, silly. You were my write-in!" she said cheerfully. Homecoming was handled very differently at Mountainview High compared to Lexi's old school. Seniors who had a certain GPA and participated in extracurricular activities were eligible to run for king or queen themselves, or they could cast write-in votes for their fellow classmates. As long as they met the pre-requisites, write-ins could technically win. But why on earth would Helen waste her vote on Lexi— the new girl?

Well, come to think of it, Helen *was* her closest friend at Mountainview High. But still. Finally, the irony struck her as she said, "But I chose *you* as my write-in!"

Helen giggled, giving Lexi's shoulder a playful shove. "Oh, stop! Me?"

"No, I'm serious," Lexi insisted as they fell into step beside each other and made their way to the cafeteria. "You're totally Homecoming Queen material."

Helen shook her head. "So are you! You're so popular. Everyone either knows you or wants to know you."

"That's just because I'm the new girl," Lexi reminded her, pushing open the double doors and heading into the breezeway between buildings. "You've been here since Freshman year. You went to middle school with most of our class! Everybody knows you."

"But that's just my point. They know *you* too," Helen pointed out. "You've been here barely a year, and you're already one of the most popular girls in our year. You made the varsity cheerleading squad—that's super competitive at MV High, and impressive for a transfer student."

"Yeah, because I was a cheerleader back at Cythera High," Lexi retorted. She had been cheering for her old high school in her hometown in Cythera, California since Freshman year. She thought back to the perfect dark orange and white uniforms they'd had, pleated skirts, with a black stripe down the bottom. At least she'd gotten to keep her shiny silver and orange pom-poms as a memento after she transferred schools. Not that her new cheerleading uniform wasn't equally cute, with the straight crimson red skirt and halter top, and matching crimson and gold pom-poms.

Helen shrugged. "I'm just saying, don't be surprised when you take home the crown."

Lexi ducked her head, not wanting Helen to see that she was holding back laughter. Homecoming Queen? *As if.*

"Ack, look out!" Helen cried suddenly.

Lexi lifted her head just as a football whizzed through the air and connected with her shoulder. "Ouch!" she exclaimed, the binder she'd been clutching falling to the ground.

"Are you okay?" Helen asked, before scooping up the football. "All right, which nitwit threw that?"

Massaging her shoulder, Lexi was about to respond when she heard several male voices clamoring at once.

"Whoa, man! You hit Lexi!" one of them said.

"Good job, dude. Take out one of the cheerleaders," another voice added.

"Dammit! Is she okay?" Lexi recognized the voice of Aidan Shields, quarterback and team captain of the Spartan's football team. She watched as he jogged over their way, flanked by half the football team.

"What kind of toss was that?" Parker Hecuba asked incredulously as he followed Aidan.

Mason Gerard, the Spartan's burly fullback, scoffed. "Maybe if you learned to catch, Parker. Good thing you don't play wide receiver."

"Shove it, Mason," Parker retorted, running a hand through his curly brown hair.

Aidan slowed his steps once he reached them. "Hey, Lexi, sorry about that. The ball was meant for Parker, not you ladies."

Helen furrowed her brow, looking to Aidan and then to the other players. "Maybe if you didn't play in the breezeway this wouldn't happen," she said severely.

Parker looked sheepish under Helen's stare. "Sorry."

"I would have caught it, Helen," Mason said in a smooth tone.

"We're just practicing for the big game," Aidan said with a grin, pumping a fist. "Got to be ready to crush those Trojans."

Lexi lifted her eyebrows, tossing her hair over her shoulder. "I don't think this is what Coach Titan meant when he told you to practice more."

"Ooh, you're in trou-ble!" Lee Acheron, the team's running back, ribbed Aidan.

"Hey, Lexi's got to be used to it by now. We play way rougher out on the field," Aidan lifted his eyebrows as he stared at Lexi, a playful grin gracing his handsome features.

"You play a little too rough if you ask me," Lexi chided him as she reached up to massage her shoulder, thinking back to last Friday's football game. She remembered watching Aidan as he called out the plays when the game was going into the fourth quarter, noticing how tense he was getting.

"Hey, we play to win," Aidan said with a cocky shrug. "But are you hurt?" He reached out to lightly touch her elbow, raising his dark eyebrows.

Lexi felt her cheeks grow warm as their eyes locked. "Um…"

"Yeah, do you need to go to the nurse, Lexi?" David Argyle, one of the team's guards, asked in concern.

Tearing her gaze from Aidan, and trying to ignore how her pulse had mysteriously begun to quicken, Lexi stammered, "Um, yeah, it just hit my shoulder, that's all." Glancing around at the half-dozen pairs of eyes locked on her, she let out an embarrassed laugh. "Oh, come on, guys, I'm fine!"

The boys smiled in relief and began laughing and talking all at once. Helen rolled her eyes, tossing the football their way. "Be more careful next time!"

Parker held out his hands, but Mason stepped in front of him at the last second and caught the ball. "See you around, Helen," he said with a wink, following the other guys down the breezeway.

Only Aidan remained, and Lexi realized that his hand was still on her elbow, deep brown eyes still locked on her. "I…" he began, before dropping his gaze to the floor. "Oh, shit, your books, sorry." He bent his tall frame to crouch in the breezeway.

"Right." Lexi tucked a strand of hair behind her ear before dropping to her knees, shuffling the papers that had spilled out of the binder into a pile.

"Whoa, did you draw these?" Aidan lifted one of the papers that had a sketch of an ancient Greek temple.

Lexi nodded. "I'm working on backdrop ideas for Homecoming."

Aidan flipped through the papers, eyes taking in sketches of ancient columns, torches, and men and women dressed in chitons. "You're on the Homecoming committee? That's awesome."

Feeling oddly hot under his stare, Lexi murmured a thank you as he helped her to her feet and handed back her binder of notes and sketches. "Yeah, it's been a lot of fun so far," she said, avoiding his eyes.

"Well, I'm even more stoked for Homecoming than I was before," Aidan said. Lexi lifted her eyes just in time to see his grin before he turned and said, "See you later."

"Bye," Lexi called after his retreating form, wondering why her palms felt a little sweaty.

Helen cleared her throat, and Lexi turned to be greeted with raised eyebrows and a smirk. "What?" she asked defensively.

Helen batted her eyelashes, saying in a high-pitched tone, "Oh, Helen, why would little old *me* be chosen for Homecoming Queen?" Clasping her hands, she breathed, "When Aidan Shields, the most popular *and* hottest guy in school, was totally just flirting with me, *why oh why* would anyone think I could be Queen?"

"Har har," Lexi replied sarcastically as they continued their walk to the cafeteria. "And, he was *not* flirting with me!"

Helen rolled her eyes. "Believe what you will, I know flirting when I see it. Half the team was after you. *Especially* the Spartan's quarterback."

Yet you didn't notice that both Mason and Parker were flirting with you? Lexi thought incredulously, but instead simply said, "Because I'm a cheerleader! Of course they all know me. Knowing is not flirting."

"Oh, whatever. It's *not* just that you're on the squad. You're gorgeous," Helen insisted as they stepped into the bustling cafeteria and made their way to the lunch line.

Nudging Helen with her binder, Lexi giggled. "No, *you* are! Your face could launch a thousand ships!"

Helen lifted her eyebrows, laughing as she lifted an apple from the lineup. "Where do you come up with these things?"

Lexi began laughing herself, following Helen to a lunch table. "Oh, I don't know."

"Hm, could Aidan be your Homecoming King?" Helen pondered as she opened a bag of chips.

Setting down her bottled water a little too forcefully, Lexi protested, "How should I know? And I'm *not* going to be Queen!"

"Sure, sure," Helen said with an eyeroll. "Think about it. You're a cheerleader, he's a football player, you see each other all the time, it's a match made in Heaven!"

Or in Hades, Lexi thought grumpily. The warm feeling she'd felt when he'd asked if she was okay, and how she'd gotten lost, just for a moment, in those deep brown eyes, washed all over her. She shook her head. "I doubt he likes me. Plus…" She thought back to the various football games where she'd witnessed him on the field. "Not only is he full of himself, but he can get so… intense. It's like he *has* to win. We're total opposites. Like Mars and Venus."

"Fine, forget about Aidan," Helen waved her hand. "You're going to at least *go* to Homecoming, right?" Seeing Lexi pause, her hazel eyes widened. *"What?* You *have* to go!"

"I *do* want to go," Lexi clarified. "But I don't want to go with… just anyone." She took a shaky breath, bad memories clouding her mind.

"You have your pick of guys to go to the dance with!" Helen said with enthusiasm.

"Yeah, just because I haven't gone to school long enough to be wary of the shallow douchebags in our year like the rest of you." Lexi pushed a lock of hair behind her ear, exhaling slowly as she stared down at her lap.

Sensing the shift in her friend's mood, Helen reached for her arm and gave her a reassuring squeeze. "Hey. They're not all like Andrew."

Eyes cast downward, Lexi nodded. To this day, remembering Andrew still stung. Having been there barely a semester, she had been so flattered when Andrew Shepard, the tall, handsome boy from her English Lit class, asked her to their Junior Prom. He had seemed so nice and sweet, and at the time, she'd even hoped that they might start dating.

That had all come crashing down when he tried to get a little too friendly with her at the dance. When she'd told him, politely but firmly, that she wasn't interested in moving that fast, especially on their first date, he seemed apologetic and even a little embarrassed.

It was what happened a few days later that made her temper flare whenever she thought about it. She'd caught him in the cafeteria, talking loudly to several other boys that he'd "scored with"—in his words—the hot new girl. She could tell by the whoops and boisterous laughter that he hadn't just meant she'd kissed him—which she totally hadn't—either.

"At least you put that tool in his place," Helen said, breaking her reverie. Her gaze flicked to the next cafeteria table over. "Right at that table, if I'm not mistaken."

Lexi remembered what had happened next. After taking a deep breath to calm the hot tears that threatened to spill over, her anger overcame the hurt and she'd stomped over to the table of boys and lit into Andrew about being a creep who would only ever "score" with her in his dreams, and proceeded to give the cafeteria tray he was holding a whack, dumping his lunch on him.

"When the Jell-O oozed down his shirt—" Helen burst into fervent giggles. "His face—"

Lexi felt herself cracking a satisfied smile at the memory. "It—"

Helen smacked the table. "Got as red as the Jell-O!" After they both gave in to a fit of giggles, she finally took a deep breath and said, "That's when I said to myself, I have *got* to befriend that girl!"

"Aw! I'm so glad you did!" Lexi smiled warmly at her friend. "Now—can you tell me if these sketches for backdrops will impress at the committee meeting after school?"

"We already know they impressed *someone*," Helen said slyly.

Lexi playfully smacked her arm. "You stop!"

Later that afternoon, Lexi, Erika and a handful of other students who had volunteered for the Homecoming Committee sat in a semi-circle of chairs on the stage of the school's gymnasium. The committee was using the stage as their work station and storage space to get everything prepped for Homecoming. In addition, part of the Homecoming festivities would be a parade through downtown, so they were also tasked with designing a float to represent the school. Since the float was such a large structure that would eventually need to be connected to a car, they would be building it in the school's shop class storage shed.

Mrs. Soleil, the committee's faculty adviser, sat in the center of the circle, a notebook open on her lap as she went over things to ensure they were on track. "Has anyone given any thought to the photo booth area?"

Both Lexi and Erika raised their hands at once. Erika crinkled her nose in a silent giggle as she locked eyes with Lexi when Mrs. Soleil called on her. "Well," Erika began, "I was thinking we could have a little table with some props. But instead of goofy glasses or mustaches, we should have things that tie-in with our theme." Seeing people nodding, she went on, "Like those Greek drama masks, and flower crowns!"

"Um," Amber Shields, a petite girl with chestnut brown hair and large glasses, lifted a hand as she interjected, "Flower crowns aren't associated with ancient Greece."

Erika flicked her gray eyes to where Amber sat. "Yes, they are. Look at all of those goat dudes who wore them, or the drunk guy…"

Pushing her glasses up her nose and sitting up in her chair, Amber corrected, "I think you mean *satyrs* and *Dionysus*, the god of wine and festivity. For your information, they didn't wear 'flower crowns,'" she said, making air quotes. "They wore wreaths crafted out of laurel branches."

Erika rolled her eyes and looked like she was about to retort when Mrs. Soleil said, "That's a great idea, Erika. Amber is correct, laurel wreaths are more on par with ancient Greece, but this is what's great about a group of people coming together—we can all give each other input."

Amber smiled.

"Any other thoughts?" Mrs. Soleil asked the group.

Lexi raised her hand again, taking a deep breath when Mrs. Soleil nodded to her. "I have been working on some sketches for the backdrop. I figured if everyone likes them, we can just paint a huge piece of butcher paper." She held up her sketches, and was pleased when the other students made sounds of approval.

"Those look lovely," Mrs. Soleil said with a smile. "I especially like the columns."

"And, to make the booth more three-dimensional, I thought we could have "real" columns," Lexi said, running her hand over her sketchpad. "Like the ones we saw in the party supply catalog."

"I think our budget is much too limited for that," Mrs. Soleil said gently. "Remember, we have to save enough for the decorations, the DJ, refreshments, as well as the float."

"Sorry," Erika whispered to Lexi.

Lexi shook her head. "Oh, I didn't mean order them. I thought we could make them!"

Nodding slowly, Mrs. Soleil tapped her pencil on her notebook. "How would you suggest we make them?"

Smiling, Lexi said, "I was doing some research online last night, and I think we can make the forms out of chicken wire, and then slather them with papier-mâché."

"And then paint them!" Phillip Marsden, a tall senior from the basketball team exclaimed with a snap of his fingers. "That would be sick! We could have a few all over the gym, not just by the photos!"

"That sounds like a great idea," Mrs. Soleil said with a smile. "Relatively inexpensive materials, but we may have some of what you need in the supply room. All right, I think that wraps it up. I'll leave you to get to work!"

The students rose to their feet and spread out to various work stations. Lexi headed to the back room on the hunt for supplies. Her eyes scanned the shelving units stuffed with bolts of fabric, bins of notions, and props from previous drama productions. When she ventured a little farther back, she noticed a pile of plywood, some short pieces of metal, and a large roll of chicken wire.

"Jackpot!" she cried in triumph. It was a very thick roll, which she hoped meant it had enough to make at least a few columns. Once she'd maneuvered to the corner to unearth the wire, she struggled to lift it.

"Hey, let us help, Lexi," Phillip and his fellow basketball player, Damon Russel, called as they jogged toward her.

Lexi breathed a sigh of relief as Damon lifted the bundle of wire with ease. "Thanks. You'd think with all the lifting I have to do stunting for cheer, I'd be stronger," she said with a breathless laugh.

"No sweat," Damon said easily as he followed Phillip and Lexi back out to the main portion of the stage to set down the bundle of wire. "Don't want our Homecoming Queen to get hurt."

Phillip grinned. "Yeah, how can you wear the crown and dance the night away if you throw your back out?"

Lexi blinked rapidly, face flushing. After Helen's declaration of nominating her for Homecoming Queen that day at lunch, she had countless people stopping her in the hallway or passing her notes in class, letting her know she was their pick for Queen. It still seemed a little hard to take in. "You guys," she said with an embarrassed wave of her hand. "I'm not going to be Homecoming Queen!"

"C'mon, of course you are!" Phillip argued jovially.

Damon crossed his arms over his chest. "Yeah, who else are people going to vote for?"

"Well, you're both very sweet," Lexi said, hoping her cheeks weren't too red.

"So…" Phillip began, "How tall do you want these things to be?"

Lexi chewed her lip and looked between both Phillip and Damon, who were easily at least six foot six. "Let's say a little taller than you?"

Damon chuckled. "Deal."

"Yoo-hoo!" Erika called to Lexi from where she was seated at the rectangular table set up toward the back of the stage. "Can you help me with these flowers?"

Phillip nodded to the roll of chicken wire on the floor. "Go help her, we've got this."

"Thanks!" Lexi waved to them before joining Erika at the table. "Hey, Erika. What do you need?"

"Could you sort through those bins and find me some bling?" Erika asked, stacking various colors of paper. "I'm making 3-D flowers out of tissue paper, and I really want them to pop in the center, so they sparkle in the lights at the dance."

"Oh, sure." Lexi ducked under the table to pull out a bin filled with a jumble of beads, buttons, and metallic papers.

"So," Erika began, hands crisply making accordion folds in layers of tissue paper, "You didn't tell me you were running for Homecoming Queen."

Focused on picking rhinestones and shredded papers out of the bin, Lexi replied distractedly, "Oh, you heard that? Yeah, I'm not actually running. Damon and Phillip apparently just voted for me." *And tons of other people.* But she kept that to herself.

For a moment, the only sound Lexi could hear was the rumpling of tissue paper as Erika folded and fanned flower petals. "Well, that's great," Erika said finally before lifting her gaze. "But just so you know, I'm running, too." She watched Lexi carefully, waiting for her to react.

Lexi was puzzled. *Why would I care?* "That's great," she said, hoping her tone reflected her sincerity. "Again, I'm not actually running."

The crinkling sound resumed. "Cool," Erika said, wrinkling her nose. "Not that I'm all that in to winning, or anything. I would just hate for things to be awkward, since we're friends."

Smiling easily, Lexi shook her head. "Of course." She held out a fistful of shiny paper grass. "How's this?"

Erika fanned out the flower and put a dash of glue in the center to secure the gold paper accents. Lexi admired how the various colors of tissue paper gave the flowers such a lush, dimensional effect. Erika smiled in satisfaction at her handiwork. "Stunning. Now to make about five hundred more."

"Maybe we should enlist the football team," Lexi said with a giggle.

Erika waved her hand, rising to her feet. "I don't trust those boys to have the patience to do all the cutting properly. I think I have a sharper pair of scissors in my locker," she added, tossing the blunt red-handled scissors she'd been using onto the table. "Be right back."

Lexi took the opportunity to pull free several sheets of tissue paper and begin on a flower of her own. She studied Erika's handiwork. "Doesn't look too hard," she murmured.

"I don't buy it."

Lexi lifted her head to see Amber had appeared at her elbow. "What?" Lexi asked with a puzzled smile. "You don't buy that I can make a tissue paper flower?"

Amber dropped into the empty seat next to her. "No," she began in a low voice, "I don't buy that Erika doesn't care about who's Queen. I've known that girl since middle school, and she's very competitive."

Lexi vaguely remembered seeing Amber's name on a few awards throughout the school. She had a feeling Amber also had a competitive streak in her. "Oh, I don't care if I win," Lexi said with a chuckle.

"But Erika does. Trust me, she wants that crown," Amber continued. "And probably the one who will be King. Namely, my brother."

That's right. Amber Shields was Aidan's twin sister. There weren't many similarities between the two, and Lexi rarely saw them together.

Then again, why would their schedules even overlap? Amber was constantly studying. She was a member of the debate *and* Academic Decathlon teams. Aidan practically *lived* on the football field when he wasn't in class. Lexi couldn't even recall seeing Amber at any football games.

"Well, just keep an eye out," Amber finished, clearly displeased that Lexi wasn't interested in what she had to say about Erika.

Lexi was sure she meant well, but Erika was one of Lexi's first friends since coming to the school, and her teammate. She just couldn't believe she was like that.

"Want to help me work on these flowers?" Lexi asked, hoping to smooth the waters.

Staring at the various colors laid out on the table, Amber said, "You know, we should try to make some anemones. They pop up a lot in Greek myths."

Feeling relieved that the tenseness seemed to melt away, Lexi smiled. "Sounds great!"

"The game is tied 10 to 10… the ball is in possession of number 17, Parker Hecuba," the announcer's voice came over the loudspeaker that night in the Mountainview football field.

Lexi shook her crimson and gold pom-poms together. "Go Spartans!" she exclaimed, performing a high kick.

"Our team needs some encouragement!" Hallie Peacock, the cheerleading captain, announced to her fellow teammates from her spot on the edge of the formation. "Spartans—aim high!"

Lexi inhaled, assuming the first move. "V-I-C-T-O-R-Y!" Pivoting as she hit a low v, she clapped as her voice resounded with the other girls,

"Spartans, aim high!"

"Number 6 Quarterback Aidan Shields has the ball and is barreling down to the 52 yard line… one more touchdown and the Spartans win! Can he do it?"

"Oh my gosh, hurry, Aidan!" Erika squealed from her spot next to Lexi.

Lexi felt her adrenaline rushing, rustling her pom-poms and performing two high kicks in a row to help burn off the energy.

"And score! Touchdown—and win—for the Spartans!"

"Spartans! Spartans!" The crowd chanted as Lexi and her crew let out cheers of excitement.

Helen hurried down the bleachers breathlessly, bouncing up and down when Lexi turned to reach for her water. "That was so exciting!"

Lexi took a large sip, loving the cool feel of water soothing her dry throat. Cheering sometimes took a lot out of her, especially outside on these cool autumn nights. "I know, right?"

The football players came jogging off the field, clutching their helmets at their sides to bursts of applause. As Aidan approached the stands, Lexi couldn't help but watch as he ran a hand through his short thatch of dark brown hair.

"Whoo, yeah, Aidan!" She heard a group of girls call from the stands. She dropped her eyes. Of course. He had a horde of girls after him, as always.

"Hey, Lexi." Aidan paused at the bleachers.

Lifting her eyes in surprise, Lexi smiled and managed to say, "Good game. You were great out there."

"Thanks," Aidan said with a grin. "I'm always hustling, can't do anything less for my teammates."

"Especially since the big game is coming up, right Aidan?" Erika had appeared at Lexi's side, tossing her red hair over her shoulder as she took a bite from an apple.

Lexi's brow furrowed when she saw Aidan's expression grow

clouded. He looked almost…stressed at the mention of the Homecoming game.

The moment passed, and though Aidan was answering Erika, his eyes never left Lexi. "Yeah, it's going to be an important night for all of us. We've got to crush the Trojans."

There it was again, that intense talk. Lexi dropped her eyes, fiddling with the zipper of her duffel bag.

"You'll be cheering for me, right?"

Lexi lifted her head, and her eyes locked with his. For a moment, she was lost in the deep brown pools. "Um…" She bit her lip.

"Of *course* we will," Erika said enthusiastically, putting her arm around Lexi and giving her shoulders a squeeze.

Lexi dropped her eyes, her cheeks hot. He wasn't talking to her. He was talking to the whole squad.

"Oh, Aidan, I wanted to ask you something," Erika said sweetly, releasing Lexi and taking a step closer to him.

Well, fine, then, flirt with Erika. Lexi scowled in annoyance as she watched the two of them. She turned back to the bleachers to complain to Helen about what just happened, when she paused. *Where did Helen go?* She began walking down the track, eyes skimming the bleachers, when she saw Helen talking to Mason. By the looks of things, they seemed to be getting pretty cozy. That's when she noticed Parker was beside her, also watching them. Taking in his glum expression, she was pretty sure what this was about.

Tapping him on the shoulder, she asked, "What's up, Parker?"

"Ugh, it's nothing," Parker said, shuffling his foot.

"C'mon, you can talk to me," Lexi said encouragingly.

Parker sighed. "Well, I waved to Helen and was heading her way to ask her something, when muscle-bound meathead cut me off."

"What did you want to ask her?"

Parker avoided her piercing stare, mumbling something she couldn't make out.

"What?"

"I wanted to ask her to Homecoming," Parker said with a frustrated puff of air. "But I'm sure Mason is beating me to the punch."

Lexi eyed the pair, noticing that Mason was standing *very* close to Helen. "Well, you don't know that for sure. If you don't get the chance tonight, just try to catch her in the hall or something."

"No way she'd pick me over a guy like Mason," Parker said dejectedly. "Face it. He's the better player, and he's got girls swooning all over him."

Lexi chewed her lip, thinking hard.

"Hey, I know," Parker said, snapping his fingers. "You're her best friend—how does a guy get a girl to pay attention, and realize he likes her and that she should go out with him?"

Lexi smiled. Parker must really like Helen. "Well, Helen is a hopeless romantic. I'm sure she would *love* it if you made a romantic gesture."

Parker lifted his brows. "What kind of gesture?"

"I don't know, maybe slip a flower in her locker, or write her a little poem or something," Lexi mused.

"Is that what you'd like?" Parker asked suddenly.

Lexi furrowed her brows. "What?"

"I just mean," Parker continued hurriedly, "is that something that only Helen likes, or would most girls—like yourself—be into getting romantic notes or gifts?"

Lexi smiled. "Lots of girls like sweet, thoughtful gestures. It shows a person cares, and is putting thought into getting their attention, you know?" She paused, then shrugged. "I guess there could be some girls who don't like it, but I know both Helen and I would."

"So… a gift, or a little note may be a good way to ask you girls to the dance?" Parker asked, foot shuffling back and forth across the track.

Furrowing her brow at his choice of words, she asked, "You mean

Helen?" She couldn't help but stare at the way his shoe kept dragging across the track.

The shuffling stopped. "Yes. Right. Helen. Um—would she be into that?"

Lexi smiled. "Definitely. You need to go for it." Seeing Parker's hesitant look, she let out a grumble of frustration. "Before Mason does!"

Watching Helen and Mason, Parker nodded slowly. "Yeah, you're right. We've got to at least *try* to make our feelings known, right?"

Unsure of why he was speaking in plurals, Lexi said, "You've got it. Take a chance, Parker, you might be surprised."

Snapping his fingers, Parker took a couple of quick steps in the opposite direction. "Thanks Lexi. He was right, you really *are* awesome!"

Furrowing her brow, she called after him, "He? He who?" But he was already hurrying away.

Shrugging, Lexi felt more confused than ever, but happy she could at least help.

"Elevator!" Hallie called out the following afternoon at cheerleading practice. "One-two—"

Ensuring her feet were firmly planted on the safety mat they'd spread out on the edge of the football field, Lexi helped lift the team's flier, Erika, to stand in Penny Berry and Hallie's waiting hands.

Hallie nodded. "Good and clean. Now, Extension! One-two—"

Gripping Erika's ankles, Lexi smoothly but quickly raised her arms to their fullest. She glanced at the other stunt formation to ensure they'd done the same.

"Let's go, Spartans!" the team cheered. Erika and the team's other flier, Diana Tsuki, as well as the cheerleaders who were not in the stunt, made the motions and clapped.

"Let's go, Spartans!" Lexi chanted, finding her gaze wandering over to the field where football practice was being held. The crimson jersey with the bright white number six on the back caught her eye, and she watched as Aidan pumped his fists in the air. Resounding claps and shouts of excitement echoed off of the field as the boys gathered for a huddle.

"Cradle!" Hallie's next call snapped her back to attention. "One-two—"

Each formation tossed their fliers in the air, effortlessly catching them and setting them safely back on the ground.

"Good going, ladies!" Coach Niko exclaimed from where she sat in the bleachers.

"Was it clean looking enough, Coach?" Erika asked, tugging at the end of her shirt. "Because I'm sure we could make it even sharper."

Lexi bit her lip when she saw Hallie tense. They'd been stunting for the past hour, first perfecting the big stunts they would be unveiling at the Homecoming game, then cooling down with several Elevator and Extension stunts. Her arms were starting to get tired, and judging by Hallie's expression, she felt the same. They already had re-done several of the stunts at Erika's insistence.

Lexi was relieved to hear Coach Niko reply, "No, that's enough for tonight."

The team spent the next few minutes rolling up the practice mats and gathering other supplies to haul back to the equipment room.

Turning the key, Coach turned to the crowd of girls and said, "Rest up, and I'll see you at the next practice!"

"Anyone want to go to Hercules Hut?" Hallie asked, referring to Mountainview's local pizza place.

Pivoting on her heel and walking backward, Lexi replied, "Oh, thanks, but I'm grabbing dinner with Helen." Her back collided with something, or someone. "Ack!" she exclaimed.

She felt a shiver up her spine when the person she'd collided with chuckled. She spun around.

"Hey, Lexi. I guess this is payback for me whacking you with that football, huh?" The corner of Aidan's mouth turned up.

Feeling her cheeks grow warm, Lexi stammered, "Sorry."

Shaking his head, Aidan said with an easy grin, "No worries. How did practice go?"

"It went great," Lexi replied, trying to ignore how her pulse had mysteriously quickened.

"I caught some of the big stunt. That was awesome. It looked tricky, though," Aidan said, resting his football helmet against his side.

Lexi shrugged. "It's a little more complicated than our usual stunts, but…"

"It should definitely show those Trojans who's boss," Erika chimed in.

Lexi turned with a start, not realizing that Erika had joined them. She glanced around, noticing that the majority of the other cheerleaders and the football team had drifted toward the bleachers where their gear was stowed.

"I've made sure that we're paying extra attention to that stunt," Erika went on, tossing her head to flick some red bangs out of her gray eyes. "It has to be just *perfect* for Homecoming."

"Speaking of Homecoming," Aidan began, tilting his head in Lexi's direction, "Um, how is the decorating going? Amber mentioned you've been working on some pretty cool stuff."

Lexi smiled, thinking back to that afternoon when they'd begun to paint the backdrop they would hang in the photo booth area. "It's really coming together!"

"We've been working really hard on the planning," Erika added.

"Oh, you're on the committee, too?" Aidan glanced back at Erika.

Erika beamed. "Yeah, you're going to *love* what we've dreamed up.

Right, Lexi?"

Not liking the tense feeling that was building in her chest when Aidan turned his gaze back to her, Lexi nodded mutely.

Aidan frowned, taking a step backward. "Well, I've got to head home," he said. "See you girls later."

"Bye, Aidan!" Erika called as Lexi pivoted to head toward the bleachers. Helen would be there any minute, and she needed to grab her stuff.

"My, my, our quarterback was certainly grabbing your attention. Again," Hallie said to Lexi from where she sat on the bleachers, shrugging into her sweatshirt.

Lexi blushed, opening her mouth to stammer a reply when Erika spoke up. "Oh, I know, he's *always* flirting with us. He thinks that just because he's the hottest guy in school, he can have our undivided attention constantly." She nudged Lexi's shoulder. "Right, girl?"

Lexi furrowed her brow, unable to shake off the disappointed feeling growing in the pit of her stomach. He's always flirting with *us*? What did that mean?

Glancing between the two of them with raised eyebrows, Hallie rose to her feet and hopped off the stands. "See you at the next practice."

Lexi heaved a sigh, sitting on the bleacher and reaching for her rose-pink duffel bag. Pulling out her phone, she saw a text from Helen.

"I didn't mean to burst your bubble," Erika began, sinking into a spot beside her on the bleachers, "I know Aidan is really cute." She heaved a sigh. "But he's a huge flirt. He's not *really* interested in you. To him, you're the hot new cheerleader to go out with… just another notch in his belt."

Lexi felt her chest tighten. Just like Andrew. Why did guys only view her as a conquest?

Erika's forehead wrinkled as she leaned forward and reached for her wrist, giving it a sympathetic squeeze. "Sorry to break it to you like this, hon. I'm just trying to be a friend."

Swallowing hard, hating how her eyes suddenly felt hot with unshed tears, Lexi nodded. "I know," she managed to murmur. Her eye caught Helen walking down the track. "I have to go. Um, see you tomorrow."

"Hey, how did practice go?" Helen said with a chipper smile as Lexi approached.

Gripping the strap of her duffel bag, Lexi shrugged, trying to put the conversation she'd just had with Erika out of her mind. "Fine."

"About half of the football team were heading out when I got to the stadium," Helen went on, twirling a lock of hair between her fingers as they made their way toward downtown. "I think Mason winked at me. You have to admit, a lot of the football players are pretty darn cute. I'm so jealous you get to check them out so often."

Aidan's handsome face flashed through Lexi's mind, and her stomach twisted. "I'm *practicing*."

Helen waved a hand. "Meh, details. Anyway, I can't believe the dance is coming up so quickly! I wonder if anyone's going to ask me…"

Seeing an opening, Lexi began in a light tone, "What about Parker?"

Helen pursed her lips. "Parker? Parker Hecuba?"

Nodding enthusiastically, Lexi said, "Yeah! He's really nice, and super cute. Plus, he's one of the best players on the team."

"Wait." Helen slowed her steps. "Is that why you won't give Aidan the time of day?"

"Aidan's a jerkface playboy," Lexi found herself muttering.

"So now you have the hots for Parker?" Helen asked.

Red alert. Red alert. This was definitely not the direction Lexi wanted things to go. She may be peeved at Aidan for leading her on, but she had to remember the task at hand. Parker was her friend. Parker liked Helen. She needed to try and open Helen's eyes to what a sweet guy Parker was, without betraying his trust that he liked her. She took a moment to collect her thoughts. *Breathe, girl.* "No!" Lexi protested. "I just got to thinking: Parker's great, you're my best friend, and the two of you have so much in common…"

"There you go again, Goddess of Love," Helen replied with a teasing smile.

Lexi laughed incredulously. "What?"

"Oh, that's just what we girls call you," Helen said matter-of-factly. "Since people always come to you with their romantic woes, and you seem to always have a solution. Except to your own."

Lexi playfully stuck her tongue out. "I just want my friends to be happy! Is that so wrong?"

Helen bumped her shoulder. "Of course not! It's just… take some time for your own happiness, too."

Lexi paused to let her words sink in. Her own happiness? It was true, she really wished she could find a nice boy to date, but every time she got her hopes up, they all turned out to be jerks. Like Aidan. Her mouth went dry, and she reached to pull the water bottle from the side pouch of her cheer bag.

A piece of paper fluttered out of the pouch to land on the sidewalk.

"Here, let me get it." Helen knelt to pick up the folded piece of paper and hand it to Lexi.

"Thanks." Lexi furrowed her brow, staring at the unfamiliar notepaper. Putting her water bottle away, she carefully unfolded the paper, eyes taking in the straight lines of a handwritten note. Her heart gave a funny little leap.

"What is it?" Helen asked, watching her expression.

"Listen to this," Lexi breathed, clearing her throat. "*I know your eyes are as blue as the sea, and your hair is like golden sand. If only you would give me a chance, and I could hold your hand.*"

"Oh. My. Gosh!" Helen squealed. "A *love* note?! Who's it from?"

Lexi's eyes dropped down to the bottom of the page, and she frowned, turning the paper over. "I don't know."

Helen grabbed her arm. "Lexi—you have a secret admirer!"

Heart hammering and face flushing, Lexi shook her head. "I don't believe it."

"Oh, believe it! The Goddess of Love is finally feeling the pluck of Cupid's bow," Helen said with a grin.

The two girls continued their walk downtown, talking animatedly.

"This had better be amazing," Amber said a few days later as she, Lexi, Phillip and Damon walked toward the school's shop class to work on the Homecoming float. "I have intel that West High has a *Trojan Horse.*"

"They're riding a horse down Main Street?" Damon asked in confusion.

Lexi giggled as they weaved through a cluster of students lingering in the classroom working on their various projects. Amber rolled her eyes. "They're *building* a Trojan Horse, Damon. Like in the Trojan War?"

Damon blinked, clearly not following. "Oh. Right."

"Oh, hey, Lexi!" Parker looked up from the table saw as they passed by.

"Hi, Parker!" Lexi smiled and followed Phillip through the swinging doors that led into the back garage.

Phillip flipped on the lights. "How did you find out about their float, anyway?"

Pushing her glasses up the bridge of her nose, Amber replied with a sly smile, "I tutored someone from West High last year. She couldn't help bragging about it on her Instagram."

"They're doing an entire horse?" Phillip whistled as he took in their half-constructed float. They'd built a Greek chariot form out of chicken wire atop the trailer bed, and had begun the tedious process of gluing tissue flowers in their Spartan colors onto the form. The student body had selected Aidan to represent the school, dressed as Ares, Greek god of war and justice, and patron god of the Spartans in ancient times. Next to the chariot would be a dog, one of Ares' symbols. "They do a giant horse, we do a little dog? This is so lame in comparison."

"Oh, come on!" Lexi protested. "You just can't see the end result yet. Our float is going to be amazing. Besides, the parade is not a contest."

Damon shrugged, rifling through the boxes of materials. "I guess you're right. What needs to be done?"

Lexi patted the cardboard cut-out she'd started of a dog. "Someone could help me make this poor boy more three-dimensional?"

"And I'll keep working on the pomps," Amber said, carefully climbing on top of the trailer bed.

"Pomps?" Damon asked, a confused look on his face.

Amber sighed. "That's the proper name for the tissue paper flowers."

Phillip rolled up his sleeves. "I'll help with the dog."

The group set to work, the room fairly quiet aside from the sound of sawing and hammering in the next room. Until they heard a crash.

Amber and Lexi shared a curious look, hopping off of the platform and hurrying to the shop class door. Damon and Phillip shrugged, continuing their work.

Lexi frowned as she watched Mason standing over a crouched figure.

"What did you do that for, Mason?" Hector Smith demanded, staring at the pieces of wood on the floor.

"Because you take up too much space, Smith."

Amber gasped when Hector's face fell, but he squared his jaw and stood up, clutching the pieces of his project. "I have to work on my projects, too. If you don't like it, use another station."

"I've got a better idea," Mason said, cracking his knuckles.

Lexi flung the door open, about to go find a teacher when Aidan intervened.

"Hey, knock it off," he said, appearing behind Mason.

Lexi's eyes widened. She hadn't even realized Aidan was there. He must have been working on a project when they arrived.

Mason rolled his eyes. "Whatever, dude, butt out."

Inserting himself between Hector and Mason and crossing his arms over his broad chest, Aidan retorted, "I said lay *off*, Mason. Unless you want me to tell Coach Titan about this little incident."

Mason scoffed. "You wouldn't."

Aidan drew himself to his full height. "Want to try me?"

Looking between Hector and Aidan, Mason was quiet for a long moment. Finally, he heaved a sigh and stormed out of the room. "Whatever."

"That was a close one," Amber murmured to Lexi.

Watching as Aidan crouched to pick up the remainder of Hector's tools, Lexi nodded, heart hammering. What he did was really cool.

Then she caught herself, remembering Erika's warning. Liking Aidan would only lead to heartache. Then again, why should she care? She already had a totally sweet guy writing her romantic notes. Besides, she and Aidan were like Mars and Venus. Total opposites.

"Thanks," Hector mumbled, rubbing the back of his neck.

"No worries, man. Don't pay any attention to Mason. He's just kind of…"

"An ass?" Hector asked dryly.

Aidan chuckled. "Yeah, that too."

The pair turned and noticed Lexi and Amber lingering by the doorway.

The corner of Hector's mouth turned up in a lopsided grin as he waved, and Lexi noticed with interest that Amber was waving shyly back.

"Hey, didn't see you two there," Aidan said, approaching the doors to the storeroom.

Stepping inside, Amber began, "We were working on the float when we heard voices."

"That was really cool what you did back there," Lexi found herself saying. Then she reddened. Oh, God, how stupid did she sound right now?

Aidan shoved his hands in the pockets of his letterman jacket. "Nah, I really didn't do anything. Hector's cool. Mason just thinks that since we're on the football team, we're better than everyone else." His brown eyes narrowed. "Bullshit."

Wow. She was convinced that Aidan was just a swaggering jock. Maybe she'd misjudged him. "Totally. Um, so what do you think of the float?" she asked, trying to divert attention away from herself. She was sure she was blushing. Though why, she still had no idea. *Remember your secret admirer,* she thought desperately.

"Sweet!" Aidan exclaimed. "This is going to blow those Trojans out of the water."

"It had better," Amber said severely. "They're building a horse," she whispered to her brother.

"But will the god of war be riding the horse?" Aidan replied with a cocky grin, ruffling Amber's hair. "Nope!"

Amber wriggled free from his grasp, attempting to smooth her ruffled locks. "I told you, *stop* doing that!"

Aidan chuckled, holding up a hand. "Sorry, sis, I'm just stoked. Between this bitchin' float and the Spartans winning the game, Homecoming is going to be on fire!"

Lexi cleared her throat, tucking a strand of hair behind her ear. "Well, let's just hope we win."

Aidan stiffened, his expression growing clouded.

Amber shared a serious look with her brother. "Don't worry, Aidan," she said soothingly. "We'll win. I've been keeping a close eye on the recent scores. The Spartans have the stronger team."

Relaxing slightly, Aidan finally smiled again. "Yeah, you're right. Well, I've got to get going. See you. Lexi," he said, locking eyes with her and winking before he left the room.

Lexi felt like she'd been zapped with electricity at his wink. *Remember what Erika said,* she commanded. *Don't fall for the flirting.* "Well, that was a little… intense," she said at last.

"Mm-hm," Amber murmured distractedly, staring at her phone. "Sorry, I just got an e-mail from Dr. Mercer…" She gasped suddenly.

Lexi frowned, taking a step closer. "What's the matter?"

"I just got the rough draft back for my Russian Lit paper," Amber said in a hollow tone. "Oh my god. I was sure it was 'A' material." She inhaled sharply, her chest rising and falling rapidly.

Phillip could hear the commotion from where he was perched on the float. "Is she okay?" he asked Lexi.

"She needs to sit down," Lexi said, guiding Amber to a chair. "Amber, hey." She rubbed her hand up and down Amber's arm soothingly. "I'm sure your paper is amazing."

Amber shook her head, eyes glazed. "No, it's not good enough for Dr. Mercer, and if it's not good enough for Dr. Mercer, it's definitely not good enough for the Golden Owl award, and if I can't even win a *basic* academic paper award like the Golden Owl—" Amber began talking so fast, Lexi was sure she was going to hyperventilate.

Damon hopped off of the platform, reaching for his backpack. "Here, Amber, have some water." He held out the bottle, giving Lexi a helpless look.

"The Ivys will never consider me if I can't even pull this off! Oh, God, what will I say to Mom and Dad…" Amber rambled on, pulling at her hair.

"Should I go find Aidan?" Phillip asked nervously.

"No!" Amber squeaked. "Please, don't tell anyone." She took a long sip of Damon's water bottle, then closed her eyes, taking slower breaths.

"Scout's honor," Phillip said, holding up his hand. "It won't leave this room."

"Maybe I have time to fix this," Amber said to herself, running her fingers nervously through her long, chestnut brown locks. "Maybe Mom and Dad will never know about this poor draft."

"There you go," Lexi said with an encouraging smile. "It's just the rough draft! I'm sure you'll get the grade you want."

Lifting her eyes, Amber stared somberly at Lexi. "I don't just *want* the grade, Lexi. I need it."

"You're like, the smartest girl in school," Damon said, tilting his head to the side in confusion. "One 'bad' grade"—he curled his fingers into quotation marks—"won't do any harm."

"You guys don't understand," Amber said in a small voice. "There's no such thing as failure in my family."

Phillip and Damon exchanged concerned looks. "Don't worry, Amber," Phillip said finally, "I'm sure you've got this."

"Yeah, why don't we go to Dr. Mercer's office right now?" Lexi said, putting her arm around Amber.

"But…" Amber's wide brown eyes glanced toward their project. "What about the float?"

Damon bumped shoulders with Phillip. "Leave it to us. We'll keep working on it."

Amber finally braved a small smile, and Lexi helped her rise to her feet. "Thanks, guys."

Lexi waved to Phillip and Damon as she walked with Amber out into the hallway.

Later that week, Lexi stood in front of her open closet, cradling her cell phone as she slid various hangers down the rod in search of her denim jacket. "Yeah, Dad's still at work," she said into the phone to her mother as she spotted the jacket. "Yes, Mom, I ate. You left enough food for three weeks, not just a couple of days," she said with a giggle as she shrugged the jacket on.

"Well, I had to!" Mrs. Cypress protested. "You know your dad—he can't even cook pasta properly."

Lexi laughed, pulling down her bin of scarves from the top shelf of her closet and rifling through it. "I could have managed for us."

"No, honey, you're too busy. I was happy to take care of it. I don't like being so far away." Lexi's grandmother had fallen and sprained her wrist several days before, so her mother was currently back in California staying with her for the rest of the week. While Lexi of course missed her, she and her dad had to laugh at the fact that her mom was constantly calling and texting both of them, probably to ensure they were still breathing. "I just called to say hi. What are you up to?"

"I'm about to head back to the school, to finish up some decorations for Homecoming," Lexi said distractedly, selecting a pale pink scarf that matched her pink and white top, and wrapping it around her neck.

"At this time of night?" her mom asked sharply. "Do you really have to do this tonight?"

Lexi sighed, cradling her cell phone between her head and shoulder as she shuffled through her messenger bag, checking to make sure she had the various assignments, notebooks, and textbooks she would need for school tomorrow. "Yes, Mom. Homecoming is almost here! I'm in charge of finishing up all of the silhouettes for the gym, but I didn't get it finished in time. Extra practice."

"Aren't you afraid of spreading yourself too thin, honey?" Lexi recognized the subtle change in her mother's voice, the one she began to notice not long after moving to Mountainview, when Lexi transferred into several AP courses, snagged a much-coveted spot on the Varsity Cheerleading squad, then was invited to join the French Club. Her mother had expressed concern that she was putting too much on her plate, barely giving herself time to settle in to their new house and town.

If only Amber's parents expressed the same concerns. Fortunately for her, the prognosis on her paper wasn't nearly as bad as she'd thought. Dr.

Mercer had just wanted to go over some weak points in the essay, and he still thought it could be a strong contender for the Golden Owl. Still, to feel so pressured to perform perfectly from your own family must be nerve-wracking. No wonder Amber was so high-strung.

And it made her wonder about Aidan.

"Hey, you and Dad are the ones who plucked me out of the only town I've ever known and thrust me into this flannel-wearing wilderness," Lexi retorted. Hearing her mother's clucking sound of concern, Lexi quickly said, "I'm joking! Despite the weather being icky and damp, and having to trade my sandals for boots most of the year, I like it here." Speaking of boots, she could not seem to locate the brown knee-length boot that matched the one she had just slipped on her left foot.

"Really honey?" Her mother sighed with relief. "I just don't want you to push yourself too hard. I know that you've got the big game coming up, so I understand the extra practices, but maybe adding Homecoming Committee to your plate on top of everything else you're in the middle of was too much for your senior year. Of course, your dad and I know you always give everything you do 110%, and your grades have always been amazing, but I would hate for them to suffer during what's your most important year of high school due to spreading yourself too thin—"

"Mom, I'm fine." She knelt to the ground, peering under her bed to see if the boot had ended up under there. "Seriously. I finished my homework already." She glanced at the clock. *Ugh. I'm running out of time to get all this done.* Maybe she was overdoing it a tiny bit since senior year began—she'd been getting invited to more parties, school events, and even sports games she didn't already cheer for. However, moving to a new school, let alone a new state at her age was hard. She was just glad she fit in, that people seemed to like her. Even enough to cast their vote for her for Homecoming Queen, which still surprised her. And apparently popular enough for someone to write her love notes…

Unbidden, she felt a twist in the pit of her stomach as she remembered what had happened yesterday afternoon after cheerleading practice.

"What did Parker just slip into your bag?" Hallie had stopped Lexi as she ascended the bleacher stairs.

Frowning, Lexi had asked, "What are you talking about?"

"Parker was just up here," Hallie had gestured to the bleachers where the members of the team stashed their sweatshirts, water bottles, and duffel bags or backpacks. "And he put something in your bag."

Lexi had frozen, hurriedly unzipping her cheerleading duffel and finding the same piece of notepaper from the last love note, with the distinctive straight, large handwriting. Oh, God. Parker didn't like *her*, did he? That would mean that while she was totally aiming her arrow at Helen to fall for Parker, he wanted *her* this whole time. Do over. Do over! Maybe he was aiming for another girl's bag. Lexi then glanced at her rose-pink duffel bag with the embroidered hearts and her initials, AVC. Okay, it would be pretty hard to do that.

"What is it?" Hallie had asked, pale blue eyes shining with curiosity.

"Nothing," Lexi had said, hurriedly stuffing the note back into her bag before Hallie could see the contents and rushing down the bleachers, face flushed and heart pounding. "Got to run!"

Snapping back to the present, Lexi weighed it over in her mind for what felt like the hundredth time. She was probably jumping to conclusions. Why would Parker ask about Helen if he really liked *her?* Then again, Helen hadn't been asked out by Parker yet, nor received any romantic gestures. Parker being her secret admirer when she not only didn't like him, but was trying to fix him up with her best friend, was more than her nerves could take. She decided not to think about it. Or, at least try not to. She had way too much going on. Schoolwork and her extracurriculars were one thing, but with all of this other stuff going on, it was starting to be too much.

"Honey? What about your test?" her mom asked.

Lexi cleared her throat, wishing she could clear her mind as easily. "I studied. Besides, my test isn't for a couple of days." Out of the corner of her eye, she noticed the brown boot underneath the chair to her vanity. Crouching to fish it out, she said, "Now I just need to finish working on those cut-outs."

"Honey, it's dark out already here, which means it definitely is dark there," her mother said with a sigh.

Lexi glanced out the window, the large maple that shaded her window reflecting the soft glow of their house's exterior lights. Of course it was dark here. Not only did it just seem to get darker here earlier—probably due to being so much farther north—but it had been an overcast day. At least no rain so far. That was something to be cheerful about.

"Do it tomorrow," her mother urged. "Or at least wait until your dad gets home—"

"Mom! I can't wait around forever—he's not due home for at least another hour or two!" Sheesh, she wanted to maybe get to sleep before midnight tonight. "Besides, it's going to take me like, ten minutes to walk to campus."

"Fine," her mother conceded, her tone a mixture of exasperation and worry. "But you can't go alone. Bring Cupid."

Lexi smiled. Though their dog was as loving as his name, he was very protective of his family, especially Lexi. "I promise. He'll love a special evening walk."

"Good. Text me when you make it to school. And," she added firmly, "when you make it back home. And don't stay there too late!"

"Will do. Give Grandma a hug for me. But not too hard," Lexi added. "Don't hurt her wrist." She smiled as her mother agreed and hung up. Heaving a sigh, Lexi plucked her keys from her nightstand and hurried into the hall. "Cupid!" she called, approaching the staircase. "Want to go for a walk?"

Lexi pulled her scarf tighter around her neck as they made their way through the neighborhood to the high school, sniffling in the chilly night air. Cupid happily trotted beside her, tail wagging. As they rounded the corner and approached the edge of the school campus, Lexi felt the wind pick up and glanced up at the sky. "I don't like the look of those clouds, my boy," she mumbled to Cupid. "It didn't *say* it was going to rain, so of course I didn't bring my umbrella." Curse this unpredictable weather! Why couldn't it do what it said it was going to do on the forecast? She quickened her steps, Cupid breaking into a brisk trot beside her. "Let's just hurry and get this done."

Thirty minutes later, Lexi was sitting cross-legged on the stage, dragging her paint brush across the life-size silhouette she and Amber had made of a woman wearing a long chiton.

Cupid whined from where he sat next to her, gazing up at her with wide brown eyes.

"Don't give me that sad face," Lexi chided him. "I'm almost done, and then we'll finish our walkies." Fortunately, the gym wasn't locked yet, as football practice was just finishing up, so she had plenty of time to put the finishing touches on the silhouettes.

As she was twisting the cap back on the jar of glitter and admiring the completed effect, she felt Cupid pull on his leash. She turned to see he had walked as far away from her as the leash would allow, nudging bins of materials. "Okay, honey, you win. Let's go."

It had gotten colder—and darker—in the amount of time they'd been in the gym. Lexi suppressed a yawn as the large doors to the gym clicked behind them and they stepped into the night.

When raised voices reached her ears, she gave a start. Tensing, she glanced around at the darkened landscape. Maybe it was a stupid idea to come back to school after dark. "Come on, boy," she said, trying to pick up the pace as they headed toward the football field to make it to the edge of campus. As they got closer to the track, the voices got louder, and she realized, heart hammering, that the shouting she'd heard had come from somewhere near the football field. Taking a deep breath, she tried to stay on high alert and walk as fast as possible.

Her steps slowed when she saw Aidan up ahead, football duffel bag slung over his shoulder, in the middle of a heated conversation. Squinting, she realized he was talking to a man—tall, with dark hair. Curiosity getting the better of her, she held Cupid's leash tightly and crept closer. As she watched them, she realized how much the man resembled Aidan, despite the graying temples and the beard. This must be Aidan's father.

Cupid started to growl at the raised voices. "Shh." Lexi reached down to stroke the top of his head, eyes never leaving the two figures.

"It's absolutely unacceptable," Mr. Shields snarled.

"I did my best, Dad," Aidan said, his voice lower than before.

"Yeah?" Mr. Shields took a step closer to his son. "Well, it sure as hell didn't seem like it. This isn't just a game, son, this is your *future*."

Aidan heaved a frustrated sigh. "I hit it hard. I practice every free chance I get. We've been having extra practices, too. But I still have to study…"

Lexi inhaled sharply when Mr. Shields threw his head back and laughed. "Like that's going to help. Let's face it, son. Amber received all of the scholarly genetics."

Lexi gasped. She couldn't believe that Aidan's own father was speaking so cruelly to him.

"I know I'm not Amber"—Lexi's heart twisted when she heard the break in his voice—"but I study hard. I can't live on the football field, Dad. If I don't keep a certain GPA, I can't play."

"You'd better be prepared to live on this field," Mr. Shields continued in a hard tone. "This is where your future is. You have to be the best. Stanford won't be impressed by subpar."

"Like I said before, Dad," Aidan began, running a hand through his shock of dark hair in frustration. "I can get into another school—"

Thunder rumbled in the distance, causing the fur at the back of Cupid's neck to stiffen under Lexi's fingertips as she watched the scene unfold.

"Let me make this clear as glass to you, young man. The Shields' are not failures. Your sister is currying the favor of three different Ivy Leagues. I'm not about to show my face at the Club and tell our circle that my son is going to *a state school*." He spat the last part as if the words were too filthy for his palate.

"But…Dad…" Aidan's back was completely to Lexi and Cupid now, but her breath hitched when she heard his tone. He sounded, well…

Broken.

Yet Mr. Shields was already dismissing his son, turning on his heel and adjusting his tie. "I have work to finish up. I expect your next practice won't be so utterly disappointing."

The wind picked up just then, and Lexi could only stare in stunned silence as Mr. Shields stormed away.

Aidan heaved a sigh, pivoting on his heel. When he saw Lexi and Cupid, he gave a start, hurriedly wiping his eyes, but Lexi saw how damp they were. "Uh, Lexi… I—" He glanced over his shoulder at his father's retreating figure.

Lexi took a step closer, Cupid in tow. "Aidan, hi. Um, sorry, I wasn't trying to listen or anything, I just was putting some finishing touches on the decorations, and…" she trailed off, watching Aidan's expression carefully. "Are you okay?"

Aidan stared back at her, face guarded. "Of course. I mean, it's nothing I'm not used to," he tried to come off casually, but something in his tone betrayed him.

"Look, I totally get it," Lexi began in a gentle tone, "Your dad is putting a lot of pressure on you." Remembering how much Amber had freaked out about that paper, she went on, "It sounds like he puts a lot of pressure on both you and Amber—"

"No, you don't get it," Aidan cut her off. "Amber's the *smart* one. Amber is the captain of the Academic Decathlon team. Amber's classes are all AP. Amber is on the Dean's List. Hell, she even took some college courses over the summer. Amber's papers get *awards*. Amber is so smart and talented and brilliant and gifted, she's got her pick of Ivy League schools."

Lexi stared at him, letting his words sink in.

"Yes, I like football," he continued, "But I *have* to be the best. You don't understand. Some people may really *want* a football scholarship. I *need* one. If we don't win the Homecoming game, if the scout doesn't see me bring it home…" He took a shuddering breath. "If I don't get into Stanford—the only school that they will even consider as being worthy—well, there's no such thing as failure in the Shields' family," he muttered in a somber voice, echoing Amber's words.

Lexi took a shallow breath, shocked that his parents could be so cruel, but she'd seen how Amber crumbled at the thought of her paper being anything less than award-winning. The serious tone their conversation had taken the other day about the football game made sense now. He wasn't obsessed with winning because he was some kind of competitive, muscle-bound jock. In his family, he *had* to win. "Aidan, I—"

"I'm sorry," he stammered finally, brown eyes suspiciously bright. "I didn't mean to snap, or lay all of this on you. I just…"

"No, I understand," Lexi replied. "It's just so unfair. Neither one of you should have to deal with this kind of stress. You should be able to go to whatever college *you* want."

"Well, if we want to go to college at all, we've got to play by Dad's rules," Aidan said dejectedly.

"Then don't play by his stupid rules," Lexi found herself saying. "Look for schools that offer work-study programs. Apply for football scholarships, anything!"

Cupid chose that moment to give a resounding bark.

Aidan chuckled in surprise. "Well, I love your spirit, and apparently so does your dog."

Lexi ducked her head, knowing her cheeks must be bright red, and not just from the cold. She ran a hand over Cupid's fur. "Shh, boy." Glancing at Aidan, she cleared her throat and said, "This is Cupid."

"Cupid?"

Hearing the laughter in his voice, Lexi looked up, and caught her breath when she saw him smile. "What?"

"Nothing." Aidan grinned. "It's cute."

Lexi's blue eyes locked momentarily with his brown ones, and in spite of her best efforts, she felt her heart flutter. She could get lost in those eyes if she let herself. It should be a crime to be so handsome. Thunder rumbled again, louder this time, and Lexi glanced at the foreboding clouds. "I've got to get going."

"You shouldn't be out this late by yourself," Aidan began, shoving his hands in the pockets of his crimson letterman jacket. "Let me walk you home."

"Oh, you don't have to do that," Lexi protested. "I've got my protector."

Aidan shook his head. "It's the least I can do to thank you for listening to my drama. Besides, you can never be too careful, right, Cupid?" Cupid wagged his tail, licking Aidan's outstretched hand. "There, it's settled. Which way?"

Feeling her pulse quicken, Lexi resumed walking in the direction of home, sandwiched between Aidan and Cupid.

When they reached the sidewalk, Lexi felt Aidan's eyes on her. She cocked her head inquisitively toward him. "Hm?"

He cleared his throat, hurriedly looking away. "Nothing, it's just, uh… you look really pretty tonight, that's all. Pink is a nice color on you."

Lexi blushed, heart hammering even harder than before. "Thank you," she managed, staring down at her hands as she nervously fumbled with Cupid's leash. She was forced to look up when she felt droplets of water on her head. The clouds had finally given way, and a steady rain was falling from the sky. "Ugh," she moaned, trying in vain to shield her bare head with her free hand.

Aidan laughed, shrugging off his letterman jacket and draping it above her like an umbrella. "That better?"

"No, Aidan." Lexi shook her head. "Your jacket will get ruined."

"It can handle a little water."

"But you're getting all wet!" she protested.

Aidan chuckled. "I'm a guy, my hair will dry quickly."

"I wish I'd brought my umbrella," she said, feeling flustered.

"I really don't mind," Aidan said. Lexi's heartbeat sped up when she realized he'd had to step closer to her to keep his jacket over her. "I'm not afraid of a little rain. Not many guys carry an umbrella. Especially in the Pacific Northwest."

Trying to keep her voice even and ignore the somersaults her stomach was doing at his close proximity, Lexi said, "It's a macho thing, huh?"

Aidan shrugged. "I'll own it. But a lot of people—guys and girls— don't bother to carry one, since the rain is such a common occurrence here."

"Well, I still am going to use an umbrella," Lexi said haughtily. "The rain may be wonderful for all of the plants, but it's killer on my hair." She wrinkled her nose. "Puffy frizz factor."

Aidan laughed, breath tickling her ear. "Nothing wrong with that. You don't have to conform."

Lexi chose that moment to look up into his eyes. Big mistake. Her heart flip-flopped when she stared into them. "I don't?" *Thump-thump. Thump-thump.* Her heart pounded loudly in her ears, though she tried hard to think straight. *Remember what Erika said—he's a player. He's not really interested in you.*

Why did thinking that hurt so much?

Smiling, Aidan shook his head. "Just be yourself."

Summoning her courage, Lexi began, "Um, Aidan, I…"

Cupid chose that exact moment to shake himself off.

"Eek! Cupid, no! You're getting Aidan all wet," Lexi exclaimed, throwing up her hands.

Cupid looked at her with big, sad eyes.

"Aw, poor puppy. You don't like the water, huh?" Aidan asked.

"Actually, he loves water," Lexi told him. "He used to go swimming with me in the ocean back in California all the time!"

Grinning, Aidan replied, "That's so cool! Do you miss the beach?"

Lexi pursed her lips forlornly. "Is it that obvious?"

"Well, we're not too far from the coast," Aidan said encouragingly. "We plan trips out there all the time… you and Cupid should join us soon."

"That would be fun," Lexi said, ducking her head and allowing a cascade of hair to hide her blushing face. "Um, this is me," she added, gesturing to her house.

"Oh, great," Aidan stammered, lifting the jacket so that Lexi could step out. "Looks like your hair survived," he said with a chuckle, reaching up to tuck a piece behind her ear.

Trying to ignore how her heart started pounding even harder, Lexi nodded. "Yeah. Um, thanks."

"No problem. Bye, Lexi, Cupid," Aidan said with a grin before turning and jogging out into the night.

Lexi leaned against her front door, watching the water cascade from the sky from the shelter of her porch as she remembered how Aidan had just brushed his hand against her cheek moments ago. "I guess the rain isn't so bad after all…"

A couple of days later, Lexi wandered out of the shop classroom, staring intently at the piece of notepaper she clutched in her hands.

As a cheerleader you cheer for others, in game and out
But do you know I cheer for you?
Seriously, I'm your biggest fan
I feel like if you were with me, I could do anything.

When she'd gone to add the finishing touches to the float, she'd found the folded-up note stuffed in between the tissue flowers of the dog she'd made.

She sighed, chewing her lip. That didn't bode well for her hopes that Parker was not her secret admirer, since he took shop and she saw him almost every time she came in to work on the float. Despite her fears, the romantic words scrawled on the note made her heart race. Unbidden, Aidan's handsome face flashed through her mind. She blushed.

Why on Earth was she thinking about Aidan? Here she had a totally sweet guy writing her notes—which, true, could be Parker, which she didn't want to happen at all—but all she could think of was Aidan.

She realized with a pang that the thought of going out with anyone else was utterly disappointing.

She was so engrossed in her thoughts that she almost jumped out of her skin when she felt a hand clamp down on her shoulder.

"Hey, Earth to Lexi!" Erika smiled, leaning over her shoulder. "What's got you so engrossed?"

"Nothing." Lexi hurriedly folded the note and stuffed it into the pocket of her jeans.

Erika cocked her head inquisitively. "Um, okay. Heading to the gym?"

Lexi nodded, absentmindedly twirling a lock of her hair.

Erika pulled her phone out, tapping intently. "So, I have to finish the flower arrangements, double-check that we have enough cups, napkins, plates—oh, and at tonight's practice, I really hope we can smooth out that new cheer dance so it looks on point for half-time."

Lexi nodded absently. Erika had been very intense at the last several practices, and it was starting to grate on her nerves.

She shoved open the door to the gym with her hip as the two made their way to the stage.

Erika shot out a hand to grip Lexi's arm. Frowning at a message on her phone, she spluttered, "Wait—you're only staying for *half* of practice?! Just days before Homecoming?"

Lexi sighed as they went up the stairs to the stage, waving to the group of students already gathered as she slid her bag off of her shoulder. "I know," she said glumly. "But I have to go to the airport to pick my mom up, I can't help it."

Erika heaved a sigh, dropping her backpack into an empty chair with a dramatic thud. "I just wish we'd known about this sooner—we could have been better prepared."

Lexi frowned, not appreciating getting lectured by someone who wasn't even the team captain. "I told Coach Niko and Hallie last week."

"Lexi!" Amber called to her from where she stood near the backdrop several feet away.

Lexi smiled, relieved to have an excuse to step away from Erika, who had begun to rant about the importance of the big game coming up. "Sorry, I've got to help Amber finish this."

Erika frowned, sinking into her chair before finally focusing on the paper flower arrangements in front of her.

"Thanks," Lexi whispered to Amber as she joined her. "She was getting a little…"

"Intense?" Amber whispered back, dipping her paint brush in the white paint jar she held.

Lexi followed suit, rolling up her sleeves and reaching for a brush.

"Well, it's like… Hallie's the captain, and Hallie has no issue with me leaving early tonight." She glanced over her shoulder, praying their voices were low enough.

Amber smirked as she ran her brush across the butcher paper canvas, creating a swirling cloud over the tranquil daytime scene they'd sketched out, complete with plants and Greek vases. "I told you, that girl's got ambition. She probably wants to be captain herself."

Lexi gave her a doubtful look. "I'm sure that's not it."

Before Amber could reply, Helen rushed up the stage stairs. "Lexi! Oh my God, Lexi!"

"Helen, what are you doing here?" Lexi asked. "Is something wrong?"

Helen put a hand to her chest, trying to take a deep breath. "Wrong? No, everything's right! Sorry to interrupt," she said hurriedly to Amber before continuing, "But I had to find you to share the news."

Lexi smiled, lifting her eyebrows in anticipation. "What news?"

"Parker asked me," Helen burst out with a grin. "To Homecoming!"

Amber gave a happy gasp. "Wow, congratulations!"

Lexi felt a grin spread across her face. Her arrow hadn't missed! Parker really *did* like Helen! "That's fantastic! You told him yes, right?"

Helen nodded enthusiastically. "Of course I said yes! You were totally right, Lexi, Parker is *so* nice. He's been talking to me a lot more recently, and we have so much in common—we watch a ton of the same TV shows, he loves animals…"

"Details, girl," Lexi reached for Helen's hands. "Tell me everything. How did he ask? Was it like, super romantic?"

"Well, I was heading to my locker after class," Helen began, bouncing on the balls of her feet in excitement, "And I noticed there was something attached to my locker."

"What was it?" Amber breathed, her brown eyes wide with anticipation.

Helen heaved a lofty sigh. "A single red rose."

"Ooh," Lexi shared a look with Amber. "What else?"

Helen blinked. "Else?"

Trying to play it cool and not give away the fact that she'd been helping Parker, she prompted, "Oh, I mean, how did you know it was Parker? Did he write you a love poem, or a totally romantic note?"

Helen smiled. "Yes! There was a note taped underneath the rose. It said, "Helen, it would make me the happiest guy in the school if you would be my date to Homecoming. Love, Parker." Helen squealed. "I mean, how romantic is that? *Love*?"

"So romantic," Amber breathed wistfully.

"I'm so happy for you!" Lexi hugged Helen, a wave of relief rushing over her. Thank goodness Parker finally summoned up the courage to ask her. Not only did she think they were a great match, but now she didn't have to worry that Parker was secretly crushing on her under the guise of asking for romantic advice.

However, that begged the question… who was writing her notes?

As if reading her mind, Helen pulled away and asked, "So, has your secret admirer revealed himself yet, or asked you to the dance?"

Amber raised her eyebrows with keen interest. "Secret admirer?"

Lexi flushed, pressing a finger to her lips. "Shh!"

Helen held up her hands. "Sorry, sorry." She turned to Amber and said conspiratorially, "Someone's been getting love notes."

Amber gasped. "Wait, really? Swoon! I want someone to write *me* love notes!"

Lexi grimaced, wishing the two of them would learn how to whisper. "My admirer is still secret. Knowing my luck, I'll be dateless to the dance and he'll stay a secret forever."

"Maybe he'll reveal himself in time for Prom," Helen teased. Seeing Lexi's disgruntled look, she amended, "I'm kidding! I'm sorry, I'm still giddy from the Parker thing. But seriously, I'm sure he's just biding his time for the perfect moment to ask you to the dance."

Tugging nervously on her braid, Amber said, "Well, your mystery man had better summon up the courage and ask you soon! The dance is just days away!"

There was that knot in her stomach again. Why was her personal life getting so complicated? "I'm well aware."

"Don't worry, she'll be ready," Helen told Amber. "We went dress shopping the other day."

"Which may have been stupid if I don't get a date," Lexi said glumly, turning her attention back to the mural in front of her.

"Lots of people go dateless," Amber encouraged. "I don't have a date, and I know lots of others who don't. We'll just go and have a big party!"

Lexi nodded, feeling a little bit better. "You're right."

"But when he *does* ask you, you all can hang out with Parker and me," Helen added.

Lexi bit her lip. "Who could it be?"

Amber shrugged. "Any number of guys. You're really popular."

Lexi blushed, but Helen added, "Yeah, Aidan had better watch out, or his dream girl is going to get scooped up."

"Helen!" Lexi glanced around to make sure no one was listening. She froze. Was it just her, or had Erika tilted her chair slightly in their direction? Plus, Amber was standing right there! "I'm sure your brother doesn't like me," she told Amber.

Amber shrugged. "He very well might. He's never talked to me about things like that."

Lexi relaxed slightly, but Helen continued, "Oh, trust me, he does. I mean, how many girls does he cry in front of?"

"Keep your *voice down*," Lexi demanded. "And I didn't see him cry." She really didn't want it getting back to Aidan that she'd told Helen about the other night. Thinking of how he'd shielded her from the rain with his letterman jacket, she felt her cheeks grow warm. "He was just going through a bad time when Cupid and I ran into him, that's all."

Helen smiled impishly. "And of course your presence comforted him better than anyone else could. He's totally into you."

Lexi glanced nervously around the room, not liking how Erika was sitting very still in her chair. She was sure their entire conversation could be heard.

Oh, well. Erika was her friend, too. She supposed it wasn't that big of a deal. She was sure she wouldn't repeat anything, especially not to Aidan.

She focused on steering the conversation away from Aidan and the dance, and instead concentrated on how the photo booth backdrop was coming along.

The next day at school, Lexi walked briskly to her locker, feeling rattled. She hadn't gotten much sleep the night before—when returning from picking up her mom from the airport, they'd hit horrible traffic, and when they'd finally made it home, she'd had to stay up late to finish her homework. She couldn't wait until Homecoming was over, and she could relax a bit more. Even though she still had no date…

Opening her locker and loading up her bag with books and binders for her next couple of classes, she gave a start when a loud squeal reached her ears.

She peered with interest down the hall, blinking when she saw Erika standing there with Aidan. "Go to Homecoming? Of *course* I'll go with you, Aidan!" she practically shrieked in excitement.

Lexi felt like someone had poured a pitcher of ice water down her throat, freezing her heart. Aidan liked Erika? She remembered how he'd been so nice to walk her home in the rain, how he'd touched her cheek, told her she looked pretty. She'd thought—hoped—he liked her too.

Apparently, Erika hadn't been exaggerating when she'd said Aidan flirted with her all the time.

He just saw her as another conquest.

She couldn't bear to watch the scene. Slamming her locker shut, she turned quickly on her heel and fled down the hall, not bothering to wipe away the tears that now ran down her cheeks.

"You look gorgeous!" Helen squealed the night of the dance. "Just like a Greek goddess!"

Lexi anxiously turned to look at herself in her bedroom's full-length mirror, studying how the pale pink floor-length dress did, in fact, resemble a Greek chiton. She still couldn't quite believe that Helen had talked her into going to the dance. After finding out about Erika and Aidan, everything had passed by in a blur. She'd done her best to be home as much as possible aside from classes and finishing the decorations for Homecoming. Erika tried to brag about going with Aidan every chance she got, so Lexi made excuses to try and avoid her as much as possible. Maybe it was wrong—maybe Erika hadn't known that she also liked Aidan—but it still hurt. They'd beaten the Trojans by a hair at the big game, and she honestly just wanted nothing more than to take a hot bath and forget about stupid Homecoming. Yet here she was, getting ready to head out in just a few minutes.

"Pink is totally your color," Helen breathed as she pinned a stray piece of hair into her elaborate updo.

Lexi's heart sank at her words, remembering how Aidan had told her he thought she looked good in pink. What was the point of going to this stupid dance? Her secret admirer was a no-show, and Aidan would be with Erika. They would probably even be crowned King and Queen. She should be happy for Erika, but the truth was, she hadn't admitted to herself how hard she was falling for Aidan until she found out he chose someone else.

Taking a deep breath to rid herself of these pessimistic thoughts, she turned to Helen, admiring how the olive-green dress she was wearing brought out the green flecks in her eyes. "You're so sweet," she said with a smile. "You look beautiful! Parker is going to love you in that dress." She glanced at the clock on her nightstand. "We'd better hurry, he'll be here in just a few minutes!" Parker and Helen had very kindly offered to give Lexi a ride to the dance, where they would meet up with a larger group of friends.

Helen nervously checked her makeup in the mirror. "I guess I'm as ready as I'll ever be," she murmured.

"You look fantastic," Lexi assured her, just as the doorbell rang, and Cupid began to bark. "That's probably Parker now!"

The two girls gathered their things and made their way carefully down the stairs. "Hush, Cupid!" Lexi called up the stairs before opening the front door and stepping out onto the porch. "Hey, Parker—" She froze when she saw Aidan and Amber standing on her front porch, both dressed for the dance. "Amber. Aidan," she stammered, feeling butterflies fluttering in her stomach as she noticed how handsome he looked in his black suit and tie. "What are you doing here?"

"Where's Erika?" Helen demanded in a hard voice, joining Lexi on the porch and pulling the door closed behind her.

"Look, Lexi, I know you're upset, but we need to talk to you," Amber began gently, nervously smoothing the skirt of her knee length blue dress.

Taking a deep breath to steady herself, Lexi lifted her eyebrows. "About what?"

Aidan took a step forward. "Lexi, I didn't want to ask Erika to Homecoming," he began.

Lexi felt her temper flare. "Oh, I see. You didn't want to, but you had no choice?" The words began pouring out, all of her hurt and frustration from the past couple of days coming to the forefront. "Like someone forced you to ask her?"

"Lexi…" Amber began, but Lexi held up her hand.

"You need to make up your mind as to what it is you want. I get it. You're the hottest guy in school, the big man on campus, and you think you deserve to have some hot girl as arm candy? Well, guess what? We have feelings. You can't just kick Erika to the curb and expect that I'll suddenly want to go out with you."

"I don't see you like that at all," Aidan protested, dark eyes shining. "This is all a huge misunderstanding. I wanted to ask you to the dance, I just didn't know how. I was going to slip the last note asking you to Homecoming into your bag the other day after football practice—"

Helen's eyes widened. "Wait—you're her secret admirer?"

Lexi stared at him, feeling a blush tinge her cheeks at the thought of him writing her all of those romantic notes.

Aidan nodded. "But you'd already left for the day," he continued. "Erika saw me, and said she wanted to help. She told me she would show me which locker was yours, so I could put the note in there."

Lexi nodded slowly, the pieces falling together. "And she showed you *her* locker instead?" she asked. She couldn't believe it. She thought Erika was her friend. Why would she do something so malicious?

Helen snaked an arm around Lexi's shoulder, giving it a comforting squeeze.

Looking chagrined, Aidan nodded. "At first, I was just trying to figure out how to let her down gently after she thought I'd asked her to the dance instead of you—I thought she had just misunderstood and made a mistake—"

Amber rolled her eyes. "Again, how would she have made that big of a mistake?"

Aidan ran a hand through his short brown hair in a frustrated motion. "I don't know, okay? I didn't think she was like that!"

"I have been complaining about that viper since Freshman year," Amber protested.

"I'm sorry, okay!" Aidan said. "I thought you were just pissed off that she beat you for Student Council."

Amber rolled her eyes.

"Why would she do this?" Lexi asked softly, blue eyes wide.

"Aidan finally told me what was going on, so we confronted Erika, and she came clean about her nasty scheme," Amber explained. "I'm really sorry this happened, Lexi. This is just how she is. She likes to sow the seeds of discord."

Aidan furrowed his brow. "Speak English so the rest of us can understand, please."

"She means Erika likes to stir the pot," Helen translated for him.

Amber looked pleased. "Exactly. I'm telling you, if there was a crown tonight for Royal Bitch—"

Lexi laughed incredulously. "Amber!"

Helen shrugged, slapping Amber a high five. "Why not tell it like it is? It's true!"

Before Lexi could respond, Aidan reached for her hands. "Again, I'm really sorry I didn't just have the guts to ask you directly. I just wanted to show you how special you were with those notes, but I guess it backfired." He swallowed hard. "But, do you think maybe you could forgive me, and be my date to the dance?"

Lexi bit her lip, staring up into his imploring eyes. She had the urge to pinch herself, but it wasn't a dream. Aidan liked her, he was the one who wrote her those sweet notes, and he was asking her to the dance. A blush tingeing her cheeks, she nodded at last. "Yes."

Aidan grinned, pumping a fist. "Yes!"

Amber and Helen squealed and clapped.

Parker pulled up just then, honking his horn. "Hey, guys! Ready to hit the dance?"

Aidan held out his arm to Lexi. "Shall we?"

"We shall," Lexi said with a grin as she took his arm.

"Why, thank you," Lexi said to Aidan as he pulled out a chair at an empty table for her at the dance.

"No problem," Aidan said with a smile, adjusting his tie. "Do you want some punch?"

Lexi shook her head. "I just want to sit for a little bit." They had spent the last hour on the dance floor with their friends, and she wanted to take a breather. The gym looked amazing with the lights bouncing off all of the decorations. Her gaze wandered back to the dance floor, where Amber was dancing with Hector. Lexi couldn't help but notice that Amber was smiling shyly up at him, while Hector in return was grinning ear to ear as they moved to the beat of the music. They were all having a fantastic evening so far, but something had been bothering Lexi that she couldn't quite put her finger on. As she stared at one of the columns Phillip and Damon had made, it finally came to her. "Say, Aidan—why did Hallie see Parker sticking a note in my bag if you were my secret admirer?"

Aidan dropped his eyes, rubbing the back of his neck. "Parker was kind of helping me," he admitted. "He knew I liked you, and when you were giving him advice about asking Helen out, he thought he could give me some pointers. I had to leave practice suddenly, so I asked him to deliver the note. Discreetly," he added sarcastically.

Lexi glanced over to where Helen and Parker sat, heads together as they laughed about something. "Well, I'm just glad he wasn't my admirer.

Those two are perfect for each other." She felt eyes on her, and looked back to see Aidan staring at her.

"What?" she asked.

"It's just, I've been thinking a lot about what you said to me that night," Aidan began. "And—"

"Okay, folks," Mrs. Soleil said from the stage. "It's time to announce our Homecoming King and Queen. Please give it up for…"

Lexi took a deep breath. "I don't know why, but I'm kind of nervous," she whispered to Aidan. He smiled and extended his hand, which she gratefully took.

"Please give it up for Aidan Shields—"

Aidan rose to his feet, but didn't let go of Lexi's hand. "Aidan, what are you doing?" Lexi asked with a laugh. "Get up there!"

"And Lexi Cypress!"

Aidan grinned, squeezing her hand as he began walking toward the stage. "I didn't think I would win," he said over the loud applause of their fellow classmates, "but I had a pretty good feeling about you."

Lexi glanced around, feeling an adrenaline rush as they walked up the stage stairs. Her heart hammered as they were each crowned. She noticed with a little thrill that Aidan was still holding tightly onto her hand.

"Now, please join us in welcoming our King and Queen to the dance floor!"

Lexi was grateful that Aidan had offered her his arm as they walked down the steps and out onto the dance floor, because her knees felt like jelly. Lacing her hands behind his neck as the music started, she asked, "Why did you have a good feeling I'd win?"

Aidan smiled, snaking his hands around her waist. "Because ever since you came to our school, you made an impression on people. You're beautiful, inside and out. You've made so many friends, and you're always there for your friends."

Lexi blushed. "Aidan—"

"That's what I was going to say earlier," Aidan continued. "You really made an impression on me when we talked the other day. Our family puts way too much pressure on Amber and me. I'm going to talk to my dad. You were right. I shouldn't have to define my life by football. I'm fine going my own way if I have to."

Lexi smiled, tightening her arms around him. "That's wonderful, Aidan," she said earnestly, eyes shining. "I know you can do it—and I'll be here for you."

"I know you will," Aidan said with a grin, pulling her closer for a kiss.

THE REAL PRIZE

AMY BEARCE

I N THE TWILIGHT *realm of the sea, many years ago in the world of Aluvia, there lived a mermaid princess known for her fierce warrior skills. Destiny would see her marry and rule without question, but she chose a different path.*

The sea dragon scale blended into the back of the cave, revealing itself only by a few streaks of sullen red light in the otherwise pitch-blackness. Only a fool would risk entering a sea dragon's nest, but Atalanta pressed forward anyway. The midnight realm of the ocean held thick darkness and dangerous creatures—but Atalanta knew this cave system better than any mer, and she needed this sea dragon scale.

She drifted past a small clump of mussels clinging to the rocks, sensing, more than seeing, their shells suddenly snap closed. Deeper in the cave now, she ran her hand along the rough cave wall, using touch to replace her sight. She'd already extinguished her moonglow, the magical bioluminescence of a merfolk's skin. Blinking against the blackness, she split her attention between the entrance of the cave and the faint red light ahead of her.

The sea dragon had gone hunting—she'd sat in wait to make sure—but it could return at any time. Atalanta might be the fastest mermaid in the kingdom (and she was) but not even she could outrun a sea dragon in pursuit of its prey. Luckily, these cliffs also passed into the twilight zone, connecting yet dividing these two parts of the ocean. Once she descended the other side, it took only a quick race across a desolate plain to reach home.

The sea dragon shouldn't even be living this close. Dragons hunted these waters, yes, but usually nested in the abyss, the deepest trench in the ocean.

The power of the scale whispered against her skin, like a sunray through the shallows. All sea dragons radiated magic and power, even within the scales they shed. The elite merfolk rangers used three such scales to build their full-length shields. Rangers, rare among the mer, trained as warriors, protecting the city—and especially the royal family—from harm. Too bad the princess would rather be the one doing the protecting.

The princess in question closed in on the scale with a sigh of satisfaction. Her fingers tingled as they traced the surface of the scale, smooth as sea glass. Red lights crawled beneath her fingers, surging at her presence. She hefted the scale from the sifting soil and nearly spun backward—it was so much lighter than expected. She could make haste with such an easy burden.

Using a piece of kelp she'd brought for this exact reason, she tied the scale to her back, then hurried toward the mouth of the cave. The city of Lyr was just past the cliffs, inside the Twilight realm. It wouldn't take two shakes of a mer's tail to get there—

A dark shadow glided past the opening, barely visible to her sharp eyes, a shadow within a shadow, but she trusted her instincts. She slipped out the cave mouth and clung to the rugged cliff, barely moving her fin.

In the Twilight realm, the scale's slight glow wouldn't even be noticeable, but here in the total darkness, even the faintest light acted like a beacon.

Pressing her back to the wall, Atalanta untied her black and green hair so it floated down over the scale, and cursed herself for not moving faster in the first place. Where could she hide? Was there some place inside the cave, a nook or a cranny? She'd never make it across the flat plain to the shelter of the city, not with a sea dragon on her tail. Most merfolk avoided the sea dragon's territory with good reason.

A whuffling sound and whicker echoed through the empty water. Relief turned her joints to jelly. Not a sea dragon, merely a water horse. While water horses were often dangerous when approached, they didn't attack if left alone—and she had a special relationship with them anyway. Pushing off from the wall, she scanned the distant depths for the dull glow of the underwater beast famed for its wildness and speed.

With two front hooves and a head like the horses on land—she'd seen them from the shallows—sea horses had a strong back half formed into a strong tail. Their front hooves could cut like blades and their sharp, wicked teeth gave a strong advantage in any battle. Merfolk had found remains of giant sea squid more than once, torn limb from limb by these horses. Stories said if a merfolk dared bridle one, a water horse would take off with them magically sealed to its back, running across sea and shore until they died from starvation or until the steed ripped them to pieces. But not her. Never her.

Following the dim, pearly light, Atalanta glided to the water horse's side, placing one hand softly against its smooth scales. So, so gently. Sea horses needed respect. The beast brushed her with its long tail. Atlanta smiled.

"What are you doing here?" she whispered, running her hand along the slick kelp–like hair of the nosy creature. "Trying to frighten me?"

Though she knew this mare, the creature had no name that Atalanta knew of. The mare had always seemed beyond such a thing, too wild for such a contrivance of civilization. Water horses rescued her when she was lost as a seawee during a sea dragon raid and wandered in their herd. If the lead mare hadn't recently lost her calf, Atalanta might have become a water horse snack instead of adopted by the herd. But the mare took her to their home in the darkest part of the sea. There the water horses fed her, and kept her safe until she became strong enough to seek the merfolk on the other side of the cliffs.

She'd seen fewer of the horses over the years, yet they still sensed when she was in need, but this one probably sensed the scale, same as she did. Strong magic always drew them.

"It's good to see you." She nuzzled the horse's nose, smooth and soft, bubbles rising from its neck gills. Suddenly, the water horse reared back, giving a rough cry that sent a flurry of bubbles across her face. A chill crept through water that usually felt like silk against her magic-protected skin. Ice crystals formed along the wall of the cave.

The sea dragon had returned. She cursed with a word she'd never be permitted to use back at home. The water horse spun its body alongside hers, extending its flippered tail, preparing to run.

No point in sneaking around now, and better visibility would speed her escape. She sent magic through her body, lighting her skin by igniting a shimmery silver glow that ran along her skin to where her silver scales began. Her scales ran from her underarms and overlapped down to the tip of her tail, like a glittering evening gown. The light shone around a pattern of tattoos across her pale shoulders, back, and arms—the silhouettes of wild water horses stampeding.

She'd need to move almost as fast as them now. Lifting her hands, she sent out a shock of magical energy that flashed through the water in a brilliant blue wave. If only she'd at least brought a fishing spear, but the princess was not even permitted so simple a weapon.

The dragon pinwheeled on its long fins, extended almost like the wings of their cousins on land, screeching against the light. Normally, the magical pulse might be enough to send a dragon running, but not after sensing its own magic in her hands. No, her only choice was to try to beat the angry dragon to the city.

Atalanta leaned forward onto the water horse, wrapping her arms up to her elbows in its waving kelp mane. "Go!"

They took off. The dark water sped along her glowing skin. Shapes loomed in her vision, appearing out of the darkness up ahead, only to rush past her and vanish just as fast. The horse's muscles bunched and stretched beneath her and despite the danger looming behind them, she laughed. The speed! The freedom! *This* was living, not stilted formal dances as princess. The beast's strong tail sent bubbles furiously roiling through the water.

The water chilled near her tail fin—she glanced back over her shoulder in time to see the sea dragon blow out another breath of icy cold. Its cold breath turned jets of water to ice crystals like small daggers.

The mare sped up with a shudder—she felt it, too. They hugged the cliff wall for protection. Atalanta didn't even blink when a protruding stone gashed her arm as they flashed past. The blood left behind would look like a squid's ink jet, but they were long gone before she could see the stream of blood spread.

"Come on, now, my friend," she whispered to the horse, whose ears turned backward to catch her words. "We're almost there."

It was hard to use her tail while being pulled by a water horse's wagging motions. Few mer ever managed to ride a water horse, much less master this technique, but she'd had plenty of practice. Adding the speed from her tailfin in perfect sync, they began to pull away, darting over and around the craggy cliff edge, around the spiraling peak and heading down the other side. In the distance, the city of Lyr glowed like a beacon, the silvery blue light of the merfolk spilling upward, settling over their city like a dome of protection. The dome could not repel a true attack—they needed a way to reinforce it—but the creatures of the midnight realm did not like the light and would just as soon hunt elsewhere. Fewer of the dangerous beasts came near than used to, but a few was all it took to cause mass destruction to their peaceful home.

The sea dragon screeched behind them. It flowed up and over the top of the cliff like a nightmare come to life, black eyes flat and glinting with rage. She'd clearly underestimated the importance of the sea dragon's scale. The beast wanted it back.

Her moonglow flared and pulsed along her skin, out of control as panic stabbed at her. She took a long deep breath of water and untied the scale. She'd have to leave it behind, even as rare a find as it was. Her plans of proving herself worthy of becoming an elite ranger would have to be delayed.

She twisted one hand through the smooth mane and closed her eyes to better feel the balance of the horse beneath her. Using her other hand, she reached up and untied the string holding the scale to her. Her fingers shook, and her eyes stung with unshed tears—but luckily, merfolk almost never cried.

The scale dropped away, spinning and glinting in the dark, empty water. The sea dragon screeched one final time, but then grabbed the scale and whipped its tail, rushing back to the midnight realm beyond the cliffs.

The loss of the scale stung. She needed three sea dragon scales to make into a shield. Each ranger applicant required them. Only then could she stand before the council and ask to be accepted in the role she wanted rather than the one she'd been born into.

The city grew brighter and the horse shied away.

"I know, sweetie," she said. "This isn't a safe place for you, either." The merfolk feared water horses almost as much as sea dragons, and with good reason, mostly. But she'd missed the glory of the race, the speed, the fierceness they brought with them.

"Thank you," she whispered, unwinding herself from the mare. "Tell the others I miss them."

And then the mare was gone—a blur in the water. Atalanta had to make the last of her trip alone, with nothing to show for it, except an arm wound. She wound her kelp strip around the thin cut—at least the bleeding slowed.

She straightened her shoulders as she passed under the glowing dome. She was Princess Atalanta, and her people couldn't see her defeated. She never lost a race. She never lost, period. She'd get the scales she needed. Next time. But first, she had a tiara to wear, a ball to attend, and a bunch of suitors to kindly reject.

Atalanta had just finished cleansing her scrape when her father swished into the room. His broad shoulders always felt like they'd shatter the delicate coral doorway and walls that looked like lace, but somehow didn't.

"I hear you went beyond the Twilight realm. Again."

Atalanta pouted. "Did you have the guards spying on me? Again?"

Her father sighed and shook his head. "If by spying you mean performing their duty as lookout, then yes. And one saw you coming through the cliffs—on a water horse. What have we said about that? I know you are strong. We all know you helped fight off the kraken last year, admirably. But you shouldn't be out there alone. And certainly not with dangerous water horses."

She gritted her teeth and counted to ten. Water horses reminded her parents of the time she'd been lost to them. But to Atalanta, the wild beasts were a reminder that she'd once been free to do as she wished. A life as a royal leader? It felt impossible. "I went seeking my first dragon scale—found it, too, but had to leave it behind when the water horse drew the dragon's attention."

She spun at the groan behind her. Her father clutched at his heart. "Papa!" She swam quickly to his side. "What's wrong?"

"You'll be the death of me yet, my girl. Do you have any idea how much we worried for you, when you were gone? Or how much we worry still? Not just for you, but for our kingdom? With magic waning for unknown reasons, we will need a strong leader at your side. And it's time you made that choice. You are of age, already committed to the sea." He gestured at her water horse tattoos, given by the sea's magic.

His face looked paler than usual. His geometric pattern of tattoos reached up to his jaw bones. Each mer received a flowing tessellation of tattoos at their coming-of-age ceremony, when they pledged themselves in service of the sea. The tattoos held special meaning to each mer. In her father's, Atalanta saw the shape of a repeating crown, but others saw different images in the pattern. The sea seemed to understand everyone wished to see themselves reflected in their leader.

No facial hair obscured the king's frustrated expression—mermen never grew any. His eyes turned black as he gathered his magic and straightened. "Listen to me, Atalanta. Tonight, at the ball, you must select a bondmate and begin your training."

Tonight? No. Too soon. She wasn't ready. She didn't want this. "Father, I beg of you, let me train as an elite guard instead—if I can find three scales—"

"Arrrgh!" he growled, thrashing his tail. "This nonsense again. I tell you, daughter, we all have our duties, and yours is to the crown. There will be no time for ranger duties, even if you could find the scales."

She swallowed a cry of despair. He wasn't going to budge. Well, neither would she. She might have to be queen, but she would not compromise herself for her mate. Too many suitors thought they were the sea's gift to merfolk. She had long ago grown weary of their "Hello sweet princess" and "Let me help you, my princess…" If only she could think of a way to disqualify most of them—

She gasped as an idea burst into her mind. Of course. It was perfect. But tricky: the king would have to agree to it. And he wouldn't like it at all.

"I won't marry anyone but my equal," she spoke slowly and clearly, lifting her chin. She couldn't be seen as acting like a child. "I have a requirement. A test, for any who would want to be considered."

Her father's lips quirked. "You should never settle. Name your requirement."

Facing away, she shook her head. "It won't happen."

He turned her back toward him, hands on her shoulder. His eyes—so much like hers—gleamed. "It will. By my name, speak your requirement and it will be done. I promise you that."

Her smile spread, but without any joy to it. Only fierceness. "Such a promise deserves serious thought. I'll announce it tonight at the ball and invite those who would like to be considered to rise to the challenge."

And she meant to see to it that no one would.

The royal home was the largest in the city, located across from the temple and municipal buildings. Open courtyards showcased gently waving flowering plants and ivy, with stones set in spiraling paths. Musicians were stationed on a smooth stone overseeing the open square. Dancers would float and sway above the kaleidoscope of plants beneath them, sheltered between the taller coral buildings, lit by glow fish lanterns and their own moonglow magic.

Atalanta's ebony hair was twisted into a braid atop her head, and a pearl necklace attached round her neck. Merfolk skin was nearly translucent—allowing their moonglow to shine—and against this pale backdrop, her tattoos conveyed a sense of motion even as she waited still.

Admittedly, her silvery scales lacked practicality for a warrior—they flashed like mirrors even in the low, dispersed light that made it all the way to the sea floor here. The silver scales suited a princess well, though, looking positively royal. Her eyes outshone an amethyst jewel when not black from working magic. She didn't mind looking pretty. It just had no bearing on her future.

Swaying, dancing, whirling merfolk filled the open courtyard of the city center, all wearing their best jewels and shells to show off their tattoos. Mermaids wore their hair piled on their heads, tied back, or left loose, woven with sea flowers and pearls. Most mermen kept their long hair tied back, but a few had chopped theirs, and others wore it loose with clam shells tied throughout.

Sound carried well through the water. Despite the orchestra's small size, its conch shell flutes and trumpets led a lively tune over the beating of the drums and the quartet of singers. Atalanta loved to dance almost as much as she loved racing, so at least she had one bright spot in the evening's agenda. Her father remained on the royal dais while she descended into the crowd of merfolk. Baskets of glowfish created a warm lighting that contrasted with the pearly silver of moonglow along so many bodies.

"Princess Atalanta," a dark-haired merman said, reaching for her hand and bending low over it, kissing the back.

She tugged her hand back. "Caspian." She nodded at him. "I'm surprised to see you here. You're not much for gatherings."

His eyes matched the waters of the midnight realm, nearly black even without magic use. "I heard there will be an important announcement tonight. About you and your… future possible bondmate." He smiled slowly.

Her stomach dropped, and not in the fun way. Caspian had been flirting with her since they received their tattoos at their coming-of-age ceremonies. But he'd been flirting with every other mermaid, too. It meant nothing to him. *She* meant nothing to him, nothing but status. "Oh? You heard that, did you? My, word travels fast." Her father must have had this planned for some time. She fumed to herself. "If you'll excuse me."

She spun to confront him, but another mer slipped in her way.

"Princess." He bowed low.

She sighed. "Hello Lysander, thank you for coming tonight."

When he straightened, she had to tip her head back to meet his piercing blue gaze. "Word is, you caught and rode a water horse today. How was it?" His tone was eager— Lysander loved the chase almost as much as she did. He loved a battle even more, showcasing strength and power over speed.

She couldn't stop her grin. "Amazing." She looked past to where her father was speaking to a young merman facing away from her. "But if you'll excuse me, I need to speak with the king."

He bowed again, muscles bunching. *Would he be so bad to bond with?* a traitorous voice whispered. He'd at least understand her need for the wild, for the race. But that's all he cared about it. The chase. He didn't care about her.

"Father," she began, brushing past the young merman before him.

"Now, Atalanta," her father chided. "Is that any way to greet an old friend?"

It took her a minute to recognize him, though their community was fairly small. "Garrison?"

"At your service." He inclined his head, but didn't bow. Interesting. Merfolk didn't stand on formality, but most still acknowledged royalty. She liked that he didn't. Then again, they'd been childhood friends. Good friends, in class and beyond, until her duties kept her too busy for play.

"You—look different," she said, then cursed herself. The last time she'd really talked to him, he'd been a prepubescent seawee, taken into the scribe group to study for the position of historian. He had a brilliant mind. But his body had filled out since then, too. Not bulky like Lysander or even as defined as Caspian, but a lithe, lean frame that suited him. His jaw was square, with sharp cheekbones and deep, wideset hazel eyes currently black from magic. His pale skin glowed slightly, setting off his tattoos. He hadn't received them the last time they spoke. She couldn't quite make out the shapes—groups of curving lines that came to a peak—

"Jellyfish," he said softly. Her eyes flashed to his face and heat burned across her face. She'd just been floating there, gaping at this boy's chest and shoulder's...

She cut her gaze to her father, who looked on with amusement, a smile quirking on his craggy face.

She cleared her throat. "I don't think I've seen jellies on anyone before."

He held out an arm, where pink scars wrapped around his bicep. "I survived an encounter that should have left me dead. They'd lured me with magical glows at the end of their tentacles, and I'd reached for one, even knowing I shouldn't. I suppose the Sea felt I should remember her mercy. I use my time to record and maintain our history, so that one day, our children's children will know our stories."

His voice remained soft, but passion throbbed like bass drums beneath his words.

Her father boomed, "Why don't you two dance? Your... announcement can wait a few minutes, Atalanta."

Garrison offered her his hand.

She shouldn't take it. She didn't want to lead him on, and he was too sweet to be teased. But something in the depths of his eyes drew her. She reached out her hand to him and when their palms slid together, a low hum of magic pulsed along her skin. A small gasp slipped from her. Sharing moonglow magic was usually reserved for close friends, family... or lovers.

"Sorry," he said, dampening the effects. "I let it get away from me."

Her hands felt cooler as he pulled the magic back, dousing even his moonglow so that his dark eyes faded to hazel once again.

With his palm on her lower back, firm and strong, he guided her into the dancers. His long green hair flowed around them, somehow smelling of sunlight. She hadn't been to the surface in a long time. Royal training took too much time.

"You look lovely tonight, Princess," he said. "Wild flights on water horses suits you."

She dropped her forehead against his shoulder for a moment before glancing up with a rueful smile. He wasn't so tall she had to crane her neck to meet his gaze. "Not you, too! Has everyone heard?"

"You're an important person to us all, so yes. And after the kraken adventure, most merfolk wonder what amazing prowess you'll display next. You went seeking a dragon scale?"

"Had to leave it behind," she said grumpily. "I will never find three at this rate."

He nodded. "Well, we're all so proud of you."

She jerked her head up. "Proud?" If only her father felt the same. The loss of the queen years before had left him numb inside in too many ways. The depth of his grief had warned Atalanta that a permanent bonding could lead to misery, giving one more reason to avoid it.

"Surely. Your strength and skills benefit our city, as will your leadership when you are queen."

She looked away from him. "I'm not sure about that last part."

"You doubt yourself?" he whispered into her ear, swinging her to the gentle tune effortlessly.

"Not myself," she replied, hiding a shiver. Was he sharing magic again? "I doubt... this life for myself."

"And you want to be a ranger? Or at least to be able to roam beyond our magical border without fear? I suppose it was a shock to return after living among the wild beasts even for the time you were gone." He dipped her and spun her without missing a beat.

"It was," she said faintly.

"We all worried for you then. And your father—he worries for you now. He just wants you safe."

"I know," she said. Then tipped her head. "You worried when I was missing? You were little then, too."

He smiled, though it seemed laced with sadness. "You've always left a big impression on me."

The song came to a close and she pulled away. It felt like trying to pull apart two sides of a clamshell. Too connected. Too close. She swam back farther. "Thank you for the dance. I must go make my announcement."

He inclined his head, dark eyes following her. She felt his gaze on her back, all the way up to the dais.

When the conch horns blew, the citizens of Lyr gathered around. Accustomed to public life, her father waited until the last few whispers and mutters died away before he began to speak.

"Beloved citizens of Lyr, you have always supported me as your king. Now, I ask you to do the same for my daughter, as she begins her training to become the future leader of our realm. But for one so young, there is still another step left to take before assuming a mantle of leadership. A bondmate must be found. A partner. Someone she can lean on and trust, to share the burden." He shook his head. "I have led alone since my beloved wife passed, and lonely leadership is not a burden I would ask of my daughter. No, she must choose among suitors for a bondmate, and it shall be a formal process."

A thrum of whispers and gasps and exclamations ricocheted through the water, followed by harried shushes.

"My daughter has set a task for her would-be mate," he continued. "One she has not shared even with me, but I have agreed to this trial. After all, she must be happy and trust her partner from the start. It is no small task to lead our people. And we should all want the best mer for her partner."

Her father put one hand on her shoulder and squeezed. His support kept her steady.

Atalanta's skin practically burned from all the stares. She kept her jaw high and refused to meet the gaze of any of the young mer in the audience who might be interested. Their community wasn't so big that many would come forward, especially given the limited pool of mer the right age. Maybe none of them would dare face her challenge. She met Garrison's gaze briefly and then looked away, clenching her jaw.

She called on her moonglow, knowing it would look more impressive. "Any suitor must best me in a race."

Her father's hands dropped from her like he'd taken hold of a jelly fish stinger. She glanced over—his smile had disappeared.

"You're the fastest we have," he said. "It's a known fact. That's hardly a fair fight."

"Not a swimming race. A water horse race. Riding to the cliffs of the Midnight Realm, rounding the steepest point, and making it back first."

A roar from the crowd sent a current rippling across her body. She couldn't help but look down—heads leaned closely, whispering. Eyes flashed in the silvery lights that pulsed from distressed merfolk.

She understood why. Riding a water horse was hard enough. Deadly dangerous. But rounding the cliff meant entering the Midnight Realm… all manner of monsters lived in those depths. Only the rangers ever swam those waters. And her.

Her father coughed once, water bubbles dancing upward, vanishing in the dimness above. "Do you wish them all to die then?" His angry words were too low for others to hear. He knew what everyone did— Atalanta wouldn't hold back.

She never did. She couldn't. It simply wasn't in her to back away from a competition. She had her honor. She'd already won every race they'd ever held, both with fins and astride dolphins, whales, sharks, and more.

She'd been the one fast enough to stun the kraken with her magic, allowing its defeat by the elite rangers. But never had anyone dared to suggest a water horse race. It was madness. Folly.

Which was exactly the point.

Already, more than half the eager bachelors in the room were shaking their heads. Good.

"I can't let you require this," her father spoke urgently. "It's too risky—"

"You promised. On your word." She met her father's gaze with a steely one of her own. Their word, a promise given, meant everything. He sighed and nodded as she knew he would.

She turned to face the disturbed crowd, raising her voice. "No one has to compete at all. It's on their heads if they do. But I've been told to choose and this is how I will do so: the winner will be my bondmate—if they cross the finish line first. And survive the water horse, of course. I'll call the herd, and I believe they'll come. I need a strong partner. This is my test."

No one would be so crazy. Look at them all, backing away, muttering, rolling their eyes. Ha, yes.

"I will." A merman swam forward.

She bit back a groan at Lysander's deep voice. Of course *he'd* sign up. He never could resist a challenge. "Lysander, are you sure? You risk death. I'm not so lovely a prize."

"That's for us to decide, is it not?" He bowed, then smirked up at her as he crossed his arms across his broad, muscular chest.

Of course. He really thought he'd win and be king. That all those muscles meant he could outrun her, water horses or no. A competitive zing made her tail fin tremble. She could outrace him any day and had, many times.

"Then so be it." Her gaze grew sharp. "I will not hold back."

"I would hope not. There's no fun in a simple win."

Maybe he understood her better than she thought.

Another mer swam forward. Caspian. "I will join the race."

She frowned. "My old friend, I'd hate to see anything happen to you. Water horses—"

"Can frenzy and attack their riders, yes, I know. I've been around."

She squelched a smile. He'd certainly *been around*—he'd dated every available mer, so maybe she was just rounding out his list.

A third voice joined the two. "I'll join as well."

Oh no. Not him. Anyone but him.

Garrison swam forward, looking like a guppy next to the brawny two mermen. "I will race for your hand, princess."

Some in the audience laughed. A hot fiery rage filled her, surprising her with its protective fierceness. But Garrison smiled serenely at her, apparently not caring at all. Caspian leaned over to whisper something to him, brows drawn. Garrison only smiled more broadly and brushed off the other mer's concern.

"I… I must speak to each candidate alone tonight." Atalanta struggled to project to the back of the crowd. The mutters among the mer grew. "The race begins at dawn." She would not let her voice shake. But she also would not let her childhood friend, this gentle soul, die because of her.

"Garrison, come see me first please. Now." She swam to an enclosed room off the center square, formed of clam shells. It was where the elders met, a council of seven, advisors to the royal family. They would be angry with her, no doubt, for pulling this stunt, but royalty overruled them.

"Garrison," she hissed at him as soon as they were alone. "What are you thinking? I can't let you risk this!"

Here was one merman she wouldn't mind talking to for more than a few hours. Too bad she needed a warrior to lead at her side. And he'd never win the race.

Unfortunately.

She blinked at the unexpected thought and tried of shake off the hint of wishful wondering. She had no space for regrets.

He swam closer. The delicious scent of sunlight and sand wrapped around her, speeding her heart in a new, unfamiliar way. It had to be nerves. She feared for him, of course.

He just smiled, undisturbed if he felt the same. "Trust me. I know you, better than you might realize. And I am confident we'd be good bondmates."

She shook her head. "We're nothing alike. I want to be a member of the elite rangers, you know. Not a royal. My father is the one who wants to see me on the throne. I love the speed of a chase, the wilderness, the speed of pushing myself, of defending our city. I won't sit quietly and let others defend us."

"And I don't want you to change. Those other two out there? They'll expect you to settle down and be a pretty little princess when all this is done. Not me. I like you just the way you are."

He held out his palm, facing up. She waited a moment, then slid her hand along it. Magic hummed again between them, tugging at her heart in a strange, compelling way. "And how do you think I am?"

"Powerful. Fierce. Strong. I think you are amazing."

Her jaw dropped. He always had been soft-spoken as a seawee. Sometimes even picked on by the bigger mer boys. He was a gentle, sweet boy and had clearly grown up to be a gentle, sweet man. Where had his confidence come from? He was like a new mer. She whispered, "I never knew you felt that way."

He squeezed her hand. "I never knew before I had a chance. I'm no royal. I'm just a simple mer. Now that I can compete, I'll go to the ends of the sea for you." The sincerity of his words rang loud and clear. "May I?" He lifted her hand to his mouth, offering a kiss.

At her hesitant nod, he lifted her hand to his lips, pressing softly there. His lips were warm on her skin, caressing. His eyes never left hers. She could imagine the intensity of a kiss to the lips. She'd kissed a merboy before, but something told her a kiss from Garrison would feel… different. She gently pulled her hand back, fanning a cooler current over herself.

"But—a water horse—and to beat me is—"

He put a finger to his lips. "Shh. Don't worry about me. I have a plan."

She had one, too. She'd need to win as quickly as possible, before Garrison's water horse could hurt him. Maybe even knock him out cold and leave him safely behind. His pride would be wounded, but better than having his heart ripped out by a raging water horse. Just because he couldn't stay by her side didn't mean she wished him harm. Quite the opposite.

Her next meetings with the other two mer confirmed what Garrison had warned. They had visions of kingship in their minds, not her. But a deal was a deal. Whoever won the race would win her hand. And so she'd have to make sure none of them did. It was better for all of them this way. Especially Garrison.

After the last guest left the courtyard, her father followed her inside through the open ceiling. "We're a peaceful people, Atalanta. Why is this the test for your mate?" He tugged on his hair in frustration. "I just want you to be happy."

"Then let me join the rangers instead of being our queen." She had to try one last time. "Or at least let me rule alone."

He turned away. "I cannot do that. I promise you, the burden is hard to bear alone. I would wish it on no one, and certainly not my own daughter. As a new queen, you will need a partner more than anyone."

"Then I shall race tomorrow for my future."

But she did not sleep. She wasn't worried about winning. She knew she would. She was worried about one particular merman who was doomed to lose. His hazel eyes haunted her, and she tossed and turned in her frond basket bed. She relived the kiss to the back of her hand, tracing the spot he'd touched. Silly. But strange. His breathless intensity had all but seared her skin.

When the pale glow of sunrise many miles above filtered through the waters, the time for the race had arrived.

The three mermen waited for her, next to her father. A large crowd followed them, from the city elders and council members to common merfolk who wanted to see the competition play out.

"It's a day for the history books," Garrison said as she stared past them at the crowd, eyes wide. She met his gaze and an electric shock ran up her spine. He looked calm and steady—a mer ready to face his death.

For her.

"This won't take long," Caspian laughed.

"No. It won't," she replied and led the way.

They swam to the far edge of the city, where the cliffs of the Midnight Realm lurked in the distance. As she slipped through the magical protective border, even weak as it was, tingles of power rained upon her skin. Rangers stationed along the path held spears and nets at the ready should the horses get too dangerous, but she'd tell the beasts to not kill anyone. Hopefully, they'd listen.

She floated quietly, closing her eyes against the crowd, shutting the sounds of the crowds from her mind.

Come to me, she called to her herd, the ones who'd saved her. They didn't always treat her gently, but they watched over her still. They'd come. She told the gathered merfolk, "Give them a moment."

And then the water horses came. Rearing, whinnying, storming, stampeding, in a herd that heaved and seethed with bubbles and swirling currents until they slowed, then floated, waiting, still squirming, baring teeth, ready to run.

The rangers shifted closer before Atalanta could tell them to stop, angling their spears, lifting their shields. The horses snapped at them, baring pointy teeth. Several horses lashed out, their sharpened hooves sparking against the shields. Those shields—the sea dragon scale shields— kept the guards safe. But the riders in this race wouldn't have that protection.

"No, get back!" she told the rangers. "They won't attack if you leave them alone."

Atalanta called to the water mare who'd saved her, their leader. The call was without words, using only her magic and her heart. The mare swam forward, alone, eyes flashing with nerves. But she came, and Atlanta met her halfway. Laying her hands along the mare's neck, she shared what she needed. Her skin glowed under the dark tattoos of the stampeding shapes.

The mare whickered and three more water horses left the herd and swam to the mare's side. Their eyes rolled, tail flicking back and forth in agitation. Dread sank in her belly like a stone.

"No one should die today," she whispered to them all. "Toss your rider if you must, but no killing them, please."

They stomped their front hooves and thrashed their tails. They screeched loudly. They so rarely obeyed any directions, but she impressed on their hearts the importance of the mermen's lives. It was the best she could do. The mare snapped her teeth at the others and they settled down enough to allow the others to approach. The rest of the herd took off, disappearing quickly into the distance.

She spun to face the merfolk. "They may or may not cooperate. You can still back out."

Lysander said, "You must be joking. I've been looking forward to this all night." He flexed his arms.

Atalanta sighed. "So be it. To the Midnight Realm and back, in a circle from here to the highest point, and around the other side to return. First to cross that line, wins."

Each merman approached a water horse, whispering to them, offering their hands. The horses glared at them and snarled. She approached the smallest water horse, Garrison's pick. It was black with a red mane and red teeth. She thought hard at it, *Don't you dare kill this one. He's a good one. Understand. He's of the herd. My friend. Mine.*

The horse tossed its head, but then lowered it submissively. Garrison might get bruised and embarrassed, but at least he wouldn't have his tailfin torn in half.

She swam to her water horse, bubbles furiously rising from her neck gills. The mare wasn't happy being called here. Atalanta could sense that the mare felt this race was a party trick, not their place. They belonged in the wild.

"So take us there," Atalanta whispered to her. "To the wilderness of the Midnight Realm and back, my pretty." No seaweed halters for these beasts. You clung on to their backs for dear life and guided with arm pressure and hoped for the best.

The four young merfolk flattened themselves along the horse's backs, weaving their hands into manes up to their elbows in a desperate attempt to hold on.

Her father sent a magic flash up and called, "Go!"

The four held on and sped away across the sandy plains of the sea bottom. Their glow created a halo that would draw attention of sea dragons if this took too long, but she didn't intend to take that much time at all.

The thrill of the speed tugging on her hair—ahh, it made her feel expansive, like the universe spiraled inside her chest. She fanned her fin in unison with the water horse, increasing their speed, clinging to the body of the mare like a barnacle, so close that the water flowed around them like a single unit. She savored the sea swirling past as they thundered, laughing as they pulled ahead already. Bubbles rose furiously behind them, swishing in the dim water. Schools of glowing, translucent fish darted out of the way as she swept past.

The young mermen were shouting at their mounts behind her. She glanced over her shoulder. The brawny Lysander was in last place, his horse chomping at the seaweed bridle he'd insisted on adding at the last minute. His heavy muscles slowed down his steed. Caspian was hanging on, but shockingly, Garrison followed not far behind her. Lightweight and willing to let the horse lead, he didn't get in the way of the creature's speed. Atalanta was still faster—he had yet to learn to use his fin to double their speed—but he showed real skill. Interesting. Unexpected. Her heart lifted and raced even faster than her water horse.

Still, the rules of the race were clear. She would not hold back. She didn't need a partner. And no one should have to die to prove it. She poured on speed, whispering to her beast to go faster yet.

The cliffs loomed already, craggy and full of hidden channels and ink-black caves. But her eyes fixed on that highest point, like a lighthouse before the Midnight Realm began.

A scream made her look back again—Lysander had already been tossed. The horse was trying to stomp on him, but he pulled out a clamshell knife from his belt, shouting and waving it at the creature.

Stop it! She sent the thought to the beast, not sure it would be heard. *Just go home!*

The water horse reared and sped off, and Lysander lay in the silted sand. But bubbles rose from his gill and the king's men were already approaching to carry him back. He'd survive. But he was out.

One down, two to go.

She faced forward again, settling in. Her water horse expanded their lead as the cliffs grew closer. Going up and around would be the hardest part. Once they returned past the cliff's jagged heights, it would be a flat race to the finish.

A red flash to her left caught her eye and she gasped. The horse tossed her head and screeched, pawing her hooves in the water—and then Atalanta saw it. A dragon scale, right on the ground. Impossible.

She angled her horse to pass near it. It meant taking a slightly wider arc, but not too far out of her way. Her eyes widened—it really was a black dragon scale, exactly what she needed. The boys might pass her if she stopped, but she took the moment to lean down and scoop it up. She'd make up the time. She tied the scale to the horse's mane, hiding it under the mountains of kelp-like hair, and sped up again.

Caspian and Garrison had slipped into the lead while she stopped, but they hadn't advanced far enough to stay ahead. They labored as they moved nearly straight up the cliff face. She zipped past them with a little wave. Caspian narrowed his eyes and smacked the water horse with his tail, like the way humans used whips. Ooh, bad idea.

The horse whipped its head around and bit deeply into his arm, releasing a trail of black blood off into the water.

"Auuh!" he cried.

"Turn back!" Atalanta commanded, but the currents stole her words.

Caspian shook off the pain and urged the horse forward.

Biting her lip, Atalanta whispered to her beast, "Keep going. Get far ahead. For me. For freedom!"

Her water horse tossed her head, but her tailfin flicked faster than before and she zipped up the cliffs. They darted around overhanging rocks and jagged points. She sped over the top, plunging into inky darkness that swallowed her light like a pit. Up and around the craggy rocks they zoomed, moving in a wide circle past the highest point to avoid any predators lying in wait in the cave at the very top. Nothing grew on this side of the cliffs, nothing at all. Predators lived only by hunting. The waters repelled her light and even felt thicker, like swimming through quicksand.

A faint red light flashed off to one side, coming from the rocks. An eel? Those attacked without hesitation—she flattened herself even closer to the horse, but the horse veered toward the brightness. "Hey! What are you doing?"

The dull red crackles of faint light took form as they approached—another dragon scale, black with red magic seeking an outlet.

"Ooh," she breathed. "That's two!"

Neither boy was in sight yet around the rocky channel at the top yet, so she took the time to secure this one to her back.

Trembling with joy, she thanked the water horse for listening to her instincts. Water horses were tightly woven within the net of magic that held them all together. "You knew magic waited for us here, didn't you, girl?"

This time, no way would she give up this scale. If she found a third scale, by mer-law, she could challenge her father's refusal to let her be a ranger, especially if she had a bondmate to help rule. Why not? He could help carry out the royal duties. In fact, her goal could be easier with that kind of help.

Maybe having a bondmate would not be so bad after all. Too bad she'd set up a challenge no one else could honestly win. It wasn't even close. She should've chosen something else for a challenge—Garrison would have won a trivia game, she bet, not that it mattered—but it was too late now. She just hoped they'd all survive it.

A scream echoing through the rocks turned her blood cold. Was that one of the merfolk? Or a sea dragon, called by the light and noise, or even drawn to the blood from Caspian's wound? They weren't in the most dangerous part of their journey yet.

Hurrying, she wrapped her arms in the cool strands of mane, sensing the straining muscles ready to work. "Let's go!"

She doused her light, leaving only the soft pearly glow from the water horse as she pulled on her magic to race. They took off like a flash, thundering around the highest point and its gaping cave so fast any evil beast would barely have time to register their appearance before the darkness would hide them again.

After rounding the cliff, they headed straight toward the city. Halfway there. She didn't see the others. They must be behind the cliff already. She leaned into the ride. "Let's finish this." On this side of the divide, small clumps of sea grasses dotted the rocks beneath them. They blurred as she passed.

By the time she reached the plains, Garrison was descending the cliff himself, still atop his water horse, moving faster than a shadow.

Well, well. Impressive. The young scholar had more skills than she'd known. Caspian appeared over the top of the cliff, horse-less and haggard. He must have been tossed off his mount's back, but at least he'd not been savaged out there in the dark. He swam as fast as he could, which was fast indeed, but he'd never catch her. None of them would.

She poured on speed. But this time, the water rushing through her hair felt somehow less satisfying than usual. She'd win and keep her honor, but at what price? The crown was destined to be hers. The real question now was if she'd wear it alone. Would Garrison really be such a burden? The way her skin hummed at his touch… maybe he'd even be… a pleasant partner. One who seemed to understand her better than the others.

She checked behind them, shocked to see he'd closed half the distance between them. He'd learned to use his fin in sync—that had taken her a while to figure out. How had he'd learned so quickly?

That's what you get for letting a scholar join the challenge. What else did he know? Would her father listen to him? Would the council? They needed bright minds like his in leadership.

The glow of the mer city glimmered ahead. She felt an urge to slow her horse, just a little. Surprised, she prodded the emotion. Well, she didn't want to beat Garrison too badly, after all. He'd been laughed at—the sound had bruised his heart. If he'd given her the best run for her hand, then he could at least hold his head high about that. Should she let him win? Tempting, but she couldn't bring herself to do that.

The water horse's webbed front feet flashed as fast as its tailfin, but it suddenly veered to the right. "Hey! Wrong way!"

The beast would not stop. It cruised to something glittering red in the sand, while Garrison thundered past, making a beeline for the city.

Her throat closed tight. Another dragon scale. Here, right out in the open. How was that possible? How had the herd of water horses not carried it away—they loved magical items like this and built nests of them. But there it sat, sliding in the silt as the currents of the horse bumped into it. The third scale she needed. The mare whinnied, tossing its head.

"You're right. We're wasting time." She grabbed it, tucked it under her arm and said, "Now take me home!"

She had the three scales required to petition the rangers! This changed everything. If she had a partner for the crown, it would free her for more than just ruling their people. She could do both. But she'd need the right bondmate, if she were to properly fulfill her royal duties, too.

Releasing magic through her body, she glowed like a spotlight, and her silvery scales shimmered in her own magical moonglow. With her rush of magic, she connected more deeply to her water horse—she could sense the mare's exhaustion, sluggishness weighing them down.

Gathering magic within her, Atalanta fed it to the mare. The water horse absorbed the power hungrily and took off. Sharing magic allowed them a sort of rudimentary communication, beyond their emotional tie. The mare had shown her how to do so when they'd rescued her. Now, Atalanta fed her mare magic for a different reason—to save her life, or at least shape it to her liking.

Just up ahead, Garrison's green hair streamed behind him like ribbons, muscles in his arms showing against his moonglow light. The little black water horse slipped through the water like an eel, rising and falling with the sandy dunes of the plain floor as if part of it.

Atalanta had never raced so hard. Her arms trembled; her breath came in gasps. He'd truly made her work for this win. But the win would be hers, she could taste it. She pushed her tail harder, faster, and slowly, they inched alongside Garrison and his horse. The little black horse snarled and snapped at the mare, who screamed back and rammed into her side.

"No!" Atalanta commanded. "None of that!" The mare laid down her ears, but pushed harder forward, edging ahead by a nose. The lights of the city glowed brighter now. Everyone had gathered here, lining the path, waiting for the winner who'd rule at her side.

You don't need *help, though. Not even him.* She began to ease past him, her honor warring with regret. "I'm sorry," she called.

Garrison called, "Do what you need to! I'll love you no matter what!"

Stunned, Atalanta met his dark gaze, black eyes challenging hers. Strong and smart. The perfect partner. And all she had to do was let him win. Or least keep him from losing outright.

But no. She wouldn't begin her life with someone who needed her to diminish herself.

As they thundered up to the finish line, she pulled ahead and crossed first. Garrison followed just a heartbeat behind her. The crowd cheered wildly. Caspian arrived a few minutes later, horse-less but alive. He clasped Garrison on the shoulders and congratulated him.

Slipping from the horses, the clash of victory and strange disappointment stole her words. Atalanta's mind offered up a vision of what could have happened: if she'd let him win, Garrison would have swept her in his arms, declared himself to her right then and there, and kissed her. Just a week prior, such a thought would have made her scowl.

Now, her lips tingled with anticipation. That hum of magic they'd shared had changed something inside her.

Backing away from his frothing water horse, he bowed low to Atalanta, saying, "Excellent race, princess. I'd expect nothing less from you."

He moved without hesitation toward her and her breath caught—was he going to kiss her hand goodbye?—but he reached past her, unerringly to the hidden sea dragon scale tied within her horse's mane. He untied it and began untangling the second one from the horse. "Your mount will take off any minute now for the wilderness. You won't want to lose these, will you?"

"How did you know—" He hadn't been close when she'd collected those. How would he know, unless—

His smile flashed quick and mischievous. "You're not the only one who's ridden this path before."

Her breath caught. He'd slowed her down on purpose! Craftily lured her with something she (and her horse) wanted. No wonder he'd almost managed to beat her to the finish line. "That's—"

"Smart?" He laughed.

"Tricky." She lifted an eyebrow.

"Some would say clever." He crossed his arms and lifted one eyebrow. "Though not clever enough to win, sadly."

"But how did you get three of them? I couldn't get one yet and you're not—" She broke off, blushing. She hadn't thought he was an athlete, but he'd proved himself today.

"I'm not in your league, no. But as a historian, I studied sea dragons. I knew where they build their nests and when they leave them to go hunt."

"You must have studied water horses, too."

"Ever since you received your tattoos, I wanted to understand them. As I wanted to understand you. So yes, I used my mind." He ran his hands along her arms. "Some might say my plan was even thoughtful. A gift. It's what I wanted it to be, not a trick. Isn't this what you really wanted? Three sea dragon scales. Not a bondmate, but a chance to prove yourself beyond the crown?"

She held the scale closely, but its magic didn't touch her nearly as much as the understanding she saw in his eyes. The prickles in the back of her eyes had her blinking. "Thank you."

"Whatever my lady wishes, is my command." He swept low. "I have other ideas, too. Ideas for true leadership spread among our elders, not just one royal couple. You don't wish to be queen, as things are now—but there are other ways to lead, ways that share the burden more widely."

He was a genius. And he was hers. Or could be, if she wanted him enough to choose him.

"The competition was my idea, my insistence, you know," she said, while the crowds bustled them both to the dais in the temple. "I could change the requirement. Technically."

He faltered, stilling in the water. "What do you mean?"

"I mean, sometimes it's good to be queen."

Her father waited atop the dais, beaming. "I think that means we have a winner after all! Do you agree, Atalanta?"

She met the gaze of the boy she'd once trusted, who'd become a merman who drew her like none other. Body, heart, and mind. She could admit it to herself now. Garrison as a bondmate would provide her with challenges all her life. "I believe we will be a good match. Yes. Garrison and I will be bondmates. He doesn't mind my speed or strength. In fact, he values me for those very reasons."

The people of Lyr cheered. And then Garrison scooped her up, leaned her back, and kissed her. It was everything she had imagined and more. Magic rushed between them and its thrill was second only to the trembling joy from the love taking root in Atalanta's heart.

EPILOGUE

Atalanta and her beloved lived happily ever after. They were the last of royalty within the merfolk, as Atalanta voluntarily took off the crown and shared their power among a council of elders. Hard times followed many generations later when the merfolk, and most of Aluvia, lost magic for a time, but this determined couple's leadership served as an inspiration to those who came later. Their descendants continually served in the role of historian for generations of the merfolk—and a set of twins from their line would one day work with humans to build back their broken world. Atalanta's strength and Garrison's cleverness lives on in their great-great-many-times-great grandchildren, Tristan and Mina, whose story is told in the second book of the World of Aluvia series, *Mer-Charmer*.

LIGHT IN THE DARKNESS

SELENIA PAZ

WHAT DO YOU remember?"

The old man's voice was soft, a mercy against the throbbing pain in her head.

"I was in the forest," Artemis said, her voice dry and brittle. "The edge of the forest, where the trees meet the foot of the mountain."

There was a soft rustling as the man kneeled down next to her. She felt him grasp her hand gently as he offered her a cool cup, wrapping her fingers around it. Artemis sat up but kept her eyes closed, her head not yet ready to see the blinding light. She brought the glass up to her lips and drank slowly, cherishing every drop of the cool water.

When she finished, she set the cup down. She began to open her right eye slowly, then her left. The throbbing pain in her head didn't seem to be as strong as it had been only moments ago.

Artemis took in her surroundings. The walls around them were a mixture of rock and mud; a small square window at the front of the dwelling let her know that she was still in the forest. She closed her eyes and inhaled, searching.

She could always find Sirius using only scent. But why couldn't she catch his scent now?

"What else do you remember?" The old man picked up the cup from the floor and walked slowly to a small wooden table near the window. The light streaming in through the window illuminated the man's gray and white hair and beard. The man reminded Artemis of someone, but she couldn't remember who.

"I was…" Artemis closed her eyes again, remembering. "I was in the forest, hunting. I was hunting with Sirius."

"Sirius?" the old man asked.

"He's my dog," Artemis said, her voice cracking. She placed her hand to her chest. Where was he?

Artemis sat up straight, her eyes wide open. "He's in the forest. He stayed in the forest." She tried to stand, but her legs buckled under her.

"Careful," the man said, his voice gravelly and stern with warning. "You don't want to hurt yourself. There will be plenty of time to venture out into the forest. But first, you must try to remember."

Artemis shook her head. "My head, it's never ached this much."

The old man approached Artemis and kneeled down in front of her. He reached over and began to move strands of her hair. Artemis pulled back.

"Easy, now. I am simply checking to make sure…" His voice trailed off, his eyes narrowing as he spotted something through the dark strands of her hair.

"Here," he whispered. Raising his right hand, the old man parted Artemis's hair with his left, placing the tips of his right fingers on Artemis's scalp. The pain gave one big pulse and then vanished.

Artemis instinctively reached up to try to touch the spot where the old man's hand had just been.

"What did…"

"It appears that a small gash on the side of your head there was the cause of your pain. But not to worry, I took care of that." The old man walked back to the table and shuffled some pots around, uncovering a loaf of bread and bringing it over to her.

"I don't feel anything," Artemis said, her fingers running over her scalp slowly.

The old man smiled, the corners of his eyes crinkling. Breaking the loaf of bread in half, he handed Artemis the bigger piece. The loaf was soft and warm, as if he had only just finished baking it.

"How did you…?" Artemis began.

The old man lifted up his right hand, the tips of his fingers glowing warmly. "Baking is not my only gift."

Artemis watched him carefully.

"Who are you?" she finally asked.

The old man's gray eyes twinkled softly as he stopped eating.

"My name, Artemis, is Chiron."

Artemis stopped running. She could see the small creek up ahead, hear the rushing water. But she had no idea where she was. She had lost her sense of direction.

But that was impossible.

Chiron had reached her. He was much faster than Artemis had thought he would be.

Turning to face him, she said, "How do you know me?"

"That is a complicated question," Chiron replied, stepping past her and continuing on to the creek. Kneeling down, he pulled out a small flask and began filling it with water.

"How do you know my name, then?"

Chiron stood, closing the flask tightly.

"I was assigned to you," he finally answered.

"Assigned to me?"

"You did not get that gash on your head from a careless tumble. Someone gave it to you. Do you remember?"

Artemis looked around, trying to find her sense of direction, trying to catch the slightest whiff of Sirius's scent.

Artemis looked up at the sky, at the leaves rustling in the soft wind. The clouds were gray but bright, and Artemis shielded her eyes as they fell upon a large leaf that was floating slowly down to the creek. Artemis's fingers tingled and she reached for her bow and arrow, but was surprised to find only one arrow left in the quiver on her back.

Connecting the arrow to her bow, she pulled back on the bow and let the arrow fly through the air. The tip flew above the slowly-floating leaf, hitting the base of a tree with a small thud before falling to the ground.

Artemis's eyes widened in disbelief. "What? I never miss."

Chiron watched as the leaf landed softly on the water and was carried away.

"What is happening? Where am I?"

Chiron stood silently.

"Please, you must tell me. I don't know why, but I can't tell where I am in this forest, and it doesn't look like the place near the mountains where I had been. What happened?"

Chiron sighed and motioned for her to sit next to him on a small log near the creek.

"I can only guess at what happened that led you here. From the cut on your head, I would say you were caught—near the mountains, as you've said—and transported here. I was assigned to take care of you, to train you to make sure you are ready to compete in the lunar hunt."

"The lunar hunt?"

Chiron nodded. "The Hunter's Moon is set to appear in a few days.

During this time, the kingdom bordering these woods has a traditional hunt. The lone survivor wins a place within the kingdom, nearest the King. You were…" Chiron cleared his throat, almost as if he was trying to remove something insincere. "You were chosen to participate in the hunt due to your incredible abilities and talents as a hunter."

"But I don't want to participate in this hunt. And for what King?"

Chiron exhaled. "King Agamemnon."

Something inside Artemis clicked. "King Agamemnon," she repeated, trying to gather her thoughts.

Chiron watched her carefully.

"But why me? Why couldn't they choose some other hunter? I don't want to be part of these human events. I just want to go back home and find Sirius."

Chiron cleared his throat again. "This year, the King's own adopted son is participating in the hunt. The King would like to prove that there is no better hunter than his son, and so he has made sure to gather the best."

Artemis eyed Chiron carefully. "And you are here to make sure I don't escape?"

Chiron's kind eyes widened. "I am here to make sure you survive."

"Survive?" Artemis laughed. "Or survive long enough to give the kingdom a good show?"

Chiron smiled a sad smile.

Artemis looked down, only now noticing a small metal brace around Chiron's left ankle.

"You don't seem to be the type to be a prison guard," Artemis said carefully. "Why are you here, really?"

Chiron sighed. "You have guessed correctly. I am certainly not a volunteer. But I suppose forcing you to compete in this tournament isn't the only thing King Agamemnon can do. This certainly is not my profession of choice."

"Let me guess. You are a healer. An apothecary, maybe?" Artemis said with a small smile.

"One of my professions is medicinal, yes."

"Then what are you doing here? Why don't you leave this place and do what you love to do?"

Chiron's voice trembled slightly as he answered. "He has threatened my family."

Artemis watched Chiron carefully. He reminded her of someone, with his gray-white beard and his caring eyes. She wondered what it would be like to have a father who only wanted to help.

"I have a family," Artemis said, her eyes going over the trees around them slowly. "I have found them to not always be dependable, if I am honest. Maybe that's why I prefer the company of the animals in the forest and the mountains."

Chiron listened carefully.

"But you seem like a good man. Your family must miss you terribly. So, we must get you back to them."

Artemis bent down to take a closer look at the metal brace around Chiron's leg.

"What is this?"

"It is assurance to the King that I will not leave the boundaries of this part of the forest. I have tried to remove it, but my healing magic is no match for the magic wielded by the creator of this brace."

Artemis jumped up and ran through the creek water to retrieve her arrow. Returning to Chiron, she bent down.

"Try to hold your leg very still," she said as she gripped the arrow tightly. Pulling her hand back, she slammed the arrow down with such force that Chiron staggered back. Reaching her arms out, Artemis steadied him.

The arrow had made a small fracture in the brace, and as they watched, it began to spread until it reached from the top of the brace to the bottom. Artemis reached down and pried the brace as if she were opening it. A loud *crack* sounded through the forest as the brace broke open.

"How did you do that?" Chiron asked.

Artemis lifted up her only arrow. "These arrows are a special type of silver, forged in the oceans under the light of the moon. They can break through anything. Now, let's go find your family."

Turning back toward the path they took to the creek, Artemis closed her eyes and tried to call upon her ability to know where she was without looking.

Chiron looked straight into her eyes. "I have heard many things about you, Artemis. That you are a good hunter, merciful but graceful, and that no other hunter has been able to best you."

Artemis shook her head, laughing quietly as she tried to pick up on Sirius's scent again. "And yet, I can't find my sense of direction, I cannot sense Sirius, and my weapons... Well, all I have from my once endless supply is this single arrow."

"That is why you must remember," Chiron said, urgently now.

"Remember?"

"Remember what happened to you. How you came here."

"You said I was brought here," Artemis replied.

"But what has changed? What is different? What has happened to affect your abilities to sense your surroundings?"

"They did something to me? Was it the gash?"

Chiron shook his head.

"You're not able to tell me," Artemis said slowly. "Like the brace. You're being kept from telling me."

Chiron's eyes widened.

Artemis closed her eyes and took a deep breath. "I was walking through the forest that meets the mountains with Sirius. The sun was setting, and we were heading to the creek to gather water and fish. And then…"

Artemis was back at the creek. She could see the bright oranges on one side near the horizon, soon to be replaced by the light of the moon. Sirius, his silvery-white fur moving gently in the breeze, sat down near the edge of the creek, waiting for Artemis to begin fishing. She tried not to hunt innocent animals if not necessary; only when they were hungry did they search for food.

And then they heard it. The crack of a twig in the distance. Sirius rose slowly, but as Artemis reached back to her quiver for her arrows, something grabbed her from the water. Her quiver fell to the ground, the arrows spilling out into the water until only a lone silver arrow remained. Sirius…

What had happened? Someone hit her on the side of the head and slipped a sack over her. She could still sense Sirius. He was trying to get to her, but then someone—someone called him. Someone in the forest. He looked at Artemis, trying to reach her, but then something came out of the trees and pulled him back. Back into the forest.

"He wasn't taken," Artemis said, opening her eyes again. "Sirius was pulled into the forest, but he wasn't taken by the people that took me. He…"

Artemis closed her eyes once more. She lifted her right hand, a motion that was so familiar to her, she couldn't believe she had forgotten why.

"I had my torch," she said, her voice almost a whisper. She opened her eyes. "Sirius was pulled into the forest, and my torch went with him. I hadn't lit it yet, that's why I can't see who took him when I try to remember."

Chiron stroked his beard, the motion reminding Artemis so much of her father she had to look away.

"You were separated from your hunting dog, your weapons, and your torch."

Artemis nodded.

"Is it possible that... that part of your own essence is missing?"

"What do you mean?"

"Sirius is gone. You are separated from the one being who is always with you. The one creature who always hunts at your side. And your weapons. The objects that are a part of you."

Artemis grew quiet, considering this.

"That is why I am unable to tell North from South? Why I missed that leaf?"

Chiron breathed in deeply, then exhaled. "I believe so."

"Then we must find them. Sirius, my weapons, my torch. We must find them."

Chiron raised his right arm.

"We will. But first, you must learn to survive without them."

The sun was high up in the sky, and there was no sign of any relief from the heat coming from the cloudless sky.

"Must we train in the heat of the day?" Artemis asked, wiping the sweat off her forehead with the back of her hand. "Why can't we wait until after sun sets, when the moon is out?"

"When the moon is out and you are at your most powerful? Tell me, what will happen if the moon is out and the clouds gather, blocking the light? What will happen to you?"

Artemis smirked.

"That's right," Chiron said, taking a long sip of cool water from a cup in his hand. "You might not be as strong as if the full moon were shining down upon you. You take for granted that the hunt will be at night, but it may not be a cloudless night. A true champion prepares for everything."

Artemis sighed. "Could I at least get a drink of water?"

Chiron laughed, taking another long sip. "But what if you find yourself at a place in the woods that is far from a creek?"

Artemis rolled her eyes and laughed. "Are you sure you are an apothecary who helps people?"

Chiron set the cup down carefully on the ground.

Reaching into his pocket, he walked toward Artemis. She could see he was moving something around in his fingers, but couldn't quite tell what it was.

"We have practiced your archery with your single arrow, have carved wooden arrows for you, have practiced at all hours without food or water. Now there is one more thing we must practice—reinforcing your senses. You have an advantage over many other hunters, but now your sense of direction, sense of smell, they have been altered. We must find a way to strengthen them so that you return to your former strength."

Artemis nodded.

"I am so sorry for this, Artemis," Chiron said with a small frown.

"Sorry for what?" Artemis asked, confused.

Chiron flung what he was holding at Artemis, and the white powder covered her entire face, stinging her eyes and skin. Artemis dropped her bow and arrow, but for some reason never heard them fall. The last thing she heard was Chiron's distant voice: "But this will strengthen your senses like nothing else can."

Artemis shook her head and rubbed her eyes, trying to get the powder out. She didn't feel any pieces in her eyes, but her vision was completely obstructed. She could hear distant shuffling and caught what might have been Chiron's voice, but she could not be sure.

He blinded me, she thought. *He blinded me and took away my hearing with this powder.*

A small part of her was frustrated at not being able to see or hear, but another part of her—the part that had learned how to survive in the wild and had always loved it—realized what Chiron had done. By taking away her senses, she had to force herself to survive without them, in the dark.

Artemis smiled, then closed her eyes even though she was not able to see. She tried to catch any small sound, but either the powder Chiron had thrown at her was very potent, or he was trying his hardest to be very quiet.

Artemis kneeled slowly down to the ground, her hand reaching out to find the bow and arrow she had dropped. They had been practicing together using the wooden arrows she and Chiron had made, in order to save her one silver arrow for when it was absolutely needed.

Her hands closed upon the bow and arrow and she brought them up slowly. She inhaled deeply, trying to use her sense of smell to get any clues as to where Chiron was, but the powder had taken that sense as well.

Artemis stumbled around the woods for so long she lost track of time. She couldn't even hear her feet crunching the leaves and twigs on the ground, and she found herself hoping that Chiron was at least somewhere nearby. She wouldn't want to unexpectedly step into a creek or walk into a snake nest.

A loud *screech* broke through the silence.

Artemis stopped walking. She heard the screech again, this time moving above her. Artemis looked up and the darkness covering her eyes changed from a pitch black to more of a dark gray.

There was something in the noise that sounded familiar.

Artemis sat down on the ground, feeling the area around her with her palms. She took a deep breath, closing her eyes again and forcing herself to relax. She was a goddess, whether she liked it or not, so it shouldn't matter that her senses had been taken away from her. She should be able to see the world around her with or without them.

She thought back to her time on Mount Olympus, remembering how different she felt from the other gods. Why was it that nature called to her more strongly than it did to the others? Why did she feel so separated from them even though she was one of them? Why did the quiet and simplicity of the forest bring her peace?

She could see herself standing there, watching the other gods enjoying their bread and wine, delicious cheeses and grapes. She remembered walking over to the balcony that jutted out from the side of the mountain, watching the people going on about their business down below. Some of them were asking the gods for gifts and favors, for help.

She watched as a young boy about her age was fetching water from a well for his mother, a small white dog by his side. She stood there as a shadow, which had been lurking in the darkness, reached out its thin fingers and snatched him into the woods. She could almost feel her leg moving as her foot leapt onto the balcony's barrier, her body ready to leap over the edge of Mount Olympus, ready to help the boy. Artemis reached up to touch her shoulder, feeling Zeus's hand as he placed it there, stopping her.

"But he was taken, he was just taken…" Artemis had cried.

"It is all part of the Fates' plan," Zeus had said, his usually bright eyes now dim.

"Fates?" Artemis had breathed. "Fates? But we can save him. We can change his fate."

Zeus shook his head.

Artemis looked around at the gods, who had grown quiet, all of them watching her. Apollo took a step back, hiding behind the others, not wanting to intervene.

Artemis shook off Zeus's hand.

"Maybe you are all tied to fate, but I'm not."

Turning, she had leapt over the edge of the balcony, bracing herself for the impact that was coming. The last thing she heard was Zeus saying her name. "Artemis!"

Screech.

"Artemis."

Now her name was only a whisper, and then all grew silent. Artemis felt her heart racing, and she placed her hand across her chest, willing it to calm down.

She had not seen her family very much since then, but a part of her was glad. She could not face them. She could not face her father. Not after she failed to find the boy. The Fates had snatched him away.

"Artemis."

Now her name was much more than a whisper.

It was not Chiron. She half stood, wondering if she was still in the forest, still in the spot where she had stopped.

There was something different in the air, and Artemis got the distinct feeling that she was much higher than the forest now—she was back at Mount Olympus. She could almost make out the sweet citrusy scent from the gardens. She had loved those gardens.

"Artemis," Zeus said again.

For the first time since her training began, Artemis was glad her senses were blocked, that she could not see her father.

"Artemis, never forget."

"Forget what?" she asked, her voice small compared to his. She had always wondered what she would say to Zeus the next time she saw him. She didn't know if the other gods felt this way, but she had always felt in awe of Zeus. He was her father, but he was also a magnificent presence that she felt she would always disappoint.

"Who you are."

The wind around her picked up, and Artemis was sure she was no longer on Mount Olympus. All around her, the world was still quiet and dark. But she could feel something. A warmth, coming up slowly behind her. As it reached out to her, Artemis spun around, stopping Chiron's hand as he was about to place it on her shoulder.

As she held Chiron's hand inches above her shoulder, her vision began to clear, and the rustles of the forest slowly filled her ears.

Chiron's eyes were shining, and for a few seconds she could almost see Zeus in them.

He smiled. "I see you have found what you needed."

"Found what?"

"Yourself."

It had been a long time since Artemis had been to the village bordering the forest. The last time had been just after she left Mount Olympus. She had searched for weeks for the boy that she had seen being taken, but she'd begun to think that the Fates were watching her and laughing as they avoided her.

Now, the village square was bustling with activity, with villagers purchasing fish, fruit, and bread, and children running and chasing one another. Artemis pulled her hood further over her face, not wanting to risk anyone catching a glimpse of her.

When they had returned from their training to gather supplies and head to the ceremony that would initiate the start of the hunt, they had found the door open, their supplies scattered and their food destroyed.

"It looks like they might know I no longer have the brace on," Chiron had said.

They had quickly gathered the food that had not been crushed and Chiron had retrieved two hooded cloaks for them before they finally headed to the village square.

Artemis had never seen so many hunters in her life. She hardly ran across any in her part of the forest, and she preferred it that way.

The crowd began to cheer, and Artemis looked up, wanting to catch a glimpse of King Agamemnon. Artemis had never taken a liking to him, and now, watching as he headed up the small steps to give his speech, she felt he seemed even more malevolent.

Chiron began to walk toward the stone benches, but Artemis stopped him.

"Where are you going?" she whispered.

"To sit," Chiron said. "Come, let us take a seat, unless you want to stand through what will undoubtedly be a dull and boastful speech, and tire before you even head into the forest for the main event."

Artemis had stopped listening. A quick movement out of the corner of her eye had caught her attention, and she stood straighter as her eyes followed a figure in a green cloak—the only person moving away from the King's speech.

"I'll be right back," Artemis said, and Chiron nodded.

"I don't blame you," Chiron said, chuckling as he turned to take a seat. Artemis was sure he was about to take advantage of the boring speech for a brief nap.

Artemis weaved through the crowd soundlessly. She was so quiet, the villagers did not stop to pay her any mind as they sat and stood, enraptured by the promises of an adventurous hunt where only one would be victorious. The King made sure to point out the many delicacies and desserts he had provided for them to celebrate this evening, inviting them to delight in them as they listened to the plan for the night's events. The crowd cheered wildly. Artemis looked around at the crumbling buildings, at the muddy roads and at the thin children. She had always wondered how it was possible for people to become pacified with so little. They could overtake this King and have what they truly needed, but they settled on a one-night feast.

The figure in the green hooded cloak and Artemis were now the only two persons on the narrowing path. Artemis had not been to this village very often, but she knew where they were headed. There was a small garden outside of the western part of the village, with statues dedicated to the gods and wildflowers that seemed to bloom all year. A statue to Zeus, and one to Athena.

Artemis smirked. Athena did love her statues.

Artemis stopped just outside the garden, not wanting the person to know she had been following them. There was something about this person. The way they walked? She wasn't sure.

When she finally entered, she could instantly tell hardly anyone came to these gardens anymore. The vines that crawled up the side of the stone wall had overtaken much of one side, as well as much of Athena's statue. Artemis smirked again. She wouldn't like that.

Artemis looked around slowly, not wanting to startle the person she had been following. As her eyes looked over the garden, she froze.

The person in the green hooded cloak had taken a seat near the statue of Zeus, an open scroll in his lap. He was a young man, about Artemis's age. Seventeen, possibly eighteen? Artemis's breath caught in her throat as she took a good look at the cloak. She had only ever seen such beautiful green cloth on the gods. Artemis realized her mistake and bowed her head, not wanting the young man to see her face, but it was too late. He had turned to look at her, and his eyes caught hers. Why hadn't she made sure her hood covered her face?

"Apologies," she said quickly, lowering her eyes and bowing slightly so that she might prevent him from seeing her face.

The young man laughed, and Artemis could sense something sad and lonely in that laugh.

"None needed," he said quietly. He shifted slightly to make room for her, and Artemis's eyes fell on the scroll he held open on his lap.

"Are you here for Zeus or for Athena?" he asked, motioning next to him. He had made space for her to sit by the statue of Zeus.

Artemis swallowed. She should leave.

Looking up once more, she caught the young man's eyes again. In the light of the setting sun, the brown of his eyes was tinged with orange and yellow. There was something else.

He was tired.

"Zeus," she heard herself saying.

The young man motioned for her to sit down.

"Thank you," Artemis mumbled, sitting down next to him. She looked up at the statue, a strange sensation jolting through her as she found herself wondering what this young man would think if he knew that this statue depicted her father.

She sighed deeply.

Glancing over, she looked down at the scroll. She could see colorful illustrations of the sun and the moon, the planets dedicated to some of her siblings.

"It's about the stars and the sky," the young man said. He handed it to her. He glanced behind them, and she felt keenly aware that he was nervous. Afraid, almost.

She caught his eye.

"My"—he swallowed—"father… he wouldn't want me reading that."

"Why not?" she asked softly.

"He thinks people who read too much start getting… crazy ideas."

Artemis chuckled. "They start thinking for themselves, you mean?"

she said, smiling.

The young man smiled back and let out an unguarded laugh.

Something strange but familiar stirred deep inside of Artemis. She instinctively wanted to reach out to this young man.

"It talks a lot about stars in there," he said, pointing. "It says they're balls of gas, do you think that's true? I mean, what about constellations?"

Artemis thought about the constellations, the ones she knew.

"I think some of them are a little bit more than that," she replied.

The young man reached over to unroll a bit more of the scroll, and his hand bumped into hers. She felt a jolt, this time a real one, course through her hand. Artemis's heart clenched and she forced it to relax. The young man mumbled, "Sorry," and pulled his hand back, but she could see him looking at her from the corner of his eye.

"Do you live here in the village?" she asked him.

"I used to," he replied, almost too quickly. Clearing his throat, he said, "How about you?"

Artemis shook her head. "I like living near the forest. It's a lot calmer there."

The sun had set, and a slight darkness had blanketed the garden as the hunter's moon rose.

Artemis looked up at the moon, wondering why people were always trying to hunt the natural world as if it were a trophy, pieces of gold for their collections. She clenched her jaw at the thought that King Agamemnon was the worst of all—hunting and eliminating hunters that he forced to participate in this game. But she would change that tonight.

The hunter's moon now lit up the garden, casting a beautiful glow around the statue of Zeus.

"There's something so beautiful about the moonlight," the young man said.

Artemis smiled, a warm feeling filling her inside. "What's that?" she asked, wondering what the young man would think to know how personally she would feel what he said.

The young man looked at her, and Artemis realized he wasn't seeing her as *Artemis*. He didn't know she was a huntress, a goddess, and he wasn't looking for Zeus's reflection in her features, as everyone did. He was seeing past that. He was looking at *her*.

"It is a light in the darkness."

Artemis looked down at the scroll, feeling a blush crawling up her neck to her cheeks. But there was something… something else about this boy. Artemis shook her head. She was being silly. She glanced over at the statue of Athena. What would she think, watching Artemis falling in love with this boy when she was supposed to be getting ready to kill King Agamemnon?

Artemis sighed.

"It sounds like you're asking him for something important," the young man said, looking up at Zeus.

Artemis laughed a soft laugh. "I suppose," she answered.

"Me too," he said. Then, hesitating, "Do you think… what do you think it must be like to have Zeus as a father?"

Artemis blinked, then looked over at him.

"I mean, he must be a good father. It must be something… amazing… to have someone like Zeus watching over you."

Artemis nodded. "It must be something," she said.

Looking over at her, the young man swallowed. "I never really had a father," he said, his voice low. Artemis felt her heartbeat increase. He was whispering, almost as if he was telling her some sort of forbidden secret. "My father left my mother when I was young. It was just me and her until…"

"Until?" Artemis asked, but she already knew.

There came a rustling behind them, and the young man was about to reach over to take the scroll from Artemis's lap, when a loud, booming voice interrupted.

"There you are! My men and I have been looking everywhere for you! What were you thinking, going off on the most important night of my—" King Agamemnon stopped talking as his eyes came to rest on Artemis. Striding forward, he pulled the young man up and brought him back to the entrance of the garden.

"What have I told you about fraternizing with the commoners? They're filthy, coarse creatures." King Agamemnon looked back at Artemis. "Don't you see, she even has some vile scroll with her. Her head is probably overflowing with repulsive—"

Just then, Chiron stepped through the entrance to the garden, clearing his throat.

"Artemis, it is time. The tournament is beginning."

King Agamemnon stopped talking. Artemis stood, rolled up the scroll and tucked it under one arm, and lowered her hood.

King Agamemnon took a step back. Artemis gritted her teeth, wishing she could drive an arrow through his heart right then. But with only one silver arrow, she could not risk Chiron's life, or the life of the young man.

She looked at him fully now, not hiding any part of her face. His eyes grew lighter, sadder.

Here he was now, the reason why she came down from Mount Olympus.

"Artemis." King Agamemnon's voice was the perfect example of *coarse* and *vile*. "I didn't realize you would be introduced so soon. Son, this is one of your competitors on tonight's hunt. Artemis, goddess and huntress, daughter of Zeus himself, said to be one of the greatest hunters in the world. Artemis," he spat the name out, "this is my son, Orion."

His son.

His adopted son.

His *stolen* son.

Artemis took a step forward, but Chiron raised his hand ever so slightly. Caution, Artemis. Not yet.

Artemis bowed slightly, lowering her head.

"Well, let the games begin!" King Agamemnon said, smiling his wicked smile. "We shall see each other in the woods."

King Agamemnon. She remembered hearing as a little girl how much he'd asked Zeus for a son. Artemis had always thought Zeus unfair for not granting his wish, but Zeus would never say why he denied Agamemnon this. Now, Artemis was beginning to understand. Sometimes, Zeus did try to interfere.

Artemis chanced a glance at Orion. She thought she might see fear in his eyes, uncertainty.

Her heart tightened as he gave her a small smile.

He was afraid, but not for himself.

In his eyes, she saw his reaction as he realized he would have to try to kill her.

Their plan had been very simple, and so far, Chiron and Artemis had been able to make contact with all the other hunters to tell them what they would be doing.

As they waited, hidden in the woods, Artemis and Chiron would reach Orion, with the single goal of bringing King Agamemnon to them. Of killing him.

"One of the hunters said he had it on good authority that King Agamemnon would be with Orion and a small army who would take out any hunter on sight."

"Of course. He can't leave the palace without his army," Artemis said, rolling her eyes.

"According to my compass, we should be coming up on their location at about…"

"A thousand feet or so," Artemis said, stopping suddenly.

Chiron turned around to face her.

"Artemis, I am not sure—"

"Everything will be all right, Chiron," Artemis said, and she realized that she was eerily calm.

"But, I just can't shake…"

There was a soft wind, and Artemis lifted her nose high. There was something in the wind…

"Sirius," Artemis whispered.

"Sirius?" Chiron repeated.

"He's here."

Artemis looked up just as a group of thunderclouds began to cover the moon.

Chiron lifted his finger up. "As I said. Be prepared."

The clouds covered the full moon completely just as a flash of lightning filled the sky.

"That's strange. I didn't think it would rain tonight…" Chiron said.

"I don't think it will rain," Artemis said, looking up at the tree branches. She spotted the eagle perched near the top of a tree. She waved up at it.

As the eagle flew down, there was another flash of lightning and a rumble as Zeus transformed, landing in front of Artemis.

Chiron's eyes widened, and he took a step back.

Zeus bowed slightly to him. "Chiron. Thank you for taking such good care of my daughter."

Chiron bowed back.

Looking at Artemis, he said, "If you'll excuse me."

Artemis stood in the silence, not sure what to say.

Artemis heard rustling behind Zeus, and as she watched, a white dog with white-silver fur came around from behind him.

"Sirius," she said, opening her arms wide to embrace him.

"Pan saw what happened at the edge of the forest. He brought Sirius to me, and this."

Zeus opened his palm, revealing her silver torch.

Artemis smiled. "I might not need it anymore," she said with a sad smile.

"Yes, Chiron has done quite an excellent job."

Reaching behind him, Zeus brought out her silver arrows.

"You might need these as well."

Artemis grabbed the arrows and placed them inside her quiver.

"The boy, the one who was taken when I left Mount Olympus, he…"

"Was taken by King Agamemnon."

"Was that why you never granted him a son? Because he would use him for something like this?"

Zeus lowered his eyes.

"But something terrible still happened. He stole Orion from his home."

Zeus nodded. "The Fates have a strange way of bringing things about sometimes."

"But you're Zeus. You're a god. We are gods. We can change things."

Artemis could see the conflict in her father's eyes.

"But someone always gets the difficult role, don't they?" she finally said.

"Someone always does," Zeus answered. It was strange to see her father, always so jovial, his loud thunderous laugh filling the skies, now so sad and conflicted. Zeus towered over her, and it scared her to think that Zeus, too, could feel fear. Zeus, too, could feel sadness.

Zeus placed a hand gently on her shoulder.

"Artemis, you were always the lone wolf. From the moment you were born and I saw the moon reflected in your eyes, I knew you would never be quite like the rest of the gods. You fled to the forest and escaped the Fates, but they found you anyway. And for that, I am sorry."

Artemis looked up at Zeus, at her father. She saw the white beard and the crinkles around his eyes. Sometimes all she saw was a god, the ruler of Mount Olympus. Sometimes she forgot he was her father. She opened her mouth to speak, but Zeus raised his right hand.

"You will always be my daughter. And when you are ready… you are missed at Mount Olympus. Make sure to visit us."

Zeus bent down to stroke Sirius gently on the head. "I'll be watching you both."

A flash of lightning came down from the sky, and just like that, Zeus was gone.

A part of Artemis wanted to follow him, to go back to Mount Olympus and not have to worry about what was going to happen. Not have to feel so human.

But she had met Orion, and it was too late.

Looking down at Sirius, she said, "It's time now. Let's go find King Agamemnon."

Clouds had begun to cover the moon again, making the uneasiness in Artemis's stomach grow. This time, she knew the clouds were not her father's.

"What kind of person creates a tournament where people hunt one another? What kind of person takes pleasure in that?" she said through the darkness.

"I think, perhaps, King Agamemnon feels that, by eliminating the best hunters, he might one day be the best himself. But, as with so many things in life, there are no shortcuts."

"No," Artemis replied, "there are not."

They were at the edge of King Agamemnon's camp, and they could see the large tents that undoubtedly housed the king's army.

"Remember the plan," Chiron said. "Wait until full cloud cover, then we move in."

Artemis was just finished nodding when she saw something green out of the corner of her eye.

Orion.

Two soldiers were pulling him along, almost dragging him to a tent at the edge of the camp.

Artemis took a step forward.

"Not now, Artemis. Not now," Chiron whispered urgently. Sirius whined next to him, seemingly agreeing.

Artemis watched as the soldiers dragged Orion inside, tossing him on the ground.

"I have to help him," Artemis said, taking off down the small hill toward the tent.

"No!" Chiron called out.

Sirius caught up to her, and Artemis was grateful to have her small shadow back.

As they reached the tent, Sirius suddenly stopped. He lifted his nose in the air, then turned, heading toward a tent at the other end of the camp.

"Sirius, no!" Artemis whispered. Where was he going?

There was no time to find out. As the clouds began to completely cover the moon, Artemis pulled out her silver arrow and bow. She took one last look at the moon and ducked inside the tent.

Orion was lying on the ground, but the guards were gone. Artemis reached down to turn him on his back, trying to wake him.

"Orion," she whispered urgently.

Maybe they could just go. He could wake up and they could go to the forest, to Mount Olympus, anywhere.

"She's here."

Artemis turned to find a group of soldiers at the tent's entrance. The King stood behind them, but there was something strange about him. Two soldiers seemed to be holding him up.

Artemis lifted her bow and arrow and aimed at the King. She couldn't miss this time.

Suddenly, Artemis felt something soft brush against her leg. She looked down at Sirius, who looked confused.

Where had he gone off to?

Sirius kept his eye on the King, and as Artemis watched, something passed between them.

"Sirius," the King said.

Artemis lowered her bow slightly. "How—?"

She felt someone grab her from behind, her bow and arrow clanging as they hit the ground.

"Chiron," Artemis said to Sirius, who started to back away, then stopped. A tall, rectangular mirror stood near the tent's entrance, and Artemis could see Orion holding her tightly.

No.

"Why?" she choked out.

As she watched through the mirror, she could see Orion changing. He grew taller, thinner, his face a mask of evil. King Agamemnon.

Behind the soldiers, King Agamemnon's features changed as well. Brown hair, colorful but sad eyes. It was Orion.

"Magic," she gasped.

The same sort of strange magic that had bound the brace to Chiron's leg.

"And here she is," King Agamemnon breathed down her neck. "Daughter of Zeus, goddess of the hunt and the moon. Tell us, Artemis, how does it feel to know your father won't be able to interfere? How does it feel to know your life is in the hand of the Fates?"

Artemis found she was not afraid.

Looking at Orion, she said, "Sirius. He was your dog when you were young." The same small white dog that was with him near the well when he was taken. That's why Sirius had run off. He had smelled Orion.

Something registered in the back of Artemis's mind. Not long after she had come down to the village, Zeus had come to try to get her to return to Mount Olympus.

She could see him standing there near the creek as she said she would not return. Zeus had sighed, then turned to uncover something he had brought with him. A small white dog.

The same small white dog that had belonged to Orion. Zeus had been watching all along.

Artemis was not afraid. Orion and Sirius would be safe. Chiron could go back to his family. Everything would be right.

"And now, poor Orion gets to watch while this girl he has grown to have feelings for dies. What a tragedy, how cruel the Fates are."

"No," Artemis gasped. King Agamemnon thought she was replying to him, but she was really talking to Chiron, who was hidden in the shadows outside the tent.

"No," she said, more loudly. She would not be responsible for his death.

"You're wrong. Yes, the Fates can be cruel. But sometimes, it is people who are cruel. Here, it is you. I cannot wait to see what the Fates have in store for you."

Orion's eyes widened. He tried to step forward, but Artemis shook her head ever so slightly. She motioned with her eyes to Sirius. He had to take Sirius and go.

Artemis felt a slight shiver run through King Agamemnon's body. "Scared, are we?" she said, hoping to get his attention and the attention of the soldiers.

King Agamemnon stiffened. "What are you waiting for?" he growled at his soldiers. "Kill her."

One of the soldiers near the back released Orion and stepped forward as the others made a path, trying to get away from whatever he held in his hand.

Artemis heard Chiron outside the tent. "No."

As the soldier approached, she could see he held in his hand a clear bottle containing a small powder similar to the one Chiron had used to help her train. But this one was a dark, putrid green. She knew that this one would take her life.

It would all be over soon. They would all be safe.

As the soldier began to uncork the bottle, Sirius leapt and bit down on his arm, and Orion tackled him down to the ground. Artemis closed her eyes, expecting the powder to cover her face. When nothing happened, she opened her eyes slowly. King Agamemnon had released her and walked over to look down at Orion, who now lay covered in the green powder.

Artemis could see Sirius laying near his feet, his soft white fur sprinkled with the green powder.

"Well, I did want that powder to work in an instant. I suppose I got what I paid for." King Agamemnon kicked Orion slightly with his foot. "Such a shame."

Artemis remembered then truly who she was. She was the daughter of Zeus. Zeus, who could rain down lightning on the world, who could make a roar of thunder travel across the sky. She was the best friend of Sirius, and the student of Chiron. She was the love of Orion. And this time, the Fates would not deny her her revenge.

Artemis reached down and picked up her bow and arrow. As the soldiers approached her, a flash of lightning traveled down from the sky, setting the tent on fire. The soldiers looked at one another, then turned and ran out of the tent, leaving the king alone and unguarded.

Chiron stood at the entrance to the tent, ready to grab the king should he try to flee.

King Agamemnon turned to her.

"Wait," he said, his voice trying its best not to shake. "I-I might be able to reverse this. I might…"

Artemis saw something inside of King Agamemnon then. Behind his lush robes and his heavy gilded crown, she could see his cowardice.

Artemis only killed when absolutely necessary.

She didn't hesitate this time.

And she knew she wouldn't miss.

Artemis kneeled down and placed Sirius gently in Orion's arms. Their breathing was shallow, and she knew they would not be with her for long.

As she stroked Sirius gently, Orion placed his hand over hers.

"Thank you," he said softly.

Artemis looked at Sirius, then at Orion.

"You were the light in our darkness."

Chiron helped Artemis lay Orion and Sirius together under the light of the hunter's moon.

As they kneeled down, Artemis tried to control the grief that was threatening to overcome her.

Closing her eyes, she called Mount Olympus.

A flash of lightning brightened up the sky even more, this time unaccompanied by the thunder.

Zeus kneeled beside them, turning to look at Artemis.

"You are sure?"

Artemis nodded. She pulled the scroll out from her cloak.

"He asked me if they were balls of gas." She laughed, but the tears began to stream down her face.

"That and much more," Chiron said quietly.

"When you're ready," Zeus said as he raised his hands above Orion and Sirius.

Artemis looked at Orion without his green cloak, with his plain clothes that made him look even more real. She looked at Sirius, his shaggy white-silver hair so bright in the moonlight. She wished she could have had an eternity with them.

As Artemis watched, a bright light began to shine from Zeus's hands until it completely enveloped Orion and Sirius.

And now, Artemis waits for night, when she can look up at Orion and Sirius as they travel across the sky, waiting for the day when they can see their beloved light again.

KÁTO KÓSMOS

JANINA FRANCK

WHEN MIRA FIRST saw her, she was stunned. The sleek chrome shell alone was enough to make her hold her breath, not to mention the gorgeous greens and greys that created unfathomable intensity in that mechanical gaze. Every movement was elegant and precise, calculated to perfection. And then the capabilities…!

It was unprecedented. Robots and A.I. were one thing, plenty of those were distributed among the planets of the Old World, but this android went far beyond what the galaxy's scientists and engineers had offered thus far. Designed to consume food in order to break it down into the nutrients and soil the plants so sorely needed, this prototype was exactly what Káto Kósmos needed.

Mira's decision was an easy one. She had come to the interplanetary science and innovation expo with a vague idea for a mission, but that mission had just taken shape. She needed this android. Her planet depended on it. She had overheard a conversation an interested buyer had had with the scientist-engineer of Olympia Corp who had developed her. Dimitri, as he was known to the world, had made it very clear however, that he wasn't going to part with the prototype of the android for any sum of money.

Keeping that in mind, she wasn't left with any other options.

Even though it was unorthodox and highly illegal, she had somehow managed to arrange for her covert forces to intercept the transport just before the expo's closing in order to steal the android.

What else could she do? It wasn't like her planet had a lot of finances or time to spare for the future line of androids that Olympia Corp would develop. This situation, lax as security was during certain times of the convention, was the best opportunity she would get in her lifetime.

Now, a few hours and a speedy escape through several wormholes later, the android was sitting in a chair in Mira's home on Káto Kósmos, staring blankly ahead. It looked like a girl, a young woman, roughly the same age as Mira, with wavy aquamarine hair that reached down to its waist, silvery greenish eyes in which the tiniest gears could be seen in the iris upon closer inspection, and porcelain colored finish for skin, dressed in a simple grey gown.

"Power on," Mira ordered, but nothing happened. She frowned. This was the most common voice order for machines to start up, but it clearly had no effect on the android. What would it take to get that lifeless head to start moving?

She paced around the android, looking for a way to start it up, but she couldn't find a switch. She didn't particularly want to check underneath the clothing; somehow that felt indecent and wrong, despite the android being nothing more than a machine—it just looked too human.

Eventually, after trying plenty of the more common voice commands, Mira sat cross-legged on the ground facing the android. She sighed and yawned, brushing her long, brown hair out of her face to tie it into a messy bun. A glance at her watch told her it was already six A.M. local time.

"Good morning," she mumbled to herself, wondering how many fleets from Olympia Corp's forces were out looking for the ones who had stolen their precious invention. Who knew how long it would take them to look past the deflection shields of Káto Kósmos and find it? Mira knew the consequences would be dire, but the alternative looked just as grim.

"Good morning."

Mira's eyes shot up to see the android smiling sweetly.

"How can I help you?" The android let her gaze sweep over the room slowly, finally resting on Mira. "I don't believe Father has introduced us. My name is Persephone."

Persephone's voice was silky smooth, like a gentle wind, brushing over an almost-still lake. Goosebumps rose on Mira's arms, and she found herself smiling before she knew it. Quickly suppressing her joy, she chided herself for her folly. She couldn't let herself hope just yet; this meant virtually nothing.

She cleared her throat.

"Hi."

Suddenly, her mouth dried up, and she found herself at a loss for words. How could she even begin to explain the precarious situation in which they found themselves? How could she show the android why they needed help and how she could save them?

Perhaps that was exactly it. *Show her.*

Mira got to her feet and held out a hand to Persephone. "Come."

Persephone took her hand readily, her fingers smooth, but much warmer and softer than Mira had expected. Even though it was so much paler than Mira's own bronze complexion, it actually felt like real skin, although some aspects of cold, stark metal were still present.

She led Persephone through the hall to the large, full-framed glass doors that led out to the balcony. She pushed them open and stopped to take in the sight of Káto Kósmos. Her home.

The millions of buildings were like a patchwork of different architectural styles from all across the universe, some small, some big, some simple, some elaborate and elegant. There were a few large streets and many parks, along with a couple of plazas, but from up here, it all just looked like one big, chaotic, colorful mess.

The city's shields glinted dark purple in the sunlight, the dome stretching far—farther than seemed plausible. It always struck Mira that even from this hill at the center of the city, she couldn't even guess at the limits of the dome's reach just by looking at it.

As a young child, she had used to marvel at what lay beyond it.

As a near adult, she knew there was nothing but dead wasteland—a planet burnt and radiated into nothingness due to humanity's mistakes. The city of Káto Kósmos was the only place that thrived, a droplet of life on an otherwise dry and dead rock.

But despite its many parks, despite the forests circling the city, and despite the joy that Mira felt at gazing upon her home, days like these, the dome—protecting them from the sun's harsh light—felt oppressive. It felt like a cage, designed specifically for her.

"This is Káto Kósmos."

Now the words were easy to find. They came straight from her heart, from her innermost being, and arrived on her lips without needing to be placed there. "It's a place where those who needed to run away live. The victims of wars, or those whose lives were threatened due to political intrigue. It's a haven, a place where everyone can belong, and no one can find them. It's my home, too. It's my duty to look after these people and to make sure they can continue to live peacefully here."

She glanced at Persephone, to see if her words had any effect so far, but the android's gaze was still lingering on the city. Not a trace in her expression gave away what calculations she might be making. In the tinted light of the dome, she looked even more otherworldly and angelic than she had inside the building. Just for a moment, the breath caught in Mira's throat.

"But they're living in a prison of their own making." Mira gestured at the sky, the dome, and Persephone's eyes followed. "They can only live within the confines of the city because the rest of the planet has been destroyed. Nothing can grow there anymore. A war long ago made sure of that. It's only a matter of time until the city's resources won't be able to support the people anymore."

Mira's lower lip began to tremble, and she felt choked up. Annoyed at her lack of emotional control, she at least managed to suppress her tears. She'd worked so hard for this and risked so much, just like her parents had done before her.

"I need your help," she whispered. "All of us do. Please help us to make our planet whole again."

A long moment of silence extended between them, and all Mira could hear were some of the imported birds chirping down below in a park. She didn't dare look at Persephone. Instead, she focused on her hands. This was where the programming should kick in. Where Mira would find out how much autonomy the android really had.

"What's your name?"

Mira looked up in surprise to find Persephone smiling at her. She knew that androids were programmed to mimic human expressions to appear more lifelike, but it felt genuine, warm.

"Mira."

A clearing of a throat behind Mira made her turn to see Cerbus, her main advisor, a tall, broad man with a large nose, short brown hair, dark eyes, and a permanent scowl stuck to his face.

"Her title," he said pointedly with a stern look at Mira, "is Lady Hadmira Esril, rightful ruler of Káto Kósmos."

Mira grimaced.

"My lady," he continued unperturbed. "What you did was foolish, and it concerns me greatly that you did not take my advice." He sighed. "But I suppose what's done is done. The first reports have arrived: We've bought some time. We are not yet suspected."

Mira nodded.

"Thank you, Cerbus."

He inclined his head and withdrew.

Mira sighed once more and turned back to Persephone, who was smirking with what appeared to be amusement.

"You're a planetary ruler, then," she said, and Mira shrugged, blushing.

"Not by choice."

"Your family perished?"

Mira started at the odd choice of wording, but she let it be and nodded instead.

"Eight months ago, shortly after my sixteenth birthday."

Persephone nodded, then gestured to the city below.

"May we take a walk?"

Taking her interest as a good sign, Mira nodded hastily and led her out of the castle.

They took the safer streets first, the ones bustling with life, so Persephone could get a feeling for the people on Káto Kòsmos. There were markets, filled with everything from colorful produce to all sorts of fabrics and clothes. Books and toys were also among the available products, as were a variety of technological appliances, though there were significantly less of those. Artisans crafted beautiful things from all across the known galaxies, showing glimpses of what the world, their previous homes, had to offer. These markets were the only places Mira had ever heard of having such a variety and respect for different heritages.

Káto Kósmos was a place that didn't want to be found, for people who didn't want to be found—people who had escaped. Advanced technology was a threat to that, though it wasn't illegal here. Seeing as trade was difficult with other planets and societies, tech remained at a low level, mostly to devices that didn't connect to wider networks and could be manufactured by the city-based factories right here.

People from different stalls called out to Mira when they saw her, all smiles and friendly words. A good number of them offered some of their merchandize to her for free, the food stalls in particular.

A few of those gifts she accepted to give to Persephone to try. She wanted to show what richness could be found here, delicacies from planets who had been enemies for centuries, even millennia.

Persephone accepted each treat with grace, partaking of a few bites of everything, but didn't comment on more than the outward appearance and the diversity.

They strolled casually through town, instead of using some of the dome-wide transport systems, and soon, Mira elected to guide Persephone out to one of the many parks sprinkled throughout the city, to get away from the overwhelming amount of noise and movement and find a moment of uninterrupted peace and quiet.

Once there, they sat down on a bench and simply watched the trees' leaves sway in a gentle artificial breeze above them. A lot of them were turning brown at the edges, and they were beginning to look looser, less lush. Even within the city limits, the plants were dying. They had survived a long time, but the poison in the ground was finally reaching them. Mira expected them to have about five years left, at most.

"Why did you request my help?" Persephone asked suddenly.

Mira frowned.

"Because we need help to heal our planet, and you're quite literally designed for exactly the kind of thing we need."

Persephone shook her head.

"No, that's not what I meant. You're the first person besides Father to ever *ask* if I wanted to do something. You could have just ordered it. Everyone else always tried to do that."

Mira raised an eyebrow in misgiving.

"Why would I do that? You're an android with a highly developed A.I. You're not exactly just a machine. You have a personality, self-awareness, the ability to learn, and I believe, the presentation at the expo even mentioned the ability to forget? So you have wires instead of veins. It doesn't mean you're less of a person. Forcing you to do something you don't agree with would be akin to slavery, and that would go against everything this planet and my family stand for."

Without realizing, Mira had risen to her feet and clenched her fists as she spoke passionately.

Now, she blinked twice, unclenched her fists, and sat back down, all the while Persephone continued to smile at her.

"Sorry about that," Mira mumbled, but Persephone shook her head.

"I appreciate it," she said. "It makes me happy."

She turned her gaze back up to the trees again.

"I will gladly help make your planet whole again. But I warn you, it will take a long time."

Warmth rushed through Mira's entire body and she felt giddy.

"You mean it?"

Persephone nodded, smiling.

"Thank you," Mira gasped and threw her arms around Persephone. "Thank you so much!"

Maybe their planet didn't have to die after all.

"It was a foolish move, a proof of your immaturity as ruler. Please, you must consider aligning yourself with someone more experienced; in fact, I have already picked out several suitable candidates."

Cerbus rummaged through his papers while Mira glared at him, sullenly chewing on her fried egg.

"A husband," she murmured. "Yeah, right."

Cerbus halted and glowered at her.

"A *husband*," he emphasized, "would help you escape your current predicament. Olympia's forces are looking for you across all the known galaxies! A well-chosen partner could create a strong political alliance with one of the galaxy's major powers, thereby making you untouchable."

"Provided I return Persephone, right?"

Cerbus nodded, hesitantly, slowly. "But you don't intend to do that, do you?"

Mira smirked at him, delighted that he knew her so well. "Nope! And I'm not getting married, either." Cerbus opened his mouth to speak, but Mira raised her hand quickly to silence him. "And before you ask, I'm not open to marrying a woman, either. Or anyone for that matter."

She got to her feet and took three steps toward the large full-length glass doors leading out to the balcony. Her gaze glided across her city, her home, her people. Chimneys expelled smoke, birds sang, and the trees swayed gently in the artificial breeze. The lilac tint touching all she could see made her feel as though she were living in one of the rainbow's colors.

"I, by myself, am enough." She rested her right hand on the window, her fingers reveling in the smooth, cool sensation of the glass, reminding her of what she had expected Persephone's skin to feel like. "I don't need anyone standing beside me, to be my lover or my spouse."

She turned back to Cerbus, her back straight and her shoulders back, her jaw jutted forward, directing all her determination into her gaze, pinning him down with it.

"I'm enough. And if I am not, then I do not deserve the name of Esril."

Cerbus bowed his head, knowing full well that he had lost the argument.

Mira may have only been on the throne for a few months, but she had

Esril blood in her, and over the years, she had absorbed her family's knowledge, their determination.

Her first priority was her people. And that was exactly why she couldn't rely on a hasty political marriage to bail them out. It would destroy everything Káto Kósmos stood for—the safety they enjoyed from being hidden, from being little more than a rumor to most, from being a shadow in the dark—suspected, but never perceived, not clearly.

And for the sake of her people, she couldn't give up Persephone, not now that the android had agreed to help revive the planet.

As if on cue, the great doors to the hall opened, and Persephone entered, slowly, almost hesitantly, glancing uncertainly at the guards stationed just outside the large entrance.

Cerbus clicked his tongue, misgiving, but he retreated after Mira shot him a warning glance.

She smiled at the android. "Did you have a pleasant rest?"

Persephone tilted her head to one side. "I'm not sure, but I had a pleasant standby."

Mira laughed quietly to herself. "Of course, it's so easy to forget that you don't sleep like humans do, forgive me."

Persephone only smiled pleasantly in response.

Mira made a wide gesture at the set table. "Would you like to eat something?"

"That would be lovely, thank you."

She gracefully took a seat on one of the chairs, her movement so elegant and smooth, it barely seemed real.

Mira poured her a cup of herbal tea and Persephone helped herself to some of the pastries.

It was strange, watching her eat.

At first glance, she looked like a young woman, barely out of childhood, just having breakfast. Upon closer inspection, and Mira was watching her extremely closely, her movements didn't seem quite natural. There wasn't anything in particular that stood out, but they appeared somewhat mechanical, as though eating were more of a chore than anything else.

Mira wondered if Persephone could enjoy flavors. She gave no indication that she could—her face did not betray her, nor did she linger on any of the foods for long, biting off new pieces periodically. Mira even thought she could set her watch to the rhythm to which Persephone ate.

Eventually, Persephone finished, dropped a seed from one of the fruits she had eaten into her pocket, and raised her eyes to meet Mira's.

"Shall we go?"

Here, at the dome's edge, everything felt more tranquil. There were fields of grain, orchards, and even a lake. Animals roamed small glades, looking up briefly to assess the two approaching women with curious, cautious black eyes before bounding away to hide.

Mira kept her pace slow to give Persephone a chance to really look around and absorb the beauty that surrounded them, but also to stall the sight of the wastelands.

While she adored this part of the city, this bountiful, green biome dripping with life, she dreaded setting her eyes once more on the dead nothingness that lurked outside the dome, miasmatic air and everything.

What would Persephone say or think when she saw it? Saw what decades of war and destruction had done to this once-vibrant planet?

What if she didn't think she could help after all once she saw what an atrocious state it had been left in?

Mira didn't dare to let herself dwell on that thought for too long. Instead, she focused on pointing out the animals, observing them from the cover of the trees and bushes. Persephone responded with nods and smiles, a softness to her gaze that reassured Mira a little.

Finally, there was no further way to drag out the inevitable.

They had reached a small, unassuming cabin set into the dome itself.

Persephone inspected the phenomenon curiously—one side of the cabin was inside the forcefield, the other outside. Finally, she turned to Mira and gestured to the cabin.

"How is this possible?"

Mira smirked, proud of her ancestor's ingenuity.

"It's a repeater," she said. "The forcefield is built from energy, but it can't only be sent out from one source alone, or it wouldn't settle right. There are eight repeaters along the city's bounds; this is what we call the southern gate. The actual energy source comes from the tip of the castle."

She gestured back to her home, the highest tower actually touching the dome, creating it.

Very few people in Káto Kósmos knew the details regarding the dome, but it was one of the Esril family's responsibilities to ensure that the dome never fell. If it did, the radiation that had killed the planet would affect every living creature in the city, and Káto Kósmos would fall. For good.

"Come."

She waved for Persephone to follow her inside the cabin. There, she opened a wardrobe with a key she pulled from her pocket and grabbed two of the full-body suits hanging inside. The material was thick and rubbery, but luckily, the suit was still lighter than traditional space suits, since it didn't need to withstand a difference in pressure. It was made of special material that didn't allow radiation particles to cling on, though Mira had never asked about the details. As she pulled the clear hood over her head and secured it, she signed for Persephone to do the same. It had built-in air filters, so she could continue to speak and breathe normally.

"What's wrong?"

Mira frowned when Persephone made no attempt at putting on her own suit.

"I'll be fine." She smiled. "I'm an android, a machine. Whatever poison waits out there, it cannot harm me."

Mira accepted Persephone's explanation, but an uneasy feeling in her stomach remained.

"I promise it will be fine," Persephone said, tilting her head into Mira's downcast vision. "Besides, I won't be able to do anything if I can't touch the ground."

Hesitantly, Mira nodded and turned to the far door. With one last uncertain glance at Persephone, she entered a code into the keypad beside it and opened the lock, stepping outside quickly to close the door again right behind Persephone.

The world outside was harsh.

Blinding yellow light made Mira cover her eyes, and she needed to wait a few moments before she could see anything. Even then, her eyes burned and watered in the brightness.

Persephone didn't seem to have the same problem.

Despite the sudden heat, she walked forward easily, surveying the flat, empty horizon critically. Then she knelt down and dug her hand into the hard, reddish ground. She pulled up a handful of dirt and inspected her find, holding it up close to her eyes and sniffing it. Then, finally, she picked up a few grains with the tips of her fingers and placed them on her tongue.

Despite being aware that this would do her no harm, that she was designed for this exact purpose, Mira cringed at the sight of Persephone analyzing the dirt by ingesting it. Once, when she'd been younger, her brothers had played a trick on her, getting her to go outside the dome with some soldiers, without their parents' knowledge, and she'd seen what the air alone could do to a living being when one of the suits was damaged. She squeezed her eyes shut when the memory flashed into her mind. She didn't even want to imagine what would happen if the soldier had also eaten some of the dirt, the way Persephone did now.

"Hmm."

Persephone's voice reached her, and Mira tentatively opened her eyes and winced. She didn't at all like seeing Persephone standing there so pensively.

"Well?" Mira's voice was barely above a whisper; her throat had closed up, and breathing had become an almost impossible feat. She stared at Persephone, unblinking, as she looked up, shielding her eyes from the harsh sun.

She didn't respond.

Mira tried to be patient, to let her do her tests, but she watched with ever-growing unease, occasionally glancing up, as though she could find signs of Olympia Corp's approach.

Meanwhile, Persephone was already kneeling on the ground again, digging a little hole and stroking the sides with her hand. She spit into the hole, kneading the dirt like batter. Then, she pulled the seed from breakfast from her pocket, and placed it in her molded dirt, before rising to her feet again.

"You'll need to install an irrigation system." Persephone didn't look up from watching the ground, and Mira nodded.

"We have a prototype we can set up," Mira said, just glad that Persephone had done something, even though she wasn't sure how her little action could possibly have achieved much of anything.

Persephone nodded, and, without so much as glancing at Mira, headed straight back to the cabin, Mira hurrying after her. They opened the lock and went inside, where Mira stripped her suit quickly.

"So," Mira said, hesitantly, and yet full of urgency. "Can you heal the earth?"

Finally, Persephone looked back at her, for the first time without a smile. Slowly, she nodded.

"I can," she said as she looked back at the lock. "But it will take time.

A small area could be healed quickly, but to heal the planet will take a long, long time. More time than I think you have."

She returned her gaze to Mira, and Mira's heart plummeted.

Olympia Corp was looking for Persephone, and apparently, she knew. How much time did they have until they found her here? Until Káto Kósmos' last hope was yanked from their grasp?

"Please," Mira begged, crossing the distance to Persephone quickly and clasping her hands around hers. "I'll do anything you need me to if you can revive the planet so my people can live and thrive outside of their cage."

"Anything?"

Her expression was unreadable as her silver, mechanical eyes fixed on Mira, holding her in place, extracting the promise from deep within her being.

"Of course! Whatever you want or need, I'll give it if it's within my power."

Finally, a smile tugged around Persephone's lips once more.

Before Mira could react, Persephone had pulled one of her hands from Mira's grip, hooked it around Mira's neck, and pulled her head toward her face.

Persephone's lips were soft, warm, even, but all Mira felt was confusion. The kiss was over in the blink of an eye, and Mira stumbled back, trying to make sense of Persephone's actions.

Persephone sighed.

"And now," she said, "I must go."

She headed to the cabin's door, and Mira hurried after her, her mind in uproar.

"Do you need to rest? Can I do something?" she asked, but Persephone did not reply with anything more than a sad shake of the head. They entered the dome, Mira still rushing to keep up with Persephone's brisk pace. Cerbus met them near the city limits with a hovercraft, his face distraught just as a shadow was falling across the entirety of Káto Kósmos.

"Lady Esril," he panted, his whole body heaving with every breath, "we have a situation."

Mira stared at the screen, gnawing on her lip and curling her toes. Heat and cold rushed through her body simultaneously as she read and reread the message over and over again.

There had to be a way out. There had to be a solution to her problems, a possibility to make everything work out.

Cerbus didn't have any ideas. He stood behind her, his expression a mask of concern and distress. Persephone remained still on a chair by the table, blankly observing her.

There had to be something…! Mira began to pace.

The warning was clear. Olympia Corp didn't want money. It didn't want compensation. All it insisted on was that the return of Persephone occur swiftly. Apparently, they had even shut down any involvement from the IPF, the Intergalactic Police Force. That would have been something to be grateful for, if Olympia Corp didn't also have enough firepower to obliterate an entire galaxy in a matter of seven days.

If she gave up Persephone, Káto Kósmos was doomed. It would shrivel and die within the next decade. There wasn't enough space left to grow adequate levels of food at their current growth rate. Plus, if the city became more densely populated, it would only become a breeding ground for disease. They needed the extra space Persephone could create for them.

On the other hand, if they ignored Olympia Corp's demands, they might not survive another week because they would invade, taking Persephone back by force, obliterating anything and anyone in their way.

Mira was more than aware that her planet's military force was a joke in open combat. Their whole culture was built around not being seen. Hence, their military was really not much more than a small group of highly skilled special agents, adept at infiltration, excellent at small, close-ranged combat, and at covert theft, but no good in a battle involving a fleet of enemy ships.

Mira finally stopped at her window doors and looked out over her city.

After a moment, Persephone joined her.

"I must go," she said.

Mira couldn't respond; she looked to the ground, not uttering a word or looking at anyone, until Persephone had left the room, quickly followed by Cerbus.

She had failed.

The Olympia Corp's star fleet retreated swiftly. They sent no further messages, made no peep—they just left. Mira watched the ships lift their shadows from her world and disappear. Gusts of wind swept through the streets, as though the city were collectively giving a sigh of relief at the passing threat.

People peeked out between curtains of their homes again, and some of the braver children even returned to their games in the street. To everyone down there, it must seem like they had narrowly escaped a terrible fate.

Mira stood by her window, not watching the starship vanish, but instead focusing her attention on the city below. She watched birds take flight once more after they had huddled in the trees, watching fate unfold, sensitive to the tension in the air. She heard the low rumbling from the streets as her people collectively murmured, guessing and fretting about what had happened. She felt the fiery worry, the singeing fear, as it clawed its way up her throat, making her want to cry out in pain. It was burning her, charring her insides.

She had failed.

They'd had one chance to survive, just one, and she'd blown it to smithereens. If she'd been more careful, hadn't left any traces, made it seem like she'd destroyed Persephone instead of stealing her…

Scenarios more plentiful than stars in the skies pushed their way through her mind, forced her to accept a new layer of guilt, to acknowledge another way in which she had failed.

With every breath, her heart sank further. How long did her people have?

The doors to the hall burst open and Cerbus strutted in, his gait expressing his feelings on the matter loud and clear.

"So." He clapped his hands together. "How shall we proceed, my lady? Now that this disaster has been averted?"

She watched him tiredly. Suddenly, she found it impossible to keep her eyes open, and they burned with unshed tears. Her arms and legs were heavy, as if they were made from lead.

"I'm going to bed."

She shuffled past him and out the door, though she could still hear him shout.

"Excellent idea, my lady. Get as much rest as you can before we launch the next plan into action. I'll prepare for a discussion with the council."

Mira kept walking, not wanting to think about how he would undoubtedly bring up the dreaded subject of marriage once again. She supposed he wanted to create a new Káto Kósmos, perhaps in a hidden section of another planet, a city not known to exist beyond its own atmosphere. But it wouldn't be the same. It wouldn't be what her people deserved, what they needed, what they had come to this planet for.

It would be nothing more than a cheap consolation prize.

Káto Kósmos had fallen.

Hunger and thirst were urges of the past.

Mira got up every morning with the chiming of the bells and attended to her daily duties. But where before she had found pleasure, all that awaited her now was dread and guilt.

She did all that was necessary and ate whenever Cerbus forced her to sit down for meals, but mostly, her existence subsisted of working and sleeping. She retired to her room whenever she was finished with her duties for the day, hiding underneath a large, thick blanket—dead to the world until the morning bells chimed once more.

Cerbus brought up the subject of marriage twice more, but then even he, the most eager of advisors, had come to the conclusion that she was in no frame of mind to make such a major decision regarding the future of her country, and he left her alone outside of the tasks that required her presence and signature.

Then there was a day when it rained. It started as idle pattering against the forcefield, the water drops splashing aside like they would against an ordinary window. But soon, the rain became heavier, and the noise of the raindrops dispersing against the forcefield thundered over the city, drowning out all other sounds.

The bell hadn't chimed that morning, and it had taken a while for Mira to wake up and crawl her way out of bed. Now, still huddled in her blanket, she was sitting in her windowed alcove, looking up to the patterns shaping and vanishing across the sky in brilliant flashes of light.

They were blurred and distorted by the water streaming along the force-field, but the roaring thunder made it all too clear what she was watching. She flinched at a few of the louder, more explosive rumbles, accompanied by the brightest flashes of lightning, but mostly, she was amazed at how beautiful and destructive this spectacle of nature seemed.

It was familiar, this sight. It was a day like today when she had been forced to take the throne, a day like today when her family had perished.

They, too, had gone on a trip to find a solution to their planet's predicament. They'd been scheduled for talks with another planetary ruler, but something had happened to their ship on the way. No one could tell her any details, so all Mira knew was that only debris of her family's spacecraft was found. She'd stayed behind that day because she'd been unwell, confined to bed with a fever, and so her family had gone without her.

A chasm opened up in her chest. She had failed them just as much as she had failed her planet.

Her naked toes were getting chilled, and she covered them with her blanket, even though her entire body felt like a block of ice. Would she ever feel warm again?

A knock on the door made her look away from her window. Cerbus peeked in through the cracked door, and wafting along with him was the sweet scent of hot chocolate. Seeing that she was up, he entered, holding out a tray with a filled, steaming mug in front of him. He took a seat next to her and held out the tray, waiting for her to take the mug. She didn't hesitate.

Close to her face, the scent invoked feelings of comfort, the apparent safety of her childhood when her loved ones had still seemed invincible and nothing bad or evil in the world could befall them; back when this city still had seemed like a fortress keeping them safe from the evils of the universe, rather than a hole that would suffocate them in time.

"You didn't wake me today," Mira said quietly, her gaze once more directed outside.

"I thought you deserved a day off." His voice sounded hoarse.

Mira smiled lightly. He'd known today was going to be difficult for her. Why else would he have brought her the chocolate?

"Thanks."

Cerbus got to his feet and pinned his tray under one arm.

"Call me if you need anything. I'll be here without delay."

Mira nodded, but she didn't look back at him, not until the door fell into its lock once more.

Then the sprinklers, the artificial rain within the city, also started their work. The acid rain must have been filtered and cleaned, so now it was ready to bring life to the plants and people in the city as well.

It blasted against her window, rivulets running down the pane quickly, finding a random path, determined by nothing Mira could distinguish.

Somehow, they seemed to be drawing a face on the glass, and Persephone looked back at Mira, smiling gently.

Startled, Mira dropped her blanket and mug and stared. She blinked, and the face was gone, but the image remained in her mind.

Hadn't Persephone promised to help her? To heal the land and clean the planet from radiation?

Determined, Mira put on a pair of shoes and a coat and left the castle, heading into the rain through the city. There weren't many people out, but Mira was so determined that she wouldn't have noticed all that much anyway.

The puddles splashed up at her legs when she crossed them, and the rain seeped into all her clothing so that by the time she reached the outer wall, she was completely soaked, despite taking the transporters as far as had been possible.

She found the cabin, entered, and put on a suit before opening the far door to leave the dome.

The door shut behind her, but Mira could only stare. She took two steps forward, and dropped to her knees, the rain around her slowly fading away. She reached out with one hand to the small, luscious green sprout that had fought its way from the ground. Its tiny leaves bobbed gently with every raindrop that fell on them and Mira had to fight with herself not to cry.

It had actually worked. Persephone had truly been able to return life to the planet the universe had abandoned, given up on. And there was a clear beginning, a first touch of life, waiting to grow and reconquer its world.

She lost the battle against her tears, and they rolled down her cheeks incessantly, accompanied only by the silent shaking of her shoulders. She cried like she hadn't done in nine months.

Eventually, when the storm had cleared and her tears had dried, Mira got back to her feet.

This was far from over. There was no way she could give up now, after she'd received proof that her world could be saved. Even if she'd need to steal Persephone away a thousand times, she would do it for her planet. Even if she was forced into a marriage to keep her planet safe from Olympia Corp's powers, there was a way to save it, and she would be damned if she wasn't going to take it.

She returned to the castle quickly, ignoring Cerbus' concerned remarks when she passed him, still dripping with every step as the city hadn't finished raining yet.

Her world was colored in rainbows, both figuratively and literally, as the sunlight outside the dome reflected the rain inside, the light refracting and splitting, creating millions of beautiful illusions in the sky.

She had regained her hope. Now it was time to make a plan.

She shut herself in her room, using every device at her disposal to find out more about how she could get Persephone back, using the tools and people at her disposal.

It was hours before someone knocked gingerly on the door.

Cerbus opened and looked inside, gulping. "My lady, you have a visitor."

Mira frowned and looked back at her plans, annoyed that she would almost definitely lose her train of thought.

It couldn't be helped. Royal duties were *her* duties, and she was the only one who had the right to perform them.

She sighed and got to her feet, but Cerbus was still blocking the door. He looked her up and down.

"You may wish to dress in a fashion more appropriate to your station," he suggested, concern—no, fear—never leaving his eyes.

Irritated that she needed to shed her comfortable bed clothes, Mira complied and put on one of her official navy robes depicting her family crest.

"Good enough?" she asked, one eyebrow raised.

Cerbus looked her up and down once more and nodded, though his pale complexion and furrowed brows still portrayed his unease.

Against her wishes, Mira grew curious. Who could this visitor be that they made Cerbus so uncomfortable?

She followed him through the halls all the way to the reception room. He didn't speak. He didn't even look at her. But his tensed shoulders spoke volumes. He was scared. And he didn't think that anything he might say could help, so he trusted that she, Hadmira Esril, as the ruler of his home, would know what to do.

He opened the door, announced her, and then stepped aside, his eyes downcast, his eyes and nose twitching.

Mira strode past him, summoning all the regal energy, grace, and authority she could muster.

There was a man in the room, his face plain, his hair pale. He was of unassuming stature, with very little presence, and even his clothes were kept bland and colorless. Yet Mira recognized him instantly.

He sat uncomfortably in his chair, his diminished muscles tensed, as though he were ready to run away. Mira almost laughed. *This* was the man she'd been so afraid of. *This* was the man she'd stolen from, the head of Olympia Corp, and proverbial father of Persephone—Dimitri. He was one of those people who was only known by their first name. With power and money like his, that was all he needed.

They watched each other, carefully gauging the other's strength, neither intending to bow down.

He had no reason to be here, Mira decided. Persephone had returned to him, after all. She jutted her chin forward, determined not to back down.

"If you've come for war, you're in the wrong place," she told him.

He hesitated and shook his head. "I have neither the energy nor the will for battle. I just…"

He looked around, his eyes seeming to linger on every detailed fresco in the room. He seemed lost somehow, as though he were looking for his reason, hoping to find it somewhere on the walls.

Mira finally walked around to the armchair facing him and folded herself into it with crossed legs. Despite all his power, she decided he was not a man who required a lot of decorum.

"I thought you'd be angry."

"I was." His eyes fell on her. "But then she came back, my little Persephone." A little smile played around his lips, just big enough to reach his eyes and give them a dreamy look. But then, it faded. "I was furious. You'd taken the one thing I treasured most, and then you even made sure you'd keep her forever. I didn't think I'd ever be able to forgive that."

There was fire in his voice, real passion, and his blue eyes were blazing with the anger that had sparked from his words.

Mira frowned. "What are you talking about? She returned to you."

Dimitri shook his head, and now, he seemed sad. "Not fully. She'll never be fully mine again. She made a promise to you, and you sealed the pact."

Mira didn't know what to say, so she just stared. None of what he was saying made any sense.

Apparently, he judged her silence correctly because he sighed.

"Your DNA," he said. "She made a commitment to you, and then sealed it with your DNA in her programming. She's bound to complete it, whatever it was she promised you. So congratulations. You won."

The memory of Persephone's kiss flashed into Mira's whirring mind.

"Wait, you mean, she's coming back to help us?" she asked incredulously. "And you're not stopping her?"

He looked at her, almost defiantly.

"I could destroy your whole planet, you know. I could make sure it doesn't exist anymore. I could have you killed or put in prison."

Mira nodded, trying to calm the storm that was raging inside her. He had the power to do any of those things. But he sounded like he wasn't going to. Was he?

"But she seemed so happy, talking of you, of this place. Of helping you." He bit his lip and glared at Mira. She thought he looked like a bratty child, just for a moment. "So I can't. I don't want to destroy that happiness. I don't want her to hate me."

Finally, the pieces were falling into place.

"You actually care about her," Mira recognized. "You want her to be happy, and you actually respect her choice."

Dimitri looked away.

"What I came here to say," he grumbled, "is that if any harm befalls her—if she so much as has a scratch on her—you're going to pay for it. Bitterly."

As much as he tried to be menacing, his face was too good-natured, and his conflicted emotions too openly displayed upon it for Mira to take the threat the way he wanted her to.

All Mira could think of was what Persephone had said, that she was the first person besides Dimitri to treat her like a real person. It was crystal clear, here, in the way he acted. He cared deeply for her, like a father for his daughter.

He could never have sold her, never leased her out to anyone. Perhaps subsequent androids, but not her.

Finally, a second meaning in his words sunk in.

"You mean, Persephone, she…"

"She'll keep her promise." Dimitri stood up, grimly avoiding her eyes. "But I'm not giving her up. I'll be making sure that she spends half her time with me, at least."

Mira didn't know what to say, so she remained silent as he left the room. Her heart, frozen in so many layers of ice, was thawing rapidly. So much so that there seemed to be a sudden excess of water forcing itself out through her eyes, and she cried—in disbelief and relief.

Then, suddenly, mid-breath, ignoring all sense of decorum, she jumped up, gathered up the skirts of her robe, and fled the castle. She ran through the streets of her beloved city, ignoring the mud, still wet from the rain, as it splashed up and ruined her robe.

At one point she gave up the chase and allowed herself to be taken farther by one of the transport system's hovercraft, knowing it was significantly faster. But the moment it stopped near the edge of the dome, she ran out once more, racing toward the southern gate, barely even taking the time to pull on the suit before she burst into the outside, where the world was a harsh and dying place.

But no more.

Persephone knelt on the ground, a finger placed underneath one of the young tree's first leaves. Her face was radiating warmth and joy, a happy, hummed tune almost audible in the air.

Mira was rooted to the spot, looking at what lay before her.

Her promise. Her future. Her miracle.

THE MYTH OF MEDUSA

SLITHER

DOROTHY DREYER

ONE

THE CLOCK ON the wall chimed three times. I took my time restocking the shelf of scented candles, knowing I still had two hours of work to get through. Not that working at Athena's Temple— the local hotspot for all things metaphysical and new age—was stressful. Quite the opposite, in fact. Athena made sure to fill the place with a "zen" aura: healing gemstones, calming scents, windchimes, and lucky bamboo. She also had a section for those who wanted to delve a little deeper into the spiritual side of things, complete with tarot cards, sage bundles, and special potions.

I didn't know if I believed in all that stuff, but the salary was decent, and Athena was a great boss. Plus, it was a perfect job for someone like me, taking a break from college to figure out what I wanted to do. My parents had left me some money in their will, but I was saving that for when I really needed it. And my aunt—whom I'd lived with for the past three years—usually took care of any expenses that came up, which alleviated any pressure to earn big before I decided what I might want to study at college. If I wanted to go back to college in the first place.

The store was never without customers. Athena had started her business from scratch, had worked hard, and was now, at her young age of twenty-seven, considered the "goddess" of metaphysical healing. I had to admire her.

A whispered conversation from the precious stone section of the store reached my ears. I looked over to see two local teen girls who frequented the store—Nia and Stella—hovering over a display of gemstone bracelets.

"I don't know," Nia said. "The red one is pretty."

"But I don't need just *pretty*," Stella retorted, throwing her blond hair off her shoulder. "I need one that works."

I put on my friendly salesperson face and walked over to them. "Hey, maybe I can help."

Stella flashed me a smile. "Thanks, Meddie."

"What exactly is it you need?" I gave her a knowing smile.

Stella scanned the store, as if to make sure no one she knew was around to hear her. "Gwen was just named cheer captain, and she's got a really strong—almost bullying—way of leading us. I feel like I need to protect myself. Like, mentally. So I can still do my part but don't feel her negative energy."

"Sure." I reached for a bracelet made up of stones with dazzling flashes of green and blue. "This is labradorite. You wear this, and it'll be like putting a wall between you and anyone negative."

"Oh my God, that's perfect," Stella said.

"And it's so pretty," Nia added.

I held back a laugh. "Did you need anything else?"

Stella swayed playfully in her place. "Nope, that's it."

"I can ring you up over here." I led them to the register, catching Athena's eye.

She had just come out of the back room with a box of crystals and set them on the counter. Her dark brown hair was pinned back with sparkling barrettes, the same sea green as her eyes. I couldn't help but think the room lit up when she stepped into it. Athena was definitely gorgeous, but she also had that "it" quality, the one that made people notice her.

I gave her a smile as I rounded the counter.

Nia leaned near the cash register, staring at me as I rang up the bracelet. "Can I just say how perfect your hair is? It's like, oh my God, you must use an expensive shampoo. Zero split ends. And those waves are to die for."

"Oh." I bit the inside of my cheek. Compliments always threw me off. "Um, thank you."

"Is that your real color?" Nia asked. "Or is it from a box?"

"It's my real color."

Stella gaped at me. "It's like red and gold and copper all mixed into one. It's like fire!"

"It's gorgeous." Nia exaggerated a pout. "I'm so jealous."

Holding back an amused laugh, I reached out my hand to take the money Stella had set on the counter. I froze when Nia reached out and grabbed my wrist.

"No way. You have a tattoo?"

She gaped at the colorful snake tattoo that marked my forearm. The head of the snake faced my wrist, its tongue pointing in the direction of the back of my hand.

"I have more than one," I replied.

"What else do you have?"

"A couple more snakes. One on my hip, and one on my shoulder blade."

The two girls nodded as they smiled. "So cool," they said in unison.

"So, you like snakes, I guess," Stella put in.

"Yep." I handed her the purchase. "I have two of them as pets."

Nia crinkled her nose. "Aren't you scared of them?"

I let out a small laugh. "No. I find them peaceful. They hardly make any noise."

"Yeah, I guess that's cool." Stella took the small bag containing her bracelet. "Thanks, Meddie! I'll let you know how this works out."

"Good luck," I called after her as she and Nia left the store.

I caught Athena looking at me. Her sparkling sea green eyes seemed to be trained on my hair. Feeling self-conscious, I ran my hands over my head, almost as if I wanted to hide the red-gold strands. I was grateful to have been blessed with such a healthy head of hair, but I wasn't exactly comfortable with the attention.

The bell above the door rang, and I glanced over to see Detective Perseus enter the store. He raised his hand to signal a greeting to Athena, to which she responded by rounding the counter and strolling over to him. He waited patiently, smoothing a hand over his cleanly shaven jaw, gushing authority with his broad, squared shoulders.

Detective Perseus was a frequent customer, always confiding in Athena for whatever it was that ailed him. Athena never divulged his secret to me, and she always insisted on handling his purchases herself. Not that I was too curious; I wasn't the kind of person to insert myself in other people's business.

As Athena was tending to him, another prominent member of the community waltzed in. Mayor Paul Poseidon was a tall, muscular man, with a meticulously trimmed beard and moustache the same black hue as his hair. Both were streaked with a few strands of white. In his hand, he held a stack of fliers, which he waved at Athena before he approached the register.

"Meddie, how are you?" He gave me a wink, and I forced myself not to cringe. Most of the people in our small town of Stone Mirror Bay loved the mayor, but I found him a little too forward and intimidating. "Athena said it would be fine if I left some of these fliers in the store. You know, to spread the word about the Harbor Festival."

I made some room on the counter. "Sure. But how come you're delivering them yourself? Don't you have interns to do the grunt work for you?"

For a split second, he furrowed his brow, his mouth twisted into a bemused smirk. "I like to interact with the community myself. You know"—his gaze seemed to travel up and down my body—"get my hands dirty."

I refused to back away, no matter how much I wanted to get away from him. "Oh, that's, um, understandable."

Out of the corner of my eye, I caught Detective Perseus leaving the store. Athena sauntered over with cash in her hand.

"Hello, Mayor Poseidon. How are you today?" Athena put the money in the register and then leaned forward on the counter. I couldn't help but notice how much of her cleavage was exposed to the mayor.

"Just fine, Athena. Thanks for asking." He'd only glanced at her chest for a moment. His eyes drifted back to me, and for some reason, I felt more exposed than Athena.

I crossed my arms and took a step back from the counter.

"The Harbor Festival." Athena picked up one of the fliers and looked it over. "Sounds fun."

"Yes, indeed." Again, he only spared her a glance before continuing to ogle me. "I hope you can make it. I promise it will be worth your while."

"Oh, definitely," Athena answered. She flipped her hair, but he didn't seem to notice.

"You, too, Meddie?" He tilted his head, probably thinking it made him look charming or something.

I faked a smile. "Yeah, sure."

His smile widened, and he knocked once on the counter. "See you there."

Once he was out the door, I finally let my smile falter. "How can you stand it?" I asked Athena in hushed tones. I didn't want the other customers hearing.

"Stand what?"

I almost shivered. "I always feel like he's undressing women with his eyes."

"You don't find him attractive?" she asked.

"Not my type. He's way older than I am. And he's way too forward."

She shrugged. "I guess I'm into men who flaunt their power. But he didn't seem to notice me. He certainly had eyes for you, though."

I wrapped my arms more tightly around myself. "Like I said, he's not my type."

Athena gave me a sideways glance. "If you say so. Hey, look, do you mind if I run upstairs to my apartment for a second? I was working on next month's order last night and forgot to bring the binder down."

"Sure, no problem."

She smiled at me. "Be right back."

As she walked away, someone came into the store, and a breeze blew through. It kicked up the fliers, sending a few of them sailing off the counter. I grunted as I retrieved them. Knowing the mayor had his hands on them made me want to toss them in the trash. With a sigh, I pushed thoughts of Poseidon out of my head, wanting to erase the whole encounter with him entirely. Instead, I turned my attention to the clock. Just an hour and a half to go before I could go home and wash the feeling of filth off myself.

TWO

I wouldn't have even considered going to the festival if it hadn't been for Angelo. He'd been my best friend since we'd been in grade school, and we'd even started at Stone Mirror Bay College together. Even when I'd dropped out and he'd continued on, we'd made sure to remain close. As my best friend, he knew just what to say to get me out of the house and out of my comfort zone. Case in point: Despite my terrible fear of Ferris wheels, he'd somehow convinced me to ride one at the festival with him.

"You want the rest of my cotton candy?" he asked, practically smashing the fluffy pink sugar in my face as our car hovered at the top of the Ferris wheel. The wind from the bay played with his dark curls, and the festival lights twinkled in his heavily lashed eyes.

I laughed as I pushed the cotton candy away. "No, thank you. I get any more sugar in me, I'm not going to be able to sleep tonight."

"Of course you will. It's called a sugar crash for a reason."

"Still, I'll pass." I elbowed him with a smirk and then stared out into the distance. Not too far away, the tide danced in the bay. The festival took place at the harbor, stretching until it reached the nearby beach. Everyone attending looked like tiny insects from where I sat. Below me was a barrage of game booths, rides, and a multitude of food trucks. The people who'd flocked to the festivities seemed to be enjoying themselves. Music and laughter filled the night air.

The Ferris wheel was on the move again, and our car stopped at the loading and unloading platform.

"I'm glad I came out," I told Angelo as we stepped off the car and headed away from the Ferris wheel. "Thanks for talking me into it."

"That's what I'm here for." He swallowed another mouthful of cotton candy, pink fluff sticking to the tip of his long nose. His gaze then traveled somewhere behind me. "Hey, why is Mayor Poseidon staring at you?"

I dreaded following his gaze, but I had to see for myself. I spotted the mayor speaking with Athena, but his eyes were on me. He gave me a wink when he caught me looking. As I forced myself not to cringe, Athena shot a glance over her shoulder. She looked disappointed that I was the one who had the mayor's attention.

I quickly turned away. Angelo furrowed his brow. I shook my head to indicate it wasn't worth talking about. The whole situation was entirely too uncomfortable, and I just wanted to pretend it hadn't happened.

The festivities died down, and Angelo and I parted ways with promises to meet up again soon despite his busy schedule. Stars lit up the sky, and I wasn't quite ready to call it a night, so I decided to take a stroll on the nearby beach.

There was something on my mind I hadn't even shared with Angelo yet. I was thinking about leaving Stone Mirror Bay. My whole life, I'd never been anywhere else. Part of that was my fault—hunkering down in my comfort zone and abstaining from taking any risks. But the time had come; I needed a change. I needed an adventure. And I needed to figure out who I was outside of this small town. I'd been saving up, and all I needed was that one push to put my plans into action.

Maybe I should have told Angelo. He'd know the perfect thing to say to motivate me to go. Heck, he'd probably decide to go with me.

The winds picked up, and the air grew cooler. I turned in the sand and started heading home.

The light of the moon silhouetted a dark figure up ahead. Someone was out here with me. A shiver ran over my skin, and my teeth began to chatter. Not too far away was a lifeguard tower. I knew there was nobody in it keeping watch at this hour, but I weighed the option of climbing up into it for safety. Then again, maybe I was being paranoid.

As the distance closed between me and the mystery figure, the size of the man gave away his identity. My eyes adjusted to the lack of light, and his features became clearer.

With my arms wrapped around myself, I forced a polite smile. "Mayor Poseidon."

"Please, call me 'Paul.'" He came closer.

"Paul. Right." I cleared my throat.

In my head I tried calculating how long it would take to get off the beach. It was just a five-minute walk to where the festival had taken place. It would most likely be deserted by now, but there were more options to elude the mayor. Places to run, stands to hide behind.

I glanced at the tower again.

"What's a pretty girl like you doing alone on the beach in the middle of the night?"

"I'm… not alone," I lied. "My friend Angelo is just getting my jacket out of his car. He'll be back any second."

He came even closer, a dark shadow encompassing his face. "You and I both know that's not true. Don't we, Meddie?"

I opened my mouth to answer but couldn't find my voice.

"Angelo left more than an hour ago," he said as his eyes roamed over my body. "I saw him leave myself."

My mind scrambled to think of another lie. As I scanned the distance, hoping someone else might be around, he reached out and seized a lock of my hair in his hand.

"What are you doing?" My voice quivered.

"I've always thought you had the most sensual hair." He leaned in and pressed the lock against his nose, groaning in pleasure as he breathed it in.

I tried to back away, but his strong arm trapped me around my waist. Pushing my hands against his chest, I struggled to break free from his hold.

"Stop. Please." I stumbled back, almost losing my footing.

His smile was full of malice as he lifted me and dragged me to the legs of the lifeguard tower. I grunted when my back hit the leg of the tower, its splintering wood biting into my blouse.

He checked over his shoulder, pulling at my hair. I screamed, but the crashing of the waves onto the shore buried the sound. While a fistful of my hair was trapped in one of his hands, his other hand pushed under my blouse. I kicked and clawed, but he wouldn't let go, burying his face in my hair. I tried to move my head away from him but then cried out as he ripped a chunk of hair from my scalp.

As he moved his hand near my mouth to stop my screaming, I took a chance and bit hard into his finger. The element of surprise had been on my side, and he loosened his grip. I managed to struggle free enough to bend down and grab a handful of sand, not hesitating to throw it in his eyes. He let out a low yelp, temporarily blinded and scrubbing at his face.

I stumbled a bit, but I quickly regained my footing and took off running, heading inland. My legs burned as I fought off the suction of the sand at my feet. My tears stuck to my cheeks, and my throat felt like it was on fire from screaming, but I didn't stop running and I didn't dare look behind me.

THREE

My hands shook as I dug my keys out of my pocket. Athena's Temple was closer than my aunt's apartment, and so I ran there to find safety. My breath came out in small, desperate bursts as I struggled to get the key in the lock. Finally managing to get the door open, I hurried into the store and slammed the door closed. The bell above my head chimed violently as I locked the door and pressed my trembling hands against it. My sobs were whispers in the dark as I closed my eyes, my forehead falling forward onto the door's windowpane.

"Meddie?"

I flinched at the sound of Athena's voice. My mind was swirling so much, I had temporarily forgotten she lived in the apartment above the store. I turned to her, tears flowing down my cheeks.

Her eyes widened. "Oh my God! What happened?" Concern warped her face as she came closer.

I wrapped my arms around myself and dropped my shoulders when she reached for me. Seeing my distress, she pulled her hands back.

"Are you all right? Do I need to call the police?"

I wiped my cheeks, sniffling. "I… No. They won't believe me."

"What?" She shook her head. "Why? Who did this to you?"

I followed her gaze to find my blouse had been torn. I reached for the throbbing part of my head where Poseidon had ripped out my hair. It felt warm and wet. I looked at my fingers to find blood on them.

When I looked back up at her, I was afraid to tell her what had happened because I knew how she felt about the mayor. I knew how almost everyone felt about him. He was well known, had a big personality, and was well liked and respected. Part of me was paranoid Athena would call me a liar and kick me out of her store.

"Meddie." She took a chance and placed a gentle hand on my arm. "You can tell me."

I swallowed back the sandpaper coating my throat as I nodded. "It was… Poseidon."

Athena's jaw dropped slightly, and her eyes searched my face as if waiting for the punchline of an awful joke. I pressed my lips together, afraid of her next words.

Her expression changed to one of understanding. "What did he do to you?"

I could barely get out the words past my sobs. As I divulged the events, I let her come nearer. She embraced me, and when I checked her expression, her jaw was squared, and her eyes were full of fury.

"We should call the police," she said.

"No. You know how everyone feels about the mayor. They'll never believe my word against his." I took her hands. "Please. Don't tell anyone. I just want to forget this happened."

She looked as if she wanted to argue with me, but she eventually nodded.

"You're bleeding." She frowned as she moved my hair aside to inspect the wound.

I couldn't shake the disgust I felt knowing the part my hair had played in the attack. I couldn't stand the thought of him touching it, touching me. There was nothing I could do short of showering to get the feel of his touch off me, but I could do something about my hair.

"I need you to do me a favor," I said to Athena.

"Anything."

"Shave my hair."

Her brows plunged downward. "What?"

"Shave it off. All of it. I don't want to feel it anymore. I don't want to see it. It'll just be a reminder."

"Shave it? Are you…? Are you sure?"

I sniffled back tears. "Yes. I'd do it myself, but—"

She placed gentle hands on my shoulders. "No. Okay. I'll do it." Her expression was full of sympathy. "We can do it in my bathroom. Come upstairs."

FOUR

I tugged on the edges of my silk scarf. It was one I'd worn many times before—the green and pink snakes of the pattern pleasing to the eye—but this time I wore it on my head instead of around my neck. It wasn't to hide my buzzcut; I didn't care that my head was shaved. It was a relief, actually, to be rid of my trouble-causing hair. But my wound from where Poseidon had ripped out my hair was still healing, and a silk scarf seemed the best way to both conceal it as well as keep the wound protected.

I blew out a tense breath as I stepped into Athena's Temple. After the incident, Athena had ordered me to take a few days off. This would be my first day back, and I prayed I could keep the panic attacks at bay.

Athena eyed me as I went behind the counter to store my purse. She couldn't come over to greet me right away because she was with a customer. There was an open box on the floor that needed to be unpacked, so I made myself busy.

After Athena tended to the customer's purchase, she came over to me and put a hand on my arm. "How are you feeling?"

I gave her a half-shrug. "Better, I guess."

"Well, I have something that might help." A sly smile crept upon her face as she turned and retrieved a small white box from the drawer of the counter. "For you."

"What's this?" I took the box and opened it on the counter. Inside was a silver chain necklace. I lifted it to find a pendant with a shiny, black gemstone in the center.

"It's a black tourmaline. It's to both calm you and protect you. But it's not like any of the commercial items we sell here. I have this connection to a woman who's really into the mystical side of the occult. I think she regards herself a witch." Athena shrugged. "Anyway, I told her what happened to you—"

"You told her?"

"Don't worry!" Athena waved her hands. "I didn't say your name— or you-know-who's. I kept it totally anonymous."

I placed a hand on my heart, relieved that my secret was still a secret.

"I did have to tell her a little bit about you," Athena continued, "just so she could tune into your vibration and place a fitting protection on the stone. She performed some cleansing and meditated some intent upon it. I know you don't buy into metaphysics a hundred percent, but…"

"I love it," I said, holding it up so the light could hit the stone. "I don't know. I think it will help. Something for me to focus on, at least, when I'm feeling anxious."

She patted my back. "Exactly."

The bell above the door rang, and I turned to see Angelo walk in. His expression changed from concern to confusion when he took in the sight of the scarf on my head.

I pulled on the edges of my scarf and forced a smile. "Hey, Angelo. What brings you here?"

"You haven't been answering my texts or calls, so I got worried. What, uh, happened to your hair?"

Athena and I exchanged a look.

"I thought I could use a change," I said. "A fresh, new look. Sorry about the texts. I turned my phone off for a few days to, uh, detox."

"Oh." He tilted his head. "Is it… How much did you cut off?"

I would have shown him, but I was afraid he'd question me about my wound. Instead, I patted the scarf and put on a cocky grin. "All of it."

His eyes widened. "No way. What did your aunt say?"

"What *could* she say? I make my own decisions." I ran a hand over the silk. "Don't tell me you hate it. I did it for me."

"Whoa, that's so cool. Can I see?"

Athena stepped in beside me. "Maybe later, Angelo. Meddie's got a shipment in the back to label."

I silently thanked her with my eyes. "Yep. I'll get right on that."

"Of course," Angelo said. "I'll let you go. But, um, we're hanging out again soon, right? Happy hour at Argo's? Friday?"

I wanted to say *no*. But I knew he'd argue with me until I gave in anyway. My gaze went to the necklace Athena had given me. Even just looking at it in its box calmed me.

"Yeah," I said. "Argo's on Friday. Wouldn't miss it."

"Sweet. See you then. Glad you're okay."

He waved and left the store. Athena flashed me a sincere smile.

Picking up the necklace, I ran a finger over the smooth surface of the black tourmaline and told myself everything would be all right.

The next evening, I found myself at the laundromat. As my clothes spun around in the dryer, I sat and caught my reflection in the window. I was slowly getting used to wearing scarves on my head, and I had so many different snake-patterned ones that I didn't have to worry about wearing the same one twice in a week.

The black tourmaline of my pendant seemed to glow. It made me think back on the past couple of days. I had to admit I had been feeling calmer. I couldn't speak to the protective properties of the stone, but maybe the fact that I hadn't seen the mayor since the incident was the stone's way of protecting me. In any case, the necklace made me feel safe, and I didn't want to take it off.

By the time my last load of laundry was done, the laundromat was practically empty. I dragged my feet as I carried my basket through the strip mall's parking lot to my car. It had taken longer than I'd thought to finish my laundry, and I felt my energy depleting. I was not looking forward to getting up early the next day to open the store. I quickly texted my aunt to let her know I was on my way home.

As soon as I reached my car, a shiver ran up and down my spine. I turned around to find a man leaning against the hood of his car. His baseball cap shadowed part of his face. He was looking at his phone screen, but something told me he was secretly watching me.

Propping one side of the laundry basket on my hip, I moved my hand up to grasp my pendant. I had to calm down. My paranoia was getting to me.

When I tried to get my car keys out of my purse, I lost the grip on my basket. My newly washed clothes and half the contents of my purse scattered everywhere. I let out a curse as I crouched down to pick everything up.

"Here, let me help you." The man leaning on his car hood came toward me.

Don't trusssst him.

I flinched at the whisper in my head.

The man picked up my hairbrush and tried to hand it to me. I couldn't fight the feeling that he was trying to trick me, that he was out to get me. My heart raced, and my hands shook.

Tell him to sssstay away.

I opened my mouth but couldn't find the air to speak.

"Hey, are you all right?" The man came even closer.

Something strange happened inside me. I felt like I wanted to rip off my skin. Something inside me was telling me he meant to harm me.

In the distance, thunder boomed. My fear turned into anger, and all I could think about was snakes attacking their prey. In the next moment, my thoughts transformed into reality. Two long, fast-moving snakes appeared out of nowhere and slithered toward the man.

His eyes widened as he backed away. But he couldn't get far because two more snakes appeared behind him, stopping him in his tracks.

"What is this?" he yelled.

Thisss isss what he dessservesss.

The snakes reached him, and he stumbled, falling back on his rear end. The first snake struck, and then the next, and the next. The man's screams echoed in my ears.

I couldn't speak. I could barely breathe. I grabbed my keys from the ground and hurried into my car. The man's screams still reached me as I started the engine and tore out of the parking lot.

My mind was numb as I drove home. My pulse raced behind my ears, pounding like war drums, and I felt like I was dreaming.

What had just happened?

I couldn't wrap my head around what had just transpired. Where had the snakes come from? Why had they attacked that man?

They were protecting me.

Had I made that happen?

As I hurried into my aunt's apartment, my mind was scrambling to understand. My hand went to the black tourmaline. It felt warm to the touch. Had this been some strange magic from the necklace? Had the woman Athena had bought it from actually put some kind of spell on it to literally protect me?

I pushed myself off the door, making sure to keep quiet so I wouldn't alarm my aunt. She was probably already asleep, knowing her. And I wouldn't know what to say to her. Would she even believe me?

With shaky legs, I made my way to my room, absentmindedly heading to my snake terrariums. I found myself staring at my snakes, my mind replaying the events in the parking lot. I might have imagined it, but it looked as though my snakes were grinning at me.

I rubbed my eyes.

My snakes turned away from me and slipped back to their usual nesting spots.

I backed away from their terrariums, not knowing what to believe.

FIVE

I'd heard from the news that the man had been found dead in the parking lot. Asphyxiation, they'd said. At first, I had worried that I'd be identified because of the things I'd left behind. But my name wasn't on any of the items I'd dropped, and my wallet was still in my purse. Unless they found my lipstick and were going to test it for DNA, I didn't think they could pinpoint the murder on me.

Murder.

It wasn't really my fault, was it?

I tried to tell myself I was being paranoid, but I swore that every person who came into the store that week was staring at me like they knew what had happened. Every pair of eyes I looked at said the same thing: "You did it. It's your fault."

I even questioned Athena's thoughts when I found her looking at me. But I was too afraid to mention it. More than once, I had to escape into the stock room and lean back against the shelves, closing my eyes and holding the black tourmaline tightly in my hand. Though it tended to calm me down for the moment, the fear always crept back in.

By the time Friday afternoon rolled around, I was a nervous wreck. When Angelo texted to remind me about Happy Hour at Argo's, I was more than eager to go have a drink with him. I wasn't one to make a habit of drinking myself into oblivion, but the prospect of forgetting my troubles for a while seemed particularly inviting.

"You okay?" Athena asked as I was leaving the shop.

"Yeah." I fidgeted with my purse. That troublesome voice in my head kept insisting she knew something was amiss, but I made myself ignore it. "Headed to Argo's."

"Oh, right." She pointed to the pendant. "Is that helping you at all?"

I hoped she didn't notice how hard I swallowed. "Yeah. Yeah, it is. Thanks so much, again."

"Of course. Have a nice weekend."

I wasn't convinced her eyes weren't scrutinizing me, but I forced a smile. "Thanks. You too."

As usual, Argo's was pretty packed for Happy Hour. Angelo and I managed to get two seats at the bar, but all around me, people were shoulder to shoulder and hip to hip. I tried not to cringe at the invasion of my personal space and concentrated on Angelo's tales of his annoying college roommate.

After a couple of drinks and a bunch of laughs, Angelo narrowed his eyes. "Everything okay?"

I studied his face, wondering what he'd seen in mine to make him ask the question. "Yeah, why?"

"I don't know. You seem… off."

I took a swallow of my drink. "It's just been a stressful week. That's all."

"You sure? I feel like there's something else."

My gaze dropped to my drink. Usually, I could tell Angelo anything. But now I felt guilty for keeping two secrets from him. Three, if I was counting my plan to leave town.

I decided to go with the least dramatic secret. "I've been thinking about leaving Stone Mirror."

His brow furrowed. "What? What do you mean by 'leave'?"

I shrugged. "I mean get out of the only place I've ever lived and figure out what else is out there."

He seemed to be searching for what to say. I worried the edges of my head scarf, waiting for him to process the news.

Finally, he raised his glass. "I get it."

A weight lifted off my shoulders. "You do?"

"Sure. This place can be a drag." He slurped his beer. "If I weren't in the middle of this intense project for school, I'd come with you."

"Well, let me know when you're free. Like this summer. Maybe you could catch up."

"Sounds like a plan. I'm in."

By the time we left Argo's, I'd almost forgotten about the other two secrets looming in the back of my head. Though I knew I could tell Angelo anything, to divulge what had happened with Poseidon would be devastating. And there was no way he'd believe me if I told him about the snakes killing the man in the parking lot. I told myself I would tell him.

One day.

There was a nice warm breeze in the night air, which made our walk home comfortable.

"Look at us being responsible," Angelo slurred. "Not driving in our condition."

"Also, you always forget where you park," I teased.

"Who's going to make sure I'm responsible when you're gone?"

"Is this your way of telling me I'm your only friend?"

"I think you're the only one who can put up with me."

Our footsteps on the sidewalk seemed to grow louder. I blinked in confusion before I realized it wasn't just our footsteps. There was someone behind us.

Don't be paranoid, I told myself. *Just because someone's behind you doesn't mean you're being followed.*

We turned the corner to discover one of the streetlamps was out, causing the road to be bathed in an eerie darkness. I glanced over my shoulder to see the man behind us turning the corner as well. He had a long, black coat over a hoodie, and he kept his head lowered. My heart sped up. Maybe he *was* following us.

Angelo followed my gaze, but he didn't seem to be bothered by the man behind us. Was it because my mind was in overdrive and I was being silly? Or was this a guy thing?

As the man behind us got closer, the hairs on the back of my neck stood up.

Don't trussst him.

I wrapped my arms around myself, and my breaths came with more difficulty. It felt as if the man were breathing down my neck.

I stopped and swung around, my fingers tingling as I reached for my pendant.

The man stopped too.

"What's wrong?" Angelo asked.

I ignored him and glared at the man. "Why are you following us?"

"What?" The man scoffed. "I'm not. Get over yourself."

Liessss.

"Meddie, it's fine." Angelo put a hand on my back.

I flinched. My mind went to the snakes again. I could feel the anger bubbling up inside me.

"Look, this is my way home," the man said.

But as soon as he took another step, I screamed. In that instant, the snakes appeared. Seven of them this time. Thick and fast and hissing. In his effort to move away, the man tripped over one, losing his footing and falling to the pavement.

"Meddie?" Angelo's voice was full of disbelief.

The snakes hissed and struck the man. He screamed as he struggled, but they were already coiling around him.

Angelo, wide-eyed, pulled me back away from the snakes. "Meddie, watch out!"

He'sss jussst as bad.

Two of the snakes turned, twisting around until they faced Angelo. They slithered past me so fast, I hadn't had time to think. One snake grabbed hold of Angelo's leg while the other snapped up and struck his thigh. Angelo was knocked to the ground, and another snake joined the first two.

Angelo's screams began as the other man's ended.

"No! No!" I crouched down, trying to save my friend, but I couldn't pry the snakes off him. My heart thrashed in my chest.

The color drained from Angelo's face as one snake wrapped around his neck, strangling him.

"No! No, please! He's my friend!" I cried, but the snakes wouldn't listen.

I stood, sobbing, shaking, and helpless. I didn't know what to do. My brain was screaming for me to call the police, so I pulled out my phone.

One snake turned to me.

They dessserved it. They wanted to caussse you harm.

Its yellow eyes were locked on me, as if warning me not to use my phone.

Leave now. Sssave yourssself.

My breaths were too shaky for me to respond. Both men lay motionless. Dead. And I could be next, if I didn't do as the snakes wanted.

Scrubbing the tears from my face, I turned on my heel and raced home.

SIX

News of Angelo's death spread through Stone Mirror Bay like wildfire. Athena had actually been the one to tell me. She'd called me at home to tell me the sad news and told me to take the next couple of days off to mourn him. She knew how close we'd been.

Inside, I was falling apart. The guilt was eating away at me. Even though, logically, I couldn't possibly have been responsible for Angelo's death—for any of their deaths—I still couldn't get past the fact that I was connected to their fatalities.

And I'd run away. Every time.

A couple of days later, Detective Perseus, who was officially in charge of the investigation, held a press conference saying Angelo's death—along with the deaths of the other men—looked like the work of a serial killer.

The words burned in my brain.

Killer.

Had I somehow unleashed the snakes onto the victims? I might as well have pulled the trigger of a gun.

I was the last person seen with Angelo, so it was just a matter of time before Perseus would question me. What was I going to say? Could I flat-out lie to his face?

When he came into Athena's Temple, I knew it wasn't for his usual purchases. Sweat formed in my palms and along the hairline of my growing buzz cut as he approached me. Athena spotted him just as he reached me and came over with concern on her face.

"Meddie, can I ask you some questions?" Perseus took a small notepad out and clicked his pen.

"What's this about?" Athena asked. "Is this about Angelo?"

I was glad she'd interjected because it gave me another moment to compose myself.

"Yes," Perseus said. "It's part of the investigation."

I wiped my sweaty hands on my pants. "Of course. Anything I can do to help."

"Thank you, Meddie. I understand you were with the victim—um, Angelo—the night he was attacked."

"Yeah, we had drinks at Argo's." I fought to keep from breaking down, but there was still a somber tone to my voice.

"We have some witnesses who saw you leave together."

Athena cut in again. "But that doesn't mean—"

"Meddie's not being accused of anything," Perseus explained. "We're trying to gather all the facts. That's all."

"It's okay," I said to both of them. "Yes, we left Argo's together. But we split up outside, and I went home."

It wasn't a lie. I'd just left out the part where he'd been bitten and strangled by snakes before I'd left his side.

"You didn't see him talking with anyone else when you parted ways?"

This was a tricky one. "Um, yeah. He spoke to someone, but I didn't get a good look at him."

Technically, it was the truth.

Athena tucked her dark hair behind her ears. "You think that guy killed Angelo?"

Perseus pursed his lips. "Can't be sure. It could also have been the other victim found at the scene."

"So you, uh, don't have any leads?" I asked, wringing my hands.

"Whoever is doing this is using something unusual to suffocate his or her victims. We also found puncture wounds and swelling on each of the victims, so we think the killer is using some kind of drug or poison to incapacitate the victims before strangling them to death."

I flinched and crossed my arms over my chest.

Athena put an arm around me. "Okay, this is obviously upsetting you." She turned to Detective Perseus. "Sorry, but if there's anything else… Angelo was a very close friend of Meddie's, so this is a sensitive topic."

Perseus looked as if he had more to say, but instead he closed his notepad and tucked it away. "I'm sorry for your loss. If it's okay, I'm going to give you my card. If you think of anything else, any details about the man Angelo was talking to, give me a call."

I took his card and nodded. "I will. Thank you, Detective."

SEVEN

It was raining, which was fitting for Angelo's funeral. My head had been aching because I hadn't been sleeping well. Nightmares of the snakes attacking Angelo left me with restless nights.

But I wasn't going to let my exhaustion keep me from attending the funeral.

I was surprised at how many people showed up. A lot of them were fellow students from the university. Stone Mirror Bay's small chapel was packed. Though part of me longed to be closer to Angelo's casket and see him for myself, another part of me was relieved. The guilt was already unbearable, but seeing the lifeless body of my best friend would probably drive me over the edge.

My mind went numb during the funeral service, and before I knew it, it had ended. I was surprised to see Mayor Poseidon in the swarm of people leaving the chapel. But then again, in our small town, almost everyone knew each other.

I quickly ducked out before he could spot me. It was a shame that I missed the opportunity to give my condolences to Angelo's parents, but could I really look them in their eyes and pretend like I wasn't responsible for his death?

"Hey, Meddie."

I turned to find Athena behind me as I swiftly escaped the chapel grounds.

"Athena." I stopped, my hand moving to hold my pendant.

"How are you holding up?" she asked.

I could only shrug.

"Listen, the shop's closed up for the day. Do you want to join me for a coffee? We could talk, if you need an ear."

I let out a shaky sigh. "Yeah, I'd like that."

We went to the nearest café, where Athena treated me to a frothy cappuccino. For a while, I couldn't bring myself to say anything, but then the words became too much to contain in my head.

"Athena, who was the woman you bought the necklace from?" I watched her face, wondering if she knew why I had asked.

"Oh, just someone I knew when I was studying occult sciences and parapsychology." She took a sip of her black coffee. "She's got quite a reputation for her gemstones. Some people even claim them to be magic."

I nodded slowly. "I see. And you told her about me?"

She leaned forward and lowered her voice. "I told her what happened. On the beach. And she was immediately sympathetic. I always knew she was a feminist, but I think she's got a particular sore spot when it comes to men."

That lined up with the powers the pendant seemed to have. Whatever she had done to it, it carried with it the woman's hatred of men.

"I'm sorry about Angelo," she said, misreading where my mind was.

"Me too," was all I could say.

She waited patiently for me to open up to her, but there really wasn't anything I could say that she would believe. Plus, I didn't want to make her an accessory to murder.

After our drinks were done, we left the café and took a walk. As we crossed the small footbridge that went over the river, I noticed a building under construction near the park.

"What's happening here?" I asked, acutely aware that I hadn't been paying attention to the progress our town was making.

"They're building an aquarium," she replied, pointing. "They've just poured down the cement for the foundation, from the looks of it."

"An aquarium." I nodded. "That's nice."

"Yeah, we can go together when they open, if you want."

But it was likely that I might never see the finished product. I had to tell her my plans to leave. The only person I'd shared my plans with was Angelo, and now that he was gone, it felt even more pressing to get out of town.

"Athena," I said, taking her arm to stop her from walking. "I'm… I'm leaving Stone Mirror Bay."

Her brows plunged down. "Leaving? You mean for a retreat? Or did you find a new college to go to?"

"No. I mean for good. I've been thinking about it for a while, and I'd like see what else it out there, figure myself out."

She pursed her lips, but then she finally gave me a nod. "That's understandable. You're young. You just lost your best friend." She took my hand. "It sounds like a great idea. And if you ever do end up coming back, just look me up. You're always welcome to work at the store again, and you've always got a friend here."

I gave her the smallest smile I could muster. "Thank you."

She pulled me in for an embrace.

"Well, isn't this a pretty picture?"

We released each other and turned to find Mayor Poseidon standing on the bridge. He had a menacing look in his eyes, his lips twisted into a mischievous grin.

Athena stepped in front of me. "What do you want?"

He narrowed his eyes at her and came closer. "What do you mean, Athena? I'm just making sure my citizens are fine and well. How are you doing there, Meddie?"

My hand went to my pendant, my fingers tingling. A faint hissing began in my ears.

No, not now. Not with Athena here.

I didn't want anything to happen to her. I wouldn't let it.

I grabbed her wrist and took off running in the opposite direction. "Come on. We've got to get out of here."

She didn't question me right away. She must have understood my urgency to get away from Poseidon. But as we drew closer to the construction site, she gave me a little resistance.

"Meddie, don't worry. I won't let anything happen to you."

"No, you don't understand. It's dangerous." I turned to look at her, noticing for the first time that Poseidon was gaining on us.

She followed my gaze. "We can stand up to him."

"No," was all I could say.

If she wasn't going to listen to me, I needed to get some distance between us. To keep the snakes from attacking her.

I crossed the construction barriers and tried to find a place to hide from Poseidon.

"Meddie, wait."

I could hear her following me. I climbed a set of steel stairs that were part of the scaffolding that overlooked the aquarium's foundation. The cement looked as though it was still wet.

"Meddie, this is getting us nowhere," Athena said, catching up with me. "We need to confront him if we want to stop this."

"Athena, I don't want you to get hurt."

"I don't want you to get hurt, either, but there's a better way to deal with this."

A dark figure appeared behind her. "Is there now?"

We both backed up a few steps as Poseidon emerged on the scaffolding. I felt the cold steel of the scaffolding rails behind me.

"What do you want, Poseidon?" Athena held her chin high. "Haven't you done enough to the girl?"

"What has that little minx been telling you?" Poseidon came closer, looming over us like a monster. "You don't really believe her lies, do you?"

"Don't try turning this around," Athena said, her voice strong. "She's the victim here, not you."

He sneered at her and grabbed her wrist. "No one will take her word over mine. I'm the mayor. She's a dropout. A nobody."

He'ssss hurting her.

My mind raced. My heart pounded like a war drum in my ear. My fingers tingled and I swore I heard thunder in the distance.

"Let her go!" I shouted.

He had the audacity to laugh.

The pendant was warm on my chest, and no sooner had I thought about the snakes attacking than they were there. This time, they didn't hesitate to attack.

Athena screamed with fright. Poseidon let out a curse, his eyes wide. He released Athena and tried to back away. Athena hurried to my side, gaping at the snakes. One snake curled around Poseidon's leg. He twisted, his upper legs catching the railing of the scaffolding. Two snakes leaped at him, one catching him in the shoulder while the other snatched on to his cheek.

Poseidon screamed as his balance was thrown off, and he plummeted off the scaffolding. Athena and I could only stare as he fell and landed in the wet cement. He struggled to get free, but one snake had already coiled around his neck. His body began to sink into the cement.

A clambering filled my ears, and I turned to find Detective Perseus rushing up the stairs.

"What happened?" He quickly eyed us before turning his direction to Poseidon.

I could tell he couldn't believe what he was seeing.

"Are those… snakes?" He fumbled for his radio and rattled off numbers into it I didn't understand.

Athena pulled me closer to her. I could feel her shaking.

"Snakes. The puncture wounds. The strangulation." Perseus was saying these things to himself, but now I knew he had put the pieces together. He turned to me. "This is what happened to Angelo? And the others?"

My eyes welled up with tears. "Yes," I said through a sob. "Yes, it was me. I don't know how, but I called the snakes. It's my fault they attacked all those men." I turned to Athena. "It's the necklace."

Athena gaped at me. In the next instant, she grabbed the necklace and tore it off me. Before I could register what she had done, she tossed it over the scaffolding. It landed in the cement. The tingling in my fingers stopped.

We both looked down to find the snakes gone. Poseidon's body lay still in the disturbed cement, half-buried, his face practically blue.

"I don't… I don't know what just happened." Perseus shook his head, bewildered. "I don't know how I'm going to report this."

"You can't arrest Meddie," Athena insisted. "She had no idea she was controlling the snakes."

His eyes darted between us. "What do you suggest I do? Sooner or later, the murders are going to be connected to you. I can't just stop the investigation."

"Let me go," I pleaded. "I was leaving town anyway. I'll leave Stone Mirror Bay, and you'll never hear from me again."

He glanced down at the mayor. "And how do I explain this?"

Athena shook her head. "Another unsolved mystery. But with Meddie gone, with the necklace gone, there'll be no more attacks. Let her go. I'll get her packed today and make sure she goes. Just… you have to promise not to mention what happened here."

"I don't think anyone would believe me anyway." Perseus rubbed his jaw. "Okay, go. And for your own good, don't come back."

"I won't," I said, wiping my tears away. "I promise. You'll never see my face again."

He gave me a nod and turned away from me. Athena placed a hand on my back, and we quickly left the construction site.

This was it. The final push. I was leaving sooner than I thought, but I was leaving.

And I would never look back.

TODAY'S GODS

SARAH DALE

H EY, RIVER! YOUR tryout was fire yesterday!"

River froze in surprise. She looked up at the ridiculously handsome boy who was hovering over her locker. He was one of two seniors acting as Student Directors for the spring play, and had been one of three on the judging panel at yesterday's auditions. She reminded herself frantically not to get so distracted by his sparkling blue eyes that she lost the ability to speak. It was a thing that happened regularly around Dane.

"Um, wow! Thanks, Dane! Fingers crossed." River smiled, zipped up her backpack and clanged her locker door shut. She hoped he didn't notice her fingers fumbling. *Dang it!*

Unable to think what else to do, she began walking in the direction of the exit door nearest her route home, expecting him to go the opposite way, toward the gym where his and the other jocks' lockers were located. But he didn't. He fell into step beside her. His cologne smelled like rain after a dry spell, fresh and alive and grateful. She inhaled deeply.

"I'm all about this spring play, you know?" Dane exclaimed. "It was

Rhiannon's idea to do this version of *Prometheus Bound*. She's way into the Greeks."

"Yeah, it's a cool script!" River responded enthusiastically. "She and Dr. Bruce did a great job of adapting it and making the language current. Rhiannon is a great writer! I'm in love with the original one-act your class wrote for the Homecoming celebration. That was amazing! That's what inspired me to try out, to be honest."

Rhiannon was the other Student Director, and Dane's girlfriend. River had admired her even before she saw the Homecoming performance last October. She was divinely beautiful and deeply smart. River had found her YouTube channel over the summer and absorbed all twenty-seven videos like a thirsty sponge.

Rhiannon had everything covered in three-to-twenty-minute bites, from morning yoga to how to cold-brew coffee, master barre chords on the guitar and where to find the best SAT tutors. River had worshiped her from afar for months.

When the announcement came that she and Dane had been chosen as Student Directors for this play, River had harried her friend Simon for details. She recalled the day they strolled through the mall; he, eyeing the latest fads for design inspiration, she, needling him for the inside scoop on the Spring Play.

"Have you read the script? Who do you think they'll choose to play Io? Are you serious about trying for a part? Can you do that and make the costumes too?" River had babbled excitedly.

Simon had eyed her seriously. "River, auditions are next week and if you don't try out for that role, you will never forgive yourself."

Just then, River had felt a cool hand on her shoulder. She spun and gasped. There stood Rhiannon, her long waves of auburn hair curling effortlessly around her face and falling to her mid-back. She was dressed simply, but impeccably in a summery cream-colored shift with a metallic gold belt and strappy sandals. The handful of girls who orbited around

Rhiannon like a cluster of satellites looked like they were doing their best to look as elegant and refined as she, and succeeding about as well as a group of Midwestern high school girls could be expected to.

Rhiannon grasped River's other shoulder and turned her so they were face to face. River stared up at her nervously, noticing the gold flecks in Rhiannon's deep blue eyes and praying that she didn't have cinnamon sugar on her mouth from the pretzel bites she'd just scarfed down.

Rhiannon gave River an intense searching look, then imperiously, but not unkindly, asked Simon, "Who is this that you think should audition for a role, Simon?"

Simon tossed his shoulders back, his chest out, and sauntered over so he was standing protectively behind River, facing Rhiannon over River's shoulder.

"Rhiannon, meet my friend River," Simon said, with a note of fierce pride in his voice. "She's a dancer and a poet, and I think she'd make a great Io, if I can convince her to try out!"

"Is that so?" Rhiannon arched one perfectly styled brow at him.

River gulped.

"Yes," he replied with firm conviction. "She played the lead in the sophomore class play last semester, and she just finished a really amazing History project for Ms. Landis on ancient Greek dance."

"Really?" Rhiannon looked interested. "I've been wondering if we should incorporate any musical movement into this play."

"Oh no!" River said automatically, and then caught her breath when Rhiannon's eyebrows shot up in surprise. Simon nodded encouragingly over her shoulder and she continued. "I mean, it wouldn't be traditional, anyway. In the theater, dancing was quite limited in scope."

Rhiannon cocked her head to the side, listening, and then nodded sharply, evidently indicating to her acolytes that she'd come to a decision. They stopped whispering among themselves and came to attention.

"I want to hear more," she declared. "Come! Coffee!" Her entourage scrambled in the direction of the nearest coffee shop. Rhiannon turned River in the same direction, and caught her arm in a friendly but irresistible grasp. River fell into step, her heart pounding with dizzy excitement. Simon kept pace, his expression pleased, but watchful.

Coffee had gone blissfully well, although once River had answered Rhiannon's questions, Rhiannon had dominated the conversation. Her crew had provided a respectful chorus, nodding and laughing at all the right times. But everything she'd said was so fascinating and encouraging that by the time River and Simon were finally excused from Rhiannon's presence, River was determined to try out for the role.

Now River jerked her head out of her thoughts and tried to focus on the present as she and Dane reached the exit door.

The weather had been unsettled all day and rain was again falling. River stepped out of the flow of exiting kids and tried to extricate her umbrella from her backpack. Dane paused with her, shielding her somewhat from the rain. Of course, the umbrella snagged on something in her pack and wouldn't pull free. Kids started piling up on the stairs, some digging for rain gear, others just trying to get out the door.

River gave the umbrella a hard yank and it came free, leaving the contents of her backpack half-in and half-falling-out.

"Crap!" River exclaimed, fumbling to catch her notebooks.

"Here," Dane offered. "You fix your stuff; I'll hold the umbrella over you so we can get out of this crowd."

"Okay, yeah, thanks," River mumbled, acutely conscious her ragged voice was betraying her embarrassment and stress.

Dane took the umbrella and put one hand on River's shoulder. He guided her deftly through the throng. Once outside, he popped the umbrella open over both of them while she shoved and organized and zipped everything back into place, with more force than was strictly necessary.

"You go this way, right?" Dane asked, gesturing.

"Yeah, down Sixty-Third Street."

"Cool. I'm going the same way. Would you mind if I keep the umbrella over both of us? It's really pouring!"

"No, thanks—I, I mean, yes, sure. It's big enough to share." And it was. It was one her mom had gotten for her. The design printed on the fabric was an impressionist scene of sky and clouds reflected in water, and it was easily large enough to cover two. River took a deep breath and tried to act normal.

"I heard a Broadway cast production of *Hamilton* was going to tour this summer," Dane said, his eyes sparkling even in the gray light. He knew exactly what to say, it seemed, to distract her from her nerves.

"Oh, wow, really? Cool! Are they coming here? Or to Omaha?" River burbled.

"I haven't seen a schedule yet, but they could come here, couldn't they? If not the Lied Center, then the Arena. We're getting a lot more cool shows since it opened, that's for sure!" Dane replied enthusiastically.

"Sure have," River agreed. "I saw P!nk last December!"

"That was an amazing show!" Dane agreed.

Deftly shepherded by Dane, her anxiety eased and the chatter went on almost effortlessly for another ten minutes until they arrived at River's house. He walked her up to the covered porch and handed off the umbrella.

"Thanks! I hope you don't have much farther to go." She glanced upward. "Although I think it's clearing up."

Dane stepped gracefully backward off the porch step and reached his hands out to his sides. At exactly that moment, the sun burst out from between a widening break in the clouds. Dane stood there in a beam of light, lit up like a god.

River couldn't help but laugh—it was just too much like he'd planned the lighting cues himself.

"The cast list will be posted at nine o'clock tomorrow morning," Dane called over his shoulder as he walked away. "Good luck, River!"

"Thanks!" she called after him, and watched as his leggy stride took him down the sidewalk at a brisk pace, his personal sunbeam seeming to just keep up.

River dropped her backpack on the floor and flopped down on her bed. For a moment, a stupidly happy smile lit her face, and then reality crashed in. She cringed, clutched her head in both hands, and groaned. Conflicting thoughts buzzed around her head like a swarm of biting flies. Dane was… he was beautiful. It was impossible not to be drawn to him. He exuded charm and humor, he possessed a quick wit and natural talent, and he was hands-down the best-looking guy in school. Maybe in town. He and Rhiannon were a magical power couple. Everybody knew that someday they'd ride off into the sunset together, to LA or New York or maybe Monaco. They'd become the newest it-couple with starring roles in the movies, or on TV or some equally glamorous life. It seemed fated.

But if that was the case, then what in the wide world was Dane doing walking her home? There was *no* question that he put butterflies in her tummy, but he was so very in the *unavailable* column, what did it matter? And even if he really did like her for some unfathomable reason, what about Rhiannon? She was every bit as gloriously perfect and wonderful as Dane. River wanted to be just as amazing as Rhiannon was, but not like this. Everything about this felt so very wrong.

Distractedly, River pulled her phone from her pocket. It had been buzzing madly all the way home, but she'd ignored it. There were a jillion texts from Simon.

Where are you?
Where are we meeting in the morning?
Did you see Meredeth's new shoes, omg!!
I thought I just saw you...
Who are you with??
OMG is that Dane?
He is sooooo hot.
But but but WTH, River???
What are you thinking?
He's with Rhiannon!
Call me
Call me
Call me
Call me
Call me
OMG River! Freaking call me!!

River opened FaceTime and tapped Simon's contact. He answered on the first ring.

"I need the whole, entire story. Immediately. Leave nothing out," he exclaimed, positioning his phone on his bookshelf so she could see him and most of his bedroom, which was artistically strewn with Mardi Gras beads, origami butterflies in rainbow shades and posters of Britney and Gaga.

"Simon, help. I don't know what happened. Dane stopped to talk to me after class about the play and it was completely his idea to walk me home!"

"Ooooh, River! Did he flirt with you? Was there flirting?"

"I think yes." River sighed.

"Oh no! That's so not good. You know that's not good, right? You know this?"

"Yes, Simon! I know this!"

"Because Rhiannon is not going to…"

"I know!"

"And you…"

"I know!!"

"And was it—oh my gosh—you were sharing an umbrella? *So* romantic! Was it… How was it?" he demanded, his voice cracking with excitement.

"Ahhhhhhhhh, it was so lovely. We talked about music, and he's so funny and fine, and oh my God, his eyes…!"

"Stop, girl!"

"Oh, Simon, help!"

"This is tragic. You know you're going to get that part in the play, and then you'll be working on the same stage with both of them. This is sooooo bad…"

"Ohmigod, Simon, I *know*. I don't know what to do about it! I didn't do anything wrong, all I did was walk home!" River's voice took on a distressed edge.

"Okay, okay. Don't panic. We'll figure it out. Listen, did you get your application sent in for Arts?"

Arts and Humanities was, along with several other "focus programs" including the Zoo School and the Career Academy, an off-site school within the public school system students could apply to attend. They offered nearly all the classes you got at the regular school, and then specialty classes. They were mostly reserved for juniors and seniors, but sophomores and sometimes even freshmen were admitted, depending on their talents or special circumstances.

Simon, who was a junior, had already applied and been accepted. He was set to start next semester and had been encouraging River to apply.

Perhaps *encouraging* was too gentle a word. Insisting? Nagging? Haranguing?

The application was complex. She'd had to submit examples of both her fiction and song writing, and videos from a speech competition and a dance recital. Additionally, she'd had to ask two of her teachers for letters of recommendation. Dr. Bruce, the Drama teacher, had written one for her, and her Ballet teacher had written the other. It seemed like it had taken forever to get everything the application required put together, but she'd finally managed.

"Yes! I submitted it last night," River said. "I was just waiting for that last letter, and Ms. Romanov finally emailed it yesterday."

"Under the wire!" Simon exclaimed with relief. "They're supposed to get the letters out before the end of the semester, so that only leaves four weeks. No worries. I know you'll get in, you're an absolute shoo-in."

"We'll see," River mused, absently straightening bottles of dark nail polish on her vanity. "We've talked about this, Simon. My skill sets aren't exactly the kind of thing they're looking for. Your designs and paintings are complete works of art. There was zero doubt you'd get in. But I'm only a soph, and I don't do any kind of visual art. They may not have any room for an odd duck like me, and being a year younger than almost everybody else isn't going to help any."

"Blah blah blah. Keep your negativity to yourself, I know better. Anyway, if whatever this is with Dane blows up in your face, you're going to need someplace to escape to."

Urk.

"Jeez, Simon! What do you think is going to happen?" River's stomach churned.

"I know you think Rhiannon is all that, but you weren't around back when that whole thing blew up with Leila Marquez. Rhiannon caught

Leila making eyes at Dane, and next thing you know, Leila was off the cheer squad, then she lost the Student Council election that everyone was sure she'd win, and not even two weeks after that her car got trashed in a hit-and-run." Simon shook his finger at the camera. "Trust me, River. Trouble like that you do not want."

Crap.

"Any word from your dad yet?" Simon asked, his tone gentle. He was trying to change the subject, River knew, and she appreciated it, but unfortunately, this wasn't any better.

"No, still nothing." River sighed and continued, "Mom's getting pretty edgy. She hasn't said anything to me, but I can tell."

River's dad worked in Army Intelligence. There was a lot about what he did that she wasn't allowed to know, but she couldn't help but worry when he was abroad for weeks on end, and not calling home regularly. It had happened half a dozen times that she could think of, but never for this long. He'd been called to D.C. suddenly just after Thanksgiving. For a while they thought he'd be home for the holidays, but he wasn't. Then, shortly after New Year's, he'd gone overseas. They'd known he wouldn't be in touch for a while, but the silence had never lasted this long. It was already mid-April, and still no word from him.

River had overheard her mom and her older brother Adrian talking late at the kitchen table in low voices. She'd thought about joining them. She figured she was old enough at sixteen to be counted in on serious family discussions, but she'd stayed away.

"I'm sorry, Riv. Is there anything I can do?" Simon asked sympathetically.

River sighed heavily. "I don't know. I mean, no, but I don't even think there's anything anybody can do. He's doing his job, you know?"

"I do. And it's important. Or at least, I know your dad and he seems like a guy that would be trusted to do important work. But, like, I know you're bummed out. Anybody would be."

Tears welled up in River's eyes. She took a deep breath and pushed them away along with her fears, willing herself to stay strong. That's what her mom did, and if she could do it, so could River.

Simon was waiting for River the next morning in the hallway outside the theater room where the cast lists were to be posted. He was wearing an exotic blue feathered cape over his immaculately pressed jeans and t-shirt. Simon was not fashionably discreet, one might say. His choice to be openly queer pushed at the edges of tolerance in this small Midwestern city. It pushed at them hard. But Simon balanced his outrageousness with wry intelligence, a wide array of close friends, and the hard-won muscles of a lifetime of gymnastics practice. He had a fierce, hard-lined kind of beauty that reminded River of Daniel Craig in the *Bond* movies. It worked for him. He was rarely bullied, and he was never beaten nor alone.

Simon held his arms out to River and she allowed herself to be encircled in the cape. Only the top of her head and her sneakers showed. She hadn't slept well at all. When her busy brain wasn't assailing her with impossible visions of the thespian or romantic variety, it switched to dread. She went back and forth between conflicting wishes; one part of her insisted that she should be brave and bold. That part butted heads with the bone-deep urge to flee this whole scene. And when those thoughts faded, she was overwhelmed with wanting her dad safely home, and trying desperately not to allow the big fear that he might not be okay gain any traction. Worrying about getting accepted into Arts and Humanities had gone to a distant third on the worry parade. The safe home-base of Simon's feathered cape was a welcome sanctuary.

A small crowd, maybe a dozen kids, gathered around the bulletin board in the hall. The cast of this play was small, and unlike the large all-school productions, this would be held in the smaller theater-in-the-round that doubled as the theater classroom. Dr. Bruce scurried out of his office at precisely 8:59 carrying a sheet of posterboard. Neatly printed down the left were the names of the roles; on the right, the name of the student who'd won the role.

Zeus/Zach:	Dane Crowley
Hera/Helen:	Rhiannon Stewart
Io/Ione:	River Inaba
Argus/Agatha:	Miranda Stephens
Hermes/Hank:	Ben Adams
Gadfly/Gabby:	Jamie Loomis
Prometheus:	Simon Galpsi
Costumes:	Simon Galpsi
Makeup:	Mindy Carson
Co-Directors:	Dane Crowley and Rhiannon Stewart

"Are you breathing?" Simon whispered down into River's safe darkness.

"Yes," River answered. "Do I dare look?"

"Do you want me to just tell you?" Simon asked gently.

"No. I have to face it. I may as well start now." River straightened her spine and Simon took down the veil of feathers.

Before River had a chance to do anything more than scan the list of names, a boisterous group of kids rounded the corner and rambled past them on their way to Theater 3-4 class. Leading the pack, her long auburn hair draped artistically over her shoulder, casually out of the way of her backpack, was Rhiannon.

River stepped back, out of the way. Rhiannon paused, smiled a welcoming smile and said, "Congratulations, River! Your tryout blew everyone else away. We're happy to have you on the cast. Rehearsals begin after school today, at 3:15. Bring your calendar and be prepared to rehearse long hours. This is a small production, and we only have four weeks to rehearse, but if it's as good as we think it will be, we're going to film it for a competition for an LA Film School."

"Thanks! Wow! Yikes, no pressure, right?" River stammered. Being face to face with Rhiannon made her feel equally thrilled by the compliments and terrified, wondering how far the story of Dane walking her home in the rain yesterday had already spread. Now with this extra layer of stress-inducing expectation, River was afraid she might actually just explode right there in the hallway.

Rhiannon fixed her powerfully beautiful blue-eyed gaze on River and said, "Yes. Pressure."

Big yikes.

"Simon." Rhiannon nodded to him and moved on. River recognized the girls following closely on her heels as Miranda Stephens and Jamie Loomis, the actors chosen to play Argus and the Gadfly.

Simon put a steadying hand on River's shoulder. "You okay? C'mon, we're going to be late to second period."

"Did you know about this competition for an LA Film School?" River demanded hotly.

"I heard a whisper. To be honest, that's when I started work on my designs. She's hoping to make a splash in Los Angeles and she thinks this may be a way in. I doubt it, personally, but we'll see. I figured I'd design some utterly fabulous costumes for it, just in case." Simon had settled his book bag on his shoulder under his feathered cape and was moving toward the main hallway and his next class.

"Oh, sure, yeah. Okay." River's voice sounded far away in her own ears.

"Honey, are you in shock? Do you need to sit down?" Simon peered at her curiously.

"I'm—I'll be oka..."

"River!" Sauntering down the hallway—fashionably late, his silky blond hair perfectly mussed, his Levi's the same shade of blue as his eyes— was Dane.

"Dane, hi! Wow! Hey, whoa there!" River exclaimed as Dane grabbed her by the waist and twirled her around the hallway, now empty except for the three of them.

"Congratulations, River!" Dane said, depositing her back on her feet, but not letting go of her waist. He leaned close and said warmly, "I knew you were perfect for this role the minute I laid eyes on you. Your tryout just proved how right I was, right Simon?" Dane raised his voice slightly and glanced Simon's way. Simon looked concerned, but he nodded. Dane turned back to River and spoke quietly into her hair. "This is going to be magic, trust me," he said. His lips brushed River's ear, sending a conflictedly unwelcome thrill down her spine.

Dane turned River in Simon's direction and released her with a flourish. River stumbled, but kept her feet.

"See you both at rehearsal!" Dane called. River turned back to see Rhiannon stepping out of the theater room doorway and assessing the scene with serious eyes. Dane slung an arm around her shoulders and guided her back toward the classroom with a sweet peck on the cheek. River scurried after Simon before Rhiannon had a chance to look twice.

Simon and River jogged down the broad main hallway, trying to beat the tardy bell to their next classes. As they parted at the stairwell, River asked, "Simon, what have I gotten myself into?"

"I don't know," he replied. "But we're in it together, whatever it is. Hang in there, sweetie. I'll see you at lunch!" Simon glided away up the stairs, a vision in peacock blue. River zipped down the stairs and slid into her Biology class just as the tardy bell rang.

That afternoon began the longest month of River's life.

The script was genius, capturing the power-mad, eons-old marital squabbling between Zeus and Hera as the marriage between two chic, urban twenty-somethings, Helen and Zach, he a dreamy artist with a wandering eye and she a controlling lifestyle blogger who made bank and kept them afloat. When Helen gets wind of Zach's interest in her personal assistant, Ione, she plants a bug on her assistant and has her stalked, harried, and generally made miserable. Zach tries to interfere and just makes things worse, and Ione spends most of the play being batted back and forth by a couple of sociopaths. The dialogue was sharp and clever, the characters were witty and well drawn, and the costumes Simon had been working on for weeks already were going to be things of beauty. River had wondered mightily how he was going to convey the idea that Io gets turned into a cow—albeit a beautiful white one—or that one character was a gadfly, and another had one hundred eyes. But Simon's sketches convinced her that the end result was going to be phenomenal.

The first rehearsal was a table read, with everyone in their regular school clothes sitting around a large folding table in the classroom adjacent to the stage, reading their parts out from the script. River quickly realized she was the youngest member of the cast.

"You killed it in the tryout," Simon whispered in her ear. He sat next to River at the table with his arm on the back of her chair. The feathers from his cape tickled her neck. "You're more than good enough to be here. Listen to their advice, learn your lines and don't give up."

River relaxed slightly. Simon was such a good friend. She reminded herself of what her mom often said, that good friendship went both ways. He had that *go big or go home* look on his face. She guessed rightly that he was going to be swamped with this costuming project.

"Do you need any extra hands with the costumes?" River whispered. "You know I can't sew for beans, but I can wash and iron and organize stuff."

"Oh, you know it! I will take all the help I can get!"

While River had heard of life imitating art, she found it dizzyingly unsettling to be in the midst of it. Rhiannon began with daily after school rehearsals from 3:30-5:00. Closer to the actual performance, she'd scheduled additional hour-long morning rehearsals, and dress-rehearsal showed on the calendar as "5:00-whenever we finish" which sounded just plain ominous.

River wouldn't have minded the obsessive attention paid to how she performed her lines if the lines stayed the same from one rehearsal to the next. Rhiannon never seemed satisfied with the script and endless tweaks and updates had to be learned daily.

On top of that was the fact that whenever Rhiannon disappeared from the stage to rewrite something, there was an unscheduled ten or fifteen-minute break in which Dane invariably managed to maneuver himself into River's presence. If that happened to be in a place where they were alone, he would engage her in conversations that became increasingly difficult to extricate herself from.

"How long has this been going on? Does Dr. Bruce know about this? Did he touch you?" Simon demanded one afternoon, a little over a week into rehearsals. He'd come out of the classroom looking for her, and discovered her in an alcove with Dane, discussing some obscure element of her performance that he wanted her to improve. Simon importuned Dane to release her, saying he needed some additional measurements for her costume, and dragged her away bodily.

"No, he didn't touch me. He doesn't do that. I don't think Dr. Bruce knows, Dane avoids catching his attention. It's been going on all week." Simon glared at her and motioned for her to spill.

River sat, composed herself a moment and gave an exasperated sigh. "He is impeding my progress between places," she began, glancing at Simon and then looking down and scrubbing hard at an invisible spot on her jeans. "And he's insisting on obscure conversations about our characters that are thinly veiled ploys at emotional seduction." She met Simon's eyes full on, her eyebrows furrowed. "Which, let me tell you, are pretty transparent once you realize that his primary goal is to pleasure himself." She shook her head. "Like, no kidding, he is every inch the soulful artist in the body of an underwear model but my bullshit detector could be completely broken and I'd still read him loud and clear."

She took a deep breath and continued, "I am tolerating his behavior in the short term because I am attempting to pick his brain about actual acting concerns. To be honest, if I can get him to stop flirting with me for five seconds, he has really valuable input and amazing suggestions." She sighed. "And partly because I don't want to rock the boat," she admitted, her eyes downcast. What she wouldn't say to Simon was that she didn't want her personal drama to ruin his chance that his costumes might get noticed at the LA film school. What she wouldn't admit even to herself, was that despite everything wrong about the situation, she was still enamored by his attentions. It was a complicated mess.

"But River," Simon protested, "it's not fair! He's the Student Director. He has power over you. He shouldn't be doing any of this stuff, and you don't have to tolerate it!"

River swallowed her own lingering worries and hugged him. "It's okay. I'll be okay, I promise." Simon held his peace, but from that moment forward, he started going with her any time she stepped out of the rehearsal room.

Simon wasn't the only one who noticed what was going on, either. By the beginning of the second week of rehearsals, River had a second shadow: Rhiannon's friend Miranda.

Miranda was the school's star Volleyball Center. She was tall and strong with silky fine blonde hair in a single long braid, and what Simon called "Bette Davis Eyes," which apparently meant big, blue, a little bugged out, and oddly compelling. She came from a big, churchy family of the homemade dresses and chaperoned dates variety. Rhiannon took her under her wing the first day of freshman year and she'd been at Rhiannon's side every minute since.

At first Miranda was just hanging around River at rehearsals, but once she caught sight of Dane watching River's movements in and out of the room, she became omnipresent. After every single class, River would emerge to see Miranda leaned up against a bank of lockers, arms crossed, face stern. At lunch, she stayed no more than six feet away from River at all times, once even forcibly vacating a table full of freshmen so she could sit closer to River and Simon.

For a day or two, River sort of appreciated it, since it kept Dane's up close and personal discussions about her scenes at bay, but it wasn't too long before it became downright creepy. River endured it for the next two full weeks, counting down the days until the performance when she could get away from all of this insanity. Or this part of it anyway. They still hadn't had any word from her dad, and that knowledge was eating into her gut with a pickaxe.

On Friday of the third week, when River requested a restroom pass out of her second period History class only to find Miranda frequenting the same restroom at exactly the same time, she had to wonder just how Miranda was tracking her movements. It wasn't like they had any classes together, but regardless, she was on her, as River's dad might say, like a second coat of paint.

That random thought about her dad made River's worries surface again. *Argh.* Between the play, Miranda's lurking around, constant rewrites at rehearsals, and the anticipation of finding out whether she would get accepted into Arts and Humanities, River's stomach was constantly in knots. Which was probably why she needed a mid-morning bathroom break. *More argh.*

River emerged from the stall and stopped to wash her hands. Miranda hadn't even bothered to pretend like she needed to use the facilities. She was just standing there, leaning up against the wall by the paper towel dispenser, arms crossed.

"Hey, Miranda," River said dryly. "Fancy meeting you here."

"Just following my acting directions. I figured it couldn't hurt to get in a little extra practice keeping the *cow* tied up."

"Dude!" River exclaimed. "Over-identify with your role much?" She strode, exasperated, to the bathroom door, shoved it open, and nearly ran into Dane, who *just happened* to be standing right outside.

"Hi, River!" Dane said brightly. As annoying as it was to have not only one, but two people following her every move, River couldn't ignore the physical and mental rush she experienced whenever she laid eyes on Dane. He was just so ridiculously good looking. When she was with him, it was way too easy to ignore his vain, cocksure behavior, and be swept away on the rush of endorphins that rocked her every time he caught her eye. Which he did, just then. Right on cue, her heart pounded, her tongue tied, she was sure she was blushing, and when Miranda suddenly pushed through the door behind her and literally shoved her into Dane's outstretched arms, River stopped breathing. She was fairly sure she was going to faint.

"Miranda, hey!" Dane said, sounding a little irate. "I thought you had gym this period. Shouldn't you be out running the mile today?"

"Got a pass," the tall girl mumbled, averting her eyes. "Didn't feel so hot." She strode down the hall, turning a corner before, River was sure, pulling her phone out to text Rhiannon.

River extricated herself from the tangle of Dane's arms. She only got a few steps from him before he turned and caught up with her.

"What's going on, River? Has Miranda been bothering you?" Dane's expression was thunderous.

"No, I…" River's thoughts tumbled. While it was true that Miranda's constant spying had been a real drag, it was also true that Dane's constant attentions were just as troubling, if not more so. *Argh!* There was no right answer here. Flustered, she sputtered out, "It's cool, everything's cool. I have to get back to class. See you later, Dane."

Dane's fickle good humor was restored by that assurance. "Yeah, great! See you at rehearsal!" He reached out to touch her arm, and River ducked inside the classroom, cutting off the gesture with the heavy door. She stepped inside the room and gave a sigh of relief.

Thirty minutes later, when River emerged from History class, she spotted the lurking presence of Miranda across the hall. Before she could so much as roll her eyes, her view of anything past her nose was obscured by a hulking figure wearing a tracksuit and size-14 white Chuck Taylor high tops, the sides of which had been intricately decorated with sharpie in a winged design. She looked up, and then up some more until her neck cracked.

"Um, hi, Ben," she said. "Excuse me?"

"Hey, River! Which way are you headed?" Ben's voice was surprisingly light and lyrical for such a huge guy. She'd noticed that right away when they did the table read at play practice. She'd been surprised to see him trying out for the play at first. River wasn't much of a football fan, so when Simon said that Ben was a Wide Receiver, she'd rewarded him with a blank stare. When Simon explained that meant that he was tall enough to catch passes, smart enough to avoid defenders and fast enough to avoid collisions (and concussions), her assumptions about big, dumb football players began to crumble. Ben was a really good guy, funny and lighthearted. His semi-raucous stories, punctuated unexpectedly with terrible dad-jokes, kept the often long breaks in rehearsals from dragging. He was also Dane's best friend.

"I'm on my way to Mr. Rogge's Math class, on the second floor. I like your shoes!" River replied, snaking around him and heading for the stairs. Ben stuck to her like glue.

"Thanks! Got the idea from Simon's sketches for my character's costume. Mind if I walk with you?" Ben asked, not waiting for her reply.

"Well, it's a free country, I guess," River said dryly. "Let me guess, Dane sent you?"

Ben cracked a smile above her head. "He got the impression that maybe you needed someone to run interference. Is she bugging you?" he asked, cocking his head in the direction of Miranda, who was following at a slightly more discreet than usual distance.

"Let's just say, I'm feeling extremely looked after these days," River murmured.

"Need a little breathing space, do ya?" He chuckled. "Well, you leave her to me. I'll see if I can't free up your path a little. See you after school!"

With that, Ben peeled off. When River peeked back over her shoulder, she saw that he'd planted himself in front of Miranda and was chatting away. Miranda was obviously torn between keeping up with River and getting caught up in Ben's hilarious recounting of some party where a cheerleader they both knew had wound up blindfolded in a parka and rain boots holding a puppy on the diving board at the neighborhood swimming pool.

River was just about to celebrate a moment of relative solitude—albeit in a crowded hallway—when suddenly, Dane took her elbow.

"Hi, River! I'll walk you to your Math class! Hey, do you know about..." And he was off. This time it was something to do with the impact of cryptocurrencies on global politics, something River was pretty sure Dane misunderstood entirely.

That didn't seem to matter too much to Dane, River had discovered. He was in his own world so much of the time. He absolutely loved having an audience, but once he'd charmed and maneuvered his audience members into position, his focus reverted entirely to himself. He firmly believed that everyone was hanging on his every word, and that was exactly as it should be. For Dane, there was no scene in which he didn't play the leading man.

River stood in the doorway of her Math class, trying to extricate herself from Dane's grip on her backpack, while he went on and on. Other students pushed around her, trying to get in before the bell. Mr. Rogge finally came over and simply pulled her inside and, with a smile, firmly closed the door in Dane's face. He turned River toward her desk, gave her a little push and began passing back yesterday's quizzes.

River had just yanked her textbook and pen case out of her backpack when she felt a sharp pinch on the back of her neck. She slapped her hand at it and winced. Gingerly she plucked at it and came away with a little round burr, the kind her aunt's husky got covered in every time she took him for walks in the woods. She looked around, amazed. Who in the actual hell would have thrown a burr at her? Or, rather, not thrown—it had smacked her hard, like it had been shot at her. Like a spit wad out of a straw or something.

She heard a quiet, hissing sort of laugh coming from behind her. Glancing out of the corner of her eye, she spotted the only other kid in the room who was also in the dang play. Rhiannon's other acolyte, Jamie Loomis. She should have been hard to miss with her wild, kinky red hair and giant round glasses, but somehow the fact that she barely topped five feet in height, even with the hair, allowed her to fly under the radar.

River remembered meeting Jamie for the first time last year, a terrifying experience she later likened to meeting an angry tiger. Jamie arrived mid-semester because—according to the best gossip—she'd been kicked out of yet another school for fighting. Depending on who you listened to, rumor had it she'd spent time in foster homes and juvie before she was even a teenager.

Jamie was one of those girls who was both terrifying and sexy, and not well in control of either superpower. Rhiannon helped change that. Under her tutelage, Jamie managed to stay in school and mostly out of trouble. She also discovered hair products, which, although they didn't completely tame her wild mane, at least made it look cool instead of crazed.

The flip side of Jamie staying out of trouble was getting into a different sort at Rhiannon's direction. That business Simon had reminded her about with Leila Marquez's hit-and-run had Jamie's brush strokes all over it.

Jamie was Mr. Rogge's student assistant this period, and as such, he normally had her out doing things like making copies or alphabetizing file folders. She was rarely in the room during class. He must be short on extra projects today.

My freaking lucky day, River thought sourly, as another expertly shot burr landed painfully on her arm.

Mr. Rogge stopped by her desk and set down her quiz, adding another layer to her aggravation. *B-.* He paused and tapped his pen on the comment he'd written below the grade. *"You can do better."* Then he went on to the next person in the row.

River put her head, which was beginning to throb, in her hands. Yeah. She knew she could do better, under normal circumstances, *which these were NOT!* She felt hot tears of frustration prick at the corners of her eyes.

Thankfully, Simon was there to greet her after class and accompany her to lunch. As the usual parade of craziness began to build, he sized up the situation, and River's anguished vibe, and came to a decision.

"Oh, hey! I just remembered: I have a library book I have to return before lunch. Come with me!" With a swift and nearly acrobatic move, Simon scooped River out of the flow of kids and into the soothing quiet of the library. Simon strode in, waved at Ms. K, the librarian, and continued on past the desk without returning anything.

"What are we doing?" River asked, permitting herself to be propelled through a conference room attached to the library which led into an empty staff workroom and then onto a back hallway.

"We're going *out* to lunch," Simon replied.

"I'm not allowed! Only juniors and seniors can go off campus, Simon! You're going to get me in trouble!"

"Your call, River. If you want to go back to the caf and try to eat with those crazies lurking around, either peering over your shoulder or fighting for your attention, go for it. But trust me, this is better for your mental health!"

"Let's go!" she exclaimed.

They scurried out the exit door normally reserved for staff and cut across the campus to the student parking lot. They piled into Simon's Jeep Wrangler and drove sedately out of the lot, River squashing her instinct to duck down in the seat to avoid notice. She'd almost succeeded in telling herself it was silly, that nobody cared all *that* much, when Simon reached over and tugged her down.

"Crap, who is it?" she hissed.

"Jamie Loomis. Good grief, River! When did *she* board your own personal crazy train?"

"Just today," River groaned. She stayed scrunched down with her hands over her head until they were well past the school. A burr Jamie had shot at her earlier snagged her fingers and she winced. "And she came armed." She extricated the burr and showed it to Simon.

"What the—?" Simon looked appalled. "Oh, this calls for the big medicine." He deftly maneuvered the Jeep through the side streets that bounded the school and out onto the main drag, in the direction of the closest Starbucks.

Fifteen minutes later, coffees and caprese sandwiches in hand, Simon turned out of the parking lot.

"Now where?" River asked, savoring the joyful rush of caffeine, chocolate and whipped cream.

"My house. I need you for a costume fitting anyway, and everything is there," he replied resolutely.

"But I have class!" River protested.

"Don't worry. I already texted Dr. Bruce and told him I needed you this afternoon for costume help. He'll send passes for both of us to the office, you're in the clear."

River let that sink in. An afternoon off. Legitimized by Dr. Bruce. With coffee, and sandwiches, and Simon. She breathed in deeply and let out a great sigh. She felt a weight lift from her shoulders she hadn't even realized she was carrying.

"Thank you, Simon," she said quietly. "I needed this."

"I know," he replied, only a little smugly. "Here's the thing about Dane. He's in his own world with Rhiannon. The two of them together are on some kind of astral plane the rest of us can't visit. Problem is, *they* visit Earth every day to go to school, and forget that they're just tourists, and not gods." Simon spoke with a level of surety that told River he'd thought long and hard on this.

"They do seem to feel that they're entitled to our blood, sweat and tears on this play, that's for dang sure," River replied.

"All that and more, especially from you right now," Simon said firmly, pulling into the driveway at his house. Simon's folks were pretty well-off and their house was super nice. His dad was a film producer. He could pretty much work from anywhere, and since his longest-living grandmother lived in this particular Midwestern backwater, this is where they landed.

They'd bought a house in the historical district and renovated it. Simon, being an only child, had the run of a whole floor of four bedrooms, and one of those was a dedicated sewing room. Simon's mom was a costume designer; she'd done Broadway plays and a bunch of movies. She had taught Simon to sew when he was old enough to hold a needle. Between them, they had a ton of fancy specialty machines and exotic, interesting fabrics.

Bolts of fabric lined the walls floor to ceiling on built-in shelves, exploding with colors and patterns. Simon kept it roughly organized by color family, so there was a rainbow effect as your eye traveled around three sides of the room. The center of the room was occupied by a large table—a big, old dining room table that had been reworked with slightly taller legs so one could work while standing. The surface of the wooden table was covered with a heavy pad, on which measurements were marked for cutting fabric. Underneath the table on all sides were storage bins on wheels. Three sewing machines, each from a different decade, occupied the lower half of the fourth wall, under the windows.

Simon hooked a stool out from under the table and plunked her down on it. She'd helped him with the early stages of the project, so she'd seen the sketches and the fabrics, but he hadn't let her see any of the pieces once he'd begun constructing them.

"Sit here. I've nearly finished all the costumes except yours and one of Rhiannon's, but I'll show you all of it." With a huge grin, he strode over to the closet door and drew out a hanging rack on wheels.

The play was in three acts. In the first, everyone dressed in their street clothes. For Helen/Hera, that meant a sleeveless silk and rayon blend jumpsuit, white with gold detail, with sky-high gold pumps. Zach/Zeus got a pair of skinny leg chinos, a silk button-down, and calf-skin loafers. Each character's costume then progressively morphed over the second act, reflecting the characters becoming more and more their true selves.

Hank/Hermes changed from a fiery red track suit and running shoes into progressively sleeker running garb consisting of form-fitting black leggings and a white silk t-shirt. Simon turned the hanging mannequin the t-shirt was displayed on so she could see the back.

River gasped. "Oh, Simon, that is glorious!" The back of the t-shirt was completely covered in golden, hand-painted wings. "That is going to look so amazing on Ben!"

Simon gazed at his work, his eyes alight. Then he winked slyly at her. "I won't say I didn't enjoy having such a beautiful model to work on."

"Simon!" River laughed.

"Well, you know," Simon replied with pretend primness. "He's on the football team. He works out."

River giggled and pointed at the items still on the rack. "Is that Miranda's?"

Simon unhooked two hangers and held one in front of the other. "This lovely frock," he intoned, displaying a blue-green wrap dress covered in a mesmerizingly tiny polka dot print, "goes with the black combat boots over there." He nodded toward a nearby shelf of shoes. "And in Act Two, Miss Argus/Agatha dons her cape as she takes off in pursuit of Io." Here he drew out the second outfit, and again River gasped.

This piece, too, was painted silk. Simon had fashioned the long, hooded cape simply, saving all his energy for the painting, and it showed. River caught one corner and lifted while Simon lifted the other so the entire expanse of vibrant blue-green peacock feathers was visible. Each eyespot was exquisitely rendered in shades of iridescent blue and green, perfectly set against the elaborately detailed, golden-brown feather patterns that made up the background.

"Oh, Simon, this is... this is just... *wow*." River grinned delightedly up at her dearest friend. "I am bursting with pride just to know you."

"Oh you hush," he protested, beaming. "Take a look at the stuff for Gabby. Honestly, I think the gadfly was the toughest to imagine."

"Can't wait!" River dropped her end of the cape and stepped back while Simon carefully replaced the items on the rack.

"Here is the Act One look," he said, pulling out a lovely, fitted pair of cropped pants in a pale spring green, with a cute close-fitted top in a slightly darker shade. "It goes with the moccasins there." He gestured with his head at a pair of mid-calf height mocs in a pale shade of cream.

"I love the colors, they're so"—she struggled to find the right word—"expectant. Like, I expect sunshine and life to come bursting forth," she finally said.

Simon smiled. "What do you think of the Act Two look?" He drew forward another jacket. Where Argus's cape was elegant and flowing, the Gadfly's coat was trim and fitted. It was a soft green felted fabric. River reached a finger out to touch the detailing. Strips of fabric in browns and greens and golds gracefully outlined the bodice, the shoulders, and the waist, giving the whole a look of the most elegant of exoskeletons.

"So pretty," River intoned, examining the shiny gold buttons. She lifted an arm to see the sleeve. "Ohhhh! Look!"

Simon smiled at the delighted tone in her voice and lifted the other arm. In between the arms and the body of the jacket was intricately tatted lace in a gauzy, web-like pattern, giving the jacket a winged appearance.

"You killed it! This is beautiful and buggy, and mean old"—her voice cracked a little—"Jamie Loomis is going to look splendid in it!" River tried to keep her tone light, and nearly succeeded.

Simon, completely unfooled, rehung the garments and took River in his arms. She put her head on his shoulder and let the craziness of the last few weeks wash over her. After a moment of clinging to her friend like a life raft, she got control and breathed down the tears. Then the anger at the unfairness of it all gripped her. She straightened her back defiantly.

"Why me?" she demanded in a low, tight voice. "Why does Dane have to pick me to be interested in? I really do *not* need all of this bull on top of—" River's breath hitched. "Not with Dad—" She stopped again as tears closed up her throat and blinded her eyes.

Simon held her while she cried, murmuring soothing nonsense and patting her back in the nicest of ways. When River was breathing normally again, she looked at him and was surprised. His eyes were full of compassion for her dilemma, but his mouth was quirked up in a defiant smile.

"What?" she asked, only a little petulantly. Despite herself, she allowed his smile to lighten her darkness. A little.

"Sweet girl. It's going to be okay! All of it! Look. The play is nearly done, right? Dress rehearsal's next week and then the performances are next weekend! Look, I know this seems impossible right now, but it's going to get better. I promise. In a month, this play will all seem like just a crazy fever dream. Rhiannon and Dane will have graduated and moved away to their castle in the sky, and you and I will be on our way to bigger and better things, you just wait and see. But for right now"—he thrust the hanger at her that contained most of her Act One costume, and part of Act Two's—"let's finish your final fitting."

In her guise as Ione, River would come to work wearing a sheer white shirtdress, elegantly detailed at the collar and cuff, layered over a more concealing shift which hid the *extremely snug* faux leather trousers used for Act Two. She adored the white go-go boots that went with both costumes and wished they were her own. The final additions, a coat and veiled hat she would wear for part of Act Two and all of Act Three, Simon hadn't let her see at all until now.

Once Simon completed pinning and tucking to his satisfaction, he asked, "Are you ready to see the coat?"

"You *know* I am!" she said, grateful to let the wave of excitement she felt on the cusp of seeing this wondrous creation Simon had crafted just for her buoy her heart with happiness, even if it would be short-lived.

Simon made a production out of returning to the closet and bringing the coat out, concealed by its own personal garment bag. He held it up and triumphantly unzipped it. River covered her gaping mouth with both hands and did a happy little dance. Simon beamed.

Dress rehearsal had gone swimmingly. The first night, each new costume garnered rounds of applause from Dr. Bruce and the assembled cast and crew as it was brought out. For each, Simon took a little bow. At the end, when his character, Prometheus, was revealed, bound to the very realistic-looking painted mountain on wheels the tech crew had cooked up, he got a standing ovation. Of course, he couldn't bow, what with being bound to the rock, but he soaked it all in with tears and gratitude.

River couldn't wait to hear the audience's reaction on opening night.

Holy cats, River thought to herself when she woke up on Friday morning. *That's tonight. Opening night is tonight!*

She jumped into jeans and a clean t-shirt and skipped into the kitchen, more alert and awake than usual at this hour. Even half asleep she wouldn't have been able to miss the giant bouquet of sunflowers that graced her usual spot at the kitchen table.

"Good morning!" her mom sang out.

"Break a leg!" her brother Adrian mumbled around his mouthful of toast.

"Aw, you guys, thank you!" River grinned. She'd barely been home at all the last week. The flurry of rehearsals, last minute changes, all on top of trying to salvage her Math grade and study for finals had her at a point where she could barely remember her own name, let alone remember to keep her mom and brother posted about opening night.

"Your dad will be so sorry he missed it!" said her mom.

Everything got quiet for a minute around the table.

Adrian cleared his throat. "He won't miss a thing. I'll be filming every second of it. He'll be home before you know it, kid."

"Adrian's right. No time for moping. Your dad is doing his job, let's us do ours!" Mom smiled and energetically rose to clear the dishes.

Adrian and River rose as well and without a look, converged on their mom for a group hug.

River scrambled to get out the door on time for school. She'd just made it to the corner when she heard a deep rumbling sound. She glanced up and beheld Dane on a motorcycle. Her heart skipped a beat.

River didn't know a whole lot about motorcycles, but judging from the amount of shiny chrome on display, she assumed this was a really nice one.

Dane rumbled to a stop in front of her and turned gracefully to unhook a second helmet from the back of the bike. He flipped the visor up on his own and smiled at her. The sun took that moment to burst forth, lighting up his gorgeous blue eyes and kissing curly tendrils of hair that escaped the helmet with perfect golden light.

River blinked to clear her eyes, and then blinked again to clear her brain.

"Hi, Dane."

"C'mon, I'll give you a ride in!" The sun gave his eyes a break and danced around on his perfect white teeth while he smiled.

"Dane, really. It's only a couple of blocks," River protested. She'd never ridden on a motorcycle, and it looked both fun and terrifying. Sort of like everything that involved Dane.

"Are you afraid?" he asked, not unkindly. It was more like he somehow knew exactly how she felt, and wanted to make her feel safe with him. It was more than a little bit intoxicating. It energized her.

"Gimme that brain bucket," she said, hand extended. He obliged.

By the end of the block, she understood that in order to do her part to balance them, she'd need to have her arms around Dane's waist. She wasted a second freaking out that he'd be able to feel her heart's staccato beat through his jacket, and then turned her focus on the ride. The sun was warm on her back, the bike was powerful underneath her, and Dane smelled sort of earthy and wonderful and she was suddenly and overwhelmingly glad to be alive. He took the long way around the school, pulling out of the neighborhood onto an arterial long enough to speed up a little. River's breath caught. It felt like they were flying.

When Dane finally pulled into the student lot, he maneuvered them right up next to the building. He parked his bike in a little grassy area next to the teacher's lot.

"Is this even a parking spot?" River asked.

"It is for me," he replied.

All along the way, eyes had been on them, watching. She hesitated before removing her helmet, hanging on to her anonymity for another moment before the *schist*, as her Physical Sciences teacher would joke, *hit the fan*. She knew it wouldn't take long. Rhiannon would find out about this and it would be awful. For a little bit. Another few days. Then this unbearably freaky school year would be over and she could spend the summer recovering from the weirdness. Rhiannon and Dane would graduate and go out and conquer the world, and leave her and Simon in the relative peace of their boring hometown. Even if she didn't make it into the Arts and Humanities focus program, she'd still be able to hang out with Simon after school next year.

She sighed sadly. Not ideal, but bearable.

Her mopey musings were cut off by a sharp pinch on the back of her neck. She straightened her shoulders, reached around and retrieved the burr. Without looking around, she flicked the burr off into the bushes and called out wryly, "Good morning, Jamie!"

Their parade gathered steam as they approached the school. Dane didn't seem to notice. He was off on a rambling monologue about the play, how great opening night was going to be, and all about the film crew they were working with to make the tape they'd use to enter the film school competition.

Miranda and Ben joined them at the front doors, she furiously texting, he skillfully blocking her attempts to shoot video. Jamie was landing a burr about every minute. That girl had unbelievable aim. River made an internal bet with herself on whether or not she'd get nailed once more before she hit the door to the Biology room. She thought she could just make it.

She didn't.

The day passed quickly. River fluctuated between freaking out about the upcoming test in English and freaking out about forgetting the latest line changes, which was great, because it kept her from freaking out about what Rhiannon was going to do to her. Or worse yet, if her dad was in the same kind of trouble she was in, fighting to hang in there and get through it, whatever *it* was.

River and Simon skipped lunch and hid out in the empty band room. She made him quiz her on *One Flew Over the Cuckoo's Nest* for her English test next period. They managed to avoid the notice of Rhiannon's flunkies until they emerged into the main hall with the surge of kids heading to fourth period classes and second lunch.

At every possible turn, River was harried. Relentlessly. Between classes, in class, in the restroom. She felt like she had a retinue. Dane at one shoulder, Simon at the other, Miranda and Ben on their heels, Jamie lurking about like a freaking ninja, regularly nailing her with burrs. She started checking her hair regularly. She felt like a scruffy puppy.

She dreaded sixth period. Dr. Bruce had regularly been excusing her from the second half of class to go get an early start with the rest of the cast onstage. Today would be no exception. Rhiannon had exhorted them all the night before to be sure to be there at 2:30. It would be the last chance for changes before everyone left to get dinner and then returned at 6:00 to get into makeup and costumes and do lighting checks.

At 2:25, Simon slipped into the drama classroom and looked at Dr.

Bruce, who nodded to him, and then at River. She got up and gathered her things. Outside the door, she looked left, to the door that led to the stage. Ben stood in front of it, arms crossed, brow furrowed, shaking his head. Simon pulled her the other direction, toward the stairs.

"What's up? Where are we going?" River asked.

"Just trust me," Simon hissed. "You do not want to go in there right now."

"Why? What's going on?" River whispered as they scurried downstairs toward the outside door near the Custodians' office.

"It's Rhiannon. She's out-of-her-mind angry about that motorcycle stunt this morning. Dane is in there with her right now and sparks are definitely flying. Ben grabbed me out of class to come and run interference. We'll have to go back in time for the opening curtain. Let's just hope she and Dane have managed to sort their stuff out by then."

"What about our makeup and costumes? You don't think she'd do anything to my costume, do you? Or yours? Oh no, Simon!"

"Don't worry, I thought of that too. I had Mindy grab our things. She's meeting us at my place. We can get dressed there. She'll do our makeup there and then head back to the school to get the others ready. She said there's no way Rhiannon is going to permit them to look anything less than perfect tonight. They were only able book the film crew for one night, so this is it. This is their big chance. They won't want anything to get in the way of that. No matter what else, the show must go on."

"Won't our being AWOL make her even crazier?" River demanded.

"Ben said this was the best way. I don't know if he's right, but I saw Rhiannon lay into Leila Marquez last year, and trust me, any option is better than that." Simon shook his head and pulled his car briskly out of the lot.

Yikes.

They made it to Simon's without incident, and Mindy was already there waiting. She had the garment bags laid carefully across the back seat of her old Honda Civic. Simon retrieved them while River helped Mindy get her makeup kits out of the trunk.

Opening curtain was scheduled for 7:30 pm. They snuck in the same door they'd exited at 7:25 exactly, in full costume and makeup, River ready for Act One, Simon ready to be strapped to a mountain backstage by a gaggle of stagehands, both with acid churning in their stomachs. Again, Ben was waiting for them. He ushered them up the stairs and stayed by River's side when Simon peeled off to stash River's Act Two coat with Mindy before taking his place.

Rhiannon and Dane were already in their places onstage. River took her spot in the wings, ready to enter. When the curtain rose, she peered into the audience, trying to see her mom or her brother. But the lights muddled her eyes and everything other than the stage was just a confusing blur. River turned her focus to the stage, anxious not to miss her cue.

> *Fade In:*
>
> Act 1
>
> *Zach and Helen's beautiful, white, spacious kitchen. Zach is leaning on the counter in front of the coffee machine, sipping, looking at his phone. Helen is working at the office nook set-up so she can work while riding her exercise bike. Ione enters enthusiastically through the French doors leading out to the backyard.*

IONE/IO

    Good morning, Helen… Zach.
Ione smiles professionally at Helen, eyes Zach out of the corner of her eye. Sets box of fancy Danish on counter.

HELEN/HERA

    Good morning, dear heart. We have a busy day today! Did you get that last video I sent you submitted to the editor?

Rhiannon eyed River over her iPhone. She never broke character, never ceased constantly scrolling, but the look in her eyes made River's extremities icy cold and her guts clench up.

Gulp.

IONE/IO

    Yes, she said she'd have it ready to post this afternoon.

HELEN/HERA

Helen stops scrolling and glares at Ione.
    What time this afternoon? That video needs to be up on the site no later than 2:00!

IONE/IO

Ione eyes Helen while gathering up piles of clothing, boxes and bags as Helen points at each imperiously.
    I told her 1:30, but I'll touch base with her and make sure she's on track.

```
HELEN/HERA
     Oh, Ione, darling. What would I do without
     you? Now don't let that scarf drop. I need all
     those back from the cleaners by first thing
     tomorrow morning. And these papers to the
     attorney's office, and don't forget, Mr.
     Sprinkles needs to be at the groomer's by
     9:00!


Helen tosses dog leash to Ione. Ione catches,
sighs, smiles, heads back outside. Zach
surreptitiously follows.
```

And the play went on.

River managed to keep entirely out of Rhiannon's way backstage, with a little continued help from Ben. At the end of Act One when Zeus transforms Io into a beautiful white heifer to hide her from Hera, River disappeared behind a tree onstage, where she shucked off the sheer shirtdress and sheath and slipped into the coat handed to her by a hidden stagehand.

She emerged into the spotlight to an audible gasp from the audience. The coat was another of Simon's masterpieces, but this one was dyed rather than painted. He'd tightly woven the fabric for the coat using silk and wool he'd first dyed into multitudes of iridescent shades of white. The fabric glistened and glowed under the lights, giving the effect of a short-haired, variegated hide, in every imaginable shade, shadow and highlight of white. The coat was a fashion-forward modern cut, minimal but not austere. The white leather, square-heeled boots added a little whimsy, and a tall rounded black felt hat with a white veil finished it off.

Audible over the audience's delighted response was a totally unscripted explosion of angry laughter from backstage.

Chills ran down River's arms.

She spent most of Act Two running away from Hera's first acolyte, Agatha/Argus of the Hundred Eyes. River began to feel strangely that Miranda's constant tracking of her for the last three weeks had been practice for the play. This, here and now, this was the real thing. The eyespots on the peacock cloak seemed less beautiful than they had on the hanger in Simon's safe, sunny sewing room, and more coldly dangerous. River's stomach churned.

During the scene where Agatha/Argus fights with Hank/Hermes, River was alone in the wings. Simon was already strapped to his mountain, ready to be pushed out onstage. She tried to conceal herself in a fold of the curtains, but Jamie spotted her. She looked positively evil in her gadfly costume, her wild red hair twisted into wild red spikes.

Watching Jamie with one eye and the stage with the other, River ducked and dodged, keeping out of range of her wretched little pea shooter until she heard their cue. Then she fled onstage as Gabby the Gadfly pursued her. The minute she had a clear shot, she nailed River in the neck and River yelped in surprise. Whatever she was using, it hurt worse than the burrs she'd been nailing her with for days.

River slapped at her neck, and her fingers came away bloody.

Then all hell broke loose. Zeus and Hera, now gloriously garbed as the gods they were, had retired to Mt. Olympus, atop another of the Stagecraft crew's rolling mountains, this one far lovelier and greener than poor Prometheus's crag. From there they screamed at one another about Io, they screamed at Hermes and Argus, and when Argus was felled, Hera continued to screech orders to the Gadfly.

River knew full well that she'd missed the final rehearsal, but she suspected a whole lot of what was happening right now was ad-libbed.

ZEUS

> Darling, you know none of the mortals mean anything to me. How could they possibly? You are my only love. Of course, I'll gift you that heifer, if it means so much to you. It means nothing to me.

HERA

> If the <u>heifer</u> meant nothing to you, then why did you give it a ride to school on your bike?

to GABBY/GADFLY

> Don't you lay off her, not for a second! Do you hear me? She does not leave this place until I have had a chance to <u>speak</u> with her, myself!

at IONE/IO

> You can't hide from me, HEIFER!

Big yikes.

On her final pass through backstage, fleeing Jamie and her evil pea shooter, now bleeding from several spots on her hands and neck, River saw a flash of golden wings. Ben! She heard Jamie's *oof* when he snagged her around the waist and held her, squirming, off the ground. Her parting shot before Mt. Olympus was rolled back offstage between them pinged into the wall by River's head. She stared at it in horror.

Jamie had driven shiny, silver needles through the burrs she was shooting. The one near her head had been shot with enough force to drive it into the wooden wall behind her. She reached up to touch it, and saw blood dripping off her hand where another of the projectiles had struck her. For a moment, the floor tilted in a funny way and River saw bright flashes. Then her stomach lurched. She grabbed for the wall to steady herself and hoped it would pass.

This was insane. This was too much. It was all too much. She'd been harried and chased, pestered and ordered about, tested to her limits. If it had just been this, only this play, maybe she could have kept it together. But the play on top of the worry that she might be separated from her best friend next year because she probably wasn't good enough to get into the Arts and Humanities program, and then her dad…

River staggered and fell to one knee.

Her dad. What would he do right now? She didn't know exactly, but she knew for sure he wouldn't give up. He told her once, "Even if you can't see the light at the end of the tunnel, you can't stop moving. It's only when you stop moving that you run out of options."

River braced her hands on the ground and pushed herself up. She just had to keep moving. Her breath hitched hard, then eased. Her stomach steadied and her vision cleared enough to see the spotlight as it lit Simon as Prometheus, bound to the mountain. Once again, the audience burst into gasps and exclamations.

Simon's costume was a bodysuit, painted like a body. A beautiful, godlike body. Each muscle, each sinew was gracefully and beautifully drawn and overlaid atop Simon's gymnast frame. Exposed on his chest, just below his breastbone, was painted a wound, nearly healed. And on top of that were his manacles.

They were molded from plastic, but they'd been painted to look metallic. It was like a suit with metal bars that held him in place, with his feet pinned slightly back and his head pitched slightly forward, and his arms held straight out behind him, held in place with another metal bar, and the whole contraption was bolted into the mountain. Simon appeared to hang, held in place by the bindings.

It looked terribly, awfully painful, and terribly, awfully beautiful.

The audience gasped and fell silent.

IO

Io staggers out onstage.

PROMETHEUS

Come here, child. Come here and rest. Tell me your troubles.

IO

Io leans against the stones, looking up at Prometheus.

Tell you mine? When you cannot free yourself from your own?

PROMETHEUS

Trouble yourself not about my worries, child. Sit and rest.

IO

I cannot rest, sir. Zeus has transformed me into this wretched form, and Hera has sent a terrible gadfly to harass me. I've been running and running and I'm so very tired. All I want is to live in peace.

PROMETHEUS

Zeus isn't one to allow anyone to live in peace all that often: not his favorites, not his enemies.

Prometheus indicates his manacles with a flick of his fingers.

He is both fickle and heartless with his favors, as you have learned. But do not give

    up hope, my daughter. For I have the gift of
    foresight and I can see into your future, as
    well as my own.

IO
    I cannot imagine anything you can tell me that
    would ease my heart.

And here River staggered to one knee and went off script.

"And even if there was anything, I'm nearly done for. It's getting worse and scarier and I don't know if I'm strong enough to make it." She looked up at Simon. A tear ran down one cheek and mingled with drops of blood from the cut under her eye. Her heart felt like it was quietly breaking. Her throat was tight and hot.

Simon's kind eyes filled with tears. He glanced sharply at someone in the audience and motioned with his head. He responded with the scripted line, his eyes begging her to stay with him.

PROMETHEUS
    Dear child, you must not despair! Listen to
    me. I see your future as clearly as I can see
    my own! You shall be set free, dear child.
    Zeus will see you safely to a new land and
    return you to your human form. And you will
    thrive, and your children will thrive!

    Stand up, child!

River tried to stand. She really did. She just couldn't seem to make her legs and arms move the right way. She sprawled like an ungainly bug, and sobbed.

The audience was silent. Everyone was holding their breath. Simon struggled with his prop manacles. Tears fell from his eyes and splashed on the stage near River's outstretched hand.

She heard footsteps, and was confused. Nobody was supposed to run out onstage just now, unless it was the damned Gadfly again! She struggled to move, and felt strong hands helping her to sit up.

She flinched, afraid to see who it was, terrified it was Dane, or worse, Rhiannon.

A low, rumbly voice sounded in her ear. "It's okay, honey. It's okay. Everything is going to be okay." Familiar whiskers scratched her cheek.

"Dad? Daddy?" She turned to see and there he was, big and brown and wearing rumpled green BDUs that didn't look like they fit him very well. He knelt over her and held her in his strong arms.

"Yeah, baby. I'm home. Are you okay?" His amber eyes peered down at her appraisingly. "You're bleeding. It doesn't look too bad, but I want to get you checked out. You're way too pale. Can you stand?"

River heard murmuring from the audience, people looking around, wondering if this was part of the play or what the heck was going on.

"Yeah, I think so," River said. "I think I can." She grinned hugely at him and, with his help, struggled to get up. Simon had gotten himself unhooked and shimmied down the mountain. He stood close by, watching them intently. She could hear whispers and scuffling as the rest of the cast and crew backstage peered around the curtains trying to see what was happening. When River got to her feet, Simon let out a happy shout and the audience echoed it, applauding as River's dad steadied her.

Dr. Bruce strode to the front of the stage and addressed the audience directly.

"Thank you all for attending this evening's performance of *Today's Gods*. As you can see, we've had a real life hero make a surprise appearance onstage, the father of one of our actors who has been away on active duty with the US Army. He returned in time to see the play, and fortunately, just in time to rescue his daughter, our own River Inaba, who is clearly suffering from exhaustion and is about to receive medical attention backstage. She, like our whole cast, has been consumed by the play for the past four weeks, and has been giving one hundred and ten percent!

"Thank you all again for attending the play, and while we make sure everyone is attended to and cared for, please take a moment to sign the book at the back of the auditorium as you leave. We'll open up the additional balcony seating, and you're all invited, free of charge, to attend either tomorrow's matinee or tomorrow evening's performance."

The audience rose and applauded. Dr. Bruce gestured at River who, steadied between Simon and her dad, managed a weak bow before being bundled offstage. Her mom and brother were waiting there, with the school nurse.

While she sat on the table provided and was poked and prodded and each of the tiny cuts inflicted by the needle-filled burrs was dabbed with antiseptic by the nurse, her family filled her in on the details.

"Our team managed to get a ride out of the city a few days after our communications went down, but it was another seventy-two hours after that before we were able to contact headquarters and organize a lift back to the States," said her dad.

"I asked to be flown home as directly as possible. I thought I could, just maybe, make it home in time for the performance," her dad told her. "Sorry I didn't have time to pick up flowers!"

Her mom supplied, "He showed up at the house just as we were leaving. He didn't even want to take time to change!"

"We did take time to check the mail, though," interjected Adrian, smiling mischievously.

River looked at him, confused. She had consumed half the bottle of water the nurse had pressed on her and her head was clearing, but the significance wasn't clicking. "And?" she asked.

"And this came for you," Adrian said, grinning hugely. She took the envelope from him and stared at it.

"Open it, dummy!" he cried. Simon elbowed him in the arm and he rubbed at it ruefully. He grinned at Simon hard and Simon's smile blossomed.

River stared at the envelope. It was something from school. It was already open so she clumsily drew out the single page and began to read.

Congratulations, River Inaba! You have been selected to attend the Arts and Humanities Focus Program beginning the Fall Semester of next year.

River stared. Simon crowed. Her parents beamed. Adrian whooped.

An avalanche of emotions collapsed all the breathable air around River for a moment, and she had to close her eyes and focus on inhaling and exhaling. Once she had ahold of herself she opened her eyes and grinned hugely. With that smile, all of the exhaustion and fear and pain slipped off her like a skin, and all at once, she felt like she could fly.

"It's all—it's so—I have no words! I love you all so very much!"

The giant group hug that followed lasted until Mindy timidly tapped Simon on the shoulder.

"So, hey, a bunch of us are going to Village Inn after, to celebrate. Did either of you feel like coming along?"

"Simon, if you want to go that's great," River's mom interjected firmly but kindly. "But I'm hereby declaring River grounded until at least nine a.m. tomorrow. She needs soup and quiet rest if she's going to be back onstage tomorrow for the matinee!"

River looked at Simon, a little surprised. "Tomorrow? I don't know, after tonight do you think Rhiannon and Dane will still want me in the production?"

"I believe I can answer that question," came a haughty, regal voice from behind her. River turned to see Rhiannon, still resplendently clad in her Hera costume and looking every bit the displeased goddess.

"We'll excuse you from this evening's activities as it's not every day one's father comes home from service." River heard her brother give a little snort at her pomposity. It didn't faze Rhiannon. "But we expect to see you at eleven on the dot tomorrow, ready for hair and makeup."

Rhiannon held River's gaze for a powerful moment, then leaned in and whispered, "You have to come, tomorrow, dear heart. You killed the role and we've talked the film crew into giving us a second session tomorrow, at no charge, given the unusual circumstances." She tilted her head toward River's dad and smiled engagingly at River.

River looked Rhiannon square in the eyes and said, "If you disarm Jamie and keep Miranda off my back, I'll finish the two performances. Do you agree? Will you keep your flunkies under control?"

Rhiannon was taken aback. She was entirely unaccustomed to being confronted. She glanced around at the crowd of folks surrounding River, looking at her in varying shades of fierce expectation.

"I…" she began. She looked around again, her gaze holding longest with River's dad, then decisively she said, "They will be contained." She graced everyone assembled with an imperious nod, as though everything was settled precisely to her satisfaction. Then she spun on her heel and hooked her arm through Dane's, who had just strolled up, smiling his megawatt smile.

Together, they exited, stage left.

LAST CALL AT THE RIM OF THE CENTRAL WELL

LEIGH HELLMAN

T WO STRANGERS SAT at a bar, three narrow chrome seats empty between them. They drank in slow, heavy gulps and traced sigils through the dents in the metal countertop and never said a word to each other.

They'd been like that for hours, days, weeks. It was the kind of place where nights smudged into one another and the waking world couldn't quite keep up.

Lines of harsh neon ran up the walls and along the low ceiling seams of Club Gaudia, hacking blunt chunks out of the shadows that soaked through the rest of the room. It was all icy edges without shading; everyone and everything raised out of the darkness like severe stone reliefs. Something disharmonic pumped out of the speakers—like a white noise wailing that pulsed to a beat—while a cluster of patrons stood and swayed, less with than against it.

It was the kind of place that couldn't be found unless it wanted to be.

From the outside it was nothing more than a crooked set of stairs sinking halfway into the concrete earth, dead-ended at an unmarked and dented steel door. The narrow windows bit out just above ground level but were blacked over so that nothing could be seen except a faint glow through the cracks in the paint. There was no street number, no sign, not even a handwritten note inviting you to come in or warning you to stay out. Hundreds of people walked past it every day without knowing—without needing to know—that it existed.

For those who did know, none of them seemed to remember how they'd heard about it or who'd first brought them there; most folks who ended up there never really seemed to leave. They'd climb up the stairs to the street level when the lights came up and then drift back down when the city went dark again, night after day after day after night. It was a hazy cycle—like smoke funneling into a ventless room—that ground on until all the painful shards of the outside world dulled away.

One of the bartenders slid out from behind the thick curtains that lined the back wall, separating the public area from the private back room. Her skin whirred, gleaming smooth and strange like an oil slick under the jagged lights, as she crossed the room and slipped behind the bar.

"So what about tonight?" The young man on the left, sitting closest to the street door, leaned across the counter and only slurred a little. "Will she see me tonight?"

The bartender paused, limbs locked at awkward angles. "The Mistress is still considering your request."

The man swung back on his stool—so fast that it tottered on its thin legs—and blew out a hard breath. "What's to consider? She won't even listen… she doesn't even know my story."

The bartender's lips stretched out like the calculations of a smile; she topped off his murky drink and pushed it back into his hands.

"The Mistress is always listening."

The young man scoffed into his copper mug and pushed his messy hair out of his eyes. He watched the bartender glide toward a new couple sitting at the far end of the bar; the augmentations made her movements precise but not off-putting, at least not to customers. If her expressions weren't quite natural, the couple didn't notice—or maybe they were too busy swapping whispers and giggles to notice much of anything else.

"I'm looking for someone," the young man announced it like a ribbon pulled out from the middle of a book that no one had been reading.

Four seats away, another young man glanced up from his still-full drink. Just a flinch really, like he didn't want to do it but couldn't stop himself. He was sturdier than the other man and tucked in at all the corners that the other man was rumpled and frayed at, but it seemed like something had pulled loose now. Loose enough, at least, for the other man to start tugging at it.

"I'm looking for someone," the rumpled man repeated as he shuffled one stool closer and then one more. "Not just anyone, but *someone*. Someone I knew… know… who left. Disappeared, I guess, but I know she's still out there somewhere. She's out here—in the Six Rivers, I mean, that's where I traced her to—and I'm gonna find her. That's why I'm here again, why I keep coming back, and why I've got to meet with The Mistress."

The tucked-in man tapped one finger against the lip of his mug. "I heard that The Mistress makes appointments, not the other way around."

"She'd take my appointment if she knew my story," the rumpled man grumbled. "It's worth her time, if she'd just listen."

"It must be a hell of a story," the tucked-in man looked up at the long line of crystalline bottles stacked against the bar wall. "But I wouldn't know unless I heard it."

I guess you could call it a love story if you couldn't think of anything else to call it, but that's not really what it is. Sure, it's about love, but a lot of stories are about love without being love stories. I wouldn't waste The Mistress's time with a love story that's just like the half-dozen others she could trip over any day of the week.

No, this is not a love story. It's a story about me, and her, and us.

We met at an open mic night, which was just as bad as you'd think it'd be and even worse because I was actually hosting this one. It was a few years ago when I was just out of high school and had no job and fifty journals full of art with nowhere to showcase it. So I begged a friend to beg his uncle who had a stage to give me one night a month to bring a little culture to his upstreet café; it got me an audience and it got him fresh customers, so it worked out for us both.

Then one night, it got her.

"I didn't come for the show," she told me. "But I'll stay for it."

She sat in the front row with her legs crossed and her hands folded in her lap like she was there to grade me. I started sweating under the house lights, and I never sweat. That night my songs, my poems, my art—it was all for her. I spilled them out for her to gather up and swallow down. I wanted her to digest me like a meal she didn't know she'd been craving.

But she was a picky eater; she applauded politely at the end of each piece, but I could tell that they didn't satisfy her. She was hungry for something more, a meal I hadn't learned how to make yet. I cut my set short and shoved through the huddle of regulars to catch her before she left.

"Come back next month?" I hadn't meant it to be a question, but it was.

She hesitated; maybe she didn't want to be rude, or maybe she didn't want to make a promise she wouldn't keep.

"I'll think about it," she said finally, smiling without any teeth.

"Come back tomorrow then." I wasn't brave, but something like bravery uncurled behind my ribs as I stood in front of her. "Come back for a coffee with me, or to split some overpriced café food. Come back to talk. I—I want to talk. Come back and I promise I won't hum a single chorus."

"Or recite a stanza," she added with a laugh.

"Not even a couplet." And I laughed, too.

We laughed into the next night and then the night after that. Another week, another month, another year and we kept laughing until it felt like we'd never stop. Until I believed that we wouldn't need to stop—not for anything—that we'd laugh ourselves right into our graves, chuckling into that cold yawn of death together.

The tucked-in man snorted, soft and not unkind.

"What?" The rumpled man's face pinched sour. "What's so funny about that?"

"It's not funny. I mean, I'm not laughing at you." The tucked-in man took a small sip from his mug. "It's just… that can't be right, right? No relationship is all laughter for weeks and months and years."

The rumpled man huffed. "I didn't say it was all laughter, er… what's your name?"

The tucked-in man wavered for a beat before answering. "Kenrick, but you can call me Kenny."

The rumpled man stuck out a hand. "I'm Dougal. Can't really call me anything but Dougal, though. I guess Doug could work, but I hate Doug. Don't call me Doug."

"Okay." Kenrick shook his hand, brief but firm. "I won't."

Dougal nodded. "Good. So anyway, Kenny, I didn't say it was all laughter. I said that we kept laughing. Doesn't mean that we didn't do other things too, but the laughing was what mattered. The laughing was the important part."

Kenrick crossed his arms and pivoted toward Dougal on his stool.

"Sure, the laughing's important. But maybe there's other important stuff too. Or else… why would you be here with me instead of out there with her?"

Dougal's voice dropped low. "The other stuff comes later, at the end. I've got to tell the whole story—you've got to let me tell the whole story—to really understand it. You've got to know about the laughing first though, because that's the only way I can make sense of it from the other side."

She laughed the first time I asked her to marry me. It'd been four and a half months since we met, and when I asked her as she made us both sandwiches one afternoon she laughed right in my face. Not a mean, nasty laugh, but a loud, absurd one that doubled her over the kitchen table. She laughed for a full minute and seemed so delighted that I couldn't even be mad at her about it.

I never got an answer that first time, not an absolute yes or no. So I kept asking and each time she laughed a little less until finally she didn't laugh at all.

"Why?" she asked from the other side of the bench in one of the sector transit exchanges.

It was late—dark outside the windows with only a trickle of passengers coming and going between the terminals—and we were waiting for a connection back home.

"Because"—I reached for her hand—"that's what you do when you want to spend the rest of your life with someone."

Her hand was limp in mine, but I took that to mean a healthy sort of hesitation on her part.

"You want to spend the rest of your life with me?" She echoed it back out into the wide hall. "Which me?"

It was my turn to laugh, and I did.

"The you that's sitting next to me right now. That's all the you I need." I squeezed her fingers and didn't mind that she didn't squeeze back. It was a big step, a big moment, and I knew she just needed time to bring it into focus for herself.

"I probably sound like a sucker, huh?" Dougal scratched at the nape of his neck. "Like some pathetic lovesick fool who still hasn't tossed out his rose-colored goggles."

Kenrick coughed. "No, that's not how you sound."

Dougal scoffed. "I am a fool—I'll admit that. And lovesick… well, I'm an artist after all. A poet, a creator. You can't carry all that around with you and not be a little delusional when it comes to hope and heart. But I'm *not* pathetic, so you can shuffle that pity right back into your deck."

He gulped down his drink, then dropped the copper mug onto the countertop with a sharp clang. "Even if I was pathetic, even if I was a sucker, she wouldn't have shook me down for it. I know leeches and fakes and she wasn't either of 'em. She was just shaky about commitment and settling down and all that forever stuff, that's all."

Dougal glanced at Kenrick, his features peeled out of neon and shadows. There was something interesting about the arch of his eyebrows and the bow of his lips; Dougal stared for a sticky few seconds like he was trying to figure out how he would describe that face in his next story.

"How did you know?" Kenrick asked, and it caught in his throat like it wasn't quite sure it wanted out. "How did you know that those things were what she was worried about?"

"Because I knew her—I *know* her. She didn't have to tell me. Hell, she didn't have to say anything. I knew just by looking at her, just by hearing the rattle in her voice." Dougal closed his eyes and leaned back. "It's the same way that I knew she loved me, so it didn't matter if she had doubts. She'd come around and I'd be there and it'd be the simplest thing in the world. And it was."

Kenrick turned back to the bar. "So she finally said yes?"

"She did, like I knew she would." Dougal grinned; it flashed bright before souring. "But by then the laughter had begun to dry up. The other stuff jostled around like loose bolts and before I knew what'd happened the whole thing had gone unstable under us."

You'd think that the age thing was why we held off on a ceremony—everyone was always telling us that we were too young for that kind of commitment, that we didn't understand what marriage really meant and that we'd end up regretting it.

But none of that ever bothered me.

The main reason we waited was credit. Honest art is never lucrative and the gig work I ran on the side didn't pull in much credit beyond essentials. She worked the front desk at a local free clinic, which didn't exactly rake in credit either.

I told her over and over to quit, that they didn't pay her enough and that they'd never promote her to an augmentation counselor like she wanted to be. I told her that there were hundreds of private clinics in the city that could give her the experience and the credit rate that she deserved, if she really didn't want to leave the field.

I never much liked it myself: a whole industry standing by ready to chop you up and reassemble you into something they tell you is better. Humanity is imperfection, I always say. Its beauty is in its frailty. We're built to break and I believe that gives us meaning. When you take away our flaws, our defects, our pain and disease… you take something else away, too.

But I'm getting off-topic now. I may have had a philosophical aversion to it, but if augmentation work made her happy then I wasn't going to force her out of it.

Only—it didn't seem to make her happy. She'd come home to our little sub-level unit every evening more miserable than she'd left it in the morning. She'd sulk and pick fights and eventually I stopped asking her to come to my performances. Since the night we met I'd been able to feel her energy burrowing into me onstage from her seat in the audience; I used to crave it, but now it just made my stomach turn.

"Do you want to talk about it?" I asked her carefully one day, over a reheated dinner.

She didn't look up from her plastic plate. "Talk about what?"

"This." I motioned with my fork between us. "This bitterness that's growing here. Whatever's going on with you that's feeding it. I can't ignore it anymore, or fight around it. Is it the clinic? I'm stressed about the credits too, but like I said before—"

"I wish you wouldn't do that," she snapped. "I wish you wouldn't keep blaming everything on the clinic, or on augmentation in general. You know that it saves lives—that I help to save lives by working there, even if I am just a receptionist right now. For every vanity procedure that we book, there are a dozen critical ones that are our patients' last chance for treatment."

That was a little melodramatic, but I leaned into the sincerity. "I know, I know, and I love that you care so deeply for the world. It's your art and I get that. You know that all I want is for you to be fulfilled, so if you tell me that this job is fulfilling then I'll believe you."

She still wouldn't look at me. "It's fulfilling."

"Okay." And it wasn't and we weren't, but I wasn't ready to crack that egg yet. "I believe you."

Later that night, as we lay in bed silent but not asleep, she whispered something into the dark stillness.

"What if I was augmented?"

The question floated above me but I didn't reach for it; I didn't know if I was supposed to have heard it and I wasn't in the mood for another fight. I had a gallery interview in the morning that I needed to be up for.

So I let it dissipate into the room without an answer, at least not one I said out loud. In my mind I'd already responded: *But you're not, so what does it matter?*

The neon hues in the club shifted abruptly from cool purples and blues to scratchy yellows and oranges. The main room lit up like it had caught fire; the remaining patrons recoiled from the surge of light.

It was a cue: thirty minutes to curfew. Time to start crawling out of the shadows.

The music turned down to half-volume and another augmented bartender appeared to begin collecting stray bottles and mugs. People still swayed on the dance floor but their movements were stilted now, like the fun was already over.

Dougal rummaged through his pockets and pulled out a handful of tokens; he dropped them on the bartop and they clattered like tiny fists pounding out for attention.

"This should be enough credits for my tab." He pushed the pile toward the bartender as she made her way down the bar to settle up. "And for my friend's drinks too, for listening to my tale of woe tonight."

He clapped Kenrick on the shoulder and his hand lingered heavy for a moment too long.

Kenrick shook his head. "You really don't have to—"

Dougal waved him off.

"No, no, I insist. Chivalry's not dead yet, you know." He chuckled, dry and brittle. "I used to say that to Justine, but I don't think she ever really believed me."

The bartender looked between them before scooping the tokens into her credit pouch.

"Justine?" Kenrick nodded to himself. "That was her name?"

"*Is* her name," Dougal snapped back. "It's not like she's dead."

"Isn't she?" Kenrick murmured. "I mean, how can you be so sure?"

"Because I know her, and I'd know if she wasn't here anymore!" Dougal slammed a palm against the counter loud enough to turn a few curious heads. "I know her better than she knows herself and I know that she's stubborn enough to run off after a fight and wait it out just to teach me a lesson! And I've learned that lesson—I swear I have—so it's time for her to come home now. I just… I need her to come home now."

He hit the counter again, but this time it landed dull and weak.

Kenrick stared hard at him. "What's the lesson?"

Dougal blinked. "What?"

"The lesson you learned," Kenrick repeated it slowly. "What was it?"

Dougal hesitated and, like a summoning, someone else filled the empty space.

"Now *that's* a question worth asking, ain't it, honey bee?"

A deep, rich voice seeped out of the tall, dark woman who suddenly loomed over them both. Her body was strong; lush velvet robes wrapped around her broad shoulders and gathered loose around her waist before tumbling to the floor. Her lips were stained black and she was bald, nothing but a sheen to cover the hills and valleys of her skull. She grinned down at them, not really menacing but not entirely friendly either.

Her teeth were bone-white against the darkness. "Now I've been listening—you know, I'm always listening—and it sounds like you're certain about your story. But I'm not so sure, and I can't make judgments with not-so-sures."

"You're The Mistress," Dougal's eyes went wide. "But—but you haven't heard the whole thing yet! Once you hear it, you'll be sure too."

The Mistress's gaze pierced Dougal like pins through a balloon, but he didn't wither away. Then she glanced at Kenrick and—with a hand coated in glittering jewels—swept them off their stools and toward the heavy curtains that guarded the fabled back room.

It was a small space, nothing more than an annex really, but the sparse furnishings and long shadows made it seem bigger somehow. It heaved like it was full of something intangible—secrets, pleas, verdicts—but there was nothing physically there beyond an old fainting couch upholstered in a shock of pink and several scattered sitting pillows in a confetti of prints and colors. The walls were lined with splotched mirrors that threw reflections in every direction. Three augmented bartenders were already there, sprawled out on a cluster of pillows in the far corner of the room.

The Mistress draped herself over the long pink couch and gestured for the boys to sit. Kenrick rearranged a pillow covered in soft curls while Dougal dropped down onto the naked stone floor.

"You've got a tale to finish weaving, don't you, lover boy?" The Mistress cooed like honey smoothed over a glue trap. "Well, get to it then."

Dougal bristled against the directive. He hemmed and hawed for a few seconds, shifting around on the hard ground, before climbing back into his story.

Justine was gone on a Sunday. I say gone because that's what she was, that's what I know her to be. Not left, not vanished, not missing or dead—just gone. With me and then not.

We were out at the District Gardens that day. It'd been raining all morning so they'd put up the holodome by the time we got there. I never really cared for the Gardens; they always felt too outlined and manicured to truly be beautiful. I'd talk about taking a road trip to the Overgrowth and roughing it out there for a while. See what the world humanity left behind is like. That's nature's beauty—the Gardens are just an easy little reproduction for us to consume and discard.

Justine didn't see it that way, which seemed to be happening more and more with my opinions, but she never pushed me to go either. She'd go by herself on her days off, and once in a while she'd take a half day and spend her afternoon there. It was two sectors from the clinic in the opposite direction from our unit, but it didn't seem to matter. I asked her once why she liked the place so much and she just shrugged.

"Nothing else in this city decays," she told me. "I think we need that. It reminds us that we're made for change."

That day was my idea; I got up early to pack two lunches and threw out the suggestion over breakfast.

"Why?" she asked between mouthfuls of bran squares. "You hate the Gardens."

"I don't *hate* them," I countered. "I just don't believe in their artistic thesis."

She rolled her eyes and grunted.

"But, more importantly, you like them. And I like you, in case that wasn't clear." I punctuated my point with my spoon. "I'm trying to make that clear."

I meant that; I'd tucked a little box with a thin silver ring inside the lunch packs. It didn't have any stones but it was stamped on the inside with the date that we'd first met at my open mic night and—when she said "I do"—I was going to have it stamped with that date too. It had been collecting lint in my pockets for a few months, ever since I'd saved up enough credits for it and the paperwork that went along with making it all legal, but the whole prospect of a ceremony had seemed to be tying her up in knots. So I was gonna take her to her favorite place, let her smell some hothouse flowers, and then bring her over to the judicial center and get it over with. It was just across the street from the Gardens' west gate, like the double-trip was expected, and then it would be done and there'd be nothing else for her to worry about.

No expensive one-time outfits, no uncomfortably distant relatives, no complaints that the food was too bland or the music was too loud or there weren't enough drinks to go around. Just us, me and her, like it was supposed to be.

It was busier than I thought it'd be and I had to hustle us along if we were going to make it to the judicial center before all the clerks clocked out for the day. We meandered through hall after hall of greenery; it was pretty enough but I couldn't see much difference from one collection to the next. What I knew was that there was a sculpted waterfall that tumbled over the ledge at the last hall and framed a huge window that looked out onto the western row of municipal government buildings, and that was where I was gonna sweep her into my arms and tell her that today was the day.

It was in the second to last hall—one that was full of the syrup-sweet smell of tropical flowers and piped-in loops of bird chirps and squawks—that she stopped and bent over a bush full of white blooms that bled into bright centers.

She breathed their scent in deep; when she spoke she was looking at them and not me.

"These are classified as perfect flowers—did you know that?"

"Uh-huh." I glanced at the timefeed on my wristband. "They're nice."

"I envy them." She paused, then straightened back up. "I've got to go to the toilets. I'll be right back."

"Sure thing." I watched her walk away before turning back toward the exit signs to the next hall.

I thought about moving to wait by the doors so that I could wave her over as soon as she came back. I thought about taking her hand and leading her through the droves of aimless tourists, swearing that I had a big surprise for her. I thought about just telling her now and skipping the waterfall bit altogether. The ring box—tucked into the inner pocket of my coat—thudded against my chest; it matched the pounding of my heart on the other side of my ribcage.

I thought and I waited. I was so distracted by my plans that I didn't realize how long it'd been until the crowd started to thin. I went over to the toilets, knocked, asked people coming out if there was anyone who looked like Justine still in there. I shouted past the jammed-up line and didn't get an answer. I wrangled a few security officers, begged them to put out an announcement. I retraced our steps back to the welcome desk, and then followed them again all the way to the waterfall. I tried to call her, but her line was dead.

I stood there, staring out the great wide west window with the setting sun in my eyes and her wedding ring hanging like a stone against my heart.

That was it—she was gone.

"But that's not really right, is it, lover boy?" The Mistress cut in. "If this person were truly gone, you wouldn't have been able to track them here like you claimed you did."

She leaned forward; one sleeve of her lush gown slid off her shoulder.

"Unless, of course, you were lying about that." She clicked her tongue and turned to Kenrick. "What do you think?"

Kenrick's spine went stiff. "What do I think?"

The Mistress hummed. "That's what I said."

There was a long beat, the tick of time muffled in the humid air.

"I—I think," Kenrick stuttered, "I think that Dougal's telling the truth."

"Whose truth?" The Mistress let the gown slide off her other shoulder too, revealing thick lines of over-healed scars.

Only augmentation left scars as deep as that—augmentation that had been done decades ago, or at least using decades-old equipment, from before the seamless technology came into the mainstream. Back when it was still done in dank downstreet operating rooms, unlicensed and off-the-books. Back when you had to know someone who knew someone to even get on a list, when you didn't use full names and no one kept you on file. You'd get the cuts and then get wrapped up in discount gauze and shuffled out the back way with two little bottles: one full of antibiotic tabs and the other full of pain tabs. You'd heal however you healed, if you healed at all, and you wore the scars along with the rest of the new you.

Dougal didn't know about any of that, didn't know augmentation unless it was shiny and slick, so he stared.

Kenrick did not.

"His truth," Kenrick answered. "Our truth is the only one any of us can really tell."

"She was gone that day," Dougal elbowed back into the conversation. "I didn't lie about that. Folks said they saw her here or talked to her there, and I kept hearing about the Six Rivers, but I never saw her again. She was gone to me."

"Gone to you, but you still want to reclaim them." The Mistress reached out and petted the bartender nearest to her. "Why?"

Dougal stood up so fast that he rocked on his heels. "Because I love her! And because I—she—I deserve—I need to know what happened!"

The Mistress narrowed her eyes. "Are you sure about that?"

"That I need to know? Yes, I'm sure!" Dougal began to pace. "If I knew what happened, I'd know how to fix it. If I knew how to fix it, I'd do it and she'd come back to me."

"If she wanted to," Kenrick added quietly.

"Yeah, yeah, of course if she wanted to." Dougal nodded him off. "Once I clear all of this up, she'll want to. I've searched for her, after all. I didn't give up. I've come to save her."

"So you say." The Mistress watched the two men carefully, lingering on the twitches of their faces. "All right, come with me."

She sailed up from the sofa and out through the curtains, leaving the boys and the bartenders in her wake. Dougal scrambled after her; Kenrick followed slower, like he was dragging weight behind him.

The customers—still foggy from the pulsing darkness—wandered toward the stairs that lead up to the street. The door near the top kept opening and closing, cutting into the dim club with shards of fluorescent light and the soft pricks of the morning sun.

The Mistress stood behind the bar with her hands splayed out along the metal counter, counting off the midnight citizens as they emptied out of her realm.

She pointed toward the light. "You will leave now, and once you're gone you'll have the answers you need."

"What? What's that supposed to mean? Is that all I get for my story—some cryptic mystical riddle mumbo jumbo?" Dougal frowned. "Where's Justine?"

"She's gone, and you already know that." The Mistress's smile burned like salt in a wound. "Now if you want to know why, you'll go up those stairs and not look back. And you'll answer one more question for us."

Dougal crossed his arms and stood stock still, but The Mistress shook her head.

"You don't get the question until you're at the door."

He threw up his hands. "Fine, whatever! If some jacked-up sphinx game will get me to her, I'll play along."

Dougal took one last look around—past The Mistress and the bartenders who now flanked her, past the discarded stools that clustered around the bar and the spinning lights that still skipped across the empty dance floor, past Kenrick who stood off to the side with his hands stuffed in his pockets—and then trailed after the stragglers toward the exit.

He walked up the steps one by one, momentarily blinded each time the door creaked open ahead of him. At the top he propped the door open, letting the last customers push past him and up to the street.

"So"—he turned back toward the shadows of the club—"what's this last ques...tion...?"

He stammered, then fell silent. Kenrick stood at the bottom of the stairs with his overshirt peeled off, exposing his arms and shoulders and a deep 'V' at his neckline.

"What's my favorite flower?" Kenrick asked, quiet like a pack of dirt in a steel trough.

Dougal's eyes went big and wild. "What?"

"My favorite flower," Kenrick repeated. "The one that I told you I envied that day at the District Gardens. What's it called?"

Dougal sputtered, his gaze tracing the broad scar lines that sliced along Kenrick's exposed skin. They were fresh, pulled tighter and redder than The Mistress's were, and carved out something new from a suddenly-familiar pattern. The veins in the hands, the shell of the ears, the curve of the eyelids—Dougal recognized them now.

"Justine?" His voice rattled out of his throat.

"*Kenrick*." The other man climbed the first step, and then the second. "What's the name of my favorite flower?"

Dougal blinked fast, tried to blot the light glare out. Kenrick was backlit—ringed in a tinge of bright against blackness—which kept him from coming completely into focus.

"The perfect flower?" It was tentative, hesitant like he'd crawled back into his memories and sifted through the puzzle pieces of his story to find it, but there was nothing there.

Just a hole.

"Does it matter? Would that fix things?" Dougal's voice cracked as he staggered back through the doorway. "Is that why all of this happened?"

A moment stretched out like a chasm between them and within it neither one made the move to jump.

"No," Kenrick sighed as he took the last few steps to meet him. "But it's hibiscus, Dougal. It's always been hibiscus."

Then Kenrick reached past him for the door handle and pulled, leaving Dougal to stumble out onto the street and watch as the windowless steel door slammed shut behind him.

IΠ PURSUIT

JESSICA GUNN

ORION

AMARA LEANED BACK in her seat against the window. Sun poured in, lighting her tanned complexion and bright green eyes with a warm glow. She was beautiful like this, bathed in sunlight. She had a graceful sort of face that reminded me of all the marble statues from ancient Greece.

The moment was interrupted by a table full of werewolves laughing and talking in hushed tones as they looked at both of us. I glanced away from my best friend long enough to shoot one of them a glare.

Amara chuckled, a sound that made happiness rush through me, and leaned in. "I think he's into you, Pheme. That's no reason to glare."

"Well, it's not going to happen," I said a little louder than was necessary. Aside from the fact that I really wasn't into guys, he was also a werewolf. They all were. And supernaturals, to me, were big no-gos.

The werewolf men—fellow students at our local college—voiced their disappointment and howled at the "he" Amara was talking about. They patted him on the back as if to soothe his ego as he tried to hide his flushed face. As if it was impossible for him to be rejected.

I flicked my long, blonde hair over my shoulder and focused on the coffee in front of me. "And here I thought the last final of our freshman year would be the hardest part of today."

Amara made a face. "Oh, come on. It's not that bad."

"They're *werewolves*." That should have explained enough.

Supernaturals and humans may have lived together for some time now, but that coexistence wasn't entirely peaceful. I'd been raised to believe that most wanted to prey on humans. Especially the more predatory breeds like werewolves and vampires. And even if they didn't actively attack humans, many of the other supernatural races still made great sport out of tricking or enchanting us.

That was where the Midnight Order came in. *My* Order, the one my parents had made me join as a young teenager. The Midnight Order had trained me to covertly fight against all supernaturals, starting with the deadliest—a list where werewolves were second from the top. One by one, our Order would rid the world of all supernaturals until, with any luck, none more would survive.

It was a little extreme, granted. But it was all I'd ever really known.

Amara sipped her hot chai latte. "They're also still human. They live just like the rest of us, Pheme. Live and work and love and *be*."

I glanced at her over the top of my coffee. "Well, they should *be* elsewhere. Not in college with us." And certainly not intermingling as though they couldn't rip out our hearts if they got pissed enough.

A shudder rolled down my spine. Just last week, another member of the Order had gotten into a nasty fight with a couple of werewolves. We'd been trying to track their pack's den in retribution ever since.

The facade of supernaturals coexisting peacefully beside humans only stood up if you didn't examine it that closely. If you didn't look past the sharing of colleges and stores and homes to all the vampire attacks and faerie death circles and shifter violence.

That was why, even though the Midnight Order was a bit extreme, our work was important.

Amara had no idea what I'd been doing. Every night, I pretended to do time as a cashier at a store outside the city. And every night, I lied to my best friend so she wouldn't know that when the sun went down, my alter ego, Orion—and her anti-supernatural work—took over my life.

Amara sighed heavily and rolled her eyes. "It's too early in the morning to be having this argument with you again. Besides, I hate it when we fight."

"This isn't a fight," I said. "It's just facts."

Amara leaned over the table and pointed as subtly as one could to another table of werewolves in the corner. These were a family, with a father, a mother, and three kids. They appeared almost human in their non-shifted forms except for the excessive hair and yellowed eyes. "Do they look dangerous to you? No. They're parents and some kids. They're not what you hear about on the news."

I wanted to believe Amara. But while I may not have ascribed to the intense black and white moral world views of the Midnight Order, I'd certainly seen my fair share of violence from both humans *and* supernaturals. Otherwise, I wouldn't do what I do. "The news doesn't tell you everything."

"No," Amara admitted as she relaxed back into the sunlit window.

Outside, spring was in full bloom with summer right around the corner. I wanted to forget all of this and spend it with her. Every single day as long as possible. Amara had been my best friend for as long as I could remember. But lately, it had begun to feel like there was something more between us. Something a lot different than friendship. Even if we didn't agree on supernaturals and their inherent danger. At least with my skills, I could keep her safe if any of them ever tried to prove to Amara just how dangerous they could be.

Suddenly, Amara sat up straight again with a finger held in front of her. "You know what the news *does* tell me, though?"

"What's that?" I asked before sipping more of my coffee.

"That Orion's been busy again." She clicked her tongue. "They're so active lately. Those poor victims' families."

I kept the coffee up to my mouth for a moment longer than necessary to hide the twitch of my lips and the hitch in my breath. If Amara only knew what she was saying… to *whom* she was saying it. "Yeah. That's crazy."

To the rest of the world, Orion was some agent of the Midnight Order who ruthlessly attacked supernaturals seemingly on a whim. There wasn't a pattern to the kills that they could find. Not even a trace of what their identity could be since they attacked from afar. All specialized arrows, each marked with their name.

My name. My alter ego's name, anyway. The one with which the Midnight Order had awarded me after I'd completed my training.

"Maybe they just see the evil supernaturals—" I started, but Amara shot me a glance that had me changing my words immediately. "What they *can* bring. The bad things. The attacks and the faerie deals. Maybe Orion is trying to stop that."

Amara's eyes narrowed. "You're trying awfully hard to justify murder, Pheme. Should I be worried?"

My heart leapt up into my throat. "No. I'm just saying—" My phone vibrated loudly on the table before us. *Saved by the text.* I grabbed it and began reading as I continued with, "Maybe there's a reason for Orion's actions, too. There're three sides to every story, after all. Right? Isn't that what our entire Journalism final was about?"

Amara chuckled dryly. "Fine, fine." But she didn't sound the least bit convinced.

Mom: We've located the den. You're on for tonight. Be safe, honey. They're ferocious.

All werewolves were. Mom didn't need to remind me.

And yet I couldn't help that my gaze traveled back to the family of werewolf shifters. Amara was right. *They* didn't seem that ferocious. They seemed… normal.

I didn't know what to believe. Only that it was easier to do as I was told.

Amara drank the rest of her chai in a hurry. "We should get going. We have to get ready for the party tonight."

Every time Amara's parents left on a business trip, Amara threw a party. It was as predictable as a clock. And honestly, I could use the distraction. But first I had work to do.

I grinned. "You know I'll be there."

Amara's eyes narrowed playfully. "I sense a 'but' coming."

"But," I relented, my grin growing wider, "I do still have to go to work first."

"*Pheme*." She groaned. "For real? You can't call out this one night?"

I couldn't call out the last several times she'd thrown a party, either. But I couldn't exactly tell my friend that one doesn't simply call out sick on the Midnight Order. "I'll get out as early as I can. I'll be there."

Amara reached across the table and touched a hand to mine. Freckles reflected back at me there, arranged like the constellation Scorpius. Even that small contact alone sent butterflies somersaulting in my stomach. "Do you promise?"

"I promise."

I'd always be there for Amara no matter what I did for the Midnight Order.

My phone vibrated in my pocket. I cringed, imagining the sound of it carrying farther out into the night than it really did. It *shouldn't* have been a problem except werewolves had superhuman hearing. Usually, my phone wasn't even *on* during a mission. How had I forgotten?

What a rookie move.

I slowly notched an arrow with calloused fingers in case that text message drew my prey to me. Werewolves were vicious, resourceful creatures that hunted in packs. And no matter what Amara had said to me earlier, I was no more ready to make myself an easy target than shrug off my duty to the Midnight Order. At least for tonight. My words to Amara earlier about there being three sides to every story had made me begin to reconsider some things, even if I was using it against her at the time. I *was* right about that. But an order was an order, and my oath mattered. Whatever their story, all supernaturals had the capacity for true evil—far beyond that of humans.

A bead of sweat rolled down the side of my temple, and it wasn't from the extreme heatwave we'd been dealing with for days now. I realized, belatedly, that when I'd been given this order, I'd forgotten that part about hunting in packs. Not because I didn't know that information—I was the best in the city's supernatural hunting business. But because for *some reason*, I'd thought I would never fight an entire pack at once alone. My targets tended to be single in nature at the time of the hunt.

Human like us, Amara had said. Amara must have never seen a pack of werewolves attack a lone person before—regardless of who'd instigated it.

More footfalls echoed down the alley below. I crouched down the fire escape on which I was currently perched. Near the top, there was no chance anyone from inside the building would notice me, nor anyone from below. On the other side of the alley, nestled between two four-story tall brick buildings, was a secret entrance to a *supposed* werewolf den. The one my Order had been looking for since we'd nearly lost one of our own.

I wasn't intending to go after the entire den. I didn't think I'd have to. But as my mark—an overly hairy man in his thirties, not yet shifted for the rising full moon tomorrow night—made his way down the alley, another two showed up. Two that, with a sinking dread thick in my stomach, I realized I recognized.

It was the parents from the coffee shop earlier this morning.

Oh no.

For a split second, my resolve wavered. The memory of them with their kids, having an everyday experience out and about. So *normal* despite being a supernatural.

Remember your oath. Remember how many have died.

I swallowed down any wavering feelings and focused on the silver-tipped arrow waiting on my bow. I was a good shot. But I wasn't sure if I could get all three at once. And if I *didn't* get all three, they might see me and make everything so much worse. While Orion's identity was a secret, my mask was not. Neither were my arrows. Each was a calling card announcing my presence.

Holding the arrow in place with one hand, I drew three more. Two for the additional targets. One for good luck. I positioned them in the hand holding the bowstring, precariously balancing them between my ring and pinky fingers.

Other supernatural hunters preferred guns for this very reason. Not me. Guns could be loud. Messy. Too easily tracked.

My phone vibrated again. Louder this time, if possible. A prolonged vibration that indicated a phone call.

I hissed. Too loudly. The werewolves turned in unison and glanced up to my exact perch on the fire escape. My mark opened his mouth, about to call out a warning, but I let the notched arrow fly right into his chest.

The other two werewolves froze. Just for a moment long enough for me to stand and notch another arrow.

"Run!" the male told his wife, and they turned and sprinted for the mouth of the alley—*not* to the entrance to the werewolf den. Clever. I, as well as my Order, knew the door was there, but not exactly *where* it was. Magic doors were fickle things.

I let loose a second arrow as they began to run. This one found its home easily into the male. I tried not to think of what his children would think about what I'd done. About all my victims' families.

He slumped to the ground almost immediately as the silver poisoned his body. While his heart gave out. Just like that, it was over. Another werewolf out of the picture. Another human who might be safer because of it.

I smiled, although keeping the smile was tough, given how Amara's words had made my resolve waver. This was my gift, though. My entire oath to my Order. To rid the world of supernatural creatures and to do so with the mercy of a swift end. So that humans might be safe in a way we hadn't been in so long.

One werewolf left. She began running, her footsteps pounding on the pavement.

I moved fast, climbing down staircase after staircase to reach the bottom quicker. I'd lost sight of her from where I'd been perched, and she was moving too swiftly for me to have any hope of hitting her at such a weird angle.

She was almost to the mouth of the alley when I'd given up on the stairs and, with only a story drop, jumped from the fire escape and rolled into a landing that only *sort of* forced air from my lungs and pain into my legs.

I stood immediately and fired. The arrow went wide, narrowly missing her shoulder.

"Stay away from me!" she screamed. "I'm innocent!"

I cringed again. Her voice carried through the night as if on a stereo. This was supposed to have been a quiet job. A quick one. And already I'd had too many setbacks, not least of all wavering when it came to my duty.

I notched the last of my silver-tipped arrows and aimed for her back, right where her heart would have been.

"Help!" she screamed even louder. "Orion is—"

I let the arrow go as she spoke my Order name. My identity. My calling card.

Orion. The best supernatural hunter in this entire city.

A sharp *thwack* sounded. A second later, the arrow found a home exactly where I'd aimed.

I rested for only a moment, allowing a single second of satisfaction over a job completed, before jumping up and grabbing on to the fire escape again. With a heave, I landed on the metal and ran up its many staircases. I had to get out of here before anybody saw me or, worse, tracked me back to Order headquarters.

Let my arrows do the talking for me.

Only when I was safe several streets away did I pull out my phone to make sure it wasn't the Midnight Order trying to contact me. Two texts. One missed call. All from Amara.

A relieved smile graced my lips, followed by an overwhelming sense of warm and calmness. No matter how sideways a job went or how bad my night had gone, a single message from Amara chased away everything bad.

Amara: You're still coming tonight, riiiight?

Amara: Pheme? Come on. You said you wouldn't be this late! The party's already started.

I bit the inside of my cheek. As much as I'd wanted nothing more than to dance the night away with Amara and her friends, this was my duty. My oath.

But my oath and my heart saw two different paths. And right now, my heart was winning. *Amara.* She'd be buzzed by now with a constant blush lighting her face. I loved her like that, smiling and carefree.

Pheme: Finally off shift! Be there in twenty. Just had to sneak past the werewolf guarding the door.

I'd meant my "boss"—and she'd assume as much. But before going to Amara's, I'd need to report in to the Order about this werewolf job.

I was already on my way to headquarters when Amara replied.

Amara: Ha ha. Funny. Some might find that offensive. Get here soon!

Amara had always been a supernatural fan.

I wondered what she'd think of me if she knew what I did at night.

SCORPIO

"Everything okay?" Pheme's voice carried over the pop music blaring from the speakers of my family's house. It was here, between ostentatious and expensive paintings and more bottles of fine liquor than any college freshman should have access to, that I felt most free these days. At least when my parents weren't around and the house was instead filled with friends. Around us, they danced the night away to the tune of finals ending.

When I didn't respond right away, Pheme laid a hand on my arm. She ducked down so our eyes were level, a concerned twist in her brow. "Amara?"

I clicked the lock button on my phone to hide the text messages.

Orion struck again tonight. Your mother has moved you to the top of the task force. Bring Orion in for justice, Scorpio.

I gulped. The last thing Pheme needed tonight was learning that my parents weren't only heads of the Peacekeeper Task Force in the city, but that I'd been recruited into it too. Four years ago, at the start of high school, I'd taken an oath to keep peace within the city, and to protect all of its citizens from the supernatural hunters and civilian dissent.

All of that training, along with a heavy dose of preternatural talent, had turned me into the best in the force.

It also didn't help that I happened to be a master with poisons. That had been thanks to my family's scorpion-shifter heritage despite the fact that we'd lost our access to those shifter forms some time ago.

Pheme snapped her fingers and laughed. "Earth to Amara. What's going on?"

I chuckled too, although it was a little too empty a sound. "My parents' trip got extended, that's all."

Which wasn't totally a lie. They *were* away on official task force business, and those trips tended to get extended at the last second. That was what happened when you owned and ran such a task force. Other cities wanted to model theirs after yours, and now my parents traveled often.

Pheme's smile fell for a single moment before a downright mischievous look overtook her face. One that sent butterflies fluttering through my belly. She had fair skin but bright, vivid eyes that always made me feel as though she could see right through me. Pheme's high cheekbones and sharp nose gave her an intimidating appearance, but I knew better. "You know what that means, right?"

I know what I *wanted* it to mean. But Pheme had never stayed the night. Not once, even as kids. She'd always blamed it on her parents. But now that we were in college, the excuses sort of fell apart. I'd taken to attributing it to some sort of weird fear of sleeping in unfamiliar places. I had the same issue when traveling myself. Besides, she'd been my best friend for years. I'd never hold this against her.

But I'd also wished we'd been more than best friends for almost as long.

I raised an eyebrow and leaned in conspiratorially. "I'm guessing you have an idea or two?"

Pheme lifted a finger. "Several, in fact. Including an extra shopping trip, raiding your parents' special liquor cabinet, and having *at least* two more parties."

I pushed her finger down. "Or we ask Philip to buy us the alcohol, stream some cute movies, and have a night in instead." I hoped my tone wasn't too telling. I was okay with partying and our friend, Philip, buying us all the alcohol we'd ever need. But a night with Pheme to myself sounded leagues better. Even if we weren't *a thing*.

Weren't we, though?

The chemistry was there. Tension, too. Or maybe that was just the raging beat of my own heart thudding in my ears. Maybe she didn't feel it at all.

I pulled in a breath to steady myself, but it sounded a bit too much like a sigh instead.

"Oh," Pheme said, sounding a little disappointed herself. "I mean, sure. Yeah, we can do that, too. Saturday?"

"Not Saturday. I have to be at the gala event at the art museum—"

Pheme rose in her seat and took on an arrogant pose and terrible British accent. "To represent the family." She rolled her eyes. "I know, I know. I'm sorry I forgot. You know, your parents could have seriously just asked someone else to go instead. Then you could just be, I don't know, a normal college student?"

There's no normal when your parents own the city's peacekeeping task force.

"Maybe next time," I offered. In truth, my parents were also wealthy art dealers, and that was what the gala event was about. A charity auction for the museum. Wealth begot wealth, and with it, strange rules and expectations. Such as your college-aged daughter representing a multimillion-dollar company in your absence.

An idea dawned on me. I grinned. "You should come. Be my plus one?"

Pheme cringed. "I don't know. That's not really my scene."

I took her hands and tried not to completely melt from the way her fingers seemed to fit between mine as if we'd been made for each other.

Her fair skin was warm but not clammy, her fingers strong and calloused on one hand from years of playing the cello. I loved the way her hands felt in mine even more than I loved listening to her play. "Oh, come on. There will be free food and maybe even drinks depending on who's working the bar."

"Amara…"

"Please?" I asked, my turn to meet her beautiful green eyes and put on a mask of pleading. I knew she'd cave, but I had to work on her first. "It'll be fun, Pheme. I promise."

A look of genuine uncertainty crossed her eyes. "I don't know."

"All you have to do is show up on time." My tone raised by the end, a joke.

At this, Pheme finally laughed and relented. "Fine, fine. I'll be there *and* on time."

"Good! You owe me for tonight."

Pheme raised an eyebrow. "Oh, do I?"

I stood and dragged her with me as a particularly bouncy song came on. Back toward the crowd of our dancing friends. "Yes! You owe me a dance."

"Okay," she said slowly, but with a grin that told me she was mine for at least this song. A playful smile that lit the deepest parts of myself with warmth and happiness.

My cheeks flushed and I tried not to stumble as we joined our friends. The way she smiled at me now, maybe she really *was* mine. At least for a few minutes.

But those thoughts didn't stand the test of duty. Because as soon as I was able to put my nerves away, my mother's text message came flying back to me.

Bring Orion in for justice.

ORION

Something in my gut told me to return to the werewolf den. Given the death of three of their own just outside their secret door, logic would say that the rest of the pack might move house. That I didn't mind. We'd track them down again the same as always *and* hopefully find their secret door this time.

What worried me was the possibility of witnesses to last night's hunt.

I gripped my bow tightly as I hopped from rooftop to rooftop. In a city as packed as this, it was easy enough to do. I savored it.

As cautiously as I dared, I edged closer to the end of the rooftop overlooking the fire escape I'd perched on last night and the alleyway below. I scouted out the nearby buildings. *Someone* had to have heard the werewolves shouting—someone beside their kind inside. Call it intuition. A gut feeling. And right now, that feeling was twisting my gut into writhing snakes.

I didn't care if someone pinned the murders on me. That was why I used marked arrows after all. What I cared about was if someone had identified me somehow. If they had caught me in the act.

Usually, my jobs were conducted away from prying eyes.

I set the bow down beside me and peered over the edge. No movement in the alley below. No lights on in any of the windows nearby. No unnatural sounds for this area of the city. It was as if I'd entered a completely abandoned section of the city.

Movement. I caught the shuffling of feet behind me and the tail end of a siren in the distance. I turned, already pulling my bow to me with one hand and reaching for an arrow to notch with the other. A flash of metal soared toward me. A knife bounced off the arrow with a *pling*. The arrow fell out of my hand and down over the edge of the roof, echoing against the fire escape below.

I looked up. Another masked individual. But they didn't wear the black-and-purple colors of my Order, nor a monstrous mask like mine.

They wore *peace keeper* armor. The sleek, government-issued black armor and facemask over military boots that held a utility belt around their middle. *Her* middle, I realized, as my eyes adjusted. Her armor hugged the curves of her body.

She withdrew more knives from sheaths at her waist and on her forearms.

I tilted my head and quickly assessed her, but nothing about her stance or the way she carried herself gave me any indication of how tough she might be in a fight.

Except her aim. She could have put that knife right through my hand but hadn't. Why? Why had she knocked the arrow away instead?

My arrow fingers flexed, itching to notch one to my bow.

They want to take me in. The realization slid over me like cool water. I licked my lips behind my mask and took in several quick but soothing breaths, steeling myself.

I wouldn't be taken in to justice. No supernatural bounty hunter ever made it out of the peace keepers' headquarters alive.

I reached for an arrow at the same time I stepped backward. She immediately threw another knife as I'd expected, but I sidestepped it and launched myself over the edge of the roof, landing heavily on the fire escape below.

A squeak of surprise sounded on her lips. I grinned as I jumped off the fire escape again, rolling into a landing in the alleyway. My legs screamed with the impact, but I forced them to keep moving. Especially as the peace keeper landed deftly behind me a little *too* gracefully.

With the agile movements of a supernatural.

I notched an arrow before she fully recovered and stared her down, ever aware that her backup could be right behind her. With my back to the mouth of the alley, it *should* assure me an exit still within reach. But it could also lead to me being trapped if I wasn't careful.

"Don't make this difficult," she said, although her voice had been scrambled by some sort of voice-changing technology. She sounded more like a government robot than a woman. "You're wanted for the murder of at least three of this pack's werewolves, not to mention dozens of other—"

I let the arrow loose. She sidestepped it and threw a knife. I dodged it easily enough and rushed her, already notching another arrow. I didn't need to listen to my crimes being read off by a supernatural sympathizer. My kills had been done in the name of making civilization safe from supernaturals again. No more vampires killing freely. No more necromancers raising the dead against their will. No more humans assisting when half their population was falling victims to the monsters.

My second arrow caught her in the shoulder. She hissed loudly as I notched another, but she managed to throw her other knife at me with unfettered force. It skimmed off the armor piece on my shoulder. She knocked away my third arrow, shot from only a few feet away, with armored plating on her hand.

I cursed loudly. The peace keepers had armor that blocked most metal. Those unfair bastards.

But still… The force of the arrow knocked the armor plating aside and the poison at the tip of this specific one ate through part of her glove almost immediately. And although I briefly caught sight of it dripping onto her skin, she didn't seem affected by it. Which was… impossible.

Last night, I'd carried silver-tipped arrows specifically for the werewolves. But normally I carried arrows tipped in my signature poison, a concoction that killed even if a mark got away from me like the werewolves almost had last night.

She took a few steps back, losing a split second to glance at her own hand. Tanned skin shown there thanks to the poison eating away at her gloves like an acid, and a smattering of freckles in a place people usually didn't have them.

Arranged in a way only one person I'd ever known had.

Arranged like the constellation Scorpius.

No. Could it be? That was impossible. My breath whooshed from my lungs as an impossible realization hit. It froze me in place, precious seconds ticking by.

Seconds the peace keeper—*Amara*, somehow—used to recover and draw another knife. I was too slow. This swipe slashed right across my arm. She followed up quickly with a lunge and a barrage of punches that battered my face and forced me to drop my bow to defend. It clattered on the alleyway ground.

I didn't want to hurt my best friend. I still didn't believe it was her. Amara *clearly* didn't know it was me beneath this mask, either.

But *she* was a peace keeper. *Amara.*

A flash of her dancing with a blush on her face clashed with the government warrior I saw before me. With the poison that didn't seem to affect her. The visage knocked me off guard.

Amara tackled me to the ground. She pinned me, but I flipped, rolling us over and over again until we slammed into a wall. She reached for *another* knife—how many did she have?—but I knocked her hand away and pinned it above her head. I grabbed her free hand before she had any more knife-related ideas.

But I didn't speak. Didn't reveal myself. I couldn't. My throat had run dry. My mouth felt full of unmovable cotton. My heart pounded in my chest to the rhythm of unheard drums.

"End it then," Amara spat, the voice-changer still altering her voice. But now that I knew it was her, I could hear the parts of the robot-tone that *were* hers. Her cadence. Her sweetness even in the taunt.

I sat astride her now and wondered how I'd missed it entirely. Every curve of her body, the way she moved. I'd known Amara almost my entire life and in this very moment, she seemed like a complete stranger.

"Don't you get it?" she asked. "Your poison doesn't affect me. I'm a shifter. You hate them. You and your Order have made a sport of killing us supernaturals. So if you're going to do it, just do it."

Fear sounded her in voice. The slightest shake of her words. But mostly I recognized the daring and her frustration.

She'd led herself into an alley with Orion and thought she might get out of it alive. Hell, I'd thought *I'd* be the one arrested and taken in for a moment.

I tightened my grip on her wrists just in case.

Amara moved her chin to her shoulder and worked off her mask before staring right into the eyes of mine. "Maybe if you have to look your prey right in their eyes, you'll see we're all the same. Human, supernatural. We live on this world *together*."

And, oh, was she right. Looking into her eyes right now, with the way we were positioned, I no longer wanted to fight her. I hadn't even been prepared to kill another supernatural tonight, let alone fight one. But never in a million years would I ever want to kill my best friend.

A *shifter*. How had I not seen it? How had I not known? I'd somehow missed my best friend being a supernatural even while she'd stood there day after day defending them.

My oath meant nothing in that moment. All my training. The number of kills I'd executed.

I wouldn't kill Amara. Even if she identified me in the very next moment. No matter what that might mean.

Which meant I couldn't uphold my oath, either.

Amara's chest heaved beneath me. Seeing her breathless twisted my stomach into butterflies. But she didn't speak more, only stared directly into my eyes as if there were no mask at all.

"What?" she asked. "Do you suddenly have cold feet? The infamous Orion can't finish the job? I wonder what made the others so *scared* of you." She nearly sang the word 'scared,' a taunt that jabbed right into my heart.

"The others are scared because I kill without remorse."

Her eyes went wide. Her mouth parted immediately, a retort on her lips, but I let go of her wrist.

I didn't have the luxury of a voice-changer. I knew as soon as I spoke that Amara realized it was me. I didn't even have to remove my mask. "You have no idea what you're getting yourself into by being a government pawn."

Amara squirmed beneath me. I didn't move. She was quick in combat but still lithe compared to me. All graceful like a dancer where I'd been built and trained to fight. "Pheme?"

"*Orion*," I corrected.

Her brow furrowed as her eyes widened impossibly more. But then they narrowed. "How does this end?"

"I don't know." That was the truth. I had sworn an oath to the Midnight Order, but an oath of friendship was deeper rooted. More important. And yet… My duty called—and Amara was a supernatural. I glanced at her hand again, so unaffected by my poison. "What are you?"

"Your *friend*," she spat. "Now get off of me."

I tightened my hold on the wrist I still held. "No."

I reached for her free hand again, but she slapped my hand away as she twisted beneath me. I thought I had her secured, but she moved fast, throwing me from her with a sudden burst of strength. Amara slid free of my hold as I rolled and she drew up onto her feet, a knife in hand.

My gaze found my bow lying several feet away. I'd lost a few arrows in the roll, too, and they also lay scattered on the ground. I moved toward the bow, but Amara threw a knife at my feet.

"No. Don't even think about it," she said, a hard glint in her tone. Clearly, she'd gotten over her shock.

Friends or not, we both had our duties.

"We don't have to do this," she said. "Come with me and you won't get hurt."

I let out a harsh laugh. "But you'll let vampires roam free hurting humans. You'll let werewolves tear people apart once a month."

"Pheme—"

I swiped at the air in front of me with a hand. "No. I won't stand by and let you peace keepers rule the way you do. I don't care how much I care about you."

Except I did. I cared for Amara so much—more than she knew—and I cared about every single moment we'd ever had together and all that we might have had if *tonight* hadn't happened.

But with a sinking feeling roiling in my gut—a gut that was never wrong—I realized that after tonight, nothing would ever be the same again. Ever.

There'd be no more parties. No more dancing breathlessly. No more long days at the shore or long nights by a campfire spent gossiping.

After tonight, Amara and I were simply two parties on opposite sides of an ancient war. That thought squeezed my chest tight and tore open a hole in my heart, letting out all hope I had and inviting in dread and desperation.

"How much I *love* you," I added. Because in that moment, I knew it was true. And I didn't mean I loved her as a friend. I *loved* her. Gods, I did.

For a moment, Amara didn't say anything. Her lips moved and her cheeks flushed, but no sound came out. When it was clear the sentiment wouldn't be returned—that maybe tonight had ruined everything entirely—I used her hesitation to make my move, reaching for an arrow again. That snapped her out of her frozen moment. Amara threw another knife at me. I rolled away from it and toward my bow, swiping up a free arrow at the same time. When I came up again, it was with an arrow already notched that I let fly right at my best friend. Someone I could have never thought I'd ever aim at except that *she* was aiming directly at *me* too. Enemies of war.

At the very last moment, Amara slipped out of the way. The sleeve of her armor was torn open by the arrowhead.

In the moment it took her to recover, I sprinted. Out of the alley. Around the corner and into the night.

My feet pounded on the pavement. My chest heaved as I ran, pushing my legs and lungs as hard as they could go and then some.

I didn't stop running until I'd crossed half the city and ducked into an abandoned building. I slid down a dusty wall and let the darkness hold me tight as I tried to piece together every moment I should have known that Amara, my *best friend*, was not only a supernatural, but a government pawn.

Only then had I realized what should have been obvious. The wealth her family had. The clandestine careers. The numerous trips out of the city. The secret texts she got from her parents that she had always refused to show me. The way they kept her busy at night when she didn't have a job that I could see.

No, Amara had a job. A job keeping the peace when people like those in my Order tried to do the same.

I ripped off my mask and buried my face in my hands. My chest hurt from breathing so hard. It also stung with the wound from Amara's knife.

She might as well have stabbed me in the heart.

My phone vibrated in my pocket. I reached for it with shaking fingers, half-expecting to find a text from Amara asking me how my night was going and if I'd be home to hang out soon. Or maybe I'd find a text with her asking me to turn myself in. Or even a call that she could use to trace my position.

No. Instead, a calendar reminder bounced on the screen.

Everett Gold Star Gala Event - In 12 Hours

I threw my phone to the side and gripped both sides of my head again. My breaths came in gasps.

In twelve hours, Amara and I would be in a room together. More importantly, if Amara was a peace keeper and her parents were in charge of *all of them*, in twelve hours, I'd be surrounded by the enemy. It might be my only chance to end this. Because whether or not Amara would still want me there, it would be the *only* time I knew where she would be after tonight.

I let out a shaky exhale and pulled myself together.

With my identity and enemies revealed, there was only one way this could end.

As my Order had trained me.

As my oath demanded of me.

With one last successful hunt.

SCORPIO

I didn't stop until I was home, the doors locked behind me, and I stood in front of my bathroom mirror. The house was deadly silent, save for my thundering heartbeat pounding away in my ears. With my parents still out of town, no one would be here for days yet.

Pheme would be. She'd normally be here first thing now that school was out for the semester. I highly doubted that'd be the case tomorrow.

I stared at myself in the mirror, all messed-up hair and red, tear-filled eyes. My hands shook. Luckily, the poison from Orion's—*Pheme's*—arrow had dried on my run back to my house. At least it wouldn't drip all over the bathroom counter.

Pheme was Orion.

Pheme was Orion. And she loved me. The infamous supernatural bounty hunter loved *me*, a supernatural. Orion, the hunter responsible for so many supernatural deaths. For those poor werewolves who'd gathered in that den to celebrate the birth of a new member of their pack. They'd been slaughtered for it.

Humanity and supernaturals had never gotten along together perfectly. Not even at the beginning. But over time, we'd grown more accustomed to sharing this world together.

Or so I had believed until tonight. Before meeting Pheme in that alleyway under the guises of our respective duties, I'd believed in the organization my parents had made. That peace was possible and we'd forge it with one apprehension of a vigilante like Orion after another.

But that was before I'd known Orion was Pheme. My best friend.

Gods. Every night she'd been busy swam back to me like a tidal wave. Or the other night of my party when she'd shown up late and out of breath, as if she'd been running.

I'd just done the same run. From that werewolf den to my house.

I was just as out of breath as she had been.

A disbelieving chuckle escaped my lips before turning into a full laugh that made my chest ache. Nothing about this was funny.

I choked on a laugh as tears began to fall. All these years, I'd regretted not telling Pheme about me being a supernatural. It was so easy to hide my lineage, as my parents had wanted. *They* hadn't wanted anyone to know the truth of us. They had thought that it'd be in bad taste if a supernatural ran the peace keeper organization. But they'd had the funds and societal sway to create the organization in the first place.

The relief that Pheme had never known until tonight, that a single lie by omission had potentially saved me an early death at her hands, made bile slick my throat.

I began hyperventilating with the shock of it all. I looked at myself in the mirror as my fingers gripped the edges of the bathroom counter and forced myself to take several deep breaths. When some semblance of calm came, it was with the realization that even if I'd let her go tonight, even if Pheme had escaped *tonight*, I'd be forced to report this to my parents and the rest of the peace keepers.

I knew who Orion was. I was the first peace keeper to learn her identity.

I knew where she lived during the day. How she operated. I knew teal was her favorite color and that she hated pink. That she'd rather drive all the way to Maine for lobster than eat a roll made in New York. I knew she loved the smell of leaves in autumn and the air after it rained.

Hands pressed to my face, I kept focusing on my breathing. Nothing would ever be the same again. Nothing *could* be.

If we hadn't run into each other tonight, if she hadn't been foolish enough to return to the scene of her crime, if she hadn't hit me with an arrow that had torn away my gloves with acidic poison, we could have walked away from that encounter still best friends.

I backed away from the mirror, still gasping for breath, and slid down the wall behind me to the ground.

We couldn't be friends.

Pheme was Orion. A vigilante hunter killing supernatural citizens of New York. And I was a peace keeper, tasked with bringing people like her in for justice.

My phone pinged with notifications back to back. With one shaking hand, I pulled it from my pocket. A text message and a calendar reminder.

Mom: Any luck with Orion? We know you're the best. If you can't bring them in, no one can.

Everett Gold Star Gala Event - In 12 Hours

I stared at both notifications sitting there innocuously. As if either the text message or the calendar reminder didn't completely shatter my entire world.

My parents would say that as soon as I'd discovered Pheme was behind Orion and all those killings, it didn't matter that she was my best friend. I had my duty, and Pheme deserved to be brought to justice.

But my heart told me I couldn't do it. It seized with the idea of even hurting Pheme, let alone arresting her and bringing her in.

My heart wanted us to enjoy the gala event as we'd planned. To go together all dressed up in beautiful gowns and makeup and laugh at the pompous air of it all. To dance together.

To be friends. To be *more* than friends?

My heart told me I loved her too.

I threw my phone across the room. It hit the tiled wall of the shower and clattered against the ground.

Because as much as my parents would want me to do my duty, I had no doubt that the Midnight Order would want Pheme to do the same. If Pheme didn't struggle as much with her duty as I did, there was every chance she would kill me at this event.

Which meant I had to very publicly apprehend her first when all I wanted to do was sit on the couch and watch movies with her and make fun of corny dialogue and silly rom-coms until the sun came up.

I stared at the back of my hand for a long time, wishing the freckles in the shape of the Scorpius constellation as well as my immunity to acid and poison had never given me away.

Wishing that I, like my ancestors, could turn into a tiny little scorpion and sneak away from this entire situation.

ORION

The Midnight Order was not happy with me. When I hadn't reported in with news after finally returning home last night, they'd come to *me*. They were worried that with another identity revealed, they may lose their ability to operate in total secrecy. They were worried that my *feelings* about my best friend might put the entire Order at risk.

I couldn't hide what happened, not entirely. My parents had seen right through every one of my attempted lies to hide Amara's identity. But, given how high profile her parents were and the fact that they ran the peace keeper organization, she would likely be safe—for now, at least.

Maybe they were right. As I woke today, my mind played over last night's events in my head again and again. It'd been foolish of me to return to that den. I'd known it even at the time. But *something* had dragged me there.

Fate, apparently. And she was having a fun time of this, no doubt. Pitting me against my best friend. My oath against my feelings for Amara that had, certainly in no short order, grown from simple friendship to something more. I'd known there was more. I'd cared for her in ways I didn't care for others. But pinning her in the alleyway, both of our truths revealed with nothing left to bare, I'd known it then.

I couldn't kill someone I loved. Even if we were from two different sides of this war. Even my final shot at her last night was aimed to miss.

But I couldn't know for sure that she'd feel the same, much less be able to not come after me. Those government dogs, the peace keepers who hunted my Order for sport, would not let this go. Not now that one of their own had gotten so close to bringing me in.

I had to know for sure. Had Amara reported me? Was my life at risk?

I'd have to put myself entirely at her mercy in order to find out. And to do so in an extremely public, vulnerable place.

So, while I dressed in a beautiful olive-green and sheer gown, I made sure it had a bit of an overskirt at the back and tucked two knives of my own underneath. There was no chance I'd be able to hide an entire bow and quiver.

I hoped against all hope that Amara wouldn't make a scene. And that I wasn't walking directly into a trap or a room full of secret peace keepers. But if I had to throw myself at her mercy—and *theirs*—I'd be damned if I did so unarmed. Assuming I could even walk in the front doors of the event. If Amara had taken me off the guest list, I'd have to sneak inside.

After some makeup, heels, and doing my hair, I steeled my nerves and made my way toward the venue for tonight's event… and hoped to the gods that event wouldn't end in my apprehension.

I had no remorse for the supernaturals I'd killed. But I definitely did not want to go to jail for the rest of my life for it. Least of all because of my best friend.

The gala event was at a place downtown. I wasn't entirely sure what to expect, given the situation, but from the outside, the flashing cameras, fancy ballgowns, and expensive limos dropping off guests seemed the same as every other event Amara's family had ever held.

My heartbeat thundered in my ears as I made my way up the stone steps of the four-story theater. No show would be playing today, but the massive space in the atrium held the party—and wow, did I stand out. Most of the women wore expensive gowns that flowed from their waists, the opposite of my more functional attire.

I ignored the few glances I received as I walked up the front steps of the building and into the atrium event space. A pair of security guards stopped me before I crossed the threshold, each dressed in fine suits that barely hid their sleek body armor beneath.

"Do you have your invite, miss?" one of them asked. He was the taller of the pair, and the unnatural tinge of orange in his eyes gave him away as some sort of big cat shifter even more than the stripes in his hair did. Tiger, if I had to guess.

Disgusting. I tried to hide that disgust with as genuine a smile as I could muster.

"Not on me, I'm afraid." I batted my eyelashes and tried to be cordial. I glanced to the other security guard and realized I recognized him. I couldn't for the life of me remember this man's name, but I knew he'd been around Amara's house before. Maybe as part of her family's security detail?

For so long, I'd thought they'd hired a detail like that because of how much money they had. It only made sense, especially in a world with supernaturals that preyed on humans. Now, I realized their security detail was due to their association with the peace keepers.

"You know me," I said as I smiled at the blond guard. "I've seen you around Amara's before. Amara Caras? She's my best friend. She invited me."

The two security guards exchanged a pair of neutral expressions. For a moment, I thought they simply wouldn't let me pass—and to be honest, the relief from that was sweet. But then they nodded to each other with some unheard message and stepped aside.

The blond guard gestured for me to pass. "Have a good evening, Miss Gabris."

I kept smiling. But inside, dread filled me to the brim. I was sure he knew me… just not my name.

Maybe it was a coincidence. I *hoped* it was a coincidence. Otherwise, my worst fears about tonight were coming true.

I nodded back to both guards and proceeded into the event without another word. Nothing to increase my chances of being found out or caught.

Why the hell had I even come tonight? Would it have looked weird without me here by Amara's side? Sure, maybe. Only to those who paid enough attention to know we'd been friends forever. But this wasn't an event run by my family, nor was it for a venue owned by my family. I was a guest, and if I'd not come at all, Amara would be the only person who'd likely *actually* miss me.

So why was I chancing this, knowing I might have been entirely surrounded by enemies?

My answer came twofold. First as a text arriving on my phone, loudly buzzing from my purse, sent by the Midnight Order. It made my heart leap into my throat.

Arrive for debrief in one hour. Icarus protocol is in effect.

Icarus had gotten too close to the sun and burned. I had no doubt that by "debrief," they meant to erase my identity and move me before the peace keepers could capture me. I'd seen it done to Order operatives before, but only the best ones. The operatives they couldn't afford to lose in their fight against supernaturals.

Orion was one such operative. But Orion and I were increasingly becoming two different people. And me, *not Orion*, was gobsmacked by the sight of Amara descending a set of spiral stairs that came down from the second floor, her golden dress beautiful against a deep red, lush carpet. Her presence, her energy, the very sight of her stole my breath away. Like me, she'd opted for a bit more functional of a gown that collected in a corset-like bodice and had full sleeves—sleeves that likely held knives.

Amara descended the stairs like a sun setting down low over the ocean. Graceful. Beautiful. Determined in finality.

Our eyes met as she stepped off the last stair and I swore it was like every single other being in the room had suddenly disappeared. Like it was just she and I, and the gaping abyss that had formed in our friendship.

And still, all I wanted to do was embrace her.

SCORPIO

Pheme's secrets. Her betrayal. Both of our lies. Everything fell away the moment I laid eyes on Pheme and saw how stunning she looked tonight in that olive-green dress. A blush crept up her cheeks despite her stoic appearance. It made a blush of my own bloom, warming my cheeks.

I hadn't expected Pheme to attend the gala event after last night. I wasn't sure *I* still wanted to. But I, unlike she, was required to make an appearance here.

So why did it feel like Pheme had stolen the show?

I didn't even care. Not now that I saw her again.

When Pheme didn't immediately run, I began to make my way toward her in cautious steps. Not slow enough to draw attention or questions from my parents' friends, but enough that I could attempt to assess the situation. She'd so easily fought me last night. No hesitation, no reserve save for not killing me. Which I supposed was a good thing. But her reputation as Orion preceded her. And without knowing where we stood as friends, I couldn't let my guard down for a single second.

I put on a smile, hoping it would draw away some of the prying eyes we'd attracted. "Pheme! I'm so glad you could make it."

She hesitated for only a moment. So minute a resistance that no one not watching closely would've noticed. "You look beautiful. This venue is amazing."

Pheme held out her arms as she'd done hundreds of times before. For the first time, I was scared to hug her. For the first time, I knew what she was *really* capable of.

I leaned into her embrace with a held breath. The hug was more like the one you'd give a distant relative you only see once a year than your best friend.

More gala guests poured in through the entrance. I nodded to Pheme and gestured for us to move aside as the string quartet began to play. Their music filtered louder above the crowd and around the open space until guests either stopped to listen or began dancing. It felt more like a ball than an event for an art museum.

As soon as we were off to the side of the crowd, Pheme's hand closed around my wrist. I inhaled sharply and placed a hand over hers in case she was up to something.

"We need to talk," she said.

I nodded to the event behind us. "Don't you think this isn't the best time?"

My thoughts drifted back to my brief text conversation with my mother earlier today. I'd told her I'd fought Orion and they'd gotten away. In return, I'd received orders to "try harder." Now that I'd gotten closer than anyone else ever had, the peace keepers were not going to let this go.

"*Is* there a good time?" Her curt tone cut me deeply, but then her gaze softened. "Why didn't you tell me?"

I scoffed. "Why didn't *you* tell *me*, Orion?"

Pheme let go and pressed a finger against my lips. A move so brazen, it made my eyes go wide with shock. I found, in that moment, that I didn't mind it so much. "Don't use that name in public."

"Why not?" I asked after removing her finger. "You do every time you leave arrows at a scene."

Pheme tore her hand from my grip. "And *you* allow supernaturals to coexist with us when they prey on us—*humans*." She all but spat the last word. "All this time and I didn't know."

"My shifter blood isn't strong," I said, as if it were some decent excuse for hiding who I was from my best friend. But Pheme had also been hiding who *she* was. "Not all supernaturals are bad, Pheme. Clearly."

A mix of disgust and shame crossed her fair features. I hated seeing those emotions on her. Like all friends, we'd had off days. Arguments that hadn't lasted. We'd always recovered from them before.

This felt different. It felt final in a way that didn't match the hunch I had that she'd saved my life and let me go rather than kill me to hide her identity because she too felt the way I did. Like maybe over the past few years this had been less of a friendship and trending toward something more—at least if the butterflies doing somersaults in my stomach were any indication. Gone was the hesitation and dread at seeing her here. Now, *even now*, her presence calmed my nerves and brought joy into my life.

"I should have run away instead of revealing myself," Pheme said. "This would have been miles easier."

My brow furrowed. I wanted to question what specifically she meant by "easier," as the weight with which she'd said it gave me the impression something more was going on. But instead, I asked, "If you hate supernaturals so much that you're clearly disgusted by your best friend, why didn't you end my awful existence then?"

Hurt narrowed her eyes. "You think I could kill you just like that?"

"Isn't it what you're trained to do?"

"I could ask the same of you, *peace keeper.*"

Pheme's disgust was back again, a venom dripping from her words that coiled the butterflies tightly in my stomach. Had she lost someone close to her because of the peace keepers? Had we arrested or even killed a friend of hers?

This. This was what Pheme had meant by "easier." Because as wrapped up as we were in this veritable war between humans who hated supernaturals and those supernaturals just trying to survive, all semblance of innocence was lost. To the peace keepers, there were no shades of gray. And it was clear that Pheme had been taught or trained the same way.

And yet here we were, friends amidst it all. A friendship unraveling at the seams of decisions not our own.

"So what now?" I was almost terrified to speak the words. Because this very moment, the two of us as alone as we could be in a crowded room, neither acting upon our oaths, seemed normal. Like nothing at all had changed.

Except that I had to bring Orion in. Even if she was my best friend. Because if I didn't, if I explained to my parents *why* I hadn't brought her in, they'd learn her identity anyway. And they knew where Pheme lived and worked and studied. They knew everything about her that I did.

Except that she was Orion. They'd be a lot less forgiving about that than I.

Pheme placed her hands on her hips. A flash of a gold bracelet around her wrist caught my eye. "You tell me. I'm probably surrounded, aren't I?"

I didn't need to glance around to know that wasn't true. "A few guests here are peace keepers, yes. However, *surrounded* is a strong way to put it."

Pheme's shoulders dropped, visibly relaxing. "I'm glad, because coming here was a big risk."

I reached for her hand and was surprised when she let me take it again. "Then why risk it?"

A faint smile curled her pink lips. Pheme didn't normally wear makeup—I supposed it clashed with hunting supernaturals every night—but she was tonight. "Isn't it obvious?"

I glanced around briefly. All I saw was a room of people who *could have* been peace keepers and suddenly I understood why she'd looked so scared. "No." And yet, had our situations been reversed, I thought I would have risked it, too.

"I wanted to see you," she murmured. "Gods, Amara. I wanted to see you. To talk. To attempt to figure this out." She raised her other hand and waved it around some, like she always did when flustered.

I took it in mine, now holding both. Her cheeks flushed again and the sight of it made my stomach flutter. I wanted to reach out and hold her face but didn't. I wasn't sure how she'd react. Moreover, I couldn't stop a suddenly sinking feeling in my gut that *maybe* this might all be an act. Not the friendship, but this now unguarded version of Pheme. The change in her rang alarms in my mind that I hated existed at all.

Pheme closed her eyes and let out a deep breath that ruffled some of the loose curls around my forehead. We were so close now that a single half-step would have me in her arms. "I hate this."

"Really?" I asked, looking down to where our fingers intertwined. "I kind of like this."

Pheme shook her head. "I wish I'd never known what you are. That you hadn't come looking for me at that den. It's going to change everything and I don't want to let you go." This time when Pheme pulled her hand away from mine, *she* held *my* face.

I turned into her palm and savored her light touch. "You don't have to let me go."

I didn't know why I said it. She knew as well as I did that if I didn't bring her in, the peace keepers would eventually find out who she was. They'd arrest her and throw her in jail, and I'd lose her that way. And there was every chance that once the Midnight Order learned what had happened—assuming Pheme hadn't already told them—they'd order her to kill me. Not just for knowing Orion's identity, but also for being a scorpion shifter.

Our oaths had pitted us against each other.

The quartet's music grew louder and now more people had begun to dance. The tune wasn't quite a waltz and yet I found myself swaying to the music all the same as Pheme held me there.

"I'm going to lose you," Pheme said, breaking the reverie. "They want me gone."

My heart dropped. "Gone? As in?"

Her lips formed a thin line. "Out of the city. Disappeared. I'll never be back here again, Amara. We'll never be able to be together."

The way she said "be together" rather than "be friends" made my heart soar again. It'd always felt like we'd danced around each other and now—now I wanted nothing more than to lean in and kiss her.

"Can they do that?" I asked. I didn't want to believe it, but I knew what lengths the peace keepers would go to in order to protect their own. The Midnight Order wouldn't be any less careful.

Pheme nodded. "I got the notification as I arrived tonight. By tomorrow, I'll be gone."

"No." I touched a hand to hers, gripping her fingers as though they were a lifeline. "They can't. I need you, Pheme. You're my best friend."

Her smile returned, a little sad this time. "And you're mine. I… really wanted more for us."

"You can't give up yet. There's got to be something we can do."

"The only way to get me out of my Order's sight is for you to arrest me." The way Pheme said it, all listless and with surrender, made me think that was actually what she wanted. But Pheme didn't understand. Sure, she'd be thrown in jail. But she'd also be questioned relentlessly. She'd be forced to give up contacts and information—aggressively, even.

I wouldn't consign Pheme to that fate. No matter how much I hated what Orion had done. No matter how many broken families Orion had created. No matter how much blood had been spilled.

I was sure I'd torn apart families she knew, too.

Pawns. That was all we were.

An idea formed in my head—risky but promising. I closed the distance between Pheme and me until our lips were inches apart. "I have a better plan."

Her lips parted in surprise. Then her eyes narrowed and she leaned in. "And that involves us being this close?"

"I don't want anyone to hear. Here." I tugged her back toward the crowd and led us into a dance. She followed as though nothing were wrong, as if dancing was the best and only thing we ever did.

We fell in step with the others. The lighthearted atmosphere completely clashed with the turmoil happening between Pheme and me.

"Amara…" She trailed off, curious but with a smile gracing her lips that sent a chill of excitement down my spine.

"The music hides our voices," I explained.

"And dancing draws attention to us."

I grinned. "I can't help it if we're the best-dressed couple here."

Pheme relented and laughed—and it was the sweetest sound I'd ever heard. After what had happened yesterday, I'd thought I'd never hear her laugh again, let alone be in the same room with her, touching her, dancing with her—

"What's your plan, Amara?" Pheme asked, dragging me out of my happy thoughts.

My plan was simple but effective. "When this song ends, we leave."

"Leave? *Can* you leave?" she asked. "Don't your parents require you to be here on their behalf?"

I shrugged. "Not if something comes up that's so important, being *here* is an issue."

Pheme didn't look convinced. "And what would that be?"

"An Orion sighting." At this, Pheme's eyes narrowed. She opened her mouth to protest, but I continued. "We fake a fight. It's bad. I get injured. You 'don't make it.'" I air-quoted the last words. "Orion's body goes missing. Your Order never needs to know what happened."

"Except there's one problem with this plan," she said as she retook my hand and got us dancing again. "The Order knows who I am beneath the mask. They're related to me."

Her parents, I guessed. It was almost funny how our parents had unknowingly set us against each other while encouraging our decade-long friendship.

I didn't know what to say to that. Faking her own death to her family seemed too far. But if we didn't do *something*, we'd never see each other again and *that* was not something I was willing to deal with.

Pheme seemed to consider this for long enough that I'd forgotten we were plotting her freedom at all. It was easy to get lost in the music and the dance steps, especially here with Pheme. Since we'd unmasked each other, it felt as though all the other layers of words unsaid had fallen away too. All that existed now was she and I and this feeling between us. About us. About our future, whatever it may hold.

Finally, she said, "What if Orion defects and disappears?"

My brow furrowed. "Your family—"

"What if Pheme disappears, too," she said before I could say more. "I mean, they'd miss me for sure, but…" She shrugged.

"Pheme, no." I held her face in my hands. More brazen moves brought on by the thought of this possibly being the last time I'd ever see her. If this was the last time, then let it be memorable. "Does it make us not have to turn each other in or hurt each other? *Yes.* But someone still gets hurt. I never should have suggested it."

"Then…" Pheme shook her head and sighed before dislodging my hands. The song we were dancing to stopped and a new one, much slower, began. "I'll run away. No one will think I'm dead, but I can duck in and out of the city. Then you don't have to bring me in, and I don't have to disappear."

I held her gaze for a moment that seemed to stretch into minutes and simultaneously last no time at all. "Is that something you can live with? Is that what you want?"

Pheme smiled softly. "I've always wanted to travel. If we play this right, maybe you can get a personal assignment to follow me. Hunt me down. It could be a fun game of cat and mouse that ends in us together every time."

I couldn't say I hated the idea. It'd be fun and, given that my parents had sent me after Orion last night, they'd been inclined to do it again. Still… "How long do you think that will really last?"

"As long as it needs to," Pheme said. "Maybe I can pass down the mantle somehow. If you can lie about who Orion is long enough for me to do that, it could work. And you… I mean, even if they knew you're a peace keeper they can't just take you out. Not as the daughter of those who run that organization. Which is good news, right?"

"I guess." I wasn't as confident. It depended on how much people already knew. But I wouldn't know that until my parents got back from their trip and we were all briefed.

The only surety in any of this was that Pheme, it seemed, was due to disappear by sunset either way. Like an evening star being chased from the sky every morning.

How had a single ten-minute encounter full of truths changed *everything*?

"Hey," Pheme said as she took my hand in hers once more. "It'll be a fun little game. I'll leave you enough clues to hand them that they won't reassign you. I can get creative too. I'll hide in places they'll never think of. We could travel the world together like this."

I couldn't help but smile back at her. She wasn't wrong. "Then let's plan a fight neither side can deny."

Pheme looked thoughtful. "I'll need a new name, too."

"How about 'Ori'? Or is that too on-the-nose?"

She chuckled. "We can work on it. I love you, you know that?"

I smiled as my cheeks flushed with warmth. I leaned in and kissed her on the tip of her nose. "I love you, too."

ORION

Amara was an incredibly convincing actress. Between the fake blood we'd purchased at a costume store on our way from the gala event to the performance of pain and frustration of letting Orion get away from her, even I was almost convinced it was real.

I watched the scene play out from a distance with a backpack slung over one shoulder and a quiver over my other. The bow in my hands made me easy to pick out in a crowd, but I'd unstring it and fold it down before leaving the rooftop. There was no way I was leaving New York without the only weapon I trusted to have my back.

The only things I'd left behind were the few personal belongings I had, my parents, my oath, and the note I'd written saying I was in too much danger to stay associated with the Midnight Order. I told my parents that I'd be around, but that I would be hiding for as long as necessary—and on my own.

Icarus be damned. He was stupid, anyway. Besides, I hadn't gotten burned by Amara. She had lit me from the inside and brought me to life. *This* was the best solution. And really, it only had to be this way for a little while.

Maybe that was why I smiled when Amara's backup arrived just in time for her to feign fainting. They loaded her up in an ambulance and drove away without inspecting the scene at all. Just as we'd assumed would happen.

I let my smile grow wide. Of course I'd rather stay in New York. To find a way to keep my oath to the Order. To take out the supernaturals who caused evil inside this city.

I could still do that. There was still evil in the city even if all supernaturals weren't so.

I'd just need a new name first. A new alias. A new oath.

And a place for Amara to find me. Like I knew she always would, no matter how much chasing happened in between.

SCORPIO

My parents had given me the permission to hunt Orion because I'd been the only one to get as close to her as I had. But I had expected Pheme to get farther away and quicker, which was why I didn't quite believe the reports when they were handed to me by the other peace keepers. A new supernatural hunter nearby. Only this hunter had gone after a well-known to us den of drug dealing vampires.

All that had remained was ash and a knife wrapped in gold foil with a name along the side.

Blade.

I recognized the gold foil as the same from our favorite chocolate shop downtown. The foil didn't have a brand name or anything on it, but I'd recognize it anywhere from having worked at that shop with Pheme for a few years in high school. Back when we'd daydreamed of escaping to California and its sun. Just the two of us. It was when I had realized I maybe had feelings for her beyond simple friendship.

I tried to hide my grin beneath the collar of my shirt and blamed it on my nose being cold when my mother asked me what was wrong. But all I could do was chuckle as the briefing continued.

I hoped Pheme had saved me some chocolate along with the next clue.

WITH DARK TRUTHS DRAW ME

MARY FAN

S HE SHOULDN'T HAVE mocked the Gods.

That's what everyone calls us, and I don't care if it's arrogant to embrace it. There are worse things for a group of friends to be called than the Gods of Olympus Prep. And, let's face it, it's kind of true.

A soft autumn breeze flutters across the dark stone courtyard, which is ringed by the school's stately walls and their elegant windows, and brings the tips of my long black hair dangerously close to the gentle flame of the white candle in my hand.

Alone, it's a pathetic little thing—cheaply made and crudely assembled—but amid a sea of identical flames, clutched by dozens of somber-faced students and teachers, it adds to a stunning image. Myriad flickers of golden light against the blackness of night... a constellation on earth. All of us wearing mournful black instead of our usual crimson-and-gray uniforms. A melancholy tune sung by the Muses, the school's selective a cappella group, who stand beneath a poster-sized, flower-wreathed photo of our fallen classmate. As far as candlelight vigils go, it's certainly a beautiful one.

She would have hated it. Just like she hated all of us.

The Muses conclude their song, and Principal Nelson thanks them as they step off the low platform that was set up for this occasion. His crinkled brown eyes shift to his small leather-bound notebook, and he adjusts his glasses, whose square, ebony-hued rims nearly blend into his brown complexion. "Next, some of our students would like to say a few words. First up is Min Wong."

I draw a breath and run my fingers through my blunt bangs, giving them a shake to make sure they don't cling to my forehead. My friends surround me, and I gingerly weave through them, squeezing between Olympic-level archer Diana and her twin brother Lucius—a singer/songwriter who landed his first record deal in middle school—and past the prettiest girl in school, Amanda, whose YouTube beauty channel, "Love, Amanda," is about to hit a million subscribers. Her boyfriend, Miles—our school's star receiver—is standing at the bottom of the short staircase to the platform, and his bulk blocks the whole thing.

"Excuse me," I whisper, and he steps out of the way, bumping into Ryder, who's half his size but has ten times his brains and whose recently launched messaging app is already racking up downloads.

They each have something special that elite universities want—hence why even the teachers sometimes call them the Gods—and I'm proud to have such accomplished friends. As for me? Well, only being good at one thing was never going to get me into Harvard, Yale, or Princeton. So I did it all, showing off my brains with AP classes and academic competitions, my physical strength with varsity sports, and my creativity with visual art. In the coming battle for the best colleges, I plan to be the best equipped.

Principal Nelson steps out of the way as I take my place before the poster-sized photo, but I refuse to look at it. I saw enough of that cocky, ungrateful girl when she was alive. I don't need to keep looking at her now that she's dead. Yet even though I won't see her with my eyes, her face burns in my mind—those narrow, judge-y black eyes, that tight, disdainful mouth always on the edge of a sneer.

"I met Arabella Zhi in first grade." The speech I wrote and memorized rings clearly in my head. "She went by Bella for the first week, and then insisted on Ara because it was more unique, even though the other kids called it weird. Already she didn't care what people said about her. Anyone who met her could tell you about how confident she was, how she would always do her own thing, and do it loudly. That's why we were all so shocked to learn that she'd... she'd... d-died by suicide..."

An unexpected sob attacks my throat, and I do my best to swallow it. Where did that come from? I never even liked Ara...

I close my eyes and take a moment to compose myself before continuing. "No one is immune to the toxic effects of cyberbullying— and no one should have to be. Because no one should be so cruel to anyone else in the first place. We should all know by now that it's never 'just the internet.' Words matter, even if they're on a screen." My voice rises. "The person who invaded Ara's privacy and posted that... that private video never considered the cascading and harmful effects it could have on someone's mental health. They probably thought it was just a joke. That shows a total lack of compassion, and I... I hope who-whoever did it is ashamed."

A few more tears fall. I gently dab them with trembling fingers. This is not how my speech was supposed to go. "There's not enough kindness in the world as it is, and the last thing anyone needs is cruelty disguised as humor. That's why I ask all of you to think deeply about how kind you truly are. Most of you were following the account that posted the video and watched Ara's private moment, which was stolen from her and spread without her consent. Think about why you did that, and how cruel it was, and how we can all be kinder in the future so nothing like this ever happens again."

I go on in this vein for a few more minutes, making sure to emphasize kindness as much as possible, because that's what people—okay, teachers and other adults whose decisions drive my fate—want to hear.

Ara would have hated every word.

After finishing my speech, I wipe my eyes, careful not to disturb my makeup.

"That was beautiful, Min," Principal Nelson says. "Thank you."

As he announces the next student speaker, I return to the crowd below. Six others are scheduled to go, plus a few teachers, and, of course, Ara's parents. This whole thing won't be over for at least another two hours. Now that I've done my part, I wish I could leave. Not only have I had enough of Ara already, but I have an AP World History test to study for, plus the big game against the Titans this weekend, plus a new painting for my studio art assignment. And that's on top of the usual mountain of homework.

"I didn't realize you loved Ara so much," Diana mutters with a sarcastic lilt.

"You know I can't pass up a chance to speak to a crowd," I whisper back.

Someone bumps my back. "How dare you?"

I whirl to see Lydia Deveraux, the only friend I'd ever seen Ara with, glaring at me. Smudged black makeup and heavy mascara tears mar her alabaster complexion. "How dare you pretend to be Ara's friend?" she hisses.

I furrow my brow. "What are you talking about? Like I said, I've known her since first grade—far longer than you."

"That doesn't matter! You—"

"Shh!" I jerk my chin at the stage, where another student is in the middle of a speech.

Lydia clenches her fists. "You can pretend to be perfect all you want, but I know who you really are, Min, and someday the world will know too." She storms off, pushing through the crowd.

I hold my face steady, but my heart trembles.

As I turn back toward the stage, a heavy item in the pocket of my black blazer bounces against my hip. I reach inside and retrieve something cold: a spider-shaped pendant, silver with long legs of cheap metal.

It's Ara's. She wore it almost every day.

Shuddering, I shove it back into my pocket.

BEFORE . . .

"What do you think of this one?" Leaning over from her spot on stone steps before Olympus Prep's arched main entrance, Diana shoves her iPhone toward me. Its glittery silver case, covered in tiny crescent moons, flashes despite the moody gray clouds muting the midday sun.

I set down my salad, wedging it between my backpack and Lucius's guitar case on the step above where I'm sitting, and take the device. Meanwhile, Lucius strums a few sunny chords. His wavy black hair, meticulously gelled into an artsy mess, falls over his dark eyes as he hums a new tune, his bright tenor swirling above the chatter of lunch period. Even though he's casually experimenting, the sound is effortlessly beautiful.

The photo displayed on Diana's phone is one she took during fall break a few weeks ago, which she spent hiking in Alaska. In it, she's sitting atop a giant rock in the middle of the mountains, staring meditatively off into the sunset, her long black ponytail fluttering. It's a lovely photo, and I admire how she angled herself so that the light would highlight her muscular arms.

I glance up at the twins and smile. I love that my closest friends have all risen to be the best at their chosen specialties, and I admire the hard work and dedication they put into it—even as I'm determined to outshine them all when it comes time for college applications.

A breeze stirs, rustling the umber and crimson leaves that cling to the majestic trees just beyond the courtyard. Their crisp scents swirl around me, and my loose striped tie flutters against my slate-gray sweater. I shiver, wishing my uniform's crimson blazer and pleated gray skirt were a little warmer.

"You look amazing in this photo… and really strong." I hand the phone back to Diana.

"Thanks! That means a lot coming from you." With a grin, Diana takes back the phone.

"Maybe just up your contrast and deepen your shadows. It'll make the colors look richer."

"Got it. I'm almost up to five thousand followers. I think these Alaska pics will put me over the mark. Hoping to go hiking in the Andes this winter."

I shake my head. Diana's always been obsessed with nature. She may be better than me at sports, but she'll never come close to my GPA when she's always running off to nature preserves during breaks and shooting arrows after school.

I grab my backpack. The Medusa-head Versace logo embossed in gold glows against the textured black leather. I unzip the front pocket, pull out my phone, and unlock it. Diana's comment led me to wonder whether I'd cracked my next follower goal—25,000.

"What are you doing?" Diana asks, craning her neck. Of course, she can't see anything with the privacy screen protector on my phone.

"Checking Insta." I tap the vaguely camera-shaped icon.

The first thing that greets me in the feed is a video of Kristen Dane, a junior like me, drinking a beer. It was posted by Olympus Prep Tea, an anonymous gossip account that shares photos, videos, and screenshots sent in by equally anonymous students. The image is grainy, and it's hard to tell exactly where Kristen is standing, but the distinctive stone-edged window behind her reveals that she must have been on school grounds. *Someone's about to get suspended…*

Guess she won't be entering the school's essay contest after all. *Which reminds me, I need to send my entry to Jun.* My stepmom will kill me if I turn it in without her approving it first.

"Ugh, what is *that?*" Amanda's high-pitched voice interrupts my thoughts. She approaches, arm-in-arm with Miles, her brown eyes fixed on something to her left and her nose wrinkled. The shimmering bronzer on her dark brown cheeks exaggerates their height and accentuates her look of disgust.

I follow her gaze. An enormous drawing of a black-and-purple spider sprawls in colored chalk in the middle of the sidewalk. I'm not surprised to see Ara crouched over it, lovingly sketching swirling patterns onto the spider's back. Though I find it grotesque, there's something undeniably beautiful about the movement she's imbued it with. A strange tightness seizes my gut, and I frown.

Ara looks up, a few strands of her chin-length, purple-streaked black hair spilling over her face, her metal spider pendant swinging against her collar. "Some of us like to paint things other than our own faces, or share images that say something more than, 'oh, look how rich and attractive I am.'" She shoots a dirty look at me and Diana.

I narrow my eyes. Ara can say whatever she wants, but the fact is that my Insta has nearly ten times as many followers as her pathetic little art account, called Color Weaver.

"And what's *that* supposed to say?" Diana gestures at the spider drawing. "Min's always been the best artist in school anyway. She's got trophies and medals from a gazillion competitions to prove it, too."

"Not all of us are obsessed with competitions." Ara rolls her eyes. "Or getting into HYP schools."

Amanda furrows her brow. "What's a hype school?"

"H-Y-P. Harvard, Yale, Princeton. You know, for those so elitist, even the whole Ivy League isn't selective enough. But it's all just hype." Ara throws me a withering look. "I don't care about trophies and medals.

I draw what I love, things that mean something to me. I remember a time when you did too, instead of imitating whichever famous dead person you think is the teacher or judge's favorite. I'd say that makes me the better artist."

I scowl. "You know that's not true. And don't forget I'm the one who taught you how to draw back in elementary school. The only reason you can even do that"—I gesture at the chalk image—"is because of me."

Ara stands. "You don't get to take credit for what I can do. You may have been the reason I got started, but my skills are my own, and they've gotten much better since we were six. If I ever felt like competing, I could beat you easily." She stalks off.

How dare she? I glare at her retreating back. *How* dare *she think she's better than me?*

PRESENTLY . . .

I toss the burn-out end of the candle from Ara's memorial into a small trash can sitting by my dorm's heavy wooden door. The meager yellow glow of the ceiling light throws pale shadows against the walls. I managed to cover most of the white plaster in framed artwork, each of which I painted and won a prize for. Some feature landscapes, some still life, and some faces... Some are photo-real, and others abstract, depending on which competition I was entering. An empty spot sits by the tall window across the room. An uncomfortable feeling creeps through my chest. I was saving that space for my next award winner, but now...

I yank my black blazer off and hang it up. It sways unevenly on its hanger, no doubt because of the metal spider necklace in one pocket. A chill washes over me. I slam the closet door shut. The full-length mirror attached to it stares back at me. I take a moment to double check that my gray eye makeup still softens my sharply angled black eyes, and that there are no streaks in the subtle bronzer on my high cheekbones. We may have retired for the night, but you never know when someone might see you.

After kicking off my shoes, I hop onto my bed and grab my thin silver laptop from where I'd left it on the pillow. The moment I log in, my AP World History notes greet me on the screen. Just thinking about how much I still need to memorize gives me a headache, especially since I hate this class. But hating something is no reason not to excel at it. *And speaking of Excel…*

I pull up the spreadsheet I've been using to track my grades. Every teacher has their own way of weighting assignments, quizzes, and tests to calculate an overall grade, and I've figured out each of their methods. Dr. Reich said that tests count for forty percent of our overall grade in his class, and he gives a test every three weeks. Considering what percentage each test counts for and how well I did on my last few…

I need to score at least a 96 to maintain my A average. Anything less and I'd slip into A- territory, and that could ruin my whole transcript. My heart pounds anxiously as I pull my notes back up. If only I'd done better last time, I'd have more wiggle room now.

No matter how I try to focus, my eyes keep drifting to the closet door. It feels wrong to leave Ara's necklace in there.

Spurred by a sudden need to take action, I rush to the closet and retrieve the necklace. That chill fills me to the core. I squeeze my eyes, digging my fingers into the metal legs. *It's not my fault you're dead, Ara…*

A tear slips down my cheek. But I don't have time for this. I shove the necklace into my desk drawer and grab my phone. Maybe I just need a quick distraction to clear my head before diving into my notes.

Of course the first thing that pops up on my Insta is an Olympus Prep Tea post. The new burner handle—a string of random letters and numbers—is a lot longer than the last one, which abruptly vanished after Ara's suicide. It took all of one day for the students following the last one to discover this new one and spread the word. That burner handle plus the fact that it's a private account keeps teachers and parents from seeing what's being posted… at least until someone decides to leak it more widely.

It's a photo of me this time, taken in the locker room after soccer practice. I'm all sweaty and gross, sitting on a bench and leaning forward. Since I'm only wearing a sports bra and shorts, every roll on my stomach spills toward my thighs.

A hot flush of embarrassment fills my face. The post already has fifty comments. Far more must have seen it—through phone screens turned toward friends or screenshots shared via texts. The caption reads:

And Min Wong wonders why she didn't make captain of the soccer team despite being the Warriors' best striker last year… Not even applying to college yet and already packing on the Freshman Fifteen.

The comments below—all from people's fake or anonymous accounts—are crueler than I could have imagined.

But I won't let them win.

Jaw tightening, I screenshot both the photo and the comments, then switch to my public account, the one I use to post photos of my prep school lifestyle and show off my art, the one that's inching toward twenty-five thousand followers.

I hesitate. This is a bold move, even for me. But I know it will work… I *know* it will.

I post the unflattering photo alongside screenshots of the nasty comments and a caption:

Someone took this picture of me without my knowledge or consent and spread it around my school. But I won't let them or the people who wrote these comments make me ashamed of how I look. Still, the fact that they thought they could use this photo to shame me says something about our society. Cyberbullying is a very real and dangerous issue. Recently, a girl at our school died by suicide after being cyberbullied. Someone had posted embarrassing images of her too. It's in her memory that I'm sharing this now, even though many won't like it. I want to be strong for her. I don't know what kind of reaction this will get, but this is what I look like after a long practice, and I won't let anyone bully me into hating my body.

I'll just leave you with this: Be kind.

Plus the required twenty-some hashtags.

The likes come in quickly, and so do the comments, calling me brave and authentic, congratulating me on my courage and lack of vanity. I smile as I continually refresh my notifications, watching the validation roll in.

I'm about to put my phone down and return to my notes when I glimpse an unusual comment amid the praise, one from a user with a private account whose name and handle I don't recognize.

It's a row of spider emojis, which Ara always used to punctuate her texts. No doubt Lydia was behind it.

I slam the phone onto my desk.

My post went viral, just as I'd hoped—cross-posted to other social media sites and picked up by content aggregators under headlines like, "Teen Influencer Shuts Down Body Shamers." Thanks to them, my follower count is up to thirty thousand, with more coming in every minute.

Smiling to myself, I stick my phone into my backpack as I enter the art studio for my next class. The smells of paint and clay fill my nose the moment I step inside. Light pours into the spacious room from the tall, stone-framed windows. Everyone else is already at their assigned work-bench, their crimson blazers hanging neatly on the backs of their chairs, their uniforms now protected by long navy-blue aprons.

I take my place at my workbench and tuck my backpack into the large drawer at the bottom. A large poster for the state-wide Voices of Our Youth art competition hangs at the front. The understated green-and-tan color palette and minimalist design bely its importance. Sponsored by a prestigious art gallery searching for the next big thing, the contest offers a prize greater than any scholarship: The winner's artwork will be displayed in the gallery alongside masterpieces by famed artists. In other words, it could skyrocket someone to international acclaim.

A cold, bitter feeling gnaws at me, and I turn away.

"Good morning, class." Lily—she's one of those "cool" teachers who wants us to call her by her first name—nods at us from the front of the room. Her red-rimmed cat-eye glasses clash against her fiery curls, and her loud yellow dress is bolder than what the teachers at Olympus Prep usually wear. "Before we begin, I have an announcement to make about the competition." She gestures at the poster. "As you know, each school invited to participate selected one student's entry to submit. Though the entries will be anonymous at the time of judging, schools are allowed to inform their students of who has been picked. With the event only a week away, some of you might be wondering why Olympus Prep hasn't announced its entry yet. The answer is… complicated. But a decision has been reached." She nods at me. "Congratulations, Min. Your painting has been selected to represent our school."

A spattering of applause follows. I smile and press my hands to my heart. But I can tell not everyone is happy. Between the congratulatory nods are a good number of eye-rolls and sighs, and I can almost hear what they're saying: *Of course it was Min Wong. She always wins everything.*

They can resent me all they want. I worked hard to become the best, and I won't let anyone bring me down.

Lily gestures for everyone to settle down. "Please take out your sketchbooks."

I retrieve mine from my backpack and flip it open.

Pencil drawings of spiders fill the textured white page, none bigger than a quarter but each lifelike in its detail.

BEFORE . . .

"Come on, Ara! Lily is practically begging you to enter!" Lydia nearly walks into me as she needles her friend.

I dodge before her gesticulating hand can punch a hole through the large painting I'm clutching. "Watch it!"

Lydia ignores me. "Why won't you at least consider it?"

Ara shrugs. "I've got nothing to prove."

That's for sure. I'm keenly aware of the slantwise look Ara gives my painting.

Ryder appears from around the corner, wearing sandals even though they're against the dress code, and stops in his tracks. "Whoa, Min, did you draw that?"

I pause in the middle of the stone corridor and face him with a smile. "No, Ryder, I'm taking some other kid's art midterm back to my dorm."

He stares admiringly at the photo-real painting of Olympus Prep's stately stone facade and elegant gothic towers. "Damn, I knew you were good, but this is something else." He runs his skinny fingers through his overgrown brown hair. "You're entering that art competition everyone's talking about, right?"

"Of course."

"You're gonna win. Not just get selected to represent the school— actually win the whole statewide thing. I mean…" He looks the painting up and down and lets out a low whistle. "If they don't pick you, I'll hack their emails and make them change their minds."

I laugh. "Please don't do that… again."

Ara lets out a derisive noise. "Not even famous yet and you're already fending off fanboys."

I shoot her an irritated look. "Ryder's my friend."

"Since when does the picture-perfect Min Wong hang out with geeks? Oh, that's right, when they develop apps on the fast-track to become the next Silicon Valley unicorn." Ara turns to Ryder. "Careful with that one, man." She jerks her head at me. "She's nice enough as long as you're not a threat, but don't get too good at anything she considers her special talent."

Ryder's sharp-featured face contorts. "Huh?"

"She used to be my friend too." Ara lifts her brows at me. "But she couldn't stay friends with someone better at painting than her."

I let out a sarcastic laugh. "Like I'd ever consider you a threat. We just started hanging out with different crowds."

"So it's a coincidence that you started ignoring me after Lily called me her most promising student freshman year?" Ara's dark eyes shift to my painting. "You know why she said that about me instead of you? Because you draw things that are generically pretty, but have nothing to say."

I clench my teeth and feel my nostrils flaring. "If you think you're better than me, then take Lydia's advice and *prove* it! Paint something for the Voices of Our Youth competition, and we'll see who the school picks."

Ara crosses her arms. "Maybe I will."

"Do it. I challenge you."

"Fine." She gives a smug smile. "If you're begging to be beaten, then I won't say no."

I narrow my eyes. "Watch yourself, Color Weaver."

PRESENTLY . . .

86. I got an *86. That brings my whole average down to a B+...* Staring in horrified disbelief at the giant blue number at the top of my history test, I resist the impulse to rip the paper to shreds. My chest tightens, and I fight the urge to cry. *How could I have failed so miserably?*

"Now, class, I'm sure many of you are disappointed by your grades." Dr. Reich, having finished handing back the tests, takes a seat behind his stately wooden desk. With his tweed jacket and salt-and-pepper beard, he looks like he stepped out of a Victorian novel. "This was a tough one, and the average was lower than usual."

Colleges won't care. All they'll see is a subpar GPA. With shaking fingers, I flip through the pages to see what I got wrong. I answered every fact-based question correctly but lost a lot of points on the short essays. Blue comments in Dr. Reich's messy handwriting swim before my eyes.

I look up, feeling sick. My gaze snags on someone else's test; a number 100 gleams at the top. I quickly look to see whose it is and glimpse a milky pale face with ruddy, acne-scarred cheeks. *Henry Davis. Of course.*

He's one of the few other students whose grades I've been tracking in my spreadsheet, and the last time I looked, he'd nearly caught up to me. *And now, he's ahead… which means he could be ranked number one academically instead of me, which means colleges would choose his transcript over mine, which means he could get in instead of me…*

I draw a deep breath and remind myself that Henry Davis might be smart, but he *only* has grades going for him. No sports, no clubs, no extracurriculars of any kind as far as I can tell, unless you count D&D. Colleges like well-rounded applicants. I might still have an edge over him.

But I can't rely on that. The closest I can come to guaranteeing I'll get into a college I want is to be number one at everything. And even then, with acceptance rates shrinking every year and students—and their parents—doing more and more to make their applications stand out…

The bell rings, and Dr. Reich dismisses the class.

I rush up to Henry. "Henry! Wait!"

He freezes, staring at me in awe. I'm not surprised by his reaction; I tend to have this effect on the school's… less popular students. "H-hi…"

"Good job on your test." I smile demurely. "Sorry for peeking at your score."

"That—That's okay." He clears his throat and tosses his head of unruly blond hair. "Did you… need something?"

"Actually, yeah, if you don't mind." I look up with the most helpless expression I can muster. "I… didn't do so well, and, well, I thought maybe you could help me on my next essay."

"You… you want *me* to help *you*? But… but you're smart."

"Clearly you know this stuff better than I do." I lift my lips sheepishly. "So, what do you say? I have practice after school, but maybe we can meet in the library around seven?"

"Um… sure. I mean, I'd be happy to." His posture relaxes, and he grins. "Sorry. I just can't believe one of the Gods of Olympus Prep needs *me*."

"Well, you mortals have your uses," I say teasingly.

"By the way… uh… I hope this isn't weird, but I saw what you posted on your Insta. For what it's worth, I thought it was super brave."

"Thanks. I had to get some things off my chest." I sigh. "The tea account wasn't completely wrong, though. If I were as fit as Bailey Mitchell, I might have been made captain instead of her."

"That's probably just because she's a senior. You'll make captain next year, I'm sure."

Since Henry's just trying to be nice, I choose not to mention how much more impressive it would look on my resume if I'd made captain as a junior. It strains every muscle in my face to give Henry one more smile. "Thanks. Anyway, I'll see you after school."

Some people don't understand that here, you're always on camera. I'd say most don't, judging by how much gets sent in to Olympus Prep Tea. I don't just mean the school's security cameras. Think about all the times you might've walked across the back of someone's video, oblivious to the fact that you were being filmed. Or, if you want to go deeper down the rabbit hole, think about how you carry a camera around in your pocket and sleep with it next to you, or how your laptop's webcam is staring at you every time you lift the lid. Even if you think it's off, how hard do you think it is for someone to hack in and turn it on when you're always connected to the WiFi?

It might sound paranoid but I'm aware—all too aware. It's why I make sure to always look my best, even when I think I'm alone. Of course, even I'm not perfect—as that gym photo proved—but at least the awareness means I'm not stupid enough to do anything I wouldn't want blasted to the whole school.

Unlike Kristen Dane, who won't be allowed back until next semester after that little beer video was sent to the principal. And unlike Bailey Mitchell, whose senioritis must've hit early for her to think she could get away with smoking pot in the woods behind the school.

A small smile creeps onto my lips as I stare at the dark yet undeniable image. Maybe I won't have to wait until next year to make captain after all.

I set my phone on my desk and check my face in the small, gold-rimmed mirror I keep beside my textbooks. Spotting a slight smudge in my modest gray eye shadow, I quickly swipe a finger to fix it.

My phone vibrates. It's my stepmom, who's right on time for her weekly check-in.

I accept the call, and her porcelain-perfect face, which has graced the covers of fashion, news, and entertainment magazines around the world, fills my phone's screen. Though she appears to be relaxing at home, with the kitchen island unmistakable behind her, every particle of makeup adorning her regal cheekbones, sharp eyes, and full lips is flawless as always. Which isn't surprising considering she's the one who taught me about the "always on camera" principle. For world-famous actress Jun Gao, that's been true since before smartphones.

"Min, honey! You look wonderful, as always." A soft Chinese accent colors her words. She spreads her pink-lipsticked mouth into a warm smile. "I saw that you're over thirty thousand followers since your antibody-shaming post went viral, and the numbers are still climbing. Good work."

"I hope she isn't spending more time on that hobby than on her studies." Dad's face edges into view, stern and hard-jawed as always. Rex Wong didn't become the CEO of a top financial firm by being friendly. Since he's from a different region of China than Jun, his accent is slightly rounder than hers. "I know colleges like extracurriculars these days, but grades are always important, especially for Asian students. The bar is higher for you. Are you still number one?"

"My last history test didn't go as planned." Though nervousness tightens my chest, my voice remains as smooth as those of the American TV anchors I grew up watching. It's funny how many people assume I was born in China even though I sound more like a Fox blonde than my own parents. "I'll make up for it on the next essay. I have a plan."

Dad shakes his head. "So you're second best in grades, just like you were second best in soccer, in art, and in writing."

"Hey, I won that essay contest!"

"Only because Kristen Dane was suspended."

"Who cares? Colleges will only see that I got the award. Oh, and it turns out I'm the best in art too. Lily chose my painting to represent our school at the Voices of Our Youth contest. And don't forget I'm still the president of several clubs, including the debate team. As for soccer and academics… I'll soon be number one in those too."

Jun sighs. "Honey, all your dad was trying to say is that if you'd worked harder, you wouldn't have had to rely on chance. What if Kristen had been better behaved? What would you have done then?"

I clench my teeth. "You never know. I might still have won."

Dad points one finger at the camera on his side. "'Might' is not good enough. Being second best *might* be enough to get you into Harvard, Yale, or Princeton, but the only way to make sure is to be the *best* of the best.

Do you understand?"

"Of course, Dad. Trust me, anything you've thought of, I have as well." I force a smile. There's no point in dragging this out. "I *will* be number one in *everything* again soon. I *will* get into one of those schools. You'll see. Anyway, I have homework."

Jun nods. "We'll let you go, then. Have a good night!"

She hangs up, and I take several deep breaths. I wish I could be mad at my parents, but I know they're right. Could they have been nicer? Sure. But I'd rather face the cold facts they spoke of than live a life of mediocrity.

It's not until several minutes later that I realize neither said a thing about Ara's death or asked how I was coping with it. A shudder runs down my spine, and I feel a strange compulsion to open the desk drawer and look at the metal spider necklace.

Like Kristen Dane, and now Bailey Mitchell, Ara didn't realize that she was always on camera, that even in her most private moments, she was never truly alone, and unlike me, she wasn't prepared to handle what might happen when an unwanted image hits the internet.

She really should have known better.

BEFORE . . .

My friends' faces shimmer in fresh paint on the canvas. The light in the studio is dimmer than I would have liked now that the sun has gone down. Those of us who want to be considered for the Voices of Our Youth competition have to turn in our entries to Lily tomorrow, and though I'm not usually a last-minute kind of person, I was too busy to put the finishing touches on my painting until now.

It's eerily quiet, with only a vague electric hum and the soft sound of my strokes surrounding me. Everyone else must be back in their dorms studying by now. Well, everyone except Ara, who didn't even start her entry until this afternoon. She was already painting by the time I got here.

On the other side of the studio, she dabs her brush against her canvas, and I wonder what she's creating. The long metal legs of her spider necklace flash as she moves to draw a wide arc. She glances at me with a smirk, as if to say, *You know I'm winning.*

I huff. We may be in competition, but this isn't a race.

Minutes tick by, and I focus on my work. The contest didn't give many guidelines, but the theme is to depict our generation. I could think of no better way to do that than to show off the best we have to offer. And so I painted the gorgeous Amanda giving a beauty tutorial, the powerful Miles scoring a touchdown, the brilliant Ryder programming his soon-to-be-famous app, the athletic Diana scoring high in archery, the talented Lucius performing with his guitar. Each portrait in the collage is surrounded by markers of my friends' achievements—their trophies and medals, headlines about them and quotes praising them. They're going to love this when I show it to them. And, of course, I had to include a self-portrait. I'm a member of this generation too, after all.

I'm so engrossed with perfecting the details that I forget about Ara's presence until she throws down her paintbrush with a flourish.

"That should do it!" She stands and turns her canvas to face me. "What do you think?"

Since it's hard to make out the details from where I am, I set down my brush and approach.

At first, I think it has to be a mistake—that maybe distance and dimness are making me see the painting inaccurately. But soon I'm right in front of it, and there's no denying what Ara has drawn.

Grotesque caricatures of me and my friends fill the canvas in bold colors and abstract lines. In one corner, Amanda is pointing out the flaws in a child's face while smiling before a camera. In another, Ryder is shaking hands with neo-Nazis and other despicable groups while encouraging them to use his app. Images of the others intertwine across the painting, each one mocking and hideous—Miles drinking from a beer bottle labeled "toxic masculinity," Diana taking selfies with a lone blossoming tree while the rest of the forest burns around her, Lucius standing on a factory conveyer belt, being manufactured by tie-wearing executives. The caricature of me is in the middle, and in it I'm holding a "For Sale" sign with an arrow pointing down at me, desperately chasing individuals wearing the letters H, Y, and P with tears in my eyes.

Yet the painting is more than just cartoons; with her distinctive style, Ara has managed to capture the desperation that drives us. The image is somehow funny and sad and strangely profound all at once. And she did it all in one afternoon, when it took me weeks to finish my painting.

A deep, rumbling anger stirs in my chest. Ara's piece is beyond insulting. If it were only me she was making fun of, I might have been able to take it, but she came after my friends. Worst of all… it's *good*. Dynamic and engaging and full of energy… It has something to say, just like Ara always boasted. My artwork looks boring in comparison, empty of meaning and downright dull.

Ara beams at the painting. "It turned out better than I'd hoped. I'm going to call it 'The Gods of Olympus Prep.'"

"How dare you?" Voice shaking, I scowl at her. "You can't submit that!"

"Why not?"

"It's—It's offensive! You didn't get our consent to paint us, and—and—I mean, look at how you've drawn me! It's racist!"

She lets out a dry laugh. "I'm Asian too, remember? I know the difference between a racist caricature and one that mocks the subject's obsession with 'worth.' You're just mad because it's better than yours."

Rage explodes through my veins, and I snatch the painting. "You can't submit this!"

"Hey!" Ara grabs the other end and rips it out of my grasp.

"You *can't*!" I lunge at her and grab her wrist, trying to tear her grip off.

We each tug, struggling and scuffling, until suddenly I slip and smash the painting down on the easel. The wood bursts through the canvas, ripping a great hole through the middle.

Ara steps back in disbelief, but I shove the painting down further, making the hole bigger and yanking to shred even more of the canvas.

"My painting! I can't believe you did that!" Ara seizes the ruined painting and stomps away.

My head clears, and I realize just what I've done. "Ara, wait!"

For a moment I fear she means to destroy my painting in retaliation, but instead she grabs her bag and heads for the door.

I rush after her. "Where are you going?"

"Let's see if Lily lets you enter the contest once she learns you attacked me and destroyed my work."

"Don't." I stop and glare. If she tells, it'll be the end of my life as I know it. Not only because I'll be disqualified, but because the school has a zero-tolerance policy for physical violence. Never mind that I barely grabbed Ara. They'll call it assault and expel me. I won't let that happen. "If you rat on me, you'll regret it."

Ara lets out a scoffing noise and continues on her way. I didn't expect her to listen, but at least I tried to warn her.

All the teachers have retired for the night. Sure, Ara can send Lily an email, but she probably won't see it until the morning.

That doesn't give me much time. But I already have a plan to stop her from ruining my life.

PRESENTLY . . .

A beautiful number 100 sits at the top of the history essay Dr. Reich hands me. I'll have to check my spreadsheet to be sure, but I think that's enough to pull my overall grade back up to an A.

A lengthy comment sits in the margin, praising me for how much I've improved since the last test. Apparently, I've grown from simply regurgitating the textbook to actually understanding and analyzing the historical events.

He doesn't need to know that Henry Davis was the one who understood and analyzed, and that Henry spent the three days before the essay was due helping me with mine. Or that he loved explaining the topic while I wrote down what he said, even though it took hours.

The bell rings, and Dr. Reich dismisses the class.

As I head out the door, Henry rushes to catch up to me. "Hey, Min!"

I face him with a smile. "Oh, hey! Thanks again for all your help."

"You're... uh... you're welcome." He gives an awkward grin. "How'd you do?"

I proudly turn my paper with that lovely number 100 toward him. "How about you?"

"Ugh, eighty-seven. Dr. Reich said my essay had good ideas but sounded rushed and messy. I guess that's what happens when you pull an all-nighter to get it done."

I give a sheepish smile. "I'm sorry... I know I took up a lot of your time."

"N-no you didn't. I mean, I liked helping you." He shifts his weight. "Um... would you want to... um..."

"Hey, I've really loved hanging out with you, but I'm super busy. Maybe we can do another study session before the next test?"

He perks up. "Yeah, sure."

"Great. See you later." I head into the hallway, internally rolling my eyes. *Poor, sweet Henry, who actually thinks he has a shot with me.* Well, he's free to go on thinking that until I figure out what it is about his writing over mine that Dr. Reich likes.

I head to my next class, which is in another building, crossing covered walkways of majestic gray stone that face the courtyard.

A pair of unfamiliar adults stand in the center, both middle-aged and somber-looking. I slow my pace and try to get a better look. They certainly don't work here, and they look too unhappy to be visiting a kid.

The answer soon arrives in the form of Bailey Mitchell and her suitcases. I quickly look away, conscious of how it would appear if I stared. Coach hasn't told us yet of what would happen to her after that pot-smoking photo was sent to the principal, but by the looks of things, there's about to be a new opening for team captain.

Bailey appears upset as she follows her parents out of the courtyard. I almost feel bad. Plenty of others have done what she did and gotten away with it. I hold no personal grudge against her. She was only doing her best.

And so was I.

"Hey!" A furious voice shoots toward me.

I whirl to find Lydia standing there, mascara tears streaking her cheeks. "What do you want?"

"Everyone else might be ready to move on after what happened to Ara, but I'm not. I won't let you forget."

"No one's forgotten Ara. She—"

"I know what you did!" Lydia's voice is practically a screech. "I know you were the one who—"

"Lydia, please!" I put on a frightened expression and shuffle backward, keenly aware of the security camera behind me and how it's angled. "Just calm down!"

"Why should I?" As expected, she takes a threatening step toward me, fists clenched by her sides. "It's only a matter of time before I find the proof I need to—"

"Stop!" I stagger. "You're hurting me!"

"What's going on here?" Mr. Petrov, one of the math teachers, steps between us.

"Tell him what you did!" Lydia points an accusing finger at me.

I hold up my hands, maintaining my frightened look. "I don't know what you're talking about." I glance up at Mr. Petrov. "She just… came at me…"

Mr. Petrov looks at Lydia. "Is this true?"

Lydia, clearly too angry to realize what she looks like, glowers at me. "We're not finished, Min."

Mr. Petrov crosses his arms. "Yes, you are. This behavior is unacceptable, Lydia. Come with me. I think you need to have a talk with the principal. Min, you should come too."

I blink. "But I have class! You witnessed everything—couldn't you tell Principal Nelson what happened, and I could come by after to corroborate it? Please, I don't want to fall behind because Lydia assaulted me."

Lydia's jaw drops. "I didn't—"

"Yes, you did! You saw, didn't you Mr. Petrov?"

Mr. Petrov frowns. "We'll have to check the security tapes to see what exactly happened, but I suppose for now, there's no sense in you missing class. Go on, then. Lydia, follow me."

"Thank you, sir." I draw a deliberate breath and continue on my way. Behind me, Lydia continues arguing with Mr. Petrov, but from the sound of it, she's having no luck.

My body would have blocked the camera from seeing exactly what she was doing with her hands. All they'll see is that I staggered as if punched.

As I head under the stone archway leading into the next building, I grab my phone and check Instagram to see if anything interesting has been posted.

Following Ara's Color Weaver account from my private, pseudonymous Insta had been my way of keeping tabs on her while she was alive. It never occurred to me to unfollow her after she died.

Which is why her artwork now sits at the top of my feed: A rough yet fluid sketch depicting spiders amid ivy. The time stamp says it was posted two hours ago. Her followers who know her only as an Instagram artist might not even realize she's dead.

I hate how… how *good* that sketch is, even though it's an empty net compared to what she used to paint. I hate that even though it's a quickly drawn work-in-progress, it still carries more life than my painstakingly crafted paintings.

I shove the phone back into my bag.

BEFORE . . .

A sobbing noise rings out from the zigzagging steps below, though I can't see who it is. I pause in the stairwell, keenly aware of how empty it is. No one ever uses the back staircase unless they're trying to remain out of sight.

"I don't know what to do, Lydia." Ara's voice floats up from below. "Ever since that gossip account posted the video of me, no one will even talk to me about anything else."

No one will talk about anything else at all. I crouch down, hoping to get a glimpse of what's going on below.

"No one will even hear my side of it!" Ara exclaims. "Someone must've hacked my webcam, but no one believes me! They think I filmed it myself—why would I do that?"

"People are stupid," Lydia murmurs. "It'll be okay."

"No, it won't. When does it end? I just want to live my life, but people keep coming after me… and now this…"

I listen for a few moments more. The two talk in circles—Ara proclaims that her life is over because of the video, Lydia tries to tell her it isn't, Ara says she doesn't understand… and so on, and so on.

The topic of Ara's fight with me never comes up. Considering it's been a whole day and Principal Nelson hasn't called me into his office yet, I guess Ara never had a chance to rat me out. The video of her appeared on Olympus Prep Tea less than an hour after our confrontation in the studio. She must've gotten distracted and forgotten.

Good.

The bell rings. I leave the stairwell, satisfied.

PRESENTLY . . .

Olympus Prep was selected to host the Voices of Our Youth competition, and paintings from across the state now fill the auditorium's stage, which is flooded with bright lights. The competition's judges and sponsors sit in a neat line across the front, each dressed in a meticulously fitted suit or gown. This might be a high school contest, but since a prestigious gallery is behind it, everyone is treating it as they would an elite exhibition.

From my spot in the audience, I surreptitiously adjust my ivory-hued dress, whose goddess-cut neckline flatters my shoulders but threatens to plunge down to an inappropriate place. Thank goodness we're in the dark.

The gallery owner, an old woman in a plum mother-of-the-bride-style gown, concludes her speech about the importance of highlighting young voices. Standing behind the podium, she glances down at a piece of paper. "And now, to announce the winners."

Beside me, Diana nudges my arm and flashes me a smile—her way of saying, *You've got this.*

I smile back, but that strange coldness creeps into my gut again. I clutch my small bag a little tighter, digging my fingers into the gold

Medusa-head medallion adorning its front. I can almost feel Ara's metal spider necklace vibrating inside. It was a stupid thing to bring, but I couldn't help it…

"Now, as you know, these entries have been anonymous," the gallery owner goes on. "Until now, that is. All the artists behind these pieces are in the audience, and I ask that you come up here and reveal yourselves when your entries are announced."

She goes on to name three honorable mentions, calling out their titles and gesturing for the stagehands to take the artwork off the easels and bring them to the front. The three contestants stand to polite applause, make their way onto the stage, introduce themselves, and shake the old woman's hand.

The same happens for the third-place winner.

And then they announce the second-place winner: "Faces of the Future."

The painting brought forth is mine.

I do what's expected and smile graciously—at the applause, at the old woman, at my hideous second-place certificate.

And then the old woman announces the winning piece, the one whose artist is about to have their work displayed in her gallery, the entry that will shoot the one behind it to fame: "The Gods of Olympus Prep."

Gasps ripple through the audience as the artwork is brought up. Unlike the other entries, it's not a painting. It's a sketch, roughly drawn in black-and-gray outlines with crude shading. But the dynamic movements and flowing shapes are unmistakable.

It's an unfinished version of the image Ara painted before she died, the one I destroyed. A draft that contains all the elements she would go on to paint in the final, but lacking the color and finesse.

No one stands to claim the prize. Confused looks pass between adults and students alike. Everyone must be wondering who's behind the winning entry.

Everyone except me.

BEFORE . . .

The waning sun, nearly smothered by gray clouds, isn't quite bright enough to illuminate the hallway, but still the automatic lights haven't come on yet. Ominous shadows drift across the walls, and a shudder runs down my spine.

But it's all in my head. It has to be.

I make my way toward Ara's dorm. I haven't been able to catch up to her since our lunch period several hours ago, and I don't like not knowing what she's up to when she might still hold my fate in her hands. The video might have distracted her and everyone else for now, but there's still a chance she could tell.

No one's seen her since sixth period, and she hasn't posted anything or messaged anyone either. I know because I set up a program on my phone to track her online activity. Ryder's not the only hacker in this school… not since I persuaded him to help me on a so-called computer science project.

I'm surprised to find Ara's door ajar. Yet no sound emits from beyond.

An uncomfortable feeling twists my gut. I approach and softly rap against the dark wood. "Ara? Are you in there?"

No response. Hesitantly, I push the door open.

Ara lies sprawled face-up on her black-and-purple dorm rug, her dark eyes staring upward into oblivion, an empty medicine bottle clutched in one still hand.

I stare in disbelief. Trembling, I approach and feel for a pulse, even though I can already tell it's too late. I drop to my knees, sobbing. *Oh, Ara…*

No one would believe me if I told them, but I never hated her. I admired her—respected her, even. I couldn't let her get in my way, but that didn't mean I wanted her gone forever… If I'd known…

Wiping my eyes, I reach for my phone to call 9-1-1, even though there's nothing they can do for her now, but freeze when I glimpse something under her bed.

It's a portfolio. I don't know why, but I feel compelled to take it. I glance through all the unfinished sketches, the experimental works-in-progress. They may be empty of detail and color—webs of pen and pencil scratches instead of tapestries of paint— but they nevertheless feel vibrant in a way my art never could.

If I leave them here, her grieving parents will stash them away in some attic, and her art will die with her. *I can't let that happen… I owe her that much…*

A new resolve fills me. I gather the portfolio and stand. As I head out, my foot meets something metal on the floor, and it slides across the dark wooden boards.

It's her spider necklace. The clasp is broken. Why she tore it off and threw it on the floor, I'll never know.

I scoop it up and clutch it to my chest.

PRESENTLY . . .

It wasn't my fault. Ara and I hadn't been close in ages—how was I supposed to know that she'd been struggling with her mental health, or that she'd been fending off online stalkers and trolls for years? How could I possibly have realized that someone so self-assured, who cared so little about what everyone else thought, was harboring such deep pain? It was just one video, no different from the images posted of Kristen Dane, or Bailey Mitchell, or even me. Kristen and Bailey dealt with it. I dealt with it… maybe that's why I did it to myself in the first place, to prove I could. I may have been the one to post the locker room picture, but I wasn't the one who took it… that was a creepy kid in my PE class who'd been texting it to his friends.

Sitting at my desk in my dorm, I stare at the Olympus Prep Tea burner account I created after finding Ara's body. The authorities are probably investigating the old one, trying to figure out who was behind it, searching for a crime to prosecute.

They won't find one. Like I said, Ryder isn't the only hacker in this school.

Really, it was society's fault that Ara felt the way she did. If they didn't judge so harshly, one hacked video wouldn't have been such a powerful trigger. It wasn't me. It was misogyny and toxic internet culture and mental health stigmas and… and…

I navigate away from Olympus Prep Tea and pull up Ara's Color Weaver account instead. No one will ever figure out how I secretly entered her sketch into the Voices of Our Youth competition, or learn how her portfolio ended up at the gallery. The owner said that, with Ara's parents' permission, she would honor the terms of the competition, award the prize posthumously to Arabella Zhi, and display the sketches.

Ara will outlive us all. I already know what will happen next. The media will sensationalize it, of course—how a dead girl's sketch won the grand prize. They'll drive themselves into a frenzy trying to figure out who's running her Insta now that she's gone.

In addition to her paper sketches, Ara left behind an impressive digital portfolio of unfinished work—plenty to keep her account full of content. I pull one up and post it under her handle. *Weave on, foolish girl… Weave on…*

My eyes sting, and I reach into my blazer pocket for the spider necklace and give it a squeeze. Maybe after Ara's work gets displayed, this compulsion will end.

I navigate back to the Olympus Prep Tea account and absentmindedly tap and scroll until I find my finger hovering over the option to delete the account.

But getting into top colleges has become a war, and a warrior doesn't throw away her most powerful weapon when she's only a few battles away from winning.

By this time next year, I might have already been accepted early by my top-choice school. After that, I can delete it. Until then…

I tap the icon to create a new post and upload a video that was submitted anonymously to the account a few weeks ago. Lydia is the one featured this time. Maybe her fight with me would have been enough to get her expelled, but in case it isn't, this should do the trick. I don't know what evidence she might have about what I did to Ara, but I can't take any risks. She has to go.

She shouldn't have challenged a God.

DARKEΠ THE ΠIGHT

AMY MCNULTY

G OT A TEMP *job in North Dakota. Be back in three weeks. Don't go out after dawn. Dad.*

Nothing like waking up at the ripe hour of six P.M. to find your dad gone, leaving nothing behind but a note and two hundred-dollar bills to tide you over for the next three weeks.

I finished towel-drying my long, frizzy black hair, tossed the towel into the laundry bin collecting an unwieldy pile of Dad's and my clothes at the top of the basement stairs, and pulled open the kitchen cupboards. A can of baked beans. Correction: A dented can of baked beans. Two cans of spinach. At least I'd get some nutrients.

Slipping on my sunglasses, I opened the fridge, wincing even through the dark lenses at the blast of white light filling the otherwise dimly illuminated room.

One gulp of milk. Correction: An expired gulp of milk. A wilting cucumber. Half a block of swiss cheese.

The freezer: A tray of ice and a wilted box of frostbitten waffles.

This was the grocery list of a man out to upend the notion of what a meal consisted of.

No wonder my dad's name was Caius. Just one short sound off from

"Chaos."

Shutting the freezer door, I slipped off my glasses and pulled back the thick light-blocking curtains over the kitchen window—similar such curtains blocked every window in our one-story three-bedroom ranch. Nightfall, as expected. I liked winter because the nights were longer. That meant I could be outside for longer, get some fresh air.

Even if the Wisconsin winters often got cold enough at night to nip off your nose.

"Don't go out after dawn," I said out loud to no one but myself. Most fathers didn't want their daughters going out after nightfall, but with my extreme light sensitivity, it was night or nothing for me.

Bright, artificial light hurt my eyes. Sunlight did that and turned my corpse-like skin into a blistering mess straight out of *The Walking Dead*.

My inbox would be full with my at-home learning assignments for the day, the pre-recorded lectures of the district's finest selection of online curriculum teachers.

My stomach rumbled.

But I wasn't going to be doing any learning until I had a decent breakfast.

"He didn't say anything about being careful after dark," I mumbled, clutching my sunglasses in one hand and slipping one of the bills in the pocket of my jeans.

A few minutes later, I was bundled up to face the cold, scratching my black cat, Charon, under the chin. He was also just waking up, but he did that several times a day regardless.

"Dad didn't pick up anything for you, either," I told him. I looked at his bowl as I slipped on my ankle-high boots. At least there were a few kibbles left. Dad must have fed him before he'd left. But there was no wet food in the cupboard.

"Looks like I'm budgeting for two."

Charon rammed the top of his head against my boots, weaving in figure eights between my legs.

He let out a pitiful purr as I headed outside and closed the door between us. I peeked at him one last time. He sat on his back legs, lifting one front paw and then the other like he was kneading the hardwood floor.

"I won't be long," I promised.

A pang of guilt hit my chest along with the slap of cold air. I really had nothing to feel guilty about—Charon would live another twenty minutes before I brought back some dinner for him. But he was practically my only friend. Sure, there was a chatroom for other district online curriculum learners and Dad had tried to get me together with some homeschooled kids once, back when he'd actually halfheartedly tried to participate in my schooling. But it had never clicked. True, there were those few hours in the evening we were all awake, but then they went to bed and I still had all those long hours ahead of me.

Long, dark, quiet hours. Even Dad was asleep half the time at night, whenever whatever job he'd floated to—if he had one at all—required him to get some rest for first shift. If he got a third-shift job, then, well, he was there and not home.

It was just me. And Charon. Whoever my mom was, I'd never met her—at least not since the days I could form memories. Dad had no pictures of her, or himself, or anything of his early days.

He was just Dad. Disheveled, loving in his own way, but chaotic. The Douglases were loners down to their DNA.

If I'd gotten a good breakfast and been able to feed Charon his dinner, I might have been able to stop by the library, get some human company in for the day via osmosis for the couple of hours before it closed. I blinked back tears as I glanced at the brick building and its piercingly bright lights filtering out through the window. We lived a decent walk away from virtually anything we needed—but I only had limited time to enjoy any place in a mid-size town like ours. Well, except for the convenience store at the gas station. At least that was open twenty-four hours a day. The grocery store a few blocks down the road would still be open right now, too, but the bottoms of my earlobes sticking out from under my knit cap were starting to throb from the cold. I hadn't thrown on a scarf. I'd figured since it wasn't snowing just yet, I could do without a layer or two for the short walk.

I'd been wrong. Summer nights may have been shorter, but I did save time on bundling up when I left the house to go anywhere.

The soft, yellow lights over the sidewalk I could usually stand without sunglasses, but the overhead lights at the convenience store and gas pump may as well have been responsible for lighting up a football stadium that could be seen on Earth's surface from Mars. Yawning, I slipped on my sunglasses and crossed over the concrete, weaving between the gas pumps. I nodded my head as I stepped into the light and a tall man by the pumps drowning in a worn Packers coat shuddered visibly. I was used to scaring people like that. Though my puffy purple down jacket had reflector tape across it vertically—affixed there by my father, who joked that we both blended into the night a little too easily—I was a creature of the night. I seemed to take the rest of Earth's denizens by surprise when I emerged from it.

A chime rang overhead the automatic convenience store door and a blast of warm air slapped across my windburned cheeks. As I slipped off my gloves and put them in my pocket, the grateful moan that escaped my lips as I blew on my frozen fingers to warm them up was like something an old man might have let out stepping into a sauna.

The clerk behind the register chuckled, and I felt my cheeks pinken— but not from an assault by Mother Nature this time.

Quickly grabbing a shopping basket with no small amount of clatter, I shuffled inside, eager to disappear behind the shelves.

There was no one else in here, even though it wasn't *that* late. It was the closest gas station to my house, but it had its share of competitors nearer the highway that were newer and cleaner, to boot.

"Can I help you?"

Now it was my turn to startle, the friction of my down coat making it impossible to hide the fact that I'd jumped in place. I glanced out of the corner of my eye. The clerk.

"No, thank you," I said, but it came out so quiet, my voice practically cracking at my efforts to speak to another human, that I wasn't sure he'd heard me. I was in front of the meager pet supply section, but I spotted Charon's favorite brand of chicken and liver pâté and started loading up the basket three cans at a time.

"Here. Let me. I'm… I'm going to hold the basket for you." He gently grabbed at the handle of the basket that hung over my elbow and I realized with a start what he thought he was doing.

"That's cat food," he said, seemingly convinced I had to be made aware of this fact.

The sunglasses inside, nighttime outside.

More than once, people had assumed I was visually impaired and, eager to do their good deed for the day, they'd swept in to act like my hero without even asking first if it was okay.

Though I knew the do-gooders had wholesome intentions, I didn't think blind people were totally fine with the invasion of personal space, either.

I turned to face my rather forceful "Good Samaritan" and explain, but he'd already slipped the basket off my arm and was loading the cat food back on the shelf.

"Hey, wait!" I said, my ice-cold pale hand shooting out and covering his dark, warm one. An explanation, a protestation, flittered at the tip of my tongue, but all of a sudden, I couldn't speak.

My gaze turned toward him and for the first time since I'd stepped inside and he'd chuckled at me, I really looked at him.

Though he was filtered through the dark lenses of my sunglasses, I could see him clearly. He was handsome—and probably somewhere around my age. Skin almost as dark as the night itself, close-cropped dark hair that almost blended in with his scalp. His eyes were a brown so deep, they were almost black, and the whites around them looked like stars in the gaps of the endless night sky. I had to stop myself from reaching over and tracing the sharp lines of his cheekbones. Instead, I focused on the trim cut of his muscles that filled out the convenience store polo shirt with such elegance, he could have been wearing a designer's ironic take on gas station clerk chic.

"I'm sorry," he said, drawing my attention back to his face. His lips drew into a frown as his eyes met mine through my dark sunglasses. "I thought you were…" He left the rest unsaid, perhaps still unsure whether or not I was blind.

I focused on refilling the basket with Charon's favorite food. "I *am* shopping for cat food." My stomach growled. "And people food." I tapped the temple of my sunglasses. "I'm light sensitive—since you seem to be wondering."

Wow, I was really doing a great job with this whole human-contact thing.

The clerk looked around and above, and even he blinked, his eyes watering. That was what happened when you stared into halogen lights. "I guess it is kind of bright in here."

"You have no idea," I said, using his diverted attention to snatch the basket back from him. "I can't stay in here too long—even with the sunglasses."

"Oh, sorry." He tucked his hands in his corduroy pants pockets and shuffled his feet. "I didn't mean to keep you. I thought I was helping."

"Thanks. But ask next time before you just assume." Yup. Not making a real human friend today.

"I will," he said quickly, surprising me. He didn't seem to have taken offense at all.

But I didn't have time to contemplate his character or dwell on the way my stomach was doing somersaults right now. I had no business dating a daywalker, for lack of a better term. At least not until I was an adult and could maybe find someone who worked a steady third shift alongside me.

True, there were those few hours each day when the rest of the world was winding down just as I was getting started, but… Most teens wanted to see their significant others *sometime* during the day.

The door to the outside opened again, and that chime rang out throughout the store. The clerk turned on his heel to welcome the man who'd been pumping his gas when I'd arrived. I used the chance to slip away to get the rest of my shopping done as the clerk went to help the customer at the register.

I didn't think I imagined the nosy stare from the customer—more discerning even than the clerk's had been—the whole time he stood there, dictating an order for cigarettes and lottery tickets. When he jogged over to the cooler and grabbed some beer, too, the clerk shouted into the backroom. "Twenty-one at register!"

A harried, balding man of around sixty with a wan dark brown complexion and a portly figure rushed out of the backroom with a scowl on his face, the smile that appeared a moment later all for show as he helped finish the customer's transactions.

So I was right. The clerk was close to my age. I was seventeen—a senior in high school—and he could have been in college. But he wasn't yet twenty-one.

The customer left and the handsome clerk said, "Thanks, Pop" to the man who'd appeared from the back. His "Pop" scowled and waved at him, as if to say it was no big deal, but he didn't say a word. His brown eyes flitted pointedly to me as I approached the register, then back to the clerk, and then back to me.

No smile for me? I was a customer, too!

But "Pop" seemed to think the clerk was up to something.

"No flirting on the clock," he snapped, then he disappeared back into the backroom.

Flirting? My heart was about to burst out of my chest.

With all the care of a baker carrying a seven-hundred-dollar thirty-tiered wedding cake, I put my basket on the counter as the clerk let out a nervous chuckle.

"That's my grandpa," he said quickly, grabbing for the half-gallon of milk. "He owns the place. Please ignore him. He thinks me smiling at a pretty face is flirting."

"*Pretty?*" I blushed.

The clerk blinked a few times, his hand frozen on the milk jug handle. "I *am* flirting now, aren't I?"

"Grandpa knows best," I said, like a total clod.

But it made him laugh.

"I haven't seen you around here before," he said, continuing to scan my order.

"I come here pretty often." I had to clear my throat to try to remain cool and collected.

"I've worked shifts here for a year now—I haven't seen you."

He spoke as if he were *positive* he'd remember.

"I guess I don't often come this early."

"Early?" He checked the dusty, grimy clock on the wall behind him. It was nearing seven now.

"I like that they're open all night."

"What are you, a vampire?"

I tapped the temple of my sunglasses again. "Light sensitivity, remember?"

"Oh, uh…" His smile faded. "Sorry." He kept scanning, the air growing quiet between us.

Yeah, I needed a lot more practice with this human contact thing.

"Do you go to Olympus?" he asked.

"Huh?" It took me a second to realize what he was asking. The high school toward the south end of town.

"No… I live just a few blocks away."

His eyes sparkled. "Me, too." Then he frowned. "But I've never seen you at Titan," he said, referring to the closer high school. "I'd definitely notice. You graduated?"

I laughed. "No. I…" I gestured at the sunglasses again. "I homeschool. Well, through the district, not my dad. I'm a senior, though."

"Me, too." His smile went broader, his thick lips parting to reveal a dazzling set of teeth. My heart was beating double time.

"So you can't go outside during the day at all?" He was scanning the cat food now, just swinging the same can back and forth until the register beeped six times.

"No. Not unless I want to get real sick."

"Shame," he added. "But kind of cool."

"Cool?"

He swallowed visibly, stacking the cans neat and tidy in a plastic bag. "It's kind of like a superpower."

"Or a super kind of curse?" I offered.

He laughed. "Ere," he said.

"Air?" I repeated, confused.

He shrugged sheepishly. "Well, Erebus Jones, but that makes me sound like a comic book character, so I just go by 'Ere.'"

"Still sounds like a comic book name to me—but that's a good thing," I qualified quickly. You didn't get to be seventeen with hardly any friends without making a few fictional ones along the way. "I'm Phoenyx Douglas. I prefer 'Nyx,' though."

"Nice to meet you, Nyx." He counted my bananas but never once took his gaze off me. "You like comics, too?"

I opened my mouth, about to launch into a list of my favorite comic book characters and the thesis I was working on for my English lit class about how they're the modern versions of myths, down to messy relationship dynamics and parables to be learned from all their escapades and mistakes, but the door chimed again.

"Hello," said Ere, quickly speaking over my head.

I realized he had finished ringing up my order, and I dug under my coat to fish out the hundred-dollar bill I'd stashed there.

The woman who'd walked in—I hadn't really noticed her at first—seemed out of place. Harried.

She wore a fur coat—I hoped it was fake—and her heels clicked hard against the scuffed, white floor as she made her way to the register, practically pushing me aside.

"Do you have any cameras?" she asked, her voice quavering. She clutched the collar of the fur coat with one hand—a hand sporting multiple, shiny rings, with different colored gems set inside. "Nothing… Nothing digital. Nothing that feeds things to the clouds."

Ere stared blankly at her, blinking.

She was… She was a lot.

Her silver-streaked honey-blonde curls drooped, as if she'd just come from a party that had lasted a night and started into the next one. At first glance, she seemed no more than forty, but the longer you stared at her makeup-caked face, the more you were certain the wrinkles she was concealing denoted a few more decades.

She growled in frustration. "Like a Polaroid! Do you know what that is? *Millennials…*"

Millennials? Try Gen Z. This from a woman who'd just mentioned cameras "feeding things to the cloud."

"No digital backup?" I offered, as much to help Ere out as to get this woman out of my way. A headache was gripping at the edges of my temples. I'd been in the halogen lights too long.

"Yes." The woman dropped her grip on her coat and slammed the counter with a fist, knocking into my empty basket.

Ere arched a brow but snapped into action. "Yeah, I think so…" He turned around and stepped past all the tobacco products to exit the counter. There was a wall of batteries there, and he crouched, his head ducking past what I thought might be a grubby small collection of blank VHS tapes.

The woman turned her gaze on me, the tap, tap, tapping of her heel echoing out throughout the store. "A bit dark out for sunglasses."

I crossed my arms and dug my boots into the dirty black rug beneath my feet.

I may not have had a lot of experience talking to other people, but I also didn't take crap from those whose intentions were less than savory.

"I have a medical condition," I retorted.

She shirked back at my tone. She looked about to say something more, but as she took me in, she snapped her mouth shut.

"Ah, here we go." Ere came back to the counter with a large, rectangular box. "Disposable camera." He blew on it and a bit of dust floated up.

The woman frowned, recoiling. "I asked for a Polaroid."

Ere cocked his head.

"I have to get that film *developed*," she gritted out through perfectly white teeth.

"Oh!" said Ere. "We actually do that here." He pointed to the sign above him. Sure enough, under a list of prices for windshield wiper fluid and cigarettes and half-faded notices about the different lotteries you could "win" here, there was a notice that read, "Photo printing. Digital and film," along with a list of sizes and prices. It looked like it might have been cheaper to buy a photo printer and print out your photos yourself.

"My grandpa does it," Ere added, as if that would seal the deal.

"Fine, whatever." The woman snapped the box out of Ere's hands, having to reach over and grab it from him since he hadn't handed it to her.

"Ma'am—"

The woman scowled. "Most people call me 'Miss.'"

Most people didn't get a close look at her, then.

"*Miss*," Ere said, though I could tell he was going into "irate customer defense" mode and wasn't at all convinced. "I need to finish with this customer before you and then I'll ring you up."

"Forget it," the woman snapped. Tucking the camera box under her armpit, she reached into an almost-invisible pocket in her oversized coat and pulled out a wallet with a shiny gold clasp. Digging out some bills, she tossed them on the counter, a flurry of twenties landing on my plastic bags and inside my empty basket.

Ere scrambled to pick them up. "Ma'am, this is way too much—"

"*Miss*," she snapped, but she was already at the door, the chime echoing out overhead.

Ere and I exchanged a look and burst into laughter.

"Well, that's a first," he said.

I ignored the piercing pain sliding across my temples, the flickering white halo of lights threatening to descend now into my vision. "Was that like…" I counted the bills. "Eighty dollars?"

"For a twelve-dollar camera," he said, shaking his head. "Overpriced, sure, but I don't think anyone else has bought one since I was born. Wonder if it still works, actually. Pop says old film expires…"

He stared at the cash register, with my total—just under sixty dollars—and the stack of cash in his hand. "Groceries are on old *Miss*, I guess." He quickly added the twelve dollars for the camera to my total and punched in the cash in hand.

"Oh, no, I couldn't," I started, unfolding the bill in my hand. I bit my lip. Three weeks with two hundred. This could really help, stretch the grocery budget longer, maybe let me order a pizza one night…

"You can and you did." Ere scraped some coins out of the till and the register chirped with the end of the transaction. He handed me the change.

"Don't be silly." My face was burning now. "You should have kept it all yourself—for putting up with *that*."

"Hey, I'm not the one who told her to *f* off," he said, dropping the bills in one of my plastic bags when my hand wasn't forthcoming.

"I did *not*," I said with a chuckle, sliding my own money back into my jeans pocket.

"You stood up to her," he said. "More than I could do—even if I weren't working right now. Rich Karens like her creep me out."

"Do you get a lot of them here?"

He laughed. "No. But she's clearly on a mission."

My head was positively searing now, but my heart was thundering and I was determined to keep my cool. "Oh?" I asked, sliding the first of the bags over my arms.

"Are you going to carry all that? In the cold? For several blocks?" He looked concerned.

"I can handle it." I flexed my bicep, but even if there had been anything to see, he wouldn't have seen it under my thick coat. "So she didn't want a camera 'feeding the clouds' because…?"

Ere shrugged. "My money is on a cheating husband."

"She insisted she was a 'miss.'"

"Women like her, they're not actually single, but they don't like not being *confused* for a young, single woman. Whereas other women might find calling them 'miss' at a later age a sign of disrespect. No winning."

"One extra problem with the gender binary," I pointed out.

He smiled. He was just too good to be true.

"A cheating husband, huh?" I asked aloud. I thought about it. A camera for what—evidence? Without a digital backup, the husband wouldn't see the pictures.

"Probably better alimony with evidence of an affair," Ere explained.

"I'm surprised she doesn't just hire a detective."

"She may yet—though I don't know if we have any around here?" Ere offered. "But she was a Karen on a mission, clearly. There's probably some deep *need* within her to prove this herself."

"But if she catches him in the act, I think that rage might blow her cover." I giggled. "I can see her popping out of the bushes, her old, dusty camera shaking in her hand as she launches into a tirade."

"The man scrambling to get his pants back up, tripping on them as they keep slipping to his ankles." He chuckled.

He shared my dark sense of humor, too. If it weren't for the silver auras growing wider and wider, maybe I could have stayed.

"I… I have to go," I said, blinking, my eyes watering as I scrambled to slide the rest of my purchases over my arms.

"Oh. I… Sorry. That was gross."

I cocked my head. Oh, the comment about the pants around the ankles? "Oh, no, that was funny. It's just…" I swallowed hard and shrugged my shoulders, my three heavy bags already wearing me down. "Too long in the lights."

"Right! I'm so sorry. Pop?" He called back to the backroom, but I was already at the door.

"I'll… I'll see you," I said.

"Wait!" he called out. "I can walk with—"

But I stepped outside, my need for the dark so much more potent than my heart's longing desire to spend as much time with him as I could.

It was only when I was in my yard, out of the lights—even the dim, yellow lights overhead the sidewalk too much—that I realized I'd never asked for his number.

Oh, well. I knew where he worked and where he went to school.

I'd find him again.

My heart lightened at the thought.

The park was familiar, the humming of the streetlight overhead like a refrain in my head. Dad used to take me here after dark, when the park had been empty. More than once, a cop would swing by, be surprised to find a dad and his child instead of a bunch of teenagers, and recommend we move along and "get that little girl to bed."

Dad would crack half a smile and pretend to comply. But when we got home, he would play with me in the yard instead. He'd never had the will to explain to the cops that I'd just woken up, that I slept during the day.

The rusty swing ahead of me was barely moving, the small figure on it merely kicking their knees to get a little motion, their feet scuffing the dirt below.

"Are you… Are you lost?" I asked, finding myself at the child's side in a blink.

"Mom!" The boy who looked up at me was a stranger—but somehow totally familiar. He had thick, dark hair, a medium brown complexion, and rich, dark eyes that reminded me with a start of the stars amid the sky, just like…

Just like…

"You came!" The boy—he couldn't be more than eight—jumped off the swing and hugged me tightly.

I patted his head and looked around, looking for his real parents. My headache had faded to something like an echo, the pain there but only a nuisance when I stopped to focus on it.

With a start, I realized I wasn't wearing my sunglasses and my heart thundered, pounding.

It was night, but there was still that light overhead—and over there… Over there at the other end of the playground.

I screamed. The light. The light was so bright there.

"Don't look," the boy embracing me said, pulling back. "That's Ethan and Emma—the day and the light."

My eyes watered, but I couldn't look away. A boy and a girl played amid the burst of sunlight, swinging from the monkey bars and laughing. They were playing in the day.

But it was night here.

My head pounded harder and I rubbed my temples, squinting my eyes.

"It's okay," said the boy, resting a warm hand on my pale elbow. I was dressed for summer. Yes, it was hot here. Day and night and hot and wrong and…

"You're dreaming," the boy said. "I'm the dreams," he added, as if that would explain it all. "Hy."

"Hi…" I repeated softly, still so confused.

He laughed. "Hypnos. But you and Dad call me 'Hy.'"

"Hy." Instinctively, I ran my hand through his thick curls, the feeling like coming home.

"I don't have much time," he said, his little face growing far too serious. "I thought you might respond better to me as a child. This is me ten years from now. I need you to save us."

"Save you?"

"Me—my brothers and sisters." He gestured toward the haunting laughter, the blinding light. "They're just two of them."

Despite everything, a sardonic chuckle escaped my throat. "If you're telling me in ten years, I'm going to have more than *three kids*…"

"Not in ten years, no, but… Never mind. Mom." Hy gripped me by both arms, all childlike demeanor gone entirely. "Mom, unless you can strike fear into Zeke's heart, I'll die. We all will."

"You'll… die?"

Hy sighed and sat back down on the swing, scuffing his feet against the dirt. "Twenty-five years from now, his wife, Helen, hires me for a job."

This *boy* had dropped all trappings of childhood, his weary little face so at odds with his angelic-like innocence.

"What kind of job? Who are Zeke and Helen?" This dream was getting weirder by the second.

Hy snatched hold of my hand and gripped it. "This isn't just any dream, Mom. I'm speaking to you through it. Like the Greek god whose name I bear, I have the power of sleep—and you, Nyx, are another coming of the goddess of night."

I ripped my hand out of his, surprised to find the boy's grip so strong—and so *real* in this dream.

He continued, undeterred. "You won't understand or fully control your powers for some time. But long before then, you have but one task if you want to save me—to save your children. Make the mayor fear you."

"The mayor?"

"Zeke Onassis. Mayor in your current time, mayor for another twenty-five years, at least. He controls this town. He does what he pleases, and there are none who would dare face him."

I thought briefly over the images I'd seen of the local mayor. Dad never discussed politics. I couldn't be sure his scattered mind even lent itself to bothering with basic matters like who led our town.

Yes, I'd seen him in the occasional news piece. Strikingly handsome for someone who had to be almost fifty, rather built with curly silver hair that fell just a bit down his neck. He always posed for photos with his hands behind his back and his knees slightly apart, like he knew he owned the place, wherever he was being photographed.

And, on occasion, beside him was…

"That woman! At Ere's store." My heart thundered as my instant-crush's name escaped my lips.

"Yes, Helen Onassis. As power-mad as her husband, but perhaps the only one who can stand up to his wrath—she's consumed with jealousy over his affairs."

"Affair*s*?" I asked, emphasizing the plural.

"And illegitimate children beyond count," Hy said, chuckling darkly. "Zeus and Hera… have not changed their natures in this modern world."

"But I don't understand. How did *you* get involved with this?" Part of me thought I was just humoring my subconscious, but a stranger, more pressing part realized I was starting to believe this was real.

That my future adult son was appearing to me in his memory as a child, that he'd projected into my seventeen-year-old brain.

Hy waved his hand and a little sparkle of light reminiscent of a puff of glitter soared into the air. It was dull enough not to bother me, even without my sunglasses. He blew on it, and it traveled across the playground to the monkey bars and into that blinding light—and then the light went out.

The two children who'd been playing there curled up on the dirt and, using their clasped hands as pillows, fell asleep on the ground.

Hy snickered. "You always yell at me for putting my siblings to sleep like that."

Sure enough, a rising bubble of aggravation shot up my throat, but I pushed it down. This was just a dream. No one had the power to put others to sleep with a wave of floating glitter. No one could send messages through sleep.

"Helen asks me to put her husband to sleep," said Hy. "I do. She gets what she wanted—control over the finances, control over the town. A husband who finally stays snug in *her* bed, and illegitimate children who come clambering for a handout and won't be given the time of day."

"You… drug him?"

Hy shakes his head. "In the original days, Zeus slumbered. But by the time I do the job for Helen, my powers have evolved. I *put him to sleep*, but he walks around. He appears able to function, but all facets of himself are gone. He's Helen's puppet."

"*Okay*… But this is you as an adult, right? How can I help you now?"

"He wakes up." Hy clasped both little hands over his eyes, as if cradling a headache. "My power is weaker than his—it doesn't last. When he figures out who was responsible, he'll kill me. He's too afraid of Helen, too prideful to risk divorce, to do much to punish her. It's me, Mom. He wants me dead."

A wave of dread came over me, my heart practically soaring through my throat. It was as if someone had threated to kill my cat—my dad. No, worse than that. Someone… Someone I'd love more than life itself.

No matter what he may have done.

To a man who seemed to me to deserve it.

I found myself on my knees, cradling my dream son against me. "What can I do?" I asked, softer now.

"Protect me. As an adult—as a child. He'll fear you."

"I don't understand," I said. "Even if what you're telling me is true—that I'm a reincarnation of an ancient god, that one day I will have powers of my own—I'm nothing right now. Nobody. Why should a powerful man thirty years my senior come to fear me when you say the only person who even intimidates him in the slightest is his wife?"

Hy pushed back, his star-like eyes dead serious. "He feared you then, and he will fear you now. Nyx, you are a goddess born of Chaos, independent of Zeus and his ridiculously large clan. He has feared you and he will fear you again. If he doesn't, I won't live to my twenty-sixth birthday—and it won't just be I who pays the price." He turned his gaze to the other children, still curled up and lost in their dreams.

"But, Hy, I…"

"Talk to Dad. You can do it—together."

"*Dad*?" I asked, but I knew without him saying.

Erebus.

He was telling me I'd just met the man I was going to marry, have kids with.

This dream was toying with my subconscious.

Something jumped on my stomach and I jolted awake.

His purr as loud as an avalanche in my ear, Charon tapped my face with a paw tentatively, then more aggressively, determined to snap me out of my dreams.

"All right, all right." I rolled over, letting my cat slide to my mattress so he'd stop squishing my organs.

I blinked in the pitch-black room at the alarm clock. 3:00. In the afternoon. It still wouldn't be dark enough for me to be up, really. Though I was still up for a chunk of most mornings. I just spent them hidden behind my black-out curtains that Dad had affixed tightly in place in my bedroom so Charon couldn't jostle them aside and burn me with the light.

Charon's thunderous purr was only outmatched by his determination as he kept ramming into my side, headbutting me and walking over my thighs at the edge of the bed.

"Okay, you're hungry, I get it." I tried thinking beyond that, my mind slow to catch up. Last night, the extra time spent in the convenience store had given me a massive headache. I'd come home, taken a nap, promising myself I'd wake up after a short while and finally get my schoolwork done…

I stared blankly at my computer. It was still on. I always turned it off before I went to bed.

I stared down at my clothes. My jeans. My sweatshirt.

I never slept in anything but tees and sweats.

That nap had lasted… I blinked at the clock again. That nap had lasted just a few hours shy of a full day!

Flinging the comforter aside, I leaped to my feet, Charon eagerly jumping to the ground beside me and trying to lead the way.

Just to make sure I wasn't in even worse trouble than I thought, I ran to get my phone off the charger and checked the date. Just one day later. But that was still certainly worrisome.

Charon settled for nibbling at my ankle now.

"All right, all right!" I thundered out of the room to the kitchen, stopping sharply at the end of the hall and blinking, my eyes watering. Charon had shifted aside the curtain in the kitchen to bathe in the sunlight.

Now he wove around my ankles, purring and purring.

"Baby, you just blocked my path to your food for another hour and a half or so at least," I said, rubbing my temples.

Charon stopped in front of me, lifting up one paw as he stared at me but hesitating, as if unsure whether or not to tap me.

"*Fine,*" I mumbled, heading back into my room. I flicked the dull, yellow lamp on and changed my clothes, this time, putting on the "has to go out in the daylight" outfit I reserved for doctor appointments, special events, and other once-in-a-blue-moon occurrences. Dad always insisted on being present for those so he could find me some shade or drape a blanket over me or generally step in whenever he thought I'd had enough.

And though Dad was never a reliably present father, there was one thing I was sure he wouldn't have wanted me to do without him here. His note had even said.

But I hadn't forgotten that dream. And frankly, the fact that I'd slept so long—even after such a headache—was proof enough for me.

Either something was seriously wrong with me, or my future son had used magic to visit me in my sleep and asked me to save him.

I slid on my sunglasses and pulled on my thick, dark hoodie, tying my wide-brimmed sunhat on top of that and sliding on my facial mask. The last thing I did was slip my hands into my thick, leather work gloves.

Charon purred at my feet.

"Okay, I'll feed you," I promised. "And then there's someone I have to see."

The only bit of my skin even exposed to the air was the small bit around my glasses—the forehead, the ears. But even those were protected by my sunhat's wide brim and the safari-like draping chunk of fabric over the back of my hoodie-covered neck.

Still, the light—even this long past noon—was blinding to me.

Through my dark, dark lenses, I was not unaware of the heads turning my way, the lingering stares, the muffled whispers. School was letting out, and everyone was either headed to the parking lot or the buses. Only a few bothered to make it as far as I stood at the sidewalk, walking off to the neighborhood houses so close you could commute to school on foot.

But if he really did live near the gas station like I did, then I figured...

"Nyx?"

The familiar husky but friendly voice caught my attention. With all of my equipment on, my neck met some resistance as I turned my head.

"How'd you know?" I asked through the muffled dark fabric of my mask.

Ere clamped his lips together as he examined me. "Good guess, I suppose, it being you under all of that."

"It's not funny, my condition." I wrung my hands together, but it was tough to get the same soothing gripping sensation I'd get without my work gloves on.

"No, of course not!" Ere scrambled to extend his hands out to apologize, but his bookbag slid down his shoulder and he had to readjust to swing it back. "I just meant... You're... You look adorable."

"*Adorable?*" I asked. I didn't know whether to be flattered or offended. I was leaning toward a mixture of both just then.

"Hey, Ere, enjoy your pandemic gardening!" shouted a boy who started laughing. "Can never be too safe from the sun or the germs!"

"Shut up, Ray!" Ere bit back at the boy.

I supposed I did look like I was trying to prevent catching the plague *and* skin cancer.

But UV rays *did* damage my skin at an accelerated rate, so he wasn't too far off with that one.

"I'm sorry about him," said Ere, rubbing his cheek as he straightened his backpack again. "He's a jackass." He leaned in closer. "But should you even be out here? Don't get me wrong, I'm glad to see you, but…"

"Can we talk?"

"Of course!" He practically bounced on his toes, but then he stopped suddenly. "Something's wrong, isn't it? This isn't a social visit."

How he could tell my lips were in a grim line with all of my equipment on, I didn't know.

"Let's go to my place," he said, then he frowned. "I mean—I can turn off the lights, and it's pretty dark in the basement. I didn't mean anything weird by it or anything. I know we just—"

I snatched his hand, cold in mine even through my thick, leather gloves. "That's perfect."

Ere didn't say anything as he led the way, but he didn't let go of my hand, either. More than a few heads turned my way as we shuffled down the sidewalk, but I didn't care.

Just then, I felt right. Ere and I went together, like the darkness and the night.

His house was just a block away, the gas station halfway between his place and mine. It was a two-story blue house, if my view through my sunglasses was accurate. There was a collection of rocking chairs on the porch, a small table that looked perfect for a pitcher of lemonade or iced tea on a hot summer day.

Not that I knew much about enjoying those.

"Ma?" Ere called out as he unlocked the door. Even to fish his key out, he didn't let go of my hand. "She's usually still at work," he said as we stepped indoors. "But I thought I'd check… It's just my mom, grandpa, and me here, and uh, they're both at work, I guess, so are you okay coming in?"

I squinted, the sunlight still streaming in through a wide window in the living room on one side and another in the kitchen on the other. "Yeah…" I said, my head starting to pound.

"Come on," he said, dropping his backpack on the ground near a coat rack and dragging me toward a door at the end of the hall. The darkness was a relief, the tension fleeing from my muscles as he opened a door, still holding tight to my hand.

"Is the overhead light all right?" he asked.

I nodded. It would be lightyears better than what I'd been dealing with the past half hour in any case, and I knew we'd need some light to get down the rickety set of stairs safely.

The bulb over the stairs hummed after Ere flicked a switch. He finally let go of my hand, but only after gently placing it on the bannister for me. "Watch your step."

The basement was dark, and my eyelids were relaxing already. The light over the stairs the only illumination, I felt safe enough to remove my glasses, putting them down on a pile of boxes, followed by my gloves, my hat, and my mask.

"This is going to sound crazy—" I started as Ere stepped up beside me.

He crossed his arms over his broad chest and nodded at me. "If you're about to tell me you dreamed about our future children, and one of them told you he would die if we didn't manage to make the fully adult, corrupt mayor fear *you*, I'm already ahead of you."

My mouth gaped open like a fish's.

Ere's teeth sparkled as he grinned. "And here I thought you might tell me *I* was crazy."

"Hy visited you in your sleep, too?"

"Even the same name!" he shouted. The smile flit off Ere's face then. "Hypnos Jones—sounded like something my subconscious would have come up with. Like I'd stick my own kid with a comic book name, too."

"And the other two?" I asked.

His eyes narrowed. We both spoke at once.

"Ethan and Emma."

"*Damn*," said Ere. Now it was his turn for his mouth to hang open. "That can't be a coincidence."

He took hold of me again, my small hands practically swallowed up in his large ones, like the darkness embracing the night sky.

Instead of voicing how remarkable this shared dream was, how unbelievable it was that the future we'd both seen could be real, he said, "You have beautiful eyes."

I blinked, surprised to find the teardrops fluttering off my eyelashes.

Few saw the violet eyes I knew reflected back his dark ones at this very moment.

But Erebus did. No one else would ever understand me, embrace me quite the same way that Erebus would.

And I knew—putting aside common sense—with a bubbly feeling that floated up from my toes to my chest, that our future was real.

"We have to blackmail the mayor," I said.

Ours was a strange relationship, halting, hesitating at moments and so sure the next.

I'd never had a boyfriend before.

He told me he'd never felt this way about any girl.

We'd just met—so there was a part of both of us that kept putting on the brakes.

If it was meant to be, we'd have plenty of time.

But there was another part of us—a deeper part I couldn't quite give voice to—that just *knew*.

He was mine and I was his. We'd face this together for the children we'd had once, in a lifetime that felt like a faded dream—the children we'd have again.

We just had to figure out how a couple of teens with average parents were going to strike fear into the heart of a corrupt mayor who could barely keep his belt buckle clipped.

"Chocolate or vanilla?" Ere asked, one hand still holding mine, the other sliding over the yellowing, crinkling instructions his grandpa had taped to a table in a makeshift storm-cellar-turned-dark-room.

"Hmm, strawberry," I answered. On top of some bins, I spotted the hydroquinone the instructions said he'd need to soak the film in and lugged it up to the table with my free hand. "Marvel or DC?"

A wide grin on his face, Ere leaned back as if I'd slapped him. "Really? You want to get things that heated this quickly?"

I shrugged. "It's a simple question."

"Okay, then, what's your simple answer?"

"Marvel. And Batman."

Ere laughed. "That's cheating."

"Batman's Rogues Gallery, to be specific," I added.

"Of course. What better figures for the goddess of night to root for?"

"Or the god of darkness?"

We stared at each other blankly for a bit. It still didn't feel real—any of it. Well, this did, actually. His hand around mine.

A phone started ringing, the ringtone futuristic and mechanical, like a spaceship calling across the vastness of the galaxy.

"Is that it already?" Ere asked, squeezing my hand once before letting it go. "Only Pop calls me. Even Mom texts."

He slipped out of the storm cellar to grab the phone. I hovered in the doorway, leaning against the doorjamb as he had his conversation.

"Film development? Really?" His brows shot up as he gazed at me—our guess was correct. "Doesn't happen too often anymore... She's paying *how much* for hour development?" He put a hand over his phone and mouthed "five hundred dollars" to me.

My shoulder practically slipped off the doorframe.

"Sure, I could come in and watch the store, but, Pop, how about I *develop* the film for you? I know you have other work to do."

He nodded, frowning, as his grandpa had some sort of response to that.

"Of course I remember how." He mouthed, "Not really" at me. "*You're* the one who taught me. You're the one who put the darkroom in our basement. You can't develop it at the store. And you're in a rush, right? So this makes sense. I can *run* to the store and back. You'd take half an hour just to carry the film to and from the house."

Ere drew the phone away from his face and winced. Whatever his grandfather was saying, I could definitely make out the tone at least. He wasn't happy.

But then he calmed down somewhat and Ere put the phone back to his ear.

"I swear to you I won't mess this up. I *swear*, Pop. Or you can deduct the five hundred dollars from my paycheck. Okay, my next *three* paychecks, whatever it takes to make up for it."

Ere gave me a thumbs-up as he finished up the call. "I knew that would seal the deal," he said after tapping the screen.

I rubbed my arms. Even with my coat and the sweatshirt, it was getting chilly down here. Or maybe it was just the realization that our plan—scraped together with guesses and a lack of any other possible connection to the man—was coming together so well.

"Stay here," said Ere, reaching for his coat, which he'd tossed down on a ping-pong table covered with a layer of dust. "I'll be back with Helen

Onassis's camera."

"What if it's not hers?" I asked, though the question felt foolish almost as soon as I'd asked it.

Of course it was hers. Who else would bring *film* to be developed? The digital photo printing they could do at the store—and even that didn't bring in a ton of business, Ere had told me.

And who else would have demanded a one-hour development service they didn't even offer and solve the problem by waving a bunch of money in the proprietor's face?

"It's almost nightfall," I said, bringing my own phone out of my pocket and checking the screen. Still nothing from Dad, but that wasn't surprising.

"Still, it's *not* quite nightfall," he said. "Just stay put. My mom shouldn't come home within the next ten minutes."

"And if she does?" I asked.

Ere came closer, a light, bouncing movement to his steps.

"You're right. Maybe I should text her that my girlfriend is over in the basement."

My stomach did a tumble at the label he'd given me.

"Isn't she going to wonder why you've never mentioned me before today?"

"Do you think she'll buy the our-future-son-talked-to-us-both-in-our-dreams angle? Nah. She won't pry like that, though. Probably will assume I didn't just meet you yesterday."

I took one of his hands, and then the other, in mine. We kept doing that. We hadn't kissed yet—too much of that common sense was weighing down my mind—but this... This still felt so right.

"We met before the beginning of time," I said softly. "The darkness and the night—they've always been one."

And someday, supposing our son truly could wield the ability to manipulate sleep, perhaps we would be as powerful as he.

Ere really *had* been taught how to develop film as a kid. His grandpa had been an amateur photographer of sorts for most of his life, and though even he'd moved on to digital cameras, he hadn't had the heart to pack up his darkroom entirely.

"Who'd have thought these skills would come in handy someday?" Ere dazzled even in—or perhaps *especially* in—the red light soaking the storm cellar like a horror movie filter from overhead.

He clipped the last of the photos up on the clothesline above us.

The film hadn't been expired—or it probably had been, but it had still worked. We'd made three copies of each of them. Ere had insisted his grandpa used the darkroom so little these days, he wouldn't notice the extra paper we'd used up.

Now we waited.

Ere slid a hand around my waist, drawing me closer to him. My head lay on his shoulder. It felt so natural.

"This is going to take longer than an hour," I said.

Ere fluffed it off. "Pop told her it would be more like two."

"I bet she took that *really* well."

Ere chuckled.

The earliest photos he'd hung up were coming in nicely now, painting a picture of an evening—and morning—Helen Onassis had spent scouring in the bushes outside of a hotel downtown.

"Did she have to climb a balcony for that shot?" I asked, pointing to one clearly taken through an upper-story window. Like *right outside* an upper-story window. Some of the images were somewhat blurry, and none were exactly framed with finesse. This one showed a railing of a balcony just to the side of the window.

"I would have loved to have seen her scale that wall with that coat on," Ere said.

He startled and his hand slipped over my eyes.

"What?" I asked, grabbing hold of him and struggling to see.

"Maybe you shouldn't be looking at some of these."

"Oh, but *you* can?"

"You said you've never had a boyfriend before."

I tugged on his hand until it finally dropped. "I have the Internet, Ere."

He swallowed noticeably, a sheepish grin on his face. "Touché." His eyes flit back to the pictures, the last of which were coming in clearly now—as clearly as Helen had managed to take them anyway.

But yes, Zeke Onassis was in every one of them, as clear as day. I'd done some research on my phone while Ere had gone to pick up the film. Zeke was every bit the blowhard—handsome, and he knew it—as I'd remembered. The more I read from the people who'd interviewed him, or the people interviewed who knew him, the clearer it was that the guy had a temper. Most writers tried to cleverly dance around it, calling him "strong-willed" or "determined to get his way." One even mentioned their conversation going from pleasant to "intense" at what he'd perceived to be the mildest of criticisms over an item in his budget.

Of course, there'd been all the flattery like "charming" and "idiosyncratic" and "intelligent," too.

The articles written by women reporters had to be the worst. The mayor's flirtations popped out between the lines in pretty much every single one of them. Or *in* the lines. One mentioned an effortless squeeze of her knee when she'd mentioned losing her dog recently. The topic had been a race to raise funds for the local humane society. She'd painted it as him being empathetic, but I'd been able to picture the moment with stunning clarity, as if I knew that man, knew what he was really up to— and hated him for it.

"These aren't the same women," said Ere, stroking his chin.

Now it was my turn to cover his eyes as he peered closer at one of the pictures. "Okay, I know you've had girlfriends and you have the Internet, but that might be a *little too much* scrutiny of these photos for my taste."

He backed up to get away from my hovering appendage that just barely managed to get to his eye level.

"I was looking at these hotel entry and exit photos," he said, pointing them out.

Flushing with embarrassment, I looked closer.

Sure enough, in the first photo, Zeke had his arm around a short, curvy woman with long, blonde hair.

In the second, he was exiting with a willowy redhead, almost as tall as he was.

"Does he manage to find every supermodel within a ten-mile radius?" I asked. "What are women like them doing in a small town like ours?"

"I could ask you the same thing." Ere nudged me.

I glared at him. "Flattery will get you nowhere just now. We have work to do."

Ere chuckled and started removing one in every three photos from the line. "First things first. I have to get these back to Pop so he can get them to our scorned wife."

"Why does she even *stay* with him?" I asked as Ere slipped the finished photos into an envelope, followed by the film, which he slid inside a smaller, almost fragile-like envelope first.

"Zeus and Hera…" Erebus grimaced as he sealed the envelope. "They have quite a history."

I supposed that explained it. If they were reincarnations in a sense like we were, old habits were going to die hard.

"So…" I said, looking at the two sets of remaining photos. "Have you ever blackmailed someone before?"

Ere snorted. Then his face grew serious. "Oh, uh, no."

"Zeus feared Nyx," I said, the bits of research on that subject I'd done while waiting not as reassuring as the fact that I just *felt it* to be true. "And he'll fear me," I said, a deepness in my voice I hadn't even thought possible.

For a moment, even Ere's eyes flickered with concern.

The darkness could be swallowed whole by the night.

I tapped my phone, bringing up something I'd found while going down the rabbit hole when it came to our fine mayor. "There's a place he'll be tomorrow, and I have a plan."

"Wow." Ere adjusted the dark blue tie at his neck, fiddling with the knot. "You look like a million bucks."

Or more like twenty at the thrift store earlier this year because Dad had thought that maybe I'd join the other online kids for prom by year's end. I wouldn't have even begun to imagine I'd be using it this way.

But the dress *worked*. A sparkly, sheen black dress with spaghetti straps, it dipped just a little over the bodice and though it reached my ankles, it had a slit up one calf to allow for better movement. I'd used a curling iron to add volume to my long, black tresses, and though I was hardly a master at makeup, I had the basics down—and I'd added some smoky black shadow.

"Do I look like I could be a reporter?" I asked. Albeit a very young one.

"You look more like you belong on a runway." Ere held the door to his navy blue sedan for me and took my hand as I approached, guiding me inside the passenger's side. It was borrowed from his mom for the evening. For a "fancy date" he was taking his new girlfriend on.

The only response she'd had was that he'd better bring this "fancy new girlfriend" over for dinner sooner rather than later.

There would be plenty of time for that—if we could pull this off.

"Models aren't usually so goth," I pointed out as I settled down and he shut the door.

"A next generation Elvira, then," he said once he got inside. He gripped the steering wheel, his face now grim. "You sure about this?" His eyes flicked to the envelope between the front seats of the car. "What if he… What if he flirts with you?"

"We *want* him to do some of that." I tapped the small black clutch I carried, at the bottom of which I'd cut out a piece of fabric so my phone's camera could record what was going on. "I'm a minor—that'll just be another bit of power we hold against him."

"Not if he doesn't *acknowledge* you're a minor," Ere said. His jaw twitched slightly as he pulled out onto the street. It was Saturday evening and the roads were a little crowded, but nothing like they'd be during the commute of the weekday. That was one thing I liked about being largely confined to the night—the world almost felt mine for the taking, with so few people out and about in the suburbs.

"I won't let it get that far," I promised. Truth was, there was a part of me that trembled at the audacity of what I was doing. But there was something lingering—something almost foreign, though it didn't feel like it was *wrong*—that was taking control.

No one threatened my family.

My family that didn't exist yet.

My family wasn't to be cowed by the likes of Zeus—Onassis—even if he held so much sway over everyone else.

"The more I think about it, the crazier I feel," Ere said. He looked *good* in a suit. More confident than he apparently felt. "We don't have an invitation to this—"

"It's a community charity event," I said, picking at a loose thread from the cut I'd made in my bag. At least it was an old thing from the back of my closet. Bought for dress-up as a child. In fact, perhaps a little *too* cheap if I was trying to project that I belonged there. "Anyone can come."

"But I bet they card you at the door," Ere said.

"Don't ask for liquor, just in case."

Ere snickered, his knuckles going just a bit white. "I hadn't planned on it, either way. Though I wonder now if everything people say about it calming nerves might come in handy."

I placed my hand over his on the steering wheel and felt it relax.

We drove the rest of the way in silence, my hand on his. Even without the car's heater blasting, there was warmth enough between us.

He found a parking spot at the country club, and we exited the car, Ere once again taking my hand, our noses in the air, like we were some sort of celebrity couple the paparazzi would be *lucky* to manage to catch a shot of.

In my purse, behind the recording phone was the envelope with one copy of Helen's incriminating pictures. What she'd done with her own, we could only guess.

Whatever it was, it hadn't resulted in either Onassis staying out of the public eye.

As we slipped into a line to head inside, more than a few eyes turned our way.

At the end of the line, greeting everyone, was Helen… and Zeke. Both dressed to the nines, both with broad smiles plastered over their faces.

"You think she showed him the pictures?" Ere asked. He hadn't been there when she'd picked them up—he hadn't wanted to give her another chance to look at his face. Not that she was the type to register clerks as human beings worth noting.

"Maybe not," I said, hushed, under my breath. "Or maybe—and they just don't want the public to know there's trouble in paradise." I tapped my purse. "We'll see."

The lights in the country club were dim, yellow, and I thanked whatever cosmic forces had led to this moment. I had my sunglasses tucked with everything else along in my clutch, but I wondered if walking inside with them might trigger some kind of recognition in Helen's brain.

As it was, her eyes went coldly to my form as we approached her, and I thought—for a moment—she *did* remember me from the convenience store.

But her gaze quickly traveled to her husband beside her, and I realized he was taking me in from head to toe.

I suppressed a shudder as a proffered hand for a handshake quickly turned into a kiss on my knuckles.

"I don't believe we've had the pleasure," Zeke Onassis said. His smirk was broad, his teeth dazzling, but there was something so thin and veneer-ish about it all. Not like the way my Ere's smile lit up the darkened night.

"Phoenyx," I said, without thinking. I at least stopped myself from giving him my last name. "I write for Humanitarian Heroes online. Perhaps you've heard of it?" There was no such publication, and if we'd been really thorough, we'd have slapped up a blog in case he'd bothered to check.

He didn't. "Yes… Yes." He stroked his chin. He couldn't possibly have heard of something I'd just made up yesterday.

But his ego wouldn't let him admit that, in case it was something he *should* have known, was my best guess.

"I was wondering if I might have a moment with you tonight? An interview for our blog?"

Ere's hand squeezed my hip, a more intimate gesture than we'd shared so far.

"Of course." Zeke's smile grew wider and Helen let out an audible grumble beside him. "Come find me after my speech." He winked.

I swallowed so as not to wince as we walked away, slipping on my glasses once I was out of sight.

Ere and I found a dark corner from which to observe the proceedings, our small town's finest dressed for the modern-day equivalent of a ballroom dance, complete with an excess of food and drinks, all in the name of raising money for the homeless, who didn't know where their next meals were coming from.

Frowning, I gazed at my own dress. Even secondhand, it felt like a waste.

Ere squeezed my shoulder, as if thinking the same.

We didn't belong here. Not with these people. Not with the wave after wave that slipped over to Zeke and Helen Onassis and laughed with them, their smiles never truly meeting their eyes.

Zeke gave his speech, and more than once he found me, even back here in the dark corner. His grin widened each time, though every time I stared my silent daggers right back at him, his smile slipped slightly and his gaze went back to fluttering around the room.

Finally, it was time.

"Is he nodding at you?" Ere asked as Zeke stepped away from the podium and gestured toward a hall.

"Stay a few steps back," I said.

Flicking my long hair over my shoulder, I was about to smile—when I decided no, the night didn't have to smile for the likes of him.

Instead, I put on that haughty face that came too naturally to me now.

"I have a minute," said Zeke, his hand slipping to the small of my back as I approached him.

I stiffened, the touch so wrong.

But I didn't weasel out of it. I just angled the hole in my clutch at him a little better.

Down past the caterers, he led me into what seemed like a storage room some distance from the bulk of the gathering.

I had to raise an eyebrow at that one.

"I *only* have a minute," Zeke said, running a hand through his golden-and-white hair. He pulled on a string overhead, illuminating the small space in a pale yellow glow. That was better for me anyway. "And I thought this would be quieter."

"Sure." I followed him inside, fumbling through my clutch and removing my sunglasses. I dropped them on the ground and cleared my throat to cover the clatter. They kept the door from shutting behind us entirely.

Zeke stared down at me, mischief sparkling in his eyes. "My wife couldn't find any Humanitarian Heroes blog like the one you described." Of course Helen had done her due diligence. "But if you want to pretend you have a story to write, you can ask me a few questions." Zeke guffawed, deep, throaty. "I love talking about myself anyway."

His hand went to my shoulder and I shrugged it off, my lips painted into a thin line.

Straight to the point of the matter, then.

Digging inside my clutch, I removed the envelope.

Zeke frowned. "What's this?"

I handed it to him.

"Copies," I said. "But not the only ones."

His jaw set, all traces of smile gone, Zeke opened the envelope and flipped through the pictures. "*Helen*," he said, like a swear word.

"I take it she hasn't discussed these with you yet?"

"She has." His jaw clenched. "We came to… an understanding. She assured me she has the original film."

So they weren't for a better divorce settlement, after all. Women like Helen would always think their husbands could be tamed, *forced* to finally like them above all others.

Me, here, in this closet with him, was proof that he hadn't learned his lesson in the least.

"Well, she's not the only one with copies," I said simply. "Seems a man like you might care about such things leaking to the press. Whispers of illegitimate children become a little easier to swallow with images like these."

Zeke shoved the pictures back into the envelope and clutched them tightly. "Who *are you*?" he snapped. "Do you even know who you're dealing with, little girl?"

"About that," I said, readjusting my clutch to make sure I got a good view of his face. "I'm seventeen."

He gulped. "I didn't know," he snapped quickly, recovering. "You look eighteen at least."

"And you're like fifty," I said. "But never mind that."

Around us, the room darkened, and Zeke's eyes grew wide. Glancing over my shoulder, I saw Ere's beautiful star-like gaze peering in through the crack I'd left in the doorway, the light practically dimming in his presence.

Maybe it was.

With a boldness I felt coming from deep within me, I stood straight, erect. "You will not follow up on this," I said. "You will not investigate who we are. Or those photos, *and a recording* of this moment"—I gestured to the hole at the bottom of my purse—"will find their way to the media. And I'm not just talking about the *local* news. Given your position in the community, this is state-wide newsworthy at minimum."

Zeke didn't seem convinced, though the longer he looked at me, toward Ere's glaring stare behind me, the more he faltered. His snobbish tone wavered as he spoke. "What do you want?"

"I want you to fear me," I said. "To know that for all your power, you can never mess with me or mine. Phoenyx—Nyx. You'll hear my name again someday."

And with that, I turned on my heel and pushed open the door.

Ere bent down to grab my glasses, then took my hand. I offered him a kiss, right there in front of Zeke. Brief, warm—full of promises of so much more to come.

Together, like the goddess and god we were deep down, we walked right out of the country club and drove off into the night.

That morning, as I went to bed, I dreamed the darkened window opened in my bedroom and revealed the cosmos, the bedroom flooding with darkness and the sparkle of starlight.

I stepped inside and found myself in the park at night.

"Mom!"

Hypnos Jones jumped off the swing as I approached. He still looked eight, but there was a twinkle in his eye that revealed his true age.

"You saved me," he said simply. "He's too afraid of you to act on his threats."

Behind him, Ethan and Emma laughed, the sunlight dancing off their little forms.

I didn't look away.

Behind me, the darkness grew stronger, as my husband and I approached our children. Even the light bouncing off them no longer made me blink. Even in this dream, this vision of the future, I could feel the warmth of their little bodies against mine.

Night and darkness were one—but night and day, darkness and light, the dreams that sleep would bring us… We all belonged together.

FEATHERS ⊕N THE WIND

LYSSA CHIAVARI

THE WATERS BENEATH me shimmered in the late summer sun. They looked cool and inviting as always. What would it feel like to run my hand through those briny waves? To dive in like a seabird and emerge with droplets glistening off the feathers of my wings?

I shook my head, as I always did whenever this longing came over me. I could never know. Harpies were forbidden to touch the land or sea—even half-harpies like myself. Such was the wrath of Queen Hera. As punishment for failing her, my mother and her sisters would never again know the firm reassurance of rock beneath their feet or the cooling relief of the waves against their skin. They would live eternally in exile from the world.

And though they'd been cursed before I was even born, their punishment had fallen on me as well.

The wind carried me higher, guiding me away from the waters that called to me. Ever since I'd been big enough to fly, the Anemoi—the four winds commanded by the storm god Aeolus—had taken me where I needed to go… and kept me from everything else. Still, my eyes stayed fixed on the sea even as I ascended. As I watched, a dolphin leapt from the sea in a majestic arc. I sighed as it slipped back into the water with barely a splash.

In the distance, shouts arose from a tiny ship, its passengers as insignificant as ants. An instant later, the cause of their distress became clear. Over the sailors' cries, I heard a high, thin melody—the song of my monstrous relations, the sirens, hungry for their next meal. I looked away, back down to where the dolphin had been. There was no sign of the creature now, save for the ever-expanding ripple on the water. I kept my eyes focused there, anywhere except on the sight that lay before me. I didn't want to see what awaited.

But even as I resisted, the wind pushed me forward. There was nowhere else for me to go. I could not forsake my duty, the duty I'd been conscripted to from the moment of my birth.

A curse at the whim of a goddess, through no fault of mine.

I squeezed my eyes closed for just a moment, wishing. Then I spread my wings, the strong wind teasing my feathers as I found my balance, and glided where the Anemoi took me.

It could have been much worse, truly.

At the end of the day, my satchel held just four souls. The sailors on the ship had had the foresight to carry beeswax with them, to shove into their ears and drown out the alluring song of the sirens. Only a few of the younger, inexperienced men had been too slow to get the sticky substance inserted in time to save them from the hypnotic song.

Four was more than enough for the sirens to eat their fill of human flesh, but the rage was still clear on their faces as they watched the ship sail away, their tails thrashing against the rocks, their large but ineffectual wings flapping uselessly in the sea spray. I tried not to look at them—and especially not at the mangled remains of the men's bodies—as I gathered the souls into my purse.

The glowing, wispy orbs were dark as the sea, each a slightly different hue. I could see the men's love of sailing reflected in the colors as I cupped each soul in my hands before gingerly placing it into the bag slung from my shoulder. Four unique souls, snuffed out in an instant. But none of them golden. None of them possessing the heart of a hero. These souls would not find rest in the fields of Elysium. I wondered what would become of them. With their bodies devoured, there would be no one to place a coin beneath their tongues to pay for passage on Charon's barge. It would be up to the gods whether they'd be allowed to cross or forced to remain on the banks of the river Acheron, listlessly wandering the Earth for eternity. Even if a god took pity and allowed them to cross, they would be entering the Underworld in debt. Were they at least virtuous enough that their shades would be allowed to dwell in the fields of Asphodel? Would they drink of the waters of the Lethe and be born again? Or would Hades cast them into the pit of Tartarus?

It would do me no good to worry about it. There was nothing I could do. I couldn't even help my own family. Not even demigoddesses like my mother and her sisters stood a chance against the whims of the gods.

The wind carried me to the edge of the sea, to a rocky outcropping of land called Tainaron. It was the closest gate of Hades to where the sirens had attacked, but also my least favorite. It had been here, three years after my birth, that Heracles had emerged from the Underworld with the captive Cerberus. The last of his great labors, marking him a hero for all time. He had overcome the Underworld, and the humans cheered his name for it.

It was because of Heracles that my family was cursed.

I descended, beating my wings to hover just above the ground. It was uncomfortable to hover like this, but far less painful than the alternative. Once, as a child, I'd landed, just to see if I could. Sharp pain like knives had shot through my feet and up my legs the moment I touched the ground. When I'd returned home to the clouds, my mother had been appalled. Blistering burns had covered the soles of my feet. It had taken nearly a month for them to heal. I'd learned then that though we were immortal, we could know pain all the same.

"Lord Hermes!" I called, and in an instant, he was there. The god was small and lithe, with golden curls atop his head. Most of the other male gods were brawny, with thick beards, but Hermes chose to appear as a youth whose first beard had not yet sprouted. On his feet were the winged sandals that the humans believed gave him his legendary speed. I always wondered if that were truly the case, or if Hermes' power simply stemmed from being a god.

"Ah, Halfling," he said, and I tried not to wince at the nickname. Hermes never called me by my real name. I was always Halfling—not a human, but not quite a harpy, either.

Just a monster, through and through.

"Four souls for you, my lord. Sailors from the Aegean," I said, taking my satchel off my shoulder. Hermes was a psychopomp, the gods' chosen emissary to guide mortal souls across the land to the Acheron, where Charon would ferry them across and into the Underworld. Hera's curse had made my family Hermes' servants. The winds of Aeolus carried us to the dying, and we would then bring their souls to Hermes. This had been my whole life. Unlike my mother and aunts, I had known nothing else.

Hermes withdrew his own satchel, holding it out to me. Gently, I removed the first of the four souls and placed it in Hermes' bag. It was cold to the touch.

"They won't have Charon's fee," I said tentatively. "The sirens…"

Hermes harrumphed disinterestedly.

I tried again. "Do you think they'll get passage?"

He shrugged. "Depends on whether one of the gods took a shining to any of them in life." My face must have betrayed me, because he softened. "The god of the Underworld is fair, Halfling," he reminded me. Hermes often said that of Lord Hades. Of all the gods of Olympus, he was the most fair. Ironic, that the only justice in this world came in death.

I hesitated before placing the last soul into Hermes' satchel. A long time ago, with my aunt Ocypete, I had traveled to the Acheron, near the western sea, and seen the shades enter Charon's barge. As the boat had moved across the river, the wispy orbs had begun to change. I'd just made out the faintest outline of their form, like a shadow of who they'd once been, with expressionless faces and eyes. Then the boat had disappeared.

"What do you think these men were like?" I asked finally, gently releasing the orb into the bag.

He harrumphed again. "Knowing sailors, they probably weren't the type of people you'd want to know."

I frowned, staggering a little in the air, coming uncomfortably close to the ground. I beat my wings harder to compensate. I had never met anyone other than my harpy family, my aunt Iris, and Hermes. At this point, I'd be happy to know *anyone* else. But I supposed he probably knew best.

The god started to turn to go; but then he paused, looking at me. "Are you lonely, Halfling?"

I opened my mouth, but didn't quite know how to answer. His question was unexpected.

A half-smile turned up one side of his boyish mouth. "You never know where the wind will take you," he said. My brows furrowed, but before I could ask him what he meant, in a streak of light, Hermes was gone.

The next morning, the wind carried me south to where the waters of the Aegean met those of the Mediterranean, near the shores of the island of Crete. The clouds hung low in the sky, nearly touching the water in places. I hated flying on days like this. It was difficult to see where I was going, and easy to lose my bearings. I always feared that I would inadvertently find myself plunging into the waters or crashing into a rocky outcropping. All I could do was trust that I had not lost my usefulness to the gods and thus that the wind would not lead me astray.

The air was unusually quiet this morning. The familiar cries of the gulls and other sea birds were nowhere to be heard, and in the thick cloud cover, the typical early-morning sounds from nearby Knossos—wagon wheels on the streets, crates and amphorae being unloaded from ships at the docks, the lowing of animals and the raised voices of the humans—were muted, nearly inaudible. All I could hear was the distant crashing of the waves below.

And something closer. The rustle of feathers. Labored breathing.

I'd barely registered what I was hearing before we collided. One moment I could see nothing but the gray swirls of the clouds around me, and suddenly there it was, a dark shape in the mist. There was no time to react, nothing to do but squeeze my eyes shut and brace for the impact.

A tangle of wings and limbs, feathers on the wind, and then I was falling. We both were falling—I hadn't collided with the cliffside, but with something living. A bird? If so, a huge bird. A vulture? No, surely whatever I had hit was bigger…

I struggled to regain my balance in the air, my wings beating frantically as I attempted to right myself. I plummeted low, arms and legs flailing, tumbling through the clouds until suddenly the air was clear, and I was close to the sea, too close for comfort. But I could see enough to tell up from down now, and I clumsily managed to regain my balance. Free of the clouds, I could now see the creature I had collided with. I gasped sharply. It was no bird. It was… a man?

But this man had wings. Not wings that grew from his back the way mine did, my monstrous extra set of limbs. His were true wings, in place of his arms, like my mother's and aunts'. Another harpy? But no, he had human legs where harpies had strong talons.

Whatever this creature was, he had not regained his balance when we broke free of the clouds. He was in a free-fall, tumbling through the air toward the sea below. Without thinking, I dove after him, beating my wings as hard as I could to reach him before he hit the water. I reached out wildly with my hands, managing to grab one of the creature's flailing ankles.

"Stop struggling!" I shouted as he kicked at me. I released his leg and beat my wings, trying to maintain my balance. "Spread your wings! Catch the wind!"

The creature looked up at me, his eyes locking with mine. Human eyes in a human face, dark and alarmed. As the creature struggled to obey my command, I realized that these wings were not part of his body—they were tied onto human arms. It *was* a man. A human man, flying through the clouds! How could this be possible?

He spread his arms, and the artificial wings expanded, the feathers fanning out in the wind. "Get your legs behind you!" I cried as he dropped below me, far too close to the sea for my liking.

For a horrified moment, I thought for sure that my instructions had come too late, that he would impact the waves like a stone and moments from now I would be bearing the orb of his soul in my satchel. I grimaced, wanting to look away but frozen in shock and horror. But to my utter unbelief, his wings caught in the wind and he rose, the Anemoi bearing him up toward me again.

He beat his artificial wings as I beat my real ones, but even with the wind's help he seemed to be struggling to keep his balance. As he drew closer, I saw the pinfeathers of his left wing had been damaged, making him off-kilter in the air. He wouldn't stay airborne long in this condition. I wanted to talk to him, find out who—what—he was and what in Zeus' name he was doing up here, but it was more important to get him to safety first.

I glanced in the direction of the nearby port as the man drew closer. Seeming to read my thoughts, he blurted out, "No, not Knossos!" I looked at him in surprise, and he added, "I can't let them see me."

I frowned at the urgency in his voice. Still, any part of me that might have been wary of the potential danger was more overcome by the giddy excitement of talking to someone—*anyone*—besides Hermes and my family. I couldn't let him get away, not until I was able to speak to him more. "Follow me, then," I said, ascending back into the clouds and hoping that he wouldn't lose sight of me in the mist.

I led him a short distance north, to a small, rocky island off the Cretan coast. Though we only flew a little way, I could hear his breathing becoming more and more labored. As we emerged from the clouds, it seemed like he could hardly bear his own weight. "Just down here," I said, guiding him down to the island. "Easy, now… Move with the wind, keep your knees bent…"

He landed much faster and harder than I would have liked. I watched fretfully, hovering above the rocks, as he got to his knees, struggling for breath. A moment later, he dusted himself off and looked up at me.

We both stared at each other in stunned silence, neither seeming to believe the other was real. His wide eyes, locked with mine, were dark like the sea, set in a square face framed by black curls. Despite his dark features, his skin was fairer than most of the Cretans I'd seen on the docks and streets of Knossos, as though he spent most of his time indoors, out of the sun. A scholar, perhaps?

I realized, looking at him more closely now, that he was quite young; I'd thought him a man when we first collided, but now I wondered if *boy* would be a more appropriate term. He looked older than Hermes (Hermes' youthful facade, anyway), but still younger than most of the men whose souls I carried to Hades. Closest in age, perhaps, to the three sailors on whom the sirens had feasted yesterday. That memory drained some of the excitement away from me, chilling me like I was up in the clouds shrouded by mist again.

Then suddenly he fixed me with a grin that warmed me like the rays of Apollo, eradicating all foreboding.

"You must have been sent by the gods," he said, his eyes wide and eager. He scrabbled up onto a tall rock to get a better look at me as I hovered, hesitantly, a safe distance above the land and waves.

"I… suppose," I managed.

"Father would be beside himself. He thought he knew of every species under Mount Olympus, but I'm sure he never could have conceived of this. A winged girl!" the boy babbled on, his eyes never holding still for an instant, looking me up and down almost studiously. "And you can speak? Yes, of course you can speak, you just spoke to me. Never mind, I have a tendency to not think before *I* speak. But what in the world are you?"

"I…" I trailed off, unsure of how to respond. I wasn't *exactly* a harpy. But I wasn't a human, either. Before her transformation, my mother had been a demigoddess. Hermes called me *Halfling*, something in between. As far as I knew, there was nothing and no one else like me in the world.

"I'm Nicothoë," I said at last. It was the best answer I could give him.

"What sort of creature is a Nicothoë?" he asked.

"It's not—It's my name," I said.

"Oh. Oh!" A blush spread across his cheeks. "I'm sorry, that was rude of me. I was preoccupied. I'm Icarus," he said, and without a moment's hesitation added, "Were you born with wings?"

I sighed. Gods, he was full of questions. I had questions of my own, but I'd never get to ask them at this rate. "Yes, I was. And I assume you weren't?"

Icarus laughed, looking down at the devices strapped to his arms. Now that we were out of the clouds, I could see that they seemed to be made of beeswax. Set into the wax were feathers of all sorts and colors, from a variety of different birds. Crow feathers as black as night, strong pinion feathers from a golden eagle, the distinct two-toned hues of the griffon vulture's underwing, all cobbled together like a strange mosaic.

"No, this is one of my father's inventions," he explained. "Surely you've heard of my father, the great inventor Daedalus?" He beamed with pride as he spoke the man's name.

"I'm afraid not," I said. Icarus looked crestfallen, and I quickly added, "I haven't encountered many humans, you see…" I trailed off awkwardly. None, in fact. At least, none who were alive. I could have explained as much, but I felt oddly shy about admitting my own isolation to this boy. Beyond that, I wasn't sure if I wanted to explain my duty as bearer of souls to him. How would he take it? The gods treated those of us in Hades' service as somehow unclean, and from what I'd gathered, humans weren't particularly fond of those who dealt in death, either. And I certainly didn't want to explain the details of my family's curse to a total stranger; that, too, would seem to invite judgment. Unsure of what more to say, I shrugged helplessly.

The flush spread across Icarus' features again. "Oh. Of course, I suppose that should have occurred to me." He ran his hand over the feathers of one wing, rumpling the feathers of the other wing in the process. "Well, my father is an inventor"—he paused, noticing my confused expression, and added—"that is, someone who creates devices to allow humans to accomplish things they ordinarily could not."

I smiled. "Such as flying?"

"Exactly. My father is in the service of King Minos of Crete… or, *was*, I suppose." A shadow seemed to pass over his face, and he said in a quieter voice, "Now he is Minos' prisoner."

I faltered on a pocket of air and my stomach leapt as I dropped closer to the water. I beat my wings harder to compensate. "What happened?" I asked.

Icarus hesitated. Whether he was unsure of how to begin his tale or unsure what he should tell me, I couldn't tell. Finally he said, quietly, "Minos is not a good man. But the gods don't care whether a person is *good* when they choose to make them great."

I looked at him in surprise. I had often thought the same thing—about Heracles, in particular—but I never would have dared voice such a thought aloud. The last thing my family needed was to further offend the gods. One family curse was more than enough. This Icarus was either very brave or incredibly reckless… and based on everything I'd seen of him so far, I was leaning toward *reckless*.

"But what did your father do to incur his wrath?" I pressed.

"He didn't do anything!" Icarus shouted, his voice echoing off the tall rocks around us. I blinked in surprise, and he looked down, avoiding my gaze. "Minos blamed my father for something that he hadn't done," he said in a much quieter voice. "So he imprisoned him in the highest tower of the palace. He doesn't belong there, he didn't—that is, my father is not to blame for Minos' defeat."

There was more to this story, but it felt wrong somehow to press Icarus about it, especially considering my own reticence to reveal details about my own life. "I'm sorry," I said.

"It's been almost a year since the last time I saw my father," he went on softly. "The Cretan guards won't allow me to visit him, and Minos refuses to consider any reprieve. As far as he's concerned, my father can just rot in the tower as punishment for a crime he didn't commit."

Punishment for a crime he didn't commit. Like a curse passed from a mother to a daughter before her child was even born.

He looked up at me, a spark in his eyes. "But then I came across the design for these wings among his things, and I thought perhaps…"

My breath caught in my throat. "You mean to rescue your father with these wings?"

He nodded. "I mean to try, at least. But I'll need to be able to fly in undetected. If Minos' guards see me, I'll be done for. One well-aimed spear or arrow is all it would take."

"So you were flying in the clouds so as not to be seen?" I asked.

"That was the intention, anyway. I hadn't bargained on colliding with a winged girl."

I grinned, feeling my own face grow hot. "I suppose I was a contingency you couldn't have planned for." Icarus laughed, making me feel strange inside. Warm. "But you still need to take care in the clouds," I added quickly, struggling to keep my head clear even as my feelings threatened to derail my every train of thought. "It's dangerous to fly when you can't see. You could hit a flock of birds, or get turned around and collide with a cliffside. Even fall into the sea."

Icarus nodded, rubbing his chin with his thumb. "I hadn't considered all of that. I suppose you know all about flying around unseen. Otherwise I'd have already heard whispers about the bird-girl of the Aegean."

I laughed, bobbing in the air as a gust of wind lifted me up higher. A thought occurred to me, and I blurted it out before I could talk myself out of it.

"Maybe I could help you," I suggested. "I could teach you how to fly, how to navigate the wind. If you've done it enough, you learn how to listen for things you can't see. And I know my way around the island from my—that is—I have flown around this island many times before," I amended.

"Really?" Icarus' face lit up. "Are you sure? I don't want to impose. I mean, my family's problems are my own, but I would appreciate the help. You saw how hopeless I was on my own—"

The wind picked up, and I could feel the change in direction and the familiar sinking feeling in the pit of my stomach. I was needed. "Yes, I would be happy to help, but not today," I said, flapping my wings hard against the Anemoi's pull. "There's… something else I need to do. And first I need to get you back to Knossos—"

"No, no, not Knossos," he reminded me. "I'm staying in the village of Stalis, on the road from Knossos to Malia."

"All right," I said, "I will take you to Stalis, but then I have to go."

"Of course, of course. But how will I find you again? And when?"

The wind tugged at me urgently. "I will find you. I don't know when. But I'll find you in Stalis."

Icarus, seeming satisfied, nodded.

"All right then," I said, looking up at the clouds. "Let's get you back in the air."

That evening when the Anemoi swept me up to the home in the clouds I shared with my mother and aunts, I felt a strange combination of exhaustion and exhilaration. I had never wanted so badly to sleep, and simultaneously felt sure that I would never be able to sleep again. I'd met a human. A *human*. A living, breathing human. I touched him, spoke to him. He was really real.

And I would see him again. That sent a secret thrill through me every time I thought it. We had agreed I would meet him in Stalis the next time the wind carried me to Crete.

I didn't know how I could possibly keep this to myself. I wanted to tell my mother, my aunts, even Hermes when I had brought him my full satchel today. But though the god had noticed that I seemed out of sorts today, I couldn't bring myself to tell him. Though I had never been expressly forbidden to speak to humans, I'd just always known that this was something we did not do. It was an unspoken rule, somehow.

But I'd done it today. Had I done the right thing? Or would my actions draw further ire from the gods onto my family?

I was so preoccupied, I nearly collided with my aunt Celaeno as she descended from the clouds. "Watch yourself, *paidi mou!*" she chided, rebalancing herself on an updraft.

"I'm sorry, Aunt," I said. "I'm—more tired than usual."

She looked at me sympathetically. "Busy day?"

I nodded. *In more ways than one.*

"Get some rest, then. Your mother is waiting for you. Iris brought us figs tonight along with our rations. You always like those."

She smiled down at me, and in that moment it struck me how different I was from the others. It had been a long time since I'd really considered it, but after today, I found myself looking at Celaeno with new eyes. She was more bird than human, really; she had a woman's face and torso, but the rest of her body was shaped like a bird of prey—massive wings, powerful feathered legs with eagle-sharp talons, strong tailfeathers. Whereas I was more human than bird. I'd only seen my reflection a few times, on smooth water or in dull, tarnished mirrors, but I knew my face was a human's face. My arms and hands, my legs and feet, all of me was human… except the wings that sprouted from my back, as long as I was tall and mottled like an owl's.

Mother had told me the story so many times. How she hadn't known that she was pregnant when she was cursed, that she didn't know she was carrying me until her belly had begun to swell. How when she gave birth to me, she thought for a moment that I'd been born human, that I'd been spared the curse she and her sisters had been forced to bear… until she turned me over and saw the small, downy wings on my back.

Punishment for a crime he didn't commit.

Celaeno, Ocypete, my mother Aello. They all looked like monsters. Maybe I looked less so. But I was still a monster just the same.

"Are you sure you're all right, Nicothoë?" My aunt was watching me with a strange expression on her face. "Nothing… happened today?"

I swallowed, wondering if she knew more than she was letting on. Part of me wanted to tell her the truth, but what if she forbade me from seeing Icarus again? I wasn't sure if I could bear that. After a lifetime spent on the outside looking in, watching the world go by but never being able to be a part of it, to finally have a chance to know someone other than my tiny cursed family and Hermes…

One little secret. It couldn't hurt. Just one little secret.

"No, nothing," I said, smiling as reassuringly as I could manage. "Have a peaceful night, Aunt."

Celaeno exhaled and nodded. "Sleep well, *paidi mou.* I will see you in the morning."

It was several days before the Anemoi allowed me to return to Crete. In the early hours of the morning, as the sun was just peeking above the horizon, I glided along the south wind until I found myself in Stalis, the village where I'd left Icarus before. The village was mostly made up of goat herders and grain farmers, though there was an inn in town where travelers would often stop over on the nine league journey from the island's capital of Knossos to the city of Malia nine leagues to the east.

When I'd left him on the sandy shore outside the village, Icarus had pointed into the hills, where I could just make out the angled roof of a small farmhouse. "I'm letting a room from that farmer," he'd said. "You can usually find me there. I'll be waiting for you."

My cheeks warmed at the memory. He said he'd wait for me. But would he still be waiting? Or did he assume when I didn't turn up the next day that I'd gone back on my promise? I couldn't help where the winds took me. I had no choice but to obey. But I hadn't explained that to him…

I could see it now—the humble clay-brick building with its thatched roof so severely angled that it nearly touched the ground on either side. In the distance, a rooster crowed, and I could hear goat herders calling to one another, their animals bleating softly.

And on top of the roof, gazing at Apollo's chariot rising up over the hills, the silhouette of a boy and a pair of wax wings.

I watched him for a moment, smiling to myself. Then I glided down to hover above the roof's peak.

"Nicothoë!" Icarus said, turning to face me with a start. "You came!"

"I promised I would. I'm sorry I couldn't come right away, though. I had… other things I needed to take care of."

"It's all right. I took advantage of the time you were away to fix these." He pulled the wax wings over, holding one up to show me. He'd removed the damaged pinion feathers and replaced them with new ones.

"Good. It's not safe to fly with an injured wing."

Icarus patted the roof beside him. "Please, won't you sit?"

"I… can't," I said hesitantly.

"You can't sit?"

I swallowed, fiddling with the strap of my empty satchel. "I can't touch the ground. Or the sea, for that matter."

He frowned. "Is it just you, or your whole species? Your kind, that is?"

"My kind, I suppose."

He nodded, crossing his arms thoughtfully. "That lets out sirens, then."

"I'm sorry?"

"I did some research about winged women, you see," he explained, and I colored. "I had a few theories. But if you can't touch the sea, you must not be a siren."

"Obviously not!" I protested. "Do I seem the type to seduce sailors to their deaths?"

"Well, not to their deaths, maybe…"

My face went from hot to burning. "What's that supposed to mean?"

Icarus laughed. "I'm just teasing you, Nico. Er… Can I call you Nico?"

I huffed, looking away from Icarus to the direction of the rising sun. "I suppose."

He grinned. "Besides, the lack of a tail was a real hole in that theory.

But I had another one. Could you be a harpy, perhaps?"

I froze, dropping too close to the roof. I tucked my feet up into my chest quickly, beating my wings hard to regain my altitude—and my composure.

"Ah, I see," Icarus said, my reaction saying it all. He ran a thumb across his chin. "You don't look at all how harpies are described in the scrolls, though."

"I'm not—" I began, struggling to put my frenzied thoughts into words. "My mother is a harpy. I'm… something else. Something in between."

"What was your father, then? You look almost human, apart from the wings."

Almost human. I thought again of my mother's story, how she thought I'd been spared the curse until she turned my newborn self over.

"My father was human, I assume." My mother didn't speak of him often. I'd been conceived in a night of passion that had sealed my mother's doom. I knew my father had been one of Heracles' men, but I was unsure whether he had been mortal or demigod like Heracles himself. Regardless, he hadn't lived to see the night after my conception. Hera had seen to that.

"I'm sorry," Icarus said softly. "I didn't mean to upset you. I'm just too curious for my own good. Father always said it would be my downfall."

"It's all right," I said. "Let's not worry about it now. I told you I would show you how to fly unseen. So we should get you into the air before the rest of Stalis wakes up."

He nodded, getting to his feet and scooping up his wax wings. "I'll show you the place I've been lifting off from," he said, scrabbling down the angled roof and jumping the short distance to the ground. He ran along a winding track higher into the hills. The wind carried me up higher above the island, and I followed the small figure of his form as it zigzagged along the path. Finally he emerged atop a cliff overlooking the sea.

"Just here," he called up to me, stopping to strap his wings to his arms. "I can get a running start, and the wind is strong enough to lift me without expending a lot of my own energy."

I fretted. It was also a steep drop down to the water. If he didn't time it just right…

"No cause for alarm, I've done this part many times before!" he shouted cheerfully. He backed up then and charged into a run. I winced at the ungainly way he spread his arms, the way the wind pulled at the feathers, so precariously affixed with wax. As he reached the precipice, I squeezed my eyes shut, certain that he would catapult down to his doom.

But no crash came, no scream. I anxiously opened one eye to see Icarus soaring on a current of wind beneath me. I smiled in relief and coasted down to meet him.

"See, I told you!" he said, grinning between his labored breaths. "I've got that part figured out."

"The strength of the wind through here is helpful," I admitted. "But you should take more advantage of the Anemoi's aid. You don't need to flap so often. Open your wings and let the wind do the work." The south wind, Notus, was blowing. I could feel its chaotic warmth beneath my wings. This wind filled the sails of ships in the summer, but it also brought powerful thunderstorms, the wrath of Zeus. "The wind can carry you up and down, east and west. Don't fight it—learn its rhythm. Learn to let it take you where it leads."

"But I want to go somewhere specific," Icarus protested.

"The wind will get you there in its time," I said. "But one of the most important parts of flying unseen is to blend with the birds, and birds go where the wind takes them. They may detour to prey if they're a hunting bird, or to escape if they're a prey bird. But in general, birds don't fight the direction of the wind."

Icarus nodded, following behind me as I allowed the Anemoi to carry me up and away, out over the sea. Higher and higher, until Crete was a mere rock beneath us.

The winds bore us gradually westward, toward Knossos. "If we stay high," I called down to Icarus, "no one below us will be able to see our shape. From a distance, we'll just appear as gulls or griffons. We should stay at this altitude for as long as we can to go undetected."

Icarus looked down at the city below us. "I don't think I've ever been this high," he said.

I grinned. "We can go much higher still."

From this altitude, the city of Knossos could fit within the palm of my hand. The fishing boats and cargo ships docked in the harbor looked like a child's playthings. The stone buildings and tile rooftops, much larger and sturdier than the clay-brick structures of Stalis, were crammed tightly together around a honeycomb of streets. Horses and wagons streamed between them like ants. And above it all stood the grand palace of Minos. I stared at its high square tower, still minuscule from this distance. *Icarus' father is in there*, I thought.

Beside me, Icarus faltered in the air, and I reached over to steady him. "What's wrong?" I asked in alarm.

He didn't answer me. I followed the direction of his stare, assuming that he'd been looking at the palace tower as I had been. But his gaze had been beyond the palace, to the massive stone maze on the outskirts of the city.

The Labyrinth.

My stomach curdled at the memory of that horrible place. The darkness, the stench… the despair…

Icarus stumbled again in the air. "Come on, let's go back before you fall," I said, guiding him along a downdraft back to the shore.

The winds bore us gently down to a secluded cove outside Stalis. Again, Icarus landed harder than I would have liked, but he showed marked improvement from the other day. His face had grown sallow, though, and he seemed unsteady on his feet, almost nauseous.

"Are you all right?" I asked, hovering above him in concern. "Are you airsick? I forgot to warn you, there are pockets in the wind that can throw you off balance—"

"It's not that," Icarus said, his voice ragged. He looked up at me, his dark eyes shadowed. "Nico, I need to ask you something."

I frowned. "What is it?"

He looked down at me, fiddling with one of the leather straps holding his wing to his left arm. "Is it… is it true that harpies are psychopomps?"

I went suddenly cold. I hadn't wanted to tell him—didn't want him to know—but of course he'd had to consult that accursed scroll—

"Hermes is a psychopomp," I hedged. Then, guiltily, I added, "But I am in Hermes' service."

Icarus watched me as I twisted the strap on my satchel uncomfortably. "There's no shame in it, Nico," he said.

I looked at him in surprise. "There's not? I just assumed…"

Icarus shrugged. "Someone has to do it. I haven't known you for very long, but what I know of you so far tells me that you guide the souls of the dead with more dignity than most would provide."

I flushed. "I… That is… Thank you?"

He smiled, but it lacked the warmth that his smiles usually possessed. He seemed distant now, as he had the other day when I'd asked him why Minos had imprisoned his father.

"I'm sorry to make you uncomfortable, Nico, I just wanted to know. So I can… ask you something," he said, so quietly I could barely hear him over the roar of the sea.

"What do you want to ask me?"

He inhaled slowly. "The… the Labyrinth. Have you been there before?"

Dark corners, wails of despair, sweat and blood and decay…

My reaction said it all. Icarus nodded, resigned. "You know what atrocities occurred in that place."

"Yes. The sacrifices to the Minotaur."

That creature was a monster. But even as I thought it, I had to acknowledge that he'd been no more monster than I. Part bull, but part man all the same. Cursed by the gods from birth through no fault of his own. Starved of all foods save human flesh. His existence had been meant as a curse on Minos by Poseidon, punishment for not offering the snow-white bull of kings as a sacrifice to the god. But Minos had used the curse to his own advantage. The Minotaur had been Minos' slave from the moment of his birth until his death at the hands of Theseus last year. But while I'd had to carry the souls of his victims to Hades after every sacrifice, there had been no wispy orb to bear after the creature's death. It was as if he'd never existed.

I wondered if he'd ever even understood the horrors he had committed.

"That… *place*," Icarus spat. "That chamber of horrors." He swallowed. "My father designed it, Nico."

I stared at him, dumbstruck. "Daedalus?" When he silently nodded, I protested, "But you said he was an inventor!"

"An inventor, an architect, a mathematician. All skills necessary for devising a maze as intricate as that one." He looked up at me imploringly.

"But he didn't know, Nico! When Minos commissioned him, my father believed that he was merely devising a prison for the creature to be kept within. It had broken free of every other dungeon Minos had attempted to confine it in. My father thought that something complex like the Labyrinth would be a sufficient challenge for the creature's intellect to prevent it escaping."

My eyes stung. Of course something so monstrous as the Minotaur had to be confined. I knew the Minotaur was dangerous—I'd seen his victims with my own eyes, held their souls in my own hands. But still… surely a bird-woman must appear just as monstrous. If the humans knew of me, would another inventor like Daedalus be commissioned to build a cage to hold me, too?

"He didn't know," Icarus was stammering, mistaking my conflicted feelings as judgment toward his father. "He didn't know what Minos was planning. About the sacrifices… When he found out the truth, he was devastated. But by then it was too late."

Suddenly a hazy memory sharpened in my head. When the hero Theseus slew the Minotaur, it had been all the gods could speak of for days. Aunt Iris had told us all about it when she brought us our weekly ration of bread and olives. She said that the rumor on Olympus was that Theseus had had help. Minos' daughter Ariadne had betrayed him, that much was known. But they'd had help from someone else, someone who knew the design of the Labyrinth…

"Your father," I interrupted. "Did he help Theseus escape the Labyrinth?"

Icarus shook his head miserably. "As angry as he was that Minos had tricked him, he never would have dared defy the king."

"Then…"

"It was me!" Icarus snapped, almost impatiently, as if it should have been obvious to me all this time.

"You?" I breathed.

"Yes. I'd helped Father draft the plans for the maze, when I was just seven years old. Father could never bring himself to betray the king to whom he'd sworn allegiance, no matter how much he disagreed with him." He looked away from me, out at the waves. "But I had no such compunction. Minos had to be stopped. It didn't occur to me that Minos would blame my father. And of course he would, why shouldn't he? As always, I acted before I thought. And now my father pays the price."

I watched him silently for a long moment, the weight of his words washing over me. It was clear Icarus had never told anyone about this before. The weight of his guilt had been crushing him. No wonder he was so desperate to rescue Daedalus.

"You did the right thing," I said softly.

He looked up at me in surprise. "What?"

I met his eyes. "You did the right thing," I repeated. "What Minos was doing was wrong. Every ill that has befallen his reign has been of his own making. He swore to Poseidon that he would sacrifice the bull of kings. Instead he kept it for his own vanity. Poseidon punished Minos' wife, forcing her to lie with that animal, and still he kept it. Even after the Minotaur burst out of Queen Pasiphaë's womb and ripped her to shreds, he kept it. And even after that accursed bull broke free of its pen and trampled his son to death, Minos placed the blame on Athens rather than himself." As little as I knew of the human world, I knew this much. There'd been no way to avoid it with the amount of death that was happening on this island, the amount of souls needing transport to the Acheron. Minos had spent nine years capturing Athenian youths who had done nothing to fault him and sacrificing them to his monstrous stepson. It never would have ended. The bloodshed would have gone on forever.

But Icarus had broken the cycle. He'd stood up to a king and defied a curse from the gods. Because of him, not one more Athenian youth or maiden would die in that horrific dungeon.

"I was born in Athens, you know," he said softly. "Those Athenians who died in the Labyrinth, they were my kin. My father's and my mother's. I couldn't just let it keep happening."

A lump in my throat kept me from responding. But I watched Icarus, staring quietly at the sea, and I thought: *Yes, he is reckless. But he's also braver than I could ever dream of being.*

I beat my wings against the wind. "We're going to save your father, Icarus," I said. "I promise you."

Through the whole of the month of Boedromion, we flew. Slowly but surely, Icarus learned the winds, became familiar with the way they blew, the way they changed direction. He learned to use them to keep himself aloft, to navigate their currents to gradually reach the place he wanted to go. Together we refined the wings, swapping out feathers and reshaping the wax to make them more aerodynamic. When I was away from him, Icarus used his time to construct a second pair—for Daedalus. If our plan was to be successful, it would rely on the inventor being able to fly on the wings he'd designed. But Icarus was confident that his father could do it.

The more we flew, the stronger Icarus became. I watched his scholar's body grow leaner, the muscles more defined. His fair skin grew tan beneath Apollo's rays. In just one moon cycle, flying became second nature to him. With each trip out, we drew closer to Knossos, closer to the palace and its high tower. We stayed out of sight of the humans below, and by the month's end, I was sure that we could do it. We could rescue Daedalus.

And what would become of them then? Icarus and his father would be fugitives. They'd have to leave Crete behind, escape to the mainland. Would I see him again after his mission was complete?

I didn't want to think about it.

The first week of Pyanepsion, Icarus told me his plan. The following week was the festival of Demeter, summer's end and the time of the harvest. Minos would be traveling from Knossos to Malia for the feast, and the palace of Knossos would be abandoned save for a threadbare staff of servants and guards. The citizens that remained in Knossos would be so distracted by the festival that they would be even less likely to notice a pair of "unusual birds." It was the perfect opportunity to sneak in unnoticed and rescue Daedalus.

I was surprised that the king was leaving the capital, though. "Does he usually celebrate feasts in Malia?" I asked. It seemed to make little sense for him to leave his main palace—and the biggest city on the island—to travel to a smaller vassal city for the festival of a major goddess.

Icarus shrugged. "A retinue of the king's men passed through Stalis two nights ago. I overheard them talking at the tavern. They said they were preparing the palace of Malia for the king's arrival on the eve of the festival."

I frowned but nodded. So little time left. Only a week…

An updraft caught me off guard, buoying me up and ruffling my feathers. I glanced upward at the clouds high above us. Hesitantly, I said, "Shall we see how high you can go now that you've been flying for a month?"

Icarus looked at me curiously. I beckoned to him as I glided into the updraft, letting the wind carry me higher, up toward the clouds… toward my home.

If I was to say goodbye to him in just a week's time, I wanted him to see my home.

Icarus followed me up, higher and higher, the north wind carrying the two of us until the clouds parted, revealing the harpies' hidden sanctuary. A world in the clouds for just the four of us. I exhaled as my feet settled into the cool, damp cloud beneath me, and I folded my wings behind my back.

We could never touch the ground, nor the sea. But Aunt Iris had found the loophole in Hera's curse—we could touch the clouds. And the clouds would hold us.

Icarus' eyes widened, beating his arms as he hovered just above the cloud. "You can stand here?"

I laughed. "Yes. Don't be afraid, it's safe here."

He lowered one foot, then the other, staring in wonder as swirls of mist settled around his ankles.

"Incredible! How is this possible?"

"A gift from a goddess," I said.

He looked around at the clouds that surrounded us, whirling into columns like those found in the temples on the earth below, clumping into small mounds like bushes and twisting above us like leafless trees. The clouds were always shifting, always changing shape and color—bluish grays, dark as night, white as snow. It never looked the same from one day to the next. Today the stratospheric landscape had a pastoral feel, the light, airy clouds resembling gently rolling hills. Other days dark storm clouds would form into craggy peaks and precipices. I was glad Icarus was here on a peaceful day.

"My aunt Iris created this place for us," I explained as Icarus gazed at the columnar clouds in wonder. "A place for us to rest." The four of us—my mother, aunts and me—took turns in our duties, some flying during the day and some at night. The Anemoi carried us home when our duty was done and it was time for us to sleep, and they stirred us awake when it was time to return to Hermes' service.

Icarus turned to me in surprise. "The rainbow goddess is your aunt? So… you are a demigoddess?"

I shrugged, sitting down on a tuft of cloud. My muscles ached as they gradually relaxed. "My mother and her sisters are demigoddesses. They share a father with Iris. He's a minor sea god."

"Yes, my scroll named Thaumas as the sire of the harpies," Icarus said, unfastening the leather straps on his bulky wings and setting them gingerly on the cloud floor.

I nodded. "They…" I swallowed, my throat feeling taut and dry. I didn't like to think about this, had never spoken it aloud. But Icarus had told me all about his past, about his father… about what had happened with Theseus and the Minotaur. His betrayal of Minos. He'd been honest with me about everything. He deserved to know. "They were raised in Themiscyra. Their mother was an Amazon."

Icarus looked at me in confusion, coming to sit beside me on the cloud tuft. "They weren't born harpies?"

I shook my head. "They were raised as humans, though they knew of their divine parentage. Ocypete, Celaeno, and the eldest, my mother, Aello. They were warriors of Queen Hippolyte. Three of her best, her most trusted."

"What happened?" Icarus asked.

I looked down at my hands. Human hands. My mother had once gripped sword and spear in hands like mine. She never would again. "A man named Heracles sailed to Themiscyra with a retinue of his men. He was on an errand for King Eurystheus."

"I've heard of Heracles," Icarus said. "He was a great hero."

I clenched my teeth involuntarily. Of course the humans all revered Heracles. Icarus would have been raised with tales of his twelve legendary labors. To the humans, all that mattered was the man's victory. The countless lives that were destroyed along his path to greatness were of little importance.

"The king asked Heracles to prove himself by retrieving the queen's belt. It had been a gift from Ares, a symbol of her queenship. But Queen Hippolyte was friends with Eurystheus' daughter Admete. She had no quarrel with Heracles. She agreed to give him the belt peacefully." There had been a great celebration in Themiscyra, to celebrate the peaceful conclusion and the alliance between the Amazons and Eurysheus' kingdom of Tiryns. And the hero's stay had stretched from one day to two, to a full week. There had been feasting, and drinking, and… other things.

"He could have just left. He could have sailed away with the girdle before Hera had a chance to intervene. But he was disappointed that there had been no challenge in this labor. He wanted a chance to prove himself. So he tarried, finding excuses to prolong his stay. It was like he was waiting for Hera to make a move. To provide him with a challenge."

"And she did," Icarus said sadly. He knew the tale.

I nodded, my eyes stinging. "When she found the Amazons feasting with Heracles' men, she flew into a rage. She… possessed the women with bloodlust. They attacked Heracles' friends viciously, with no warning. They couldn't help themselves. Not one was left alive save Heracles himself." He was the one warrior they couldn't kill.

"He killed Hippolyte and took the belt," Icarus finished. "But what of your mother and her sisters?"

"Hera was furious that the Amazons had not stopped Heracles from retrieving the belt. She smote the warriors in a fire that destroyed all of Themiscyra. But Thaumas refused to allow his children to be killed. Even though he's just a minor god, Hera didn't dare risk enraging the other gods of Olympus by murdering three demigoddesses. So instead, she… she cursed them."

A hot tear escaped from the corner of my eye and I swiped it away with the back of my hand. "They'd slain every one of Heracles' men"—even my father, Mother had once acknowledged with regret—"but it wasn't enough for her. She destroyed an entire kingdom and punished my mother and aunts for the rest of eternity out of her own jealousy and spite. And after all that, do you know what Iris told us? She said that when Heracles died five years ago, they welcomed him on Mount Olympus, and Hera decided all was forgiven. She gave him her *daughter*, Hebe, to be his wife for all eternity. And yet my mother and aunts still remain cursed." Tears were spilling from my eyes rapidly now, blurring my vision. I should have known better than to speak all this aloud, to voice my bitterness against Hera. I'd thought Icarus a fool for saying much less than I had just now. But I'd found that once I started, I couldn't stop myself. It all came spilling out of me, like rain from a storm cloud.

"And you," Icarus said softly.

"What?" I asked, my voice thick and sticky.

"And you also remain cursed. For something you had nothing to do with. This must have been before you were born."

"Yes. It was almost seventeen years ago. My mother became pregnant just before the curse. By… by one of Heracles' men." My shoulders shook. "That's why I am… how I am. Not fully harpy, but not human, either. Conceived by a woman whose womb transformed around me."

Icarus slipped off the cloud tuft, crouching in front of me. He took my hands with his left one, reaching up to wipe the tears off my cheek with his right. I couldn't look at him. I closed my eyes as I whispered, "I'm a monster."

Warm arms around me took me by surprise. My breath caught in my throat as Icarus pulled me close. Then I buried my face in his chest, my tears soaking into his chiton. "You are not a monster, Nico," he murmured into my hair.

"I am," I protested. "We all are."

"No," Icarus said firmly, pulling back to look me in the eyes. "You are anything but a monster. Minos is a monster. You are caring, and generous. You value others over yourself—you never complain about the fact that you were cursed because of something that was out of your control. After all this time, all these weeks we've spent together, I've told you about all of my troubles and you've kept yours to yourself. You care about the souls of the dead; not just the souls of the heroes, but of the ordinary drudges without even a coin to pay the ferryman. You offered to help me even though you don't even know me." He ran a gentle hand through my tangled, dark curls. "You're not a monster. You're beautiful, inside and out."

His words made my heart beat irregularly. I didn't know how to respond, though I felt warm all over, and like I was going to cry again for a completely different reason.

But I didn't need to respond. Icarus pulled me close again, and I wrapped my arms around him, my head against his chest, feeling the beating of his heart in sync with mine.

That evening, long after I'd returned Icarus to Stalis, as Apollo sank beneath the horizon and the sky was aflame in pink and orange and red, I heard my mother's voice on the wind. The Anemoi carried me up through the clouds, until I found her roosting on the misty steps of the cloud temple. Her wings were folded about her, her leather warrior's belt—a reminder of her days as an Amazon, even if she would never again grip a spear in her hands—draped like a sash across her human torso, from one shoulder across her breasts down to her waist.

"*Paidi mou*," she said, lifting her wing and beckoning me to come close. I sat beside her, and she wrapped her wing around me, drawing me close like an eagle with her chick. She hadn't done this with me for a long time.

"Is something wrong, Mother?" I asked as she rested her head against mine.

"I just worry about you, that's all. It's a mother's prerogative."

I shifted nervously. I had a suspicion that this display of motherly concern was not random. "Why should you worry about me?"

She leaned back, giving me a knowing look that told me everything.

"He's a good person, Mother. He's worthy of my help."

"I know who he is. And I heard what he said to you earlier." I winced. I had hoped we were alone in the clouds this afternoon, but I should have known better. My mother had gathered souls all night, and she had still been gone when I left this morning. Of course it had been her time to sleep.

She lifted a talon to delicately caress my cheek. "I would approve of him merely for what he told you. He's only known you for a short time, but he sees the beautiful person you are on the inside. That alone makes me love the boy."

I beamed, but she stayed me. "But you still need to be careful, Nicothoë. He is brave and caring, yes, but he has a reckless streak to him. If he keeps it up, he will attract the attention of the gods. And the gods' attention is a double-edged sword. It could bring favor, honor, and glory… or it could bring wrath. And this family has known its share of wrath."

I nodded, my good mood dampening. She was right. Of course she was right. I had known it all along. Keeping company with Icarus was anything but safe.

But he also made me feel alive, after sixteen years of living like a shadow. This past month, I had felt happiness like I'd never known. More than that—Icarus' bravery had made me feel brave. With him by my side, I felt like maybe I could face anything. Even the gods' wrath.

The thought of giving that up was far worse than any fear of the gods I had left in me.

"Icarus is doing so much to save his father from a punishment he doesn't deserve. Just like you," I said quietly. "I wish I could find a way to save you. I just don't know how. But I thought maybe if I could help him…" It wouldn't save my family. But if I could save another family, at least I'd be doing *something*, somehow fighting back against the injustice of this world.

The only justice in this world comes in death.

I shuddered, trying to drive that thought from my mind. Hermes had said it many times before, but after meeting Icarus, I couldn't believe it. Icarus was willing to fight for it, even if he had to wrest it with his bare hands. He wanted *make* justice in this life, fight back against the whims of kings and the will of the gods.

"You're a good girl, Nicothoë. I'm very proud of you," my mother said, folding her wing around me again. "But my sisters and I aren't the only ones who are cursed, you know. Of all of us, you're the one who deserves this punishment the least. If you can only save one person, I'd rather you save yourself."

The morning of the festival of Demeter dawned clear and cold. The smell of autumn was in the air, the sorrow of the goddess as her daughter returned to her throne among the dead for the long winter ahead. Something about it filled me with a sense of foreboding.

It would all be over today.

A few days before I'd finally gathered up the courage to ask Icarus what he planned to do once Daedalus was freed. They obviously couldn't stay on Crete, or anywhere Minos could find them. He told me that he had booked passage for two on a ship bound for Thera, sailing tomorrow morning. From there they would continue on until they reached Athens, Icarus' childhood home and their ultimate destination. They would need to find a place to hide until the ship sailed, which made me nervous. I would have preferred they sail immediately, but Icarus argued that he couldn't be sure how long it would take for us to sneak Daedalus out of the tower. I knew he was right, but I also knew that every moment they spent on Crete's shores after Daedalus' escape, their lives would be in danger. Minos had already demonstrated that he would resort to any measure rather than admit his own fault. It had cost him his wife, his son, and his daughter, but he still showed no remorse. The man was dangerous.

The Anemoi brought me directly to the cliffs outside Stalis with no delay. It was as if Aeolus knew what our task was today and was eager to see how it played out. I wondered how many other gods were watching on this day. My mother had said Icarus' actions would attract the attention of the gods. I was sure she was right. But would that attention bring their favor, or their wrath? I wished that I could know.

Icarus was waiting for me on the cliffside, strapping his own wax wings to his arms. The pair that we had constructed for Daedalus lay near his feet, and he paused to hand them up to me. I clutched them tightly, watching Icarus intently as he fastened the leather straps around his bicep, then his forearm, then his wrist. The rising sun made his dark hair shine with copper undertones. I remembered the way he had held me in his arms a week ago. This would be our last day flying together. It might be the last time I'd ever see him. I felt like I should say something, do something, but I couldn't think of what.

He looked up at me, his dark eyes catching mine and holding them. "Are you ready?" he asked.

I tried to answer but found that I couldn't. So I merely nodded, and together we took flight.

Despite the swiftness with which the Anemoi had brought me to Icarus' side, the winds were not on our side. By the time we managed to approach Minos' palace, it was nearly midday, and Apollo was high above us. We didn't dare fight the winds' currents, though; it was a bright, cloudless day, and with all the people on the streets for the festival, it would be too dangerous to recklessly fly against the winds. Icarus was agitated, but he knew that we had no other choice.

At last, Notus carried us low, following on the heels of a flock of geese, large enough to disguise our own larger silhouettes if we flew above them. I could hear the sounds of the festival below us over the geese's cries: The reedy notes of auloi, the banging of drums and cymbals, the thunder of thousands of dancing feet, the echoes of laughter and singing and shouting. I was afraid to look down at the revelry. Though I had spent my life flying near humans and never being spotted, today I feared that if

I looked down a human would catch my eye and we would be found out. So I kept my eyes fixed doggedly on the tower in front of us, looming larger and larger as we drew closer.

There would be no going back this time.

The tower had only one window, small and square, at the place where the stone walls met the roofline. It was enclosed with bars to keep its prisoner from escaping, but Icarus had prepared for this as well. In his satchel he carried a kit of blacksmith's tools. He landed roughly on the tile roof and quickly scrabbled over, leaning precariously over the top in a way that made my stomach lurch. With practiced skill, he hammered at the bronze bars at the window. They quickly warped, then broke with an ear-piercing *clang*. I winced at the sound, but it blended in neatly with the crashing cymbals in the festival below. Icarus had been right—this was the best day to attempt this. The festival was a better distraction than I could have hoped for.

A face appeared at the window, haggard and worn, with a long, unkempt gray beard.

"Father!" Icarus cried at the sight of him.

"Icarus?" the man said, his voice raspy with disuse. "What in the world are you doing?"

"We're here to rescue you, Father. Quick, Nico, the wings."

Daedalus stared in my direction, seeming to notice me for the first time. As he took in my wings, he started, his eyes widening in alarm. "What in Zeus' name—"

"There's no time, Father. I'll explain later. Just know that she's a friend. Quickly, we have to escape now."

"Icarus, it's far too dangerous—"

"*Father!*" Icarus snapped in frustration. "Just because Minos is away doesn't mean the palace is completely unguarded. There's no time to argue, let's just *go*."

Daedalus blinked. "Minos, away? No, boy, it's the festival of

Demeter."

"I know, but his men said that he was celebrating in Malia."

"I saw him with my very eyes this morning," Daedalus argued. "Minos is here!"

My blood ran cold. *Minos is here?*

Icarus swallowed. "It doesn't matter. It's too late to turn back now. Father, take these blasted wings and let's *go*."

I could hear, now, a sound louder than the festival. Louder and closer. Thundering feet on the ground—not dancing, but running. And the shouts of men, not in joyous celebration, but in anger.

Daedalus' hands shook as he strapped the wings on, and my heart pounded more erratically with each passing second. Minos' men were coming, and if we didn't escape now—

Daedalus was at the window now, and Icarus half dragged him out by the nape of his filthy prison tunic. The inventor scrambled up onto the roof just as the door to the prison cell banged open.

"Soldiers!" I cried.

"Father, come on!" Icarus shouted. "These wings are your invention."

Daedalus nodded, and I prayed that meant he knew what to do. Icarus ran ahead of him, spreading his arms to catch the wind. Daedalus followed, but just as he was about to launch himself into the air, an arrow whizzed past me, cold air stinging my cheek.

"Split up!" I shouted without thinking. If we weren't flying together, the soldiers wouldn't have a single target to aim for. "I'll distract them!"

I hurled myself against the wind's current, diving down into the soldiers' range. The men cried out in alarm when they realized I was not like Icarus and Daedalus with their artificial wings, but something else entirely. I swooped down on them like an eagle, spreading my wings and forming my hands into claws.

"A monster!" the men cried, shrinking back against the parapets.

"Don't look! She could be like a Gorgon, with eyes that can turn us to stone!"

"Your shields! Use your shields, like Perseus!"

"Cowards!" the captain bellowed, striding forward undaunted. "Just shoot them down before they pass out of range!"

A gust of wind burst over the parapet just then, propelling me forward with a burst of speed. This time I didn't fight it, allowing the wind to carry me up and away from the palace. Icarus and Daedalus were well ahead of me now, the guards' distraction giving them a much-needed head-start. With the aid of the wind, they were already well out of range, even as Daedalus struggled to keep his altitude. I beat my wings hard to catch up with them. We just needed to get him away from the island, that's all we needed…

As I came up alongside them, I could hear shouting behind us, but I didn't dare look back. We just needed to keep going, keep going forward… the Anemoi were helping us, the gods were on our side…

I flinched and cried as something hot touched the skin of my right arm. It lasted only a moment, but it had burned like when my feet had touched the ground all those years ago. What in Zeus' name had that been?

I turned to look at Icarus just in time to see it, but everything happened too quickly for me to react.

As I turned my head, a brilliant flash of light blinded me, like a beam of Apollo's rays directed straight from the Knossos shoreline.

Icarus cried out in pain as the beam of light connected with his left side.

The smell of hot, hot wax.

And then his wing crumbled.

One second it was there, and the next the wing was breaking into pieces, feathers scattering on the wind like a bird felled by a hunter's arrow. Icarus shouted, I screamed, and then he was falling, falling, spiraling quickly and falling like a dead weight. I dove after him, reminded for a horrific instant of the way he had plunged toward the sea on the first day we met. But this time I couldn't save him. I couldn't shout instructions for him, couldn't tell him to catch the wind, because even with wind as strong as a hurricane's gale, a bird can't fly with only one wing.

He fell faster than I could dive after him. He plummeted like a stone. I knew I could never catch him, I wasn't strong enough to hold his weight, but I dove blindly after him anyway. His eyes met mine, and though they should have been terrified they were almost calm, as if he was resigned to his fate.

No.

No.

"Icarus!" I screamed as his body crashed into the waves.

I would have dove straight in after him, but a sudden gust of wind even stronger than the one that had propelled me away from the palace caught me. I fought against it, desperately struggling to follow him into the water—if there was even the slightest chance he had survived that impact, maybe I could pull him up, prevent him from drowning… But the wind was like an invisible barrier. No matter how hard I fought it, it would not let me draw any closer to the water.

And then it came. The small, glowing orb, ascending gently toward me. I couldn't bear to look at it, but I couldn't look away, even as tears blurred my vision and sobs began to rack my body. My hands shaking, I reached out, and the wispy orb nestled between my fingers, icy cold and glowing gold.

Icarus.

He was gone.

Numbly, I managed to guide Daedalus to the same rocky isle where I'd led Icarus on the day we met. While we flew he babbled hysterically about how it was his fault—not just the fact that Icarus had risked his life to save him, but the beam of light, the beam that had melted Icarus' wing. It was his invention, you see, a weapon he had devised for Minos. It reflected the sun's rays and concentrated them into a precise weapon of fire that could burn enemies from distances far greater than could be reached by spear or arrow.

I wanted to scream at him, hurl invectives at him. *This was his fault.* All of it had been his fault, from the very beginning. To serve a king as clearly deranged as Minos! To design the Labyrinth without even considering what it might be used for! To give Minos a weapon like this, after everything that the crazed king had done! Maybe Daedalus had *deserved* to be imprisoned, and Icarus should have just left him there. But I was too numb with my grief to manage to form a word.

And of course it had been a trap. I should have followed my instincts and argued with Icarus when he'd said the king would be in Malia for the festival. Daedalus babbled about how he'd overheard the king's men talking about a plot to infiltrate the palace that Minos' spies had uncovered, but Daedalus had never guessed that it would have been his own son. Though there was no way the man could have warned us, I found myself blaming him for that, too.

Daedalus babbled and prattled between hysterical sobs, and I flew alongside him silently until at last he stood on the shore of that tiny, rocky island.

"What are we going to do now?" Daedalus asked, looking up at me frantically.

As far as I was concerned, he could just rot there. But I knew that would be a disservice to everything Icarus had fought for… had *died* for. He had sacrificed everything to save his father. I couldn't just leave him there.

But I had something else I needed to do first.

"You're going to wait here," I said.

"Are you going to leave me in this place?" The inventor's voice shook.

I squeezed my eyes shut, inhaling salty air. "I will come back for you. But first I need to take care of your son."

"You're a psychopomp, aren't you?" Daedalus asked. "A harpy? You must be. No other creature under Olympus comes close. Surely there must be something you can do for Icarus! Please, I beg you!"

I swallowed hard. *Not for you*, I wanted to snap. But I couldn't bring myself to rage at him, as much as I wanted to. The golden orb in my satchel seemed to whisper restraint to me. Icarus loved his father just as I loved my mother. He had made mistakes, but so had my family. Now wasn't the time for fury. It was the time for action. Now, before it was too late.

Finally, I managed: "I'm going to try."

"Lord Hermes!" I shouted as the Tainaron came into view. I swooped down toward the land, the wind against my back. "Lord Hermes!"

I blinked and the god was beside me, his flaxen curls mussed, his arms crossed in annoyance. "Halfling, what is the urgency?"

I struggled to catch my breath. Wordlessly, I opened my satchel. My stomach clenched as I withdrew the orb, holding it out to him. It hovered just above my hand, glowing like a tiny sun in my palm.

"A golden soul?" Hermes looked at me shrewdly, the orb's light reflected in his blue eyes. "Just who is this hero you're carrying, Halfling?"

I suspected that he knew perfectly well. It was clear from the behavior of the wind that the gods had been watching. I should have suspected sooner—the fact that I was able to steal away so frequently to help Icarus learn to fly, the fact that the Anemoi had guided us up to the clouds last week… I'd wanted to deny it, because the gods' attention was a double-edged sword. But Icarus had proven himself. Despite his death, he was a hero, and that meant favor from the gods.

I was relying on that favor now as I made my audacious request.

Hermes reached out for the orb, and I drew away, holding Icarus' soul close to my chest. "I request an audience with Lord Hades."

Hermes' eyebrows rose, though it seemed to me it was more a reaction of amusement than surprise. "What about?"

I refused to let my voice shake. "About this soul."

The corner of Hermes' mouth twitched upward. "That is an interesting request. And why should the god grant it?"

I inclined my head deferentially. "I have served you faithfully for many years, my lord. My entire life. This is very important to me."

Hermes snorted. "A master owes his servant nothing. You serve because it is your duty, not because you expect a reward."

My face grew hot with anger and shame, but I didn't move. I kept my head inclined—but I also kept my grip tight on Icarus' soul. Hermes laughed aloud. "My, you *are* determined about this, aren't you? All right, then. Come with me." He reached out his hand. Hesitantly, I replaced the soul into my satchel and took his outstretched hand.

I blinked, and we were no longer on the peninsula. Now I was suspended in midair between two high cliffs, a narrow band of aquamarine water meandering beneath my feet.

"Charon!" Hermes shouted.

The barge appeared from the shadows at the base of the cliffs. It moved slowly and silently toward where Hermes hovered above the water. "My lord?" the ferryman rasped.

"This is my servant, Nicothoë," Hermes said, and I looked at him in surprise. I had never heard him say my name before. "She requires passage to the Underworld for an audience with Lord Hades."

Charon nodded beneath his dark cloak. He looked up at me with hooded eyes and beckoned me onto the boat.

I started to descend, but Hermes stayed me. "Aeolus has no authority in the Underworld. There will be no wind. In many places the rock is barely above head-height. You won't be able to fly."

I nodded. I would just have to endure it. I remembered how difficult it had been to remain conscious when last my feet touched the ground, and I hoped I wouldn't black out as soon as I touched the barge. But there was nothing to do but try.

Hermes rolled his eyes and bent in the air, reaching down with one hand to unstrap his sandals.

"My lord!" I cried. "I couldn't—if you remove your shoes, how will you fly? How will you be able to travel?"

Hermes barked out a laugh. "Don't be ridiculous! Don't tell me you believe the humans' stories. Child, I am a *god*. I give these sandals their power, not the other way around." He handed them to me as if it were nothing, but I felt an enormous surge of affection for him as I gratefully took them from him. All these years, I had never been certain whether Hermes despised me or not. But maybe I had the favor of one god on Olympus after all.

With Hermes' sandals strapped to my feet, I turned to go, but once more he stayed me. In a low voice, he said, "One final bit of advice, Halfling. Take it from a trickster: When dealing with the gods, pay attention to what they say… and what they don't say."

"Yes, my lord," I said slowly, playing his words back in my mind, trying to understand what he meant, to commit it to memory.

He smiled at me almost sadly. "You've been a good little servant, Halfling."

With that, he disappeared. And I couldn't help but feel, with more than a slight sense of foreboding, that he had been telling me *goodbye*.

"Free the soul," said Charon as I landed in the boat, Hermes' sandals keeping my feet a hand's breadth from the deck.

"I'm sorry?" I asked in confusion.

"The one you carry in your satchel." The ferryman's voice was like gravel. "It cannot remain contained. Once in the Underworld, it will reassume its form."

Of course, I knew that. I had seen it once before, when I had been here with my aunt Ocypete. Hurriedly I opened my satchel and withdrew the orb of Icarus' soul. It hovered in the space beside me. With that, Charon pushed off, steering the barge forward with his long pole, returning to the shadows he had appeared from. I swallowed hard as we moved into the darkness. For a moment, I could see nothing around me but shadows; then the golden light beside me brightened, and I sucked in my breath. The soul was no longer a wispy orb, but a translucent shape. It was Icarus, as though he were standing right beside me. But his eyes were empty and lifeless, his face expressionless. He was a mere shade now.

I couldn't bear to look at him.

The river continued to widen until we reached a convergence, where the five rivers met: Acheron, Cocytus, Phlegethon, Lethe, and the greatest river of the Underworld, Styx. Charon navigated the convergence with practiced skill, though I struggled to keep my footing, unaccustomed to relying on them anywhere but in the cloud world. I spread my wings in an attempt to balance myself. Beside me, Icarus' shade remained vacant and unmoving.

Then the barge was through, and we were on the placid waters of the Styx. The Underworld opened out before me, huge and dark, a massive cavern with no end as far as the eye could see. There was no sky above us, only a void, blacker than the darkest night, with no stars to be seen. No light save for the lantern on the barge's front, a small, flickering candle—and the brighter glow of Icarus' golden soul beside me. I soon lost track of time; with no sky and no familiar markers to let me know how many minutes, how many hours had elapsed, I had no way of knowing whether I'd been here just a few moments or for days.

Gradually, I started to make out shapes in the darkness. I thought maybe my eyes were adjusting, but then I realized there was a light in the distance. As we drew closer, I realized I was seeing the shore—and beyond, the palace of Hades. The king of the Underworld, the lord of the dead. Anxiety set my heartbeat off-kilter.

Be brave, Nico. Like Icarus. Be brave for *Icarus.*

The barge rocked as Charon came up alongside a pier of gray wood. Flickering lamps lit the way from the dock along a path into the palace. "The god awaits," Charon rasped as I climbed off the boat, the winged sandals keeping my feet from touching the ground. Icarus' shade silently followed, its expression blank as ever. "Do not tarry."

As I stepped off the dock, a tongue of green flame flickered to life in front of me. It silently beckoned, leading the way up the cobbled road away from the pier, up the stone steps and through the colonnade into the palace. The ceiling within the palace was so high that I couldn't see it. Maybe it didn't even exist. Maybe like the Underworld's sky, it was only a void.

The green flame led me around a corner into a second chamber, and I found myself wincing at the sudden bright light after so much time in utter darkness. I blinked away stars until I finally could make out the source of the light.

On a dais in front of me were two thrones. On one sat a man with a dark beard, his face somber. He had an almost sullen look to him—or maybe it was just the impression given by his sallow skin, paler even than Icarus' scholar's pallor when I first met him. It was exacerbated by the sheer radiance of the woman seated beside him. She had golden hair and tanned skin that seemed to shine, producing a luminescence all their own. *Persephone*, I realized with a start. We were now in the month of Pyanepsion. The festival of Demeter had begun.

The goddess of spring had returned to her husband in the Underworld.

I knelt before them, my knees nearly brushing the ground but remaining just above it by the power of the winged sandals. "My lord, my lady," I said. Beside me, Icarus' shade remained motionless.

"So here they are at last." Hades' voice was deeper and richer than I'd expected from his gaunt, pale appearance. "The human and the harpy who have caused such a stir on Olympus."

I glanced up in surprise. "My lord?"

Hades smirked. "You had no idea what you were getting yourself into when you involved yourself with this boy, Halfling. Though I suspect that in itself was not mere chance. Minos has proven to be a divisive subject among the gods, you see." He shifted in his seat, propping a foot up on an ornately carved ivory footstool in front of the throne. "Poseidon has not forgotten Minos' insult with the white bull. Yet every attempt to send revenge down upon the king has failed. Minos has Zeus' favor, you see."

My stomach twisted. It was like Heracles all over again. The other gods could attempt to thwart the man, but if he had Zeus' favor, there could be no stopping him.

"All eyes on Olympus have been watching you this last month, Halfling. And many eyes off it as well. The gods were bitterly divided between those who wanted your Icarus to fail and those who wanted him to succeed—and you, Nicothoë, got yourself neatly tangled in the middle of it."

I kept my head down, silent. I didn't know what to say. I should have suspected this, though. My mother had warned me…

"Oh, don't fret, Halfling. This little drama with Minos has been going on for many years, and it will continue for many more. But now that

Daedalus is freed and Icarus is slain, your part in it is over. Zeus, Poseidon and their sycophants have already moved on. The curtain has fallen on this stage." He leaned back, crossing his arms. Beside him, Persephone watched me, frowning silently. "Which leaves the fate of this hero in my hands. That's what you're here for, after all, isn't it? To ask me for a reprieve. To beg for my mercy and forgiveness. Just like Orpheus."

I winced at the comparison. I'd heard the tale of Orpheus as a child. The legendary musician and poet whose melodic voice was renowned throughout the known world and even on Olympus. His true love, Eurydice, had succumbed to a snake bite, but Orpheus refused to give up on her. He'd managed to charm his way through the gates of Hades and made it all the way to this court. Hades had shown mercy and agreed to let Eurydice return on the condition that Orpheus not look back until they were out of the Underworld.

But he'd failed. Eurydice had paid the price for her husband's weakness, but everyone seemed to think Orpheus was the real victim of the tale.

"I'm nothing like Orpheus!" I shouted before I had a chance to think better of it. My voice echoed off the invisible ceiling above.

For a long moment, Hades and Persephone stared at me, shocked into silence by my outburst. My heart seemed to stop beating as I waited in frozen horror for the smiting that was sure to follow.

Hades raised his eyebrows. Then he burst into laugher that filled the cavernous space.

"A feisty halfling, aren't you? You think you're so different? I can promise you that you're not—"

"I want to see her try," Persephone interrupted.

Hades blinked in surprise, turning to face his wife almost as though he'd forgotten she was there—though how he could have forgotten the radiant sunshine beside him was beyond me. "My queen?"

Persephone held his gaze resolutely. "She deserves to be judged by her own merits. Remember," she added with a wry quirk of her eyebrow, "that is your own philosophy."

Hades smirked. "My wife reminds me of my own scruples. Whatever would I do without her? Very well. I shall do it to please you, my queen. And for no other reason." He stood, then, approaching the edge of the dais and looking down at me. "Nicothoë, you have before you a choice. This shade, once known as the human Icarus, has proven himself to be of valor before the gods. His future is secure in Elysium. Yet you wish to have him return to the world of suffering above."

It sounded selfish when he put it that way. And maybe it was. But even though there was suffering in life, there was also good. Icarus had fought so hard for justice in this life. He deserved to be able to experience the reward in this life, too. He deserved to see his father again.

And selfish as it was, I wanted to see him again, too.

"Yes, my lord," I said.

"If Icarus returns to the living, there can be no guarantees, Halfling. In life, there is no certainty. That can be found only in death. I cannot say whether his second life will last a hundred years or one minute. The Fates alone will know the hour of his second death, but rest assured that it will happen all the same."

I swallowed down the lump that was forming in my throat. There was no turning back now. "Yes, my lord."

"Very well." His dark eyes were hard. "I will grant your request. But in return you must make a sacrifice."

And here it was. I braced myself for his next words, my hands shaking. What would I be asked to trade in return for Icarus' life?

Hades extended his hands. Two tongues of flame burst to life in his palms, one blue and one orange. "Decide before the fire burns out." He raised his left hand, holding the orange flame. "Icarus will live, but he must never see you again. You will go on as you always have, and he will go on as he always has. It will be as if you never met."

The very thought of it cut me like a knife. How could I go back to the life I'd led before after knowing what I did now?

But if it came down to that or leaving Icarus here, I would still do it. In a heartbeat.

Hades held out his right hand now, containing the blue flame. "Icarus will live, but you will give up your own immortality. You will lose all you've ever known. You will forfeit your harpy half and become human. You will never fly on these wings again."

Forfeit my harpy half? Then I would never be able to see my mother or aunts again. I hadn't even had a chance to say goodbye to my mother. Would she ever know what became of me? And though I'd longed to feel the ground beneath my feet and the sea against my skin, to never fly again…

Never fly on these *wings.*

I inhaled shakily, remembering what Hermes had said. *"When dealing with the gods, pay attention to what they say… and what they don't say."*

Hades watched me, his gaze steady, his lips pulled up in one corner in a smirk. The flames were flickering down in his hands rapidly. "Make your choice, Nicothoë."

"The god of the Underworld is fair, Halfling."

The flames sputtered in Hades' open palms.

I got shakily to my feet, striding forward and grasping the blue flame.

The sand beneath my feet was hot, baked by Apollo's rays; but in the places where the waves lapped over it, it was cool and refreshing. I wriggled my toes through it, relishing the feeling of solid ground beneath me, the way the water snaked around my ankles and then pulled away. The white-crested waves rolled over the rocks beyond the shore, and as I watched, in the distance a dolphin leaped from the sea in a majestic arc, slipping back into the water with barely a splash. The sight of it felt like a memory from another life.

"Nico!" a voice called behind me, and I turned, smiling as Icarus picked his way over to me, across the rocks down to the beach.

"Were you able to secure passage?" I asked.

"Yes. We'll be leaving for Athens three days from now," he said.

I smiled and nodded.

Just a week had passed since that fateful day, but it felt like an eternity. I was already struggling to remember parts of it, as though it had been a dream. When I'd grasped the blue flame, the world around me had disappeared into nothingness. I'd awoken hours later, the wind whispering in my ear that it was time to rise as it had every morning. But even as I drifted back into consciousness, I'd known something was different. Every inch of my body had ached, and I was disoriented by both the hard ground beneath me—so different than the cool softness of the clouds that had been my home for sixteen years—and by the fact that I could not move my wings. I couldn't even feel them.

Then I'd opened my eyes to find myself on the rocky island where I'd left Daedalus. A warm hand was in mine, and when I opened my eyes I saw him crouching beside me, smiling down at me. Icarus. He was alive.

The moment I stirred, Daedalus had begun to babble about how Icarus' body had washed up on the shore a few hours after I'd left him, moments later followed by mine. He almost hadn't recognized me because my wings were missing, and he had no idea what had happened while I was gone. Icarus had awoken a short time before me, with no memory of anything after the moment Minos' weapon had melted his wing. Only I knew what had taken place in the Underworld.

Had I made the right decision? Only the gods could say.

Even after a week, I was still adjusting to the change in my body. The loss of my wings, having to rely on my legs to carry me everywhere. The heaviness that came from being grounded. It was a strange, uncomfortable feeling. All my life I'd longed to touch the land and the sea, to live as my mother and aunts had once. But now that I had my wish, I felt disoriented, bereft. Like a part of me was missing.

But it was the choice that I had made, and I refused to regret it.

Icarus managed to persuade Daedalus and me to allow him to fly back to Crete on Daedalus' undamaged wings and return with a boat for us. I was horrified at the thought of him flying back into Minos' clutches, but we'd had no choice. As Hades had warned me: by bringing him back to life, I had put him in danger again. I couldn't protect him forever. *"In life, there is no certainty,"* the god of the Underworld had said. *"That can be found only in death."*

I might have saved his life only for him to die again the same day, or in a week, or in a month. No one could know for sure but the Fates. It was something I would just have to live with.

But the gods had been on our side this time. Icarus returned for us within the hour. We returned to Crete, spent a harried evening in the wilderness outside Stalis, but somehow managed to evade Minos' attention. I remembered what Hades had said about this part of the drama being over. Minos' saga would continue, but Icarus and Daedalus wouldn't be a part of it. Maybe that had been more than a comment— maybe it had been a promise. Regardless, Icarus had managed to barter me onto the ship on which he'd booked passage on for himself and his father. We sailed to Thera the next morning, and I breathed a sigh of relief as I watched Crete's rocky shores disappear beyond the horizon for the last time.

Now we would be bound for Athens in a few short days, but our time on Thera hadn't been spent idly. Icarus and I had explored the island's hills and shores, the slopes of its volcanic mountains, hunting for feathers at every opportunity. After all, it would take a lot of feathers, of all shapes and sizes, to build a new set of wax wings.

My mother had told me—what felt like a lifetime ago—that if I could only save one person she wanted it to be myself. But by some twist of fate that could only be attributed to the favor of the gods, I had somehow managed to save both myself and Icarus.

I wouldn't be content to leave it there. We'd rescued Icarus' father. I had to believe there was some way I could save my family, too.

"Look what I found," Icarus said as he reached my side, taking my hand in his and gingerly pressing a long, soft feather into my fingers. It was mottled like an owl's, brown and white, but much larger than the feather of any bird I'd ever seen.

It looked almost like a harpy's.

I grinned up at him, and he put his arm around me. I rested my head on his shoulder. *"Never fly on* these *wings again,"* Hades had said. He hadn't said I'd never fly again—only on the wings I was born with.

I'd see my mother again. I was sure of it. And maybe I could still save her and my aunts, too.

I was no longer a harpy, no longer immortal. I wasn't sure who I was, in fact—a former monster, now redeemed. The daughter of an Amazon, a descendant of the gods. Someone who had faced Death and somehow come out on the other side. A stranger to the person I'd been just months before. I was unrecognizable to myself.

I didn't know who I was anymore, but something I knew for sure was that my story wasn't over.

In fact, I had a feeling it was only just beginning.

ABOUT THE AUTHORS

A voracious reader, JANE WATSON has always been a fan of romance, fantasy, adventure and especially happy endings. She is the author of the YA romantic comedies *The Taming of the Dudebro* and *A Midsummer Night's Dudebro*. She is also the author of several short stories which have been published in the anthologies *A Touch of Magic*, *Perchance to Dream*, and *Magic at Midnight*. She received her degree in Art History from the University of Puget Sound. When she is not writing, Jane works as a wedding coordinator, helping people reach their happily-ever-afters. She likes to spend her free time doting on her menagerie of pets, riding her bike, crafting, and obsessively shopping for purses. Visit Jane online at janewatsonauthor.com.

AMY BEARCE writes magical escapes for young readers and the young at heart. She is the author of the World of Aluvia series, the Secret Psychic series, and the Wish & Wander series, beginning with *Paris on Repeat*. She is also a former reading teacher and librarian. As a military kid, she moved eight times before she was eighteen, so she feels especially fortunate to be married to her high school sweetheart. Together they're raising two daughters in San Antonio. You can find her online at www.amybearce.com.

LYSSA CHIAVARI writes inclusive speculative fiction for young adults. She is the author of The Iamos Trilogy, a near-future science fiction series set on Mars, and *Cheerleaders from Planet X*, a tongue-in-cheek send-up of classic alien invasion lore. Her short fiction has appeared in *Wings of Renewal: A Solarpunk Dragon Anthology, Brave New Girls: Tales of Heroines Who Hack, A Touch of Magic,* and *Overmorrow: Stories of Our Bright Future.* She is also the editor of the anthologies *Perchance to Dream* and *Magic at Midnight* through Snowy Wings Publishing. Her first published story, "The Choice," was named one of *Ama-gi Magazine*'s Best Fiction of 2014. Lyssa lives with her family and way too many animals in the woods of Northwest Oregon. You can visit her online at lyssachiavari.com.

SARAH DALE is an author, mom, daughter, step-mom, pack member, friend, dog-walker, cat-appreciator, library book balancer, word lover, think thinker and picture-taker living in Lincoln, Nebraska, just generally trying to get things done. She is the author of the YA paranormal series Tales of the Zodiac Cusp Kids, as well as the fantasy novel *We Could Be Heroes.* She is also the co-author of the suspense thriller *Collision Course* with Welsh author David Owain Hughes. Her short story, "Something Old, Something New, Something Cursed, Something Blue" is featured in a collection of horror short stories, *What Goes Around.*

DOROTHY DREYER is a Philippine-born American living in Germany with her husband, her two college kids, and two Siberian Huskies. She is an award-winning, *USA Today*-Bestselling Author of young adult and new adult books that usually have some element of magic or the supernatural in them. Her repertoire also includes adult romance and adult thriller novels. Aside from reading, she enjoys movies, binge-watching series, chocolate, take-out, traveling, and having fun with friends and family. She tends to sing sometimes, too, so keep her away from your Karaoke bars.

MARY FAN is a sci-fi/fantasy writer hailing from Jersey City, NJ. She is the author of the *Jane Colt* sci-fi series, the *Starswept* YA sci-fi series, the *Flynn Nightsider* YA dark fantasy series, the *Fated Stars* YA high fantasy series, and *Stronger Than a Bronze Dragon*, a YA steampunk fantasy. In addition, Mary is the co-editor of the *Brave New Girls* anthologies, which feature tales about girls in STEM. Her short fiction has appeared in numerous anthologies, including *Keep Faith* (edited by Gabriela Martins), *Thrilling Adventure Yarns* (edited by Bob Greenberger), and *Magic at Midnight* (edited by Lyssa Chiavari and Amy McNulty). When she's not writing, she can usually be found punching heavy bags, singing alto in choir, swinging from a flying trapeze, or hanging upside down from aerial silks. Find her online at MaryFan.com.

Growing up in the Black Forest in Germany as a hopeless dreamer with an overactive imagination, JANINA FRANCK began writing at a young age to give a voice to the stories living inside her head.

As a teenager, she moved to the emerald isle of legends and myths, Ireland, where she completed her basic education, and went on to study Modern Languages and Multimedia.

While her surroundings changed, her desire to create stories did not, which she now pursues across various types of media, while traveling to quench her thirst for new impressions and adventures.

JESSICA GUNN writes urban fantasy adventure stories full of heart and epic journeys. Her favorite stories are those that transport the reader to other, more exciting worlds. To catch up with Jessica, follow her on Twitter (@JessGunnAuthor) or on her website, www.jessicagunn.com.

LEIGH HELLMAN is a queer writer, originally from the western suburbs of Chicago, and a graduate of the MA Program for Writers at the University of Illinois at Chicago. After gaining the ever-lucrative BA in

English, they spent five years living and teaching in South Korea before returning to their native Midwest.

Leigh's short fiction and creative nonfiction work has been featured in *Hippocampus Magazine*, *VIDA Review*, and *Fulbright Korea Infusion Magazine*. Their critical and journalistic work has been featured in the *American Book Review*, the *Gwangju News* magazine, and the *Windy City Times*.

Their debut book, *Orbit*, is a new adult speculative fiction novel available through Snowy Wings Publishing. They also have a historical fantasy piece included in the Snowy Wings Publishing anthology *Magic at Midnight*.

Leigh is a strong advocate for full-day breakfast menus, all varieties of dark chocolate, building a wardrobe based primarily on bad puns, and bathing in the tears of their enemies.

AMY MCNULTY is an editor and author of books that run the gamut from YA speculative fiction to contemporary romance. A lifelong fiction fanatic, she fangirls over books, anime, manga, comics, movies, games, and TV shows from her home state of Wisconsin. When not editing her clients' novels, she's busy fulfilling her dream by crafting fantastical worlds of her own. Learn more about Amy at amymcnulty.com.

SELENIA PAZ is the author of the Leyendas series (Book One, *Life and Death*; Book Two, *Gods and Demons*; and Book Three, *Shadows and Light*), a middle grade fantasy series inspired by Mexican folklore. She has also contributed to several anthologies, including *Perchance to Dream: Classic Tales from the Bard's World in New Skins* (2017) and *Brave New Girls: Tales of Heroines Who Hack* (2018). Selenia is a librarian and spends her free time reading, writing, and running with her dogs. You can find her online at seleniapaz.com.

⊕THER AΠTH⊕L⊕GIES
FROM SNOWY WINGS PUBLISHING

SHAKESPEARE RETELLINGS
Perchance to Dream
edited by Lyssa Chiavari

FAIRY TALE RETELLINGS
Magic at Midnight
edited by Lyssa Chiavari & Amy McNulty

MAGIC & FANTASY
A Touch of Magic
edited by Janina Franck